THAT SUMMER OF '45

BY
G. SAM PIATT

Best wishes,

G. Sam Piatt

THAT SUMMER OF '45

Copyright © 2014 by G. Sam Piatt

SOFTBACK EDITION

ISNB: 978-0-9887319-3-6

Published by:

RIGHT EYE GRAPHICS
P.O. Box 5071
Ashland, Kentucky 41105-5071
606.393.4197
www.RightEyeGraphics.com

I have had the honor and pleasure of proofing a wonderful manuscript by G. Sam Piatt — a novel about a group of boys in the summer of 1945. Sam does a great job weaving tales of their young, carefree lives into the backdrop of the Second World War and its impact on their small town. Two thumbs up.

Amanda Gilmore

Community Relations Coordinator,
Boyd County Public Library

Faculty member,
Ohio University Southern Campus

DEDICATION

To Miss Opal, a wonderful teacher who instilled in me in the 7th grade the desire to write, a desire that is within me yet today; and to Hobo and Dale, who await with great anticipation the reunion of the Braves.

HOOVERVILLE MAP

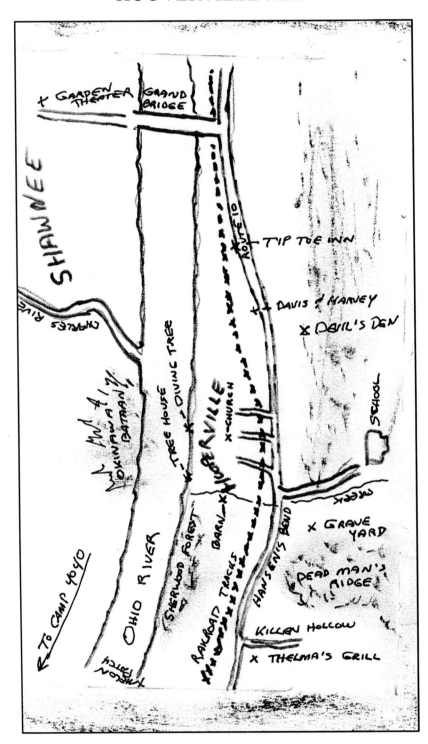

PROLOGUE

He had reached an age well past the three-score and ten that the Scriptures referred to as the allotted span of man's life on earth. So it was understandable that he spent more time these days looking back than he did in looking to the future. He wondered if others were affected by nostalgia as strongly as he was of late. For the third time in a week, he had come awake in the middle of the night, staring at the ceiling, tears flowing down the sides of his face and onto the sheet. Oh how he longed to see again the people and the places in that little Ohio River village where he spent his boyhood days.

The village, he felt certain, was still there, although it had been more than 60 years since he'd seen it. He believed Hooperville will be standing there, on the second rise back from the river – at about the halfway point between Pittsburgh and Cairo – when the Rapture comes. But the people … well, he supposed the people would most all have passed beyond the veil by now.

It was the summer of 1945 that had been calling to him most vividly from the past. He could remember the events of that summer as though they happened yesterday. How could he ever forget? It was a summer filled with more adventures than any boy had a right to expect, thanks mainly to the unloosed imagination of one Vince Royalton.

There was mystery to that summer, too. Do the spirits of the dead really hang around, trying to tell you something or accomplish something? Or is that just some deep process of the imagination at work?

It was not all good memories, of course. Life doesn't keep you on a high for long before it sends you crashing back to earth. He felt both joy and sadness when he thought of Chopper. Poor ol', good ol' Chopper. He still missed that dog.

And unrequited love. Oh boy, that smacks you down. Never trust your heart to someone who will hardly recognize you exist, then fly away like a wild bird.

Yet it was pleasant for awhile, when hope abounded.

Just a memory now too were the people who had shared that summer with him from the funny papers of The Shawnee Times and from the speaker of the big floor model radio in Gale Flanders' house – Wash Tubbs and Captain Easy, Terry and the Pirates, Orphan Annie, Red Ryder, Fibber McGee and Molly, Jack Benny, the Lone Ranger, Tom Mix, Gabriel Heater and Walter Winchell.

And the stars from the big screen at the Saturday matinees at the Garden and the Lyric theaters: the Phantom, Hopalong Cassidy, Lash LaRue, Buster Crabbe, Rita Hayworth, Victor Mature, John Wayne in "Back to Bataan."

Hooperville was probably an eight hour drive from his home. No matter. He had to go.

"So you're taking a trip into the past, hey?" his wife of more than half a century said as he loaded some things into the car.

"I've got to see what it is that's calling me," he replied. "But don't worry about me. I'll go halfway and spend the night. I won't be driving after dark."

She pulled at her chin and raised her eyebrows.

"Well, go with my blessing," she said. "I hope you find what you're looking for. And I know you'll feel better even if you don't." She leaned suddenly into the car window and kissed him on his brow.

———————

On his second day out he took the exit off the Interstate and headed along a narrow, curvy, undulating road leading north toward the river.

An hour later, as he drove along the narrow state highway leading past the village, he discovered the source of the mysterious longing – a calling almost, it seemed – that had drawn him there.

And he could scarce believe what his eyes were seeing. He gripped the wheel and leaned toward the passenger side for a better look at the towhead. He was walking the railroad tracks that parallel the highway. He balanced his bare feet on a rail and seemed to flinch a bit with each step, no doubt

10

from the heat of the rail. A slingshot stuck from the pocket of his faded, cut-off overalls. Trailing him was a ragged black-and-white dog, its pink tongue lolling out from long facial hair.

He slowed the car. The youth – eleven, perhaps twelve – waved to him! He smiled and he saw that half of one front tooth was missing.

"How in heaven's name can this be?" he muttered. "What's going on here?"

The sound of tires pounding on gravel warned him, and it took a sharp turn on the wheel to prevent the car from plunging into a deep ditch between the highway and the railroad.

Fifty yards ahead he turned into the last of the three lanes that cross the railroad and lead down into the village. He stopped short of the tracks and climbed out, thinking to cut the boy off at the crossing. He looked toward where he'd seen the boy walking the rail, but there were only empty tracks. They converged and disappeared around a bend.

Hurriedly, he made his way along the tracks, pausing now and then to peer over the slope of the railroad bed. A few weeds and saplings grew there, but there was certainly not enough cover to hide a boy and a dog.

He returned to the crossing, mystified, and stood with hands on hips.

Had it been a specter, a product of nostalgic anticipation? His gaze shifted down the dirt street that leads through the village and dead ends at the top of the riverbank.

There they were! The boy and the dog stood at the end of the street. The boy waved, motioning for him to come to him.

Quickly, he climbed back into the car and drove to the end of the street. He got just a glimpse of them before they disappeared into the tall horse-weeds growing in the narrow bottom between the first and second rises. Moving as fast as his legs would carry him, he made his way down the path leading through the weeds and on into the willows and maples growing on the slope of the first rise.

He came out of the willows and stood on the narrow strip of sandy shoreline. He looked upstream and down. Where were they?

Slowly his eyes took in the surroundings. Things were still somewhat familiar, but more than six decades had brought considerable change.

11

Looking downstream, toward Sherwood Forest, he saw that most of the big trees that he remembered growing there were gone, having fallen victim to the lapping waters of the eternal river, its level increased by construction of the high-level dams. He knew there was no need to search for the tree house.

But then he realized that he was standing right under the big tree that cast its shadow over the old swimming hole – a huge maple with friendly, spreading limbs, limbs where once the boys had perched and, during times of high water, plunged frog-like into the murky waters of the Ohio.

He rubbed his hands lovingly over its bark. He searched round the trunk, and exhilaration stirred him as he saw it was still there: Five chiseled letters – J-A-N-I-E, and below them, three more, T-O-M, and the whole thing encircled by a heart pierced with an arrow.

Where did she go? Who did she marry?

Then, not without difficulty, he found himself climbing the tree. The limbs grew big and friendly and close together. He was breathing heavily by the time he made it to a limb some twenty-five feet above the ground. One slip here and he'd never see his wife and home again. He sat down near the base of the limb and leaned back against the trunk.

There in the dappled sunlight he closed his eyes, and the memories flowed back like yesterday. Ah, yes, he recalled, just above his head was the very limb where he had taken leave of his senses and made that suicidal dive, an act that was the last of the initiation tests in his quest to become a member of the Hooperville Braves.

He looked out across the river and saw the sandbar jutting out from the Ohio shore. He remembered that beach well. It was Bataan, Corregidor, Okinawa. He thought of the great beatings they had put on the Japanese, landing in the *Reuben James* to rush ashore, slamming down on their bellies amid machine gun bullets and mortar rounds.

The sound of splashing jerked his head back toward the sandy shore below. There was the boy again! He stood in water chest-deep, rubbing wet hair back from his face, and he guessed that he had just made a running belly-whopper from the bank. The dog with the whiskers ran up and down the shore, barking, dashing belly-deep into the river.

Now other boys bolted out of the willows to join them. There was Hobo, Dale, Gale, Keith, Vince, all laughing and shouting. There was a water battle. Keith tossed a small bell out into deeper water and all five boys dove under to see who would be the first to retrieve it. Then there was a contest to see who could stay under the longest.

From around the bend downriver came the sound of a steamboat's whistle. He heard a steam calliope playing, telling all within hearing distance to *Meet me in Saint Louie, Louie, meet me at the fair…* Shouts of joy came from the boys down below. "The showboat's comin'! The showboat's comin'!"

The watch on his wrist became a joke. Time had ceased to progress in a linear way. It was as though past, present and future existed simultaneously.

Can they?

He stood up on the limb, shading his eyes with one hand, and with excited anticipation stared down toward the distant bend.

Yes, there were showboats on the river in those days, showboats like the *Gordon C. Green,* which had a paddlewheel that threw huge waves behind it.

And there was a war, and there was the Marine in the Victory Garden.

And there was the gang.

Oh, that summer of 1945 ….

CHAPTER 1:
WELCOME, STRANGER

The big cattle truck with the high board sides and tarp over the top labored up the slight incline of the bridge approach and rocked to a halt at the tollbooth.

"How much?" the man on the passenger side asked the attendant.

"Twenty-five cents for the vehicle and driver, five cents for each passenger," said the collector, his right hand extended. "Let's see…looks like it'd be thirty-five cents."

"Whew!" said the man, twisting and turning to dig some change out of his pants pocket. He looked at the woman in the middle and asked, "You got any change, Mom?"

She rummaged through her purse and handed him three nickels. He put the coins with his and placed them in the collector's hand. The collector separated the coins in his right palm with his left index finger.

"You gave me forty-five cents. Looks like ten cents too much," he said, trying to give back two nickels.

"Two boys back there," said the man, tossing his head toward the back of the truck.

The collector raised his black eyebrows and rolled his eyes in that direction. He seemed to be debating whether he should have a look.

"Just two?" he asked.

"That's all. Well, there's a dog back there. Don't charge for dogs, do ya?

"Go on!" said the collector, waving the truck toward the Kentucky side.

Tom Sycamore, 11, and his brother, Flint, 17, leaned out over the tailgate and looked down on the river, which was running heavy with drift and had pushed its brown water into the trees along the shore.

"Good gosh, Flint, we must be a hundred feet up," said Tom, his eyes wide with wonderment.

A paddlewheeler plowed under the bridge, headed downstream, pushing a string of barges loaded with coal. The angle was such that it allowed Tom a glimpse into the pilothouse. He could see the pilot standing behind the wheel.

"The mighty Ohio. Big river, Tom. Looks like a mile wide. Snakes down almost a thousand miles from Pittsburgh to Cairo."

Tom Sycamore didn't take in all that his big brother said. His mind was down there in the pilothouse. He had one hand on the wheel, the other lifting a cup of hot java the cook had brought up from the galley. His eyes were trained on the distant bend, his mind wondering what new adventures lay beyond it.

"That's what I wanna be when I grow up, a steamboat pilot," he said.

"You can do it, Tom. Set your mind to it. Steamboat pilot, fighter pilot, John Wayne, locomotive engineer – any of these things you've said you want to be when you grow up, you can be, set your mind to it, and stick with it."

"And you can be the songwriter you want to be, right?"

"At's right, at's right. Entirely up to me."

The "moving van," holding all the earthly possessions of the Sycamore family, ran smack dab into Kentucky. A little gas station squatted in an alcove dug out in the base if the hill. The wooded hill rose steeply to a height of maybe five hundred feet. The truck turned right, down river, on what was then known as Route Ten.

The sweet fragrance of spring filled the air. Redbud blooms sprinkled the ground. Dogwoods still held their pink and white flowers.

Part way up the hill, on a flat, Tom could see houses in among the trees. Far above the houses a cliff rose up from the treetops.

Tom reached over and nudged the shoulder of his brother, who was leaning out over the tailgate on the opposite side, where houses, some of them with their rear ends on columns, were scattered along the slope between the highway and the railroad tracks, all fronting on the highway. Another slope, covered with willows and maples and sycamores, slipped down from the railroad bed to the river.

"Flint! Flint, look up here. Ain't that a big cave I see up there?"

Flint moved over to Tom's side and his eyes followed his outstretched arm up to the gaping hole on the upriver side of the cliff, about a third of the way down from the top.

"Sure looks like it. Mysterious lookin,' huh?" he said.

Looking at it, for some reason he didn't understand, Tom felt the hairs on the back of his neck prickle.

He soon dismissed it from his mind, however. The sense of adventure and wonder brought by moving to a new place pervaded his being. It was overcoming the sadness he felt at leaving behind his friends at Ashville Elementary.

He moved over to Flint's side of the truck as it rolled on down the narrow paved highway. A big wooden building with a false storefront slid by. Black letters on a white sign at the top identified it as the Tip Toe Inn. A painted lady and a balding man walked arm in arm from their car to the open doorway.

The truck passed the South Shawnee depot and freight house, and a huge, black water tank with a spout, like a giant's arm, that could swing out over the tracks to give the locomotives a drink.

Davis & Harvey, a grocery and general merchandise store, came into their view and moved on.

Another half a mile and they reached their destination: Hooperville, a village of maybe 40 houses and two churches sprawling in a bottom between the railroad and the river. Three streets led from Route Ten down into the village, each served by its own railroad crossing. The truck driver intended to turn down the middle crossing, but he braked too late. So he turned into the lower crossing instead. Gammons Grocery, a small frame building, was sandwiched between the highway and the railroad.

Over the bumpy crossing and down into the village they went, stirring a little dust up from the graveled street. Here and there, people stopped what they were doing and looked up from front porches or from well-kept yards and gardens. Dogs barked. Two of them gave chase. The dog in the truck, curled up in a chair, bounded up and put his front paws on the tail-gate, yelping excitedly. The rope around his neck, which Tom had tied to a dresser leg, restrained him from leaping into the midst of the enemy and taking on all comers.

Tom ignored his dog. "Where's our house, Flint? They said it was by the Methodist Church."

Flint, preoccupied, didn't answer. The truck turned right at the end of the street onto a street – more of an alleyway, actually –just wide enough for one car, then turned right again onto the wider street leading down into the village from the middle crossing.

"There's another one! That's nine," Flint said, looking at Tom with wide eyes and mouth agape. "My good lord, Tom! I've counted nine service stars in the windows, four of them gold!"

Tom knew enough about service stars to appreciate the significance of such a small place contributing that many of its sons – and daughters? – to the war.

The truck rumbled up to the foot of the middle crossing. Mr. Bivens maneuvered it until he had backed it within a few feet of the front porch of a two-story white frame. Bruce Sycamore, the boys' father, and Mr. Bevins dropped the tailgate. Flint leaped down. Tom untied the rope from the dresser leg and held the rope in his hand as he and the dog bounded out. The woman, the boys' mother, Carrie, opened the front door and disap-peared inside.

Tom and the dog romped around the side of the house to the back. There was a cistern with a pump on the small back porch. Tom found a rusty coffee can, pumped it full of clear water, and set it down in front of the dog. As the dog eagerly half-emptied it, Tom cupped his right hand under the spout, pumped the handle with his left, and drank his fill.

They scampered into the back yard and discovered a garden growing in a strip of land between the house and the church next door. Young bean, corn, sweet pea and potato plants, along with a patch of lettuce and green onions, fought the weeds for survival. A Victory Garden, Tom thought. He wondered why anyone would go to the trouble to plow and plant and then move off in such a hurry as to leave it. It worried him, too, because he knew

18

who would no doubt wind up tending it.

The dog lunged at the rope, which was a new thing to him, and gave his best begging whine. Tom led him back around to the front. Everyone was so busy unloading household items they didn't seem to notice them. Duty called, but the urge to explore their new surroundings called louder. Tom gazed down the street, which ended in the trees on the second rise of the riverbank. He couldn't see the river for the trees, but he could smell it. And it was the aroma of adventure.

He led the bounding dog down the gravel sidewalk to the churchyard. The white frame building seemed to lean just a little atop its concrete block basement walls. Tombstones marking the sleeping places of some of the church's founders rose up in a grassy plot out front. Tom bent over to examine the dates on one of the stones.

Suddenly the dog yanked the rope from his hand and scampered into the street, growls bouncing from his throat. A brown, collie-looking dog, nearly twice as big as Tom's dog, rushed toward him from the other side of the street. They stopped five feet short of a collision. Both had their hackles up, and both flung gravels with a hind foot.

"Come back here, Chopper!" Tom shouted. "Leave that old' brown dog alone."

"At's right, Buckeye! You better call that mutt back. Leader will chew the mangy cur up and spit him out, if I say the word."

The boy belonging to the voice stood behind the fence bounding the front yard of the house across the street from the church. He tossed his head to throw a mane of red hair from his eyes. His freckled face was turned down in a scowl. Tom was not intimidated. If this boy wanted to be rude, he could be rude, too. He squared his shoulders and stuck out his chest.

"I wouldn't be too sure of that, buster," he said. "And let me straighten you out on one thing right quick: my dog's no cur. He's almost 100 percent wire-haired rat terrier. Best rat dog you'll ever see."

The redhead snickered, then threw his head back and laughed derisively. Quickly, Tom added, "You better call your ugly dog off if you don't want him turned into mince meat."

That stopped the laughing. A moment of tension passed before the redhead said, "Well, I swear. Ain't never seen such impudence. A total stranger – and a Buckeye to boot – comin' in here and. . . sic him, Leader! Eat that cur rat dog up!"

The brown dog whined and looked back at his master, careful to keep one eye on Chopper, who held his ground, lips curled back to expose white teeth. The brown dog walked back and fourth stiff-legged, hair on his back erect. He turned slowly and walked back toward the redhead. Chopper retreated, too. He circled Tom's legs, several choice dog-talk cuss words emanating from his throat.

Tom wasn't sure what to do next. He bent over and rubbed his dog's head. Here he was, he said to himself, a free man in a free country, just minding his own business, and this boy was treating him like some kind of outcast. Did Tom pose a threat to his territory? Surely there must be room for middle ground.

Something whizzed by and struck a tombstone behind him. He saw the redhead, slingshot in hand, bend over to pick up more ammo.

"Why you dirty son-of-a-gun!" Tom yelled. "This is war!" He sidestepped up the sidewalk to the big maple in front of his new house. Where was his slingshot? In one of them durn boxes, he thought.

Tom ducked behind the maple just as another stone hit it a glancing blow. The marble-sized missile struck the house and spun around on the porch floor. Tom scooped up two rocks and threw them both in quick succession. One bounced off the redhead's fence rail and the other thumped against a flower box atop a stump just as the redhead ducked behind it. He grabbed up another rock and cocked his arm. But he didn't get to pull the trigger, because a hand grabbed his forearm.

"Drop it!" his mother said. She gave him a smack on the rear and whirled him around by the ear. "James Thomas, I can't believe you! Here we are with all this work to do, dark's going to catch us, and you're out here playing games."

Games, heck. You call all-out war a game?

She pushed him toward the truck, then pointed at the redhead, who was snickering again. "And you," she said, "you stop with your throwing rocks in this direction."

20

A minute later, as Tom carried a box of clothes and curtains from the truck to the front porch, the redhead, hands cupped to his mouth, yelled, "We'll find out later how tough you are, little boy. We'll see how tough you are when you're out from behind your mother's skirts."

All Tom could do was stick his tongue out at him. As he went through the front door, he heard the redhead fire off one final verbal volley: "Up your hairy leg with a blow torch, Jack!"

CHAPTER 2:
MAN'S BEST FRIEND

A mockingbird singing from the big silver maple at the side of the house greeted Tom Sycamore as his feet hit the floor. A sweet sound it was, filled with a promise of the continuation of life. But a nagging thought of the redhead troubled his mind. If he persisted in his rude behavior, Tom decided, then he could be rude, too. Bust his nose for him, if he had to.

It was not good to taste anger before breakfast. He shook his head to clear his mind. He dressed and went downstairs, where he found that Flint and his father had hooked up the kerosene cook stove in the kitchen. His mother had fixed flour and water gravy in bacon drippings. They spooned it over slices of light bread that had been dipped in bacon grease and fried to a crispy brown in an iron skillet.

After breakfast, everybody finished unpacking and positioning things. Bruce Sycamore had walked up to Davis & Harvey's, which handled local accounts for the electric company, to sign up for power.

"Stick close here, now, and help your mother," he had told Tom before leaving. "The quicker we get the work done here, the quicker we can get down there – he motioned toward the river – and try our luck on the catfish."

His father kept a dozen cane poles rigged with line and hook and sinker, plus he had three bait-casting reels on steel casting rods. Tom remembered a time up in Ohio when his father borrowed a car from a friend and drove him and Flint out to the Charles River, where they caught a carp that covered half the rear floorboard.

Flint had peddled off on his bike for somewhere. Tom helped his mother clear the table and went out onto the back porch with a plateful of gravy and toast leftovers.

"Tale it easy!" he said as Chopper lapped it up. "You're getting gravy all over your whiskers."

His mother's voice came through the screen door: "Tom, don't get any ideas about running off nowhere. Your father wants you in that garden as soon as the dew dries."

No surprise there. But he felt a tinge of envy, of injustice. Where the devil did Flint go?

A more pressing question, though, concerned the garden.

"Why'd the people move off and leave that garden, Mom?"

Carrie Sycamore came out onto the back porch, drying her hands on a dishrag. She looked in the direction of the garden.

"It's a sad story," she said. "According to your Aunt Mary, who wrote us about this house being empty, a young Marine put this garden in. He'd finished his basic training and was home on a short leave when he did the plowing and the planting. Then he shipped out to the Pacific and . . . oh, Tom, he was killed. A place called Okinawa."

She dabbed at her eyes with the dishrag; pulled Tom in close to her bosom, unconsciously rubbing the fingers of her right hand through his blonde hair.

"Lowell Thomas was talking about that place this week," she continued. "Our boys are still dying there at the hands of the cruel Japanese. Lord knows how many will die if we have to invade the Japanese homelands, which Lowell Thomas was saying could happen."

She released Tom and continued to look out over the garden, wringing the dishrag in her hands. Tom knew she was thinking of Flint, that she lay awake nights worrying that he would have to take up a rifle and leave them.

"Mom, Dad says we've got Hitler beat and Tojo's got his tail between his legs. Flint'll not have to go."

She looked down at him with a weak attempt at a smile.

Secretly, Tom wished the war would last until he could get there.

"Anyway," his mother said finally, "the young Marine's wife – they had been married only about six months – nearly lost their baby she was carrying when she got the news of her husband's death. She didn't lose it though. Mary said she left here and moved in with her parents over in Shawnee."

24

This put a different slant on the garden chores, Tom thought. Bringing it to harvest was the least he could do to get back at the Japs. The Marine's Victory Garden would be a source of pride for him.

For now, though, it could wait until the dew dried.

Already the sun was turning the morning to gold. Chopper lapped the empty gravy pan, sliding it across the porch floor and off into the grass. Time was wasting.

"Come on, boy, let's go look around." He headed around the corner of the house for the front. The little dog excitedly circled him, pausing only to leap up and put his forepaws on Tom's legs. He would go anywhere Tom wanted to go – do anything to escape the mundane life.

Tom paused on the graveled sidewalk in front of his house and picked up several small rocks and slipped them into a pocket of his cut-off overalls. He patted the slingshot protruding from a back pocket. Chopper gave a whine mixed with excitement and anxiety as his master crossed the street and ambled down the sidewalk toward the redhead's domain.

Tom stopped short as he spotted the enemy. The redhead came around the corner of his house, walking on stilts, his eyes to the ground. He continued his unsteady gait until he reached his front fence. He stepped off onto the two-by-four railing, lifted the stilts over the fence, climbed back on them, and headed up the sidewalk straight for Tom, his attention still directed toward where his "feet" were crunching down.

Chopper growled from down deep in his throat as the redhead's dog scampered around the corner of the house and crawled through a hole in the fence. The part-collie had spotted Chopper, the rat-terrier, who had diverted his course to near the middle of the street. Growls bounced from the brown dog's throat and his hackles raised as he bounded stiff-legged toward Chopper. Chopper stiffened, ready for an assault, his hackles also raised.

The redhead broke stride and staggered a bit as he watched the dogs. Then he saw Tom. His eyebrows lowered and a scrawl crossed his face.

"Well, well. And just where do you think you're going, momma's boy?" he growled.

"I guess that's my business," Tom answered. "But it's for sure I'm going down this sidewalk, to see the river."

"And who gave you permission to cross over here and walk bare-faced down my sidewalk? You think you can just move in here and take right over? You Buckeyes are like that. I wanna know what makes people like you tick."

This boy clearly needs a lesson in Democracy.

"Nobody gave me permission. This is a public sidewalk. And this is still a free country. That's why our boys are fightin' the Krauts and the Japs – keep it safe from dictators like you."

The redhead took two long strides closer, closing the distance between him and Tom to about six feet. Tom's head came to just above his waist. He looked down at Tom as though he was an insect worthy only of crushing. Tom was thinking of ducking and running right between the stilts, just to see the look on the redhead's face. As the redhead took a step closer, one stilt landed on the side of a rock, causing him to lose his balance. He staggered like a robot out of control and toppled against the fence. One hand caught between the rail and a stilt. The redhead hit the ground, then jumped up blowing on the fingers of the hand that was pinched between the stilt and the fence.

"Oh, oh! Goshdurn it! Mashed my goshdurn fingers! Ummm-umph! All your fault, too, you dirty son-of-a-gun!"

He grabbed up one of his stilts and drew a line in the dirt and the gravels.

"Well, you ain't comin' down this sidewalk, snodgrass. You cross that line, ol' buddy buddy, and something bad is gonna happen, like gettin' your nose smashed all over your face. That's a promise!"

Now down from his lofty perch, the redhead didn't look half as formidable. He was not quite as tall as Tom, and certainly just as slim. He had a long, skinny nose and a face to match it.

Tom hesitated only a moment before stepping across the line. The redhead shot him a look, and Tom hoped he didn't have a pistol.

"Well, boy, you're a testy one, ain't 'cha! Push a man right to the limits!" said the redhead. He whirled and picked up a chip of wood from the side of the ditch. Tom backed off a step, dukes raised. The redhead laid the chip of wood atop his left shoulder.

26

"Knock that off, if you dare," he said. "And if you're crazy enough to do that, get ready to take what follows."

"And if I knock it off, what are you gonna do about it, Mr. Tough Guy?"

"Why, I'll knock your fool block off, that's what."

Their noses were hardly more than a foot apart when Tom reached out and knocked the chip off the redhead's shoulder.

"Well, I swear! I've never seen a body push a man like you do. You're taking advantage of my special good mood this morning. But you're trying my patience, boy. Don't you realize that if I give the signal, a dozen or more commandos will swoop down and whale the living tar right out of you?"

"You're in need of help, that's for sure. But you and the whole German army backin' you couldn't do that."

"*German* army! Well boy, that's it! – I'm gonna take you…"

Just then the attention of both boys was detracted from the front line by the actions of their dogs. Chopper was on his back with the brown dog on top of him. Then the brown dog leaped off and rolled down into the ditch, Chopper on top of him, feigning a death grip on his throat. They rolled over and over in the ditch, then both leaped up and the brown dog chased Chopper around a power pole. They stopped to face each other, both in a praying position, both of them wagging their tails, then leaped back into mock battle.

The enemy watched for a minute, picked up his stilts, and carried them back toward his gate. He disappeared around the corner of his house.

Tom headed on down the sidewalk toward the river. He looked back over his shoulder and called for Chopper. Chopper ran to catch up, the brown dog right on his heels. Tom heard the redhead calling to his dog, clapping his hands.

"Come on Leader. Leader! Get your hind end back up here, you traitor."

Leader stopped, looked back, whined, but continued on with Tom and Chopper. Tom hid to grin as he scrunched his shoulders up. This was wonderful, he thought. Even his dog won't have anything to do with him.

Tom stopped at the top of the bank and looked down into a narrow, weed-filled strip of bottom lying between the base of the second rise and the top of the tree-lined first rise. He had a glimpse of the river through the willows and maples.

He hadn't spotted the path, not until the redhead startled him by passing just to his right.

"I forgot I had the watch," Tom heard him say as he started down the hill. "My job to keep check on the *Reuben James*."

Tom wasn't sure if he was speaking to him or to himself. The redhead called to Leader. Leader followed him. Chopper followed Leader, nipping playfully at his heals. Tom paused for a moment, wondering if the redhead was leading him into an ambush.

But he followed after the redhead and the dogs. They crossed the narrow bottom and entered the willows. The redhead stopped at the water's edge and, hands on hips, stood looking down at a red johnboat. A rope tied to the boat's bow disappeared under the water.

"Oh my gosh, this river's coming faster than I thought," the redhead said. "Good thing you reminded me to come down here." Now Tom was certain he was talking to him.

The redhead plunged his arms into the muddy water up to his shoulders and untied the rope from an underwater tree root. He retied it to the limb of a willow, several feet above the ground. He grunted as he attempted to pull the nose of the boat up onto shore. Tom grabbed hold of the front seat and helped him. The redhead seemed to welcome the help. At least he showed no resentment.

Leader lay on his back in the sand, all four legs extended, and Chopper chewed on his ear. The redhead watched them a minute as he dried his hands on his pants legs, a smile turning up the corners of his mouth.

"Looks like our dogs have taken a liking to one another," he mumbled.

"Yeah. Sure looks like they're friends," said Tom, resting his hands in his back pockets. He pulled out his slingshot and got a rock from his front pocket. The redhead stiffened, then relaxed as he saw Tom taking aim on a can floating by with the current, just outside the willows. His shot thumped the can.

"Good shot," said the redhead, pulling out his own slingshot and some ammo. His shot landed just behind the can before it disappeared downstream. Another, bigger, can drifted by, and both boys scored a direct hit. They used up all their stones before returning the slingshots to their pockets.

"This is the *Reuben James*," the redhead said, squatting and patting the red johnboat with one hand. "We caught her from the floodwaters a month ago. We named her in honor of Keith Richards' brother, who died when a German sub torpedoed the real *Reuben James*."

Flanders added that Keith Richards had lost both his brother and his father to the war.

Tom listened with real interest. Lots of people had lost loved ones in the war, and especially so, it seemed, in the village of Hooperville.

"My mom's scared to death that my big brother, Flint, is going to have to go to the Pacific and help finish the Japs," Tom said.

"Wish I was old enough to go," the redhead said. "You ever wish that?"

"Yeah. Yeah, I do. Young Marine lived in my new house got killed on Okinawa. Left a wife and a baby on the way."

"That's true. I knew that."

They heard their dogs barking and turned to see Leader and Chopper both with their paws on the base of a big maple. A squirrel squawked at them from one of the upper limbs.

The redhead, his head cocked to one side, stole a look at Tom. He laughed and shook his head from side to side.

"Garsh," he said, "looks like our dogs have become best friends." With a sheepish grin, he added, "Maybe we ought to, too?"

"I'd think so, especially since we're neighbors."

The redhead extended his right hand, and Tom reached out to grasp it. "My name's James Thomas Sycamore," he said. "Friends call me Tom."

"Mine's Gale Flanders. Glad to meet you, Tom Sycamore. And, listen, I'm sorry I tried to bean you there yesterday."

"And I apologize for trying to rock you, Gale."

Out on the river a steamboat plowed upstream, pushing a string of empty coal barges. Tom was fascinated by the sight. Gale seemed hardly to notice it, until he saw Tom move for a better look through the leafy willows.

"That's the *Omar*," Gale said. "Look at the size of the waves she's throwing behind that paddlewheel. She's got no wave-breaker."

Gale launched into an expatiation of his domain they had entered. Not far downstream, he said, was Sherwood Forest. And down that way was where the clubhouse was.

"But you'll have to understand that, even though we're friends, I can't take an outsider to the clubhouse. Not without permission of the Major."

"The Major?"

Gale explained that "the Major" was how they sometimes referred to Vince Royalton, the undisputed leader of the Hooperville Braves. Vince Royalton, Tom was to learn, read every adventure book he could get his hands on. He liked to take fiction from the pages and turn it into real life, or maybe some kind of movie version of real life, usually with him playing the roles of producer, director and star. More often that not, though, he made up his own script as he went along.

"He comes up with the craziest things sometimes," Gale said. "But he does get us into a lot of nice adventures. See that sandbar over there?" He pointed toward the distant Ohio shore. "Well, no, you can't see it now, cause the water's up. Lots of people think that's the Ohio River bottoms. But it ain't. That's Guam, honey. Guam, Iwo Jima, Bataan. We must have killed a thousand Japs on an invasion there. The Major, leading the charge, of course, was machine-gunned twice and somersaulted by a hand grenade, but they couldn't stop him. He's like one of these cartoon characters – mash him, bash him, riddle him, he springs right back."

For now, though, Gale explained, the Major had taken on a new role. "He's Robin Hood, and we're his merry men. Down there in Sherwood, we've got ropes tied to tree branches. We can swing down and knock the king's men right off their horses. He's got that scheduled for this afternoon. Yes, for now, we've gone from carbines to bows and arrows – ha!"

The two boys fell silent as they walked back up to the village. At the street's end on top of the second rise, Gale jumped ahead of Tom to face him, placed his hands on Tom's shoulders. "Listen, Tom," he said. "The Hooperville Braves is a great organization. You've got to get in, and I think I can swing it. You're a Buckeye, I know, but you can't help that. We got no choice about where we're born. But we can convert you, especially after you see the way the Ohio boys treat us when we go over town. In a couple of weeks school will be out, and we'll have us a summer filled with more adventures than you can imagine. You talk about fun!"

Tom wondered what he would have to do to join up.

"Oh, there's nothing automatic about it. You'll have to pass an initiation, and it'll be a tough one. Vince will see to that. But I think you're a tough guy, and I don't think you'll have any trouble. After you do that, the members will vote on you. One black ball could keep you out, but that won't happen. Not if you pass the test."

Tom mulled it over as they continued on up the street. They reached Gale's gate and Tom said, "OK. When?" Gale smiled and slapped him on the back.

"There's a meeting this afternoon. I'll take you down and introduce you – sponsor you. Pick you up after dinner. Right now, I've got this grass to cut."

"And I've got weedin' and hoein' to do in that garden out back. But I'll be ready."

As Tom crossed the street, he heard his mother's voice calling from behind the house: "Tom! Oh Tom. James Thomas...."

CHAPTER 3:
TOM MEETS THE GANG

The May sun was straight overhead when Tom finished hoeing the last of the three rows of potato plants. He had also pulled the weeds from the lettuce and onion patch. Not a bad job, he thought, looking back over his work. There were still two rows of beans and two rows of peas to do, not to mention several rows of sprouting corn plants, somewhat shorter than the weeds around them. He dropped the hoe and examined a blister on his palm. A catbird called in sympathy from the cherry tree at the far end of the garden.

Suddenly he felt the presence of someone else in the garden with him.

It was almost as if he could feel a hand on his shoulder. He spun all the way around, but saw no one. Chopper, dozing in the sun between the bean rows, jerked his head up and perked his ears. He barked sharply, whined, and, with his tail between his legs, hurried off to crawl under the floor of the storage shed. Curious behavior for his normally fearless dog, Tom thought. Tom felt no fear, just curiosity. Whoever – or whatever – was there posed no threat to him, he was certain.

He shook his head vigorously from side to side.

Too much sun?

His eyes still searched the garden as he put the hoe in the shed and then went to the back door. Chopper scampered out and followed closely on his heels. His father and Flint showed up as Tom washed his hands at the sink. His mother soon had dinner on the table. She had cooked a pot of brown beans with fat pork in them and fried a pan of cornbread in an iron skillet. Tom's father spooned the thick bean soup over crumbled hot cornbread. Between bites he told Carrie they would soon have electricity.

"I got us signed up, and the man who works for the electric company lives right here in Hooperville, so he's supposed to come around and turn it on," he said.

Flint wolfed his food and was off and gone on his bike again. Bruce Sycamore looked over the work Tom had done in the garden, gave him a pat on the head, and pointed to a roll of wet newspaper lying under the spout of the cistern pump. The paper was wrapped around a dozen tomato plants.

"We'll plant them at sundown," he told Tom. "Looks like no fishing for awhile, not with that river up and swift and muddy. You hang around here and help your mother. I'm going to walk down to Killin Hollow and see about lining up my ride to work for Monday."

Back inside, Tom showed his mother the blister on his palm. She burst it with a needle and put iodine on it. Tom did a quick little dance while blowing on the wound.

"I'll see if I can't find you a pair of gloves to work in," she said.

She returned in a few minutes and handed Tom a pair of cotton gloves. Tom knew his enemy-turned-friend would soon be calling with some important business. His mind began whirling to come up with some idea to allow him to escape the garden work for a while.

"Where the heck's Flint, Momma?" he asked. "Is he going to do anything around here?"

"Your brother's got himself a job, down there on the Henson farm, I think he said. They're shoveling manure out of a barn. Do you want to do that, let him come and work the garden?"

Getting no response to her question, she told Tom to rest a minute, while she finished hanging out the wash, and then maybe she could help some with the hoeing.

Tom sat on the edge of the daybed in the front room and thumbed through a Superman comic book with his good hand. He dropped the book and leaped up when he heard Gale Flanders calling for him through the front screen door. Tom tiptoed out the door, motioning to Gale with one finger over his lips as he eased the door back shut. He leaped off the porch with a muffled cry of, "Let's git!"

And down the street for the river they flew, with Chopper and Leader flying behind them.

They sped down the narrow river bottom and entered into a grove of tall maples, sycamores and tulip poplars. Gale stopped Tom and patted him on the shoulder. "The boys are already down there," he said. "Vince sent me up to get you."

Then, turning somber, he gave Tom the password phrase he would need to repeat in order to gain entrance to the clubhouse and "go before the council."

They proceeded on for a sort distance under the shade of the trees before Gale stopped again. "Here we are," he said. "The clubhouse."

"Where?"

"Right there," Gale said, pointing upwards.

The tree house was cradled in the limbs of a huge tulip poplar, perhaps 30 feet above the ground – or water, as it was now, for the river had crept up to surround the base of the tree and lapped eight or ten feet onto the shore beyond it.

"Remember, now, after I knock on the door, it's up to you to give the pass words. You got 'em?"

"Oh yeah," Tom said, rehearsing the four words in his mind.

With that, Gale plunged through the muddy water toward the tree, which featured short lengths of two-by-fours and assorted pieces of driftwood nailed to the trunk to form a ladder of sorts up to the tree house.

Tom lingered on the shore. "How deep is that water?" he asked.

"I don't know. Maybe waist deep. There'll be a drop-off on the far side of the tree, though. Probably fifteen feet there."

Tom followed his friend, being careful to step where he had stepped. They went up the ladder and through a trapdoor in the wooden deck that fronted the tree house, which was made of various sizes of boards and had a tarpaper roof. The door was shut and a curtain or drape covered a window.

Gale rapped three times on the door. A voice from within barked, "Hark. Who goes there?"

Gale shot Tom a look. "As if they didn't know," he muttered, then said

35

aloud, "It is I, Friar Tuck."

"The passwords. You must give the passwords," said the voice.

Gale pointed at Tom and his hands made the motions of a choir director.

"Down With the Rich!" Tom shouted, feeling a little silly but enjoying himself nonetheless.

"Yea, then enter," the voice from within said.

Gale opened the door and Tom filed in behind him. The place seemed as dark as a movie house, but the flickering light cast by a single candle on top of an orange crate was enough for Tom to make out four boys, and get a pretty good look at each. One was seated behind the crate, two stood at attention, one on each side of it, and another lurked in the background.

The boy to the left of the crate was lanky and his shock of hair was such a light yellow that it almost appeared to be white. The boy on the right was stocky, broad-shouldered, with short, rusty hair and freckles. Both had bows strung over their shoulders. The boy in the background was smaller than any of the other three and had black hair and dark eyes. He seemed to be enjoying the uncomfortable position Tom found himself in.

Gale ushered Tom to a position in front of the crate, where both stood at attention. The boy seated behind the crate – who had to be Vince Royalton, the "Major," Tom figured – wore a jaunty little hat with a feather protruding from the band. He stood and looked Tom up and down. He wore a long-sleeved smock that looked like a pajama top. It was gathered at the waist by a wide, black belt. His bottom attire was a pair of tight-fitting red long johns, flap sewed up, Tom presumed. He had a bow strung over one shoulder and a quiver of arrows over the other. His light brown hair protruded from the front of the hat and spilled down onto his forehead.

He stood and looked Tom up and down. He barked a command: "Little John, throw back the arrow guards, that we might have a better look at this knave."

The broad-shouldered one leaped from his position at Royalton's left and drew back the curtains from the front window, as well as from a window facing the shore. He quickly returned to his original position, snapping to attention.

The leader turned his attention to Gale.

"Who is this stranger you have brought into our midst, Friar Tuck?" he asked.

"Sir Robin Hood, sir, this is Tom Sycamore, the new boy I was telling you about who moved into the old Sexton place, where the Marine and his wife lived?" Gale said. "He wants to join the Braves, and he's a good candidate. He's tough enough and he don't back down."

Robin Hood returned his gaze to Sycamore, who was still trying to figure out what a knave was.

"Tough, you think he is, hey? Well, we'll see how tough he is. We have our ways of finding that out. But tell me, how can you be certain he's not one of the King's loyal subjects, sent here to Sherwood Forest to spy on us?" He motioned to the one called Little John. "Go round, Little John, and check this man for weapons."

Little John stepped behind Tom and patted him down head to toe, checking the pockets of his cut-off jeans and pulling the ball cap off his head. Other than a brown pair of worn tennis shoes, they were Sycamore's only attire.

"He seems clean, sire," Little John said, then returned to his position by the crate.

"Well, gee whiz, Vince, – er, Sir Hood – I had already checked him for weapons. You don't think I would …"

Robin Hood cut him off with an uplifted hand, then directed a series of questions at Tom Sycamore – about his background, his thoughts toward the weaker sex, his skills with a bow, and, finally, about whether he was aware of any "stingy rich people" who needed robbing.

Tom stammered over an attempt to answer, but Robin Hood seemed to have grown tired of the questioning, saying the truth would come out soon enough about whether Tom was brave enough to become a Brave.

"You can go back down and wait on the shore while we decide what your initiation will be," he said, motioning for Friar Tuck to escort Tom out. Tom followed Gale out the door and down through the trapdoor in the deck. Chopper barked and leaped belly-deep into the water as Tom waded ashore.

"Wait here. We won't be long," Gale said, then went back up the ladder to rejoin the others,

After a while the others came down the tree and waded ashore single file, Gale took hold of Tom's arm and guided him off to the side. The other four, armed to the hilt with bows and arrows and swords, went on down-river through the trees.

"The Major has set three tests you'll have to pass to have a chance to get in," Gale said. "And they're not too bad. Well, one is. Stupid, really. But you can handle it."

What is it?"

"You'll find out tonight?"

"Tonight?"

"That's right. He's set two of them for tonight. Can you get out after dark? After bedtime, I mean. I can, because I've got my own room."

Tom thought about the swing-out window over the front porch. He would be sleeping with Flint, and his mom had a habit of checking on them before she retired.

"I don't know. I think so. I'll try."

"You have to, Tom. Test One and Two have to be done under cover of darkness."

He reached out and placed his hands on Tom's shoulders and looked him in the eyes. "Yes, while the rest of the world sleeps," he said, "Vince Royalton and the Hooperville Braves will be out helping the poor and the downtrodden, and trying to save this Great Republic." He tried to keep a straight face, but was not entirely successful.

Tom swallowed hard and said nothing more.

The two of them followed on down the path the others had taken. On the way, Gale explained that Tom would not be permitted to take part in the gang's activities, not until he was a bona fide member of the Braves.

But he was given a sampler. For the better part of an hour, he sat in the forks of a maple tree and watched a magnificent robbery by Robin Hood and his merry men. It was Robin himself who swung down from a tree to dispatch the armed guard seated beside he driver of the carriage. He forced the driver to move over while he took control of the reins. Then the other

38

four dropped down from the trees and trained their notched arrows on the other guards, said to be mounted on horses.

Little John and Friar Tuck mounted the carriage and threw down the chest filled with gold and jewels. But right then a rear guard of horsemen showed up, and it was hand-to-hand combat that followed. Though heavily outnumbered, Robin and his band leaped and pranced with their swords flashing, running through one of the King's men after another. Tom wasn't sure how many fell, but Robin and his crew seemed to escape with only a few minor wounds. Robin helped the carriage driver back into his seat and told him to "gather your wounded and return to the king. Tell him his gold and jewels will go to feed the poor of his realm."

Any idiot who would drive a carriage into Sherwood Forest carrying a small fortune deserved to be robbed, Tom thought.

CHAPTER 4:
THE NEWS CENTER

Other than face his mother after the abrupt departure he had made, Tom went around back to the storage shed, got a hoe, and went on into the garden. He was hoeing weeds from between the corn rows when his mother came out to check on her wash on the line.

"Oh, you, Tom. There you are," she said. "Where have you been for the past two hours?"

"Why, right here, Momma, working in this garden, just like you told me to do."

"Uh huh, oh sure. And the Ohio River runs through Arizona."

"It does? I never knew that, Momma." Tom grinned as he said it. He had a grin that allowed him to get by with lots of little things with his mother. Fun fibs, he called them.

"Well, strange it is, that, warm as it is, I don't see no sweat on your brow," she said, stepping forward and running the backs of her fingers across Tom's forehead. "But I better start seeing some. You remember what my pineapple upside down cake tastes like? Well, I was thinking of making one, but . . .."

Tom started making the hoe fly like an automatic threshing machine. She laughed as she took some clothes off the line and put them in a basket.

Tom hadn't been at his chores long before he heard someone calling his name. He looked and saw Gale peering around the corner of the house.

"Ask your mom can you come over to my house after while," he said. "Vince and all the other guys are gonna come over. We listen to our radio shows and play some games."

Carrie Sycamore came out to empty her mop bucket. She saw Gale and threw a suspicious glance at him. Gale stepped back behind the corner of the house.

"You needn't be afraid of me," she said to the corner. "I'm not some mean old woman who beats up on boys."

Gale stepped back into view and smiled sheepishly, his hands at his sides, and quickly apologized for smacking the Sycamore house with a rock. "I didn't mean it, Mrs. Sycamore. And Tom and me are best friends now. I came to get him to go over to my house for a little while this evening. Can he?"

"Tom and I," she corrected him. "Well, I forgive you. And any friend of Tom's is a friend of mine." She turned to Tom and said, "You can go over for a while after supper. But remember tonight's bath night, and you know what tomorrow is."

———————

The Flanders home, a two-story frame, was often the meeting place for the Hooperville Braves. Over on the fireplace side, one wall of the big front room held plenty of shelves filled with books, both paperbacks and classics, and the latest issues and back copies of Life and Saturday Evening Post magazines. One shelf held board games like Monopoly and checkers. There was a Victrola record machine with its crank handle and a stack of .78 rpm records.

The Flanders family included Gale's dad, Will, who worked at the steel mill in Shawnee and owned a 1941 Crosby. Well, he and the bank owned it together. His father, Grandpa Newt Flanders, who drew a pension from the steel mill, generally occupied an easy chair over in a windowed alcove. There was a floor lamp to read by and he was within reach of the big floor model Philco radio. He was a tall, heavy man whose thick eyebrows and mustache matched the color of the smoke that curled up from his pipe. His scissors and scrapbook were always handy and now he was engrossed in a fresh copy of The Shawnee Times.

Gale's mother, Lois, a slender woman with a ready smile, could make the best chocolate chip cookies and peanut butter fudge in the country – when, that is, she was able to get her hands on the rationing stamps required to get the sugar. Gale's sister, Gina, two years the younger, was playing a lively tune on the upright piano when Gale and Tom walked in that evening.

When she overheard Tom paying compliments to Gale on her piano playing, she stood up to take a bow. The piano kept on playing. Tom had heard of a player piano, but this was the first one he'd ever seen. Gina laughed at the expression on his face before sitting back down.

After Tom had been introduced to the family, the four boys he had met in the tree house showed up. They greeted the Flanderses, but hardly acknowledged Tom, filing by and soon finding things to occupy their hands and minds.

Gale pointed to each one as he introduced them to Tom. Vince Royalton, alias Robin Hood, had headed straight for the book shelves and was seated on the floor, looking scholarly, with a copy of "The Adventures of Huckleberry Finn," leafing through its pages in search of the place where he had left off. Hobo Hooper, alias Little John, looked up from where he was playing a game of checkers with Dale Riley, the dark-haired boy who stood behind Vince in the tree house, his dark eyes seeming to relish the discomfort Tom showed at going before the council. The remaining Brave, Keith Richards, the skinny one with the mop of yellow hair who had stood to Tom's left at the orange crate, had sat down beside Gina on the piano stool and was helping her install another tune roll.

There was joshing and bantering and the camaraderie was real and enjoyable. Among themselves, at least. Toward Tom, they remained standoffish. He was still an outsider, a Buckeye, even though Gale was doing his best to combat that. He got Tom a place on the floor close to the Philco as activities ceased while the gang rode with the Lone Ranger.

"Who was that masked man?"

"He left a silver bullet."

"Why, it was the Lone Ranger."

"Hi ho Silver, away."

"Get 'em up, Scout."

After the radio serials ended, Grandpa Flanders shushed the boys as H.V. Kaltenborn came on the air with the latest war news.

Later, outside, after the boys had left and gone home, Gale told Tom what he could expect for that night's initiation. He should wear long pants and a long-sleeved shirt, along with shoes and long socks. Tom pointed out where his bedroom window was above the alleyway. Gale told him to listen for a cat's meow from below the window. When he heard that, he was to come out and join the others in the alley.

The Sycamore supper consisted of warmed-over beans, potatoes fried crispy brown, and fresh baked cornbread. The electricity was on and the kerosene lamps were stored away.

Flint was excited about his new job on the Henson farm.

"The hay crop's early and Mr. Henson cut it today," Flint said. "He wants us to work tomorrow, to put it up, Momma, but he said we wouldn't have to come out until afternoon, so we could attend Sunday … er, well …."

"That's right, young man. Sunday school. You and James Thomas are going to be in the Lord's House when the first bell rings. They say this is a nice little church, and right next door – and Methodist, too."

Tom's parents hardly ever attended church, except now and then on special occasions, but ever since he was about five years old his mother had always made sure he and Flint were scrubbed and in their best clothes and in the Sunday school service in whatever church was close enough to walk to. Tom still had a small white New Testament he was awarded for going a year in the Ashville church without missing a Sunday.

It was the teaching he had learned from that book that was causing him an uneasy feeling of guilt over the bit of deceit he was planning for the coming darkness. He eased the burden of the unborn sin by taking the hoe to the garden. He had dug up the weeds from a row of potatoes by the time the sun sank into a bank of threatening clouds on the horizon downriver. A yellow light spilled from the kitchen window as he put the hoe away. Whip-poorwills called from the hills above town.

Inside, his mother was at the sewing machine. Flint had gone off with some of his newfound friends to Thelma's Grill, a gathering place for teenagers that stood near the mouth of Killin Hollow.

His father had turned on their floor model radio and tuned into a news program. A local report detailed the liberation from a German prison camp of four local soldiers, including one from Hooperville.

44

Without waiting to be told, Tom brought in the galvanized wash tub, heated a pan of water on the cook stove, and had his Saturday night bath there in the kitchen. His mother brought in his pajamas and checked behind his ears. Then Tom amazed her by heading upstairs for bed. He paused on the stairway to listen to Gabriell Heater reporting on how Allied forces continued to close in on Berlin, and of efforts to confirm the death of Hitler. In the Pacific, American infantrymen continued to advance on Okinawa.

"You're next, Tojo!" he heard his father say as he reached the top of the landing.

He paused in what was to become his brother's room. He glanced out the window toward the garden and thought he saw someone walking among the crop rows in the moonlight. There was something there. He rubbed his eyes and shook his head, and when he looked again the image was gone.

Strange.

He stripped out of his pajamas and dressed in long jeans and a long-sleeved shirt, leaving his old shoes handy at the side of the bed. He wished Flint would come on and get to bed and go to sleep. He wasn't sure what his brother's reaction would be if he came in and found him gone. He wasn't the kind of brother who would rat on his kid brother – not, at least, unless he thought Tom's escapades might get him into trouble, maybe get him hurt.

Actually, although he felt a tinge of jealousy at times for Flint's privileges, his big brother was his hero. Tom thought about the time, back last fall up in Ashville, when Flint had saved him from a black eye, or worse. Tom had strapped on his skates one Saturday and was skating down the sidewalk to the corner parlor to meet Annie and buy her a sundae. Two boys, both of them in high school, stopped him in front of the poolroom. The ugliest one pushed him around a bit, asked where he was going in such a hurry, and then demanded that Tom "loan" him a dollar. He had Tom by the collar, and Tom knew he couldn't fight with skates on. So he did the safe and sane thing. He handed over the fifty cents he had and skated home to tell Flint.

Flint went right on in the poolroom door and Tom, after pointing out the two boys at a pool table in the back, watched from just inside. The owner saw trouble coming, but before he could move to intervene, Flint had bloodied the ugly one's nose and put a whelp on his cheekbone. He started for the other boy, but he ducked out the backdoor.

"He took this from my little brother out front," Flint explained to the owner as the beaten one handed over fifty cents. Then, turning to his foe, he said, "You even think about touching him – nodding toward Tom at the front – again and you'll get worse that this."

Tom never had any more problems with either boy.

It's nice to have a big brother.

Now, as he listened for the cat's meow to float in through the window screen, he decided to make a trial run. He could go out the side window, grab a limb of the big silver maple, and descend the trunk to the ground. That was a bit chancy, though, and it would require removing the screen. He chose the other option, opening the hinged double window in the front of the room and stepping out onto the roof of the front porch. The corner post was nearly flush with the roof edge and it was no problem to shinny down it. Chopper greeted him almost as soon as his feet hit the ground, squirming and barking and wagging his tail to let his master know he was ready for whatever was up.

"Sh-h-h. Shh! No noise, Chopper. Can't have that." The dog whined and cussed when Tom locked him in the shed. "You don't have to be initiated, you lucky dog. You've already been accepted."

Getting back up the post wasn't as easy as coming down. But, by getting his feet in the lattice work at the top of the post, he was able to push and belly his way back onto the roof.

He lay down and pulled the sheet up over his chin and listened to the sounds of the night.

Flint awakened him by turning on the ceiling light and plunking some coins down on the dresser top. Seeing Tom shielding his eyes from the light, he exclaimed, "Look at that, Tom m' boy! Four beautiful half-dollar pieces. My wages for shoveling two tons of cow poop. A little more, Jimmy Tom, and I'll have enough to send my song to the publisher. We could be in the money then. I'll buy you a new bike, of course."

Tom knew about the stack of songs his brother had written. He had shared The One with him, and Tom had slipped and read some of the others. Back in Ohio, he had showed Tom the letter from his publisher. "Send us your top song and twenty dollars," it said, "and we'll have your song recorded by one of our professional singers under contract to us. You receive three copies of the record and the sheet music."

He didn't tell Flint as much, but he didn't care for the songs. They were all about starry skies and big brown eyes and moonlit nights and rose gardens, and women's lips that tasted of honey. Not one good adventure in the whole batch.

Well, he hoped Flint didn't stay up to work on songs this night. Maybe it didn't matter. Maybe he had slept right through the cat's meow. At any rate, shoveling manure had done Flint in. He rolled into bed, passing gas like a motor boat with bad plugs. He laughed when Tom fired one back at him.

"Beans, beans, good for the heart. . ." Flint said, still laughing.

Five minutes later he was snoring like a grizzly in January.

None too soon, either, for Tom heard the sound of gravel bouncing off the top window pane, and pretty soon a fine imitation of a tomcat's lovesick call. This was something right out of the pages of Tom Sawyer, he thought, as he slipped on his shoes. He pushed open the window, tiptoed across the porch roof, went down the post, and found all five of them waiting for him in the alley.

CHAPTER 5:
MOONLIGHT STRAWBERRIES

Vince, dressed again in his Robin Hood attire, came up to Tom and patted him on the back – almost put his arm around his shoulders. "You made it, Sycamore. That's good. You're working out fine," he said.

Out at a forbidden time. Tom had to admit it was exciting. He felt a strange sense of freedom, of power.

Gale's grin reached from ear to ear, but he said nothing. In fact, no one spoke as the group of six boys – single file, Tom bringing up the rear – headed down Tom's street and then scampered up an alleyway leading to the upriver part of the village. The full moon moved in and out of cloud cover. Tom thought he saw a flash of lightning downriver.

Finally, they squatted in moon shadows behind a hedgerow and some hollyhock bushes. Vince parted the foliage and pulled Tom in beside him. On the far side of the hedge, he explained, was a quarter-acre patch of strawberry plants belonging to the Widow Louella. Her house was visible just beyond the patch.

"We're going to have to act fast on this now," said Vince, handing Tom a small penlight and an empty shoebox. "These berries have come on early. I know, because I picked three quarts for the Widow Louella yesterday. There's still quiet a few green ones, though. You'll need the light. But don't lose it whatever you do. Captain Midnight sent that to me personally. Your job is to go in there and fill up the box with the best and ripest ones you can find."

Tom's mouth fell open as he looked at Vince.

"Wait a minute, now. You want me to go in there and steal strawberries? This is an initiation? I don't think so. This is what they call stealing. And the law don't cater to stealing. Neither does my dad. I'm sorry, I don't want any part of this."

Vince looked at Tom, rolled his eyes, and gave a quick little sigh. "No. No, you're wrong," he said. "It ain't stealin' at all. You're not getting these berries for us. What we're about to do here is take from the rich and give to the poor."

Tom looked at Gale, who nodded in agreement with Vince. "The widow Louella is rich, Tom," Gale said. "She bought the church that new piano. She's just got herself to look after. Well, her and that old dog, Bo. Boy I hope he don't catch you in there."

Seeing the startled look on Tom's face, he added, "She keeps him in at night, so he won't. And besides, she's got so many strawberries she won't miss a shoebox full. She probably gives away as many as she sells. If we asked her for some, she'd give them to us. But I'm like Vince on that. Where's the adventure in that?"

Well, she could qualify to represent the rich, Tom reasoned. And redistributing the wealth, not stealing, seemed to be the aim of this socialist Robin Hood guy.

Hobo voiced his support for the plan. "We're in this together," he said. "Nobody will know about it but us, so don't worry about your mom and dad finding out."

Vince reached out to place his hands on the penlight and shoe box. "Let me remind you of one thing, Sycamore," he said. "Until you've passed every test, you won't get into this organization. And if not, you can pretty well figure on bein' an outcast around here for the rest of your days. I hate to put it that way, but that's the way it is."

Tom sure didn't want to live the whole summer like a leper. He swallowed hard, pushed through the bushes, and crawled on his belly into the patch, scooting the box along and holding the light in his teeth. He saw luscious red berries hanging full and plump. He put several in the box and couldn't resist plopping one in his mouth. It was sweet, much sweeter, he thought, than any you would buy in the store.

He had the box nearly full when the back porch light of the Widow Louella's house came on! Tom flicked off Vince's Captain Midnight light and froze. A silver-haired woman came out of the door, a huge white dog at her side. The dog looked toward the patch and barked. Tom shot a glance back toward the hedgerow. Beads of sweat the size of soup beans popped out on his forehead.

The woman's voice drifted across the patch. "What is it, Bo," she said. "Why were you whining and scratching on the door so?" She followed the dog's gaze out toward the strawberry patch. Tom stiffened, trying to decide whether to hold his position or bolt for the hedgerow. That big dog called Bo would probably catch him, rip off a leg or two. He remained motionless.

"Probably just a rabbit out there," the woman said. "We'll have enough berries this year for the rabbits to have a few." She patted the dog's head with one hand while holding onto his collar with the other. "Come on Bo, it's all right. Back in the house with you. This damp night air's not good on us old folks."

Tom remained frozen until he saw the porch light and then the kitchen light go out. Then he hurried through the patch on all fours, holding the light in his teeth, filling the box with berries; probably getting a few green ones mixed in.

Back on the other side of the hedgerow, his accomplices congratulated him in excited but hushed tones. Vince, taking back his flashlight, remained focused on the task at hand. "Now come on, let's move," he said. "Hold tight to that box. Don't spill them."

They galloped down allies and streets to the lower end of the village, where it ended abruptly against the fence row of farmer Henson's farm. A dirt lane peeled off toward the river and disappeared in a grove of trees. They followed it until Vince halted under a huge willow growing just outside a broken-down picket fence. Tom could make out a dilapidated house squatting in the moonlight. Its front porch sagged. The yard was bare of grass.

"Lonnie Porter's place," Vince said. "He's got no job right now. Probably not able to work. He's got five mouths to feed. I'll bet his kids have never tasted fresh strawberries."

As they crouched behind the tree trunk, Vince pulled a piece of paper from his pocket. He flicked on his light to show the others the words written on the paper: THIS FOOD COMES FROM ROBIN HOOD AND HIS MERRY BAND WHOSE AIM IS TO HELP THEM IN NEED.

"At's good writin', Vince," Gale said.

"Makes me nearly want to cry," said Keith Richards.

Vince tucked the note in under a few berries, then reached into his tunic pocket and brought out a small brown bag. He placed that on top of the berries.

"What's that?" Hobo asked, at the same time running his hand into the bag. He withdrew it and licked his fingers. "My gosh, Vince, that's sugar! Your mom'll kill you if she finds out you're giving away sugar. That stuff's like gold."

"Course it's sugar," Vince said. "You think old Lonnie and his wife'd have sugar? You've got to have sugar for the real enjoyment of strawberries. Especially since it looks like Tom Sycamore got a few green ones mixed in."

He turned his attention to Tom. "Now, take the berries up and just set them down inside the screen door. No dogs to worry about. Lonnie used to have a couple of hounds, but he traded them off. Be careful not to lose the sugar and the note."

Tom did as instructed, leaving the box of berries behind the battered screen door. As he scampered back to the fence, he had to admit to himself he was feeling pretty good about the whole thing.

Test Number One was history. The moon was still out, but there was definitely lightning on the western horizon.

"Looks like a storm comin' upriver," Vince said. "We've got to hurry – get in Number Two Test and we're done for the night."

CHAPTER 6:
THE DEVIL'S BACKYARD

Vince Royalton wasn't exactly making up Tom's initiation as he went, but no doubt there would have been some other variation on it had not Hobo recovered the dead cat. For Test No. Two, the dead cat – a black cat at that – was necessary. Vince had put out a directive a month ago for the boys to watch the highways and byways for a dead cat, preferably a black one. So it was evident he was scheming about some kind of experiment involving the black cat before Tom ever came into the picture.

And it was on that very day of the nighttime raid on the strawberry patch that Hobo, walking up Route Ten to Davis & Harvey's, had seen the cat dart out of the weeds onto the highway – right into the path of Baldy Carver's bread truck. Hobo, seeing the cat was black, had quickly crossed his heart as it bounded right in front of him and into the path of the truck, which was headed upriver on the other side of the highway. There was an awful thump from under the truck, and the poor creature was killed instantly. Baldy drove on without realizing he had hit it. Hobo dragged it to the side of the road, and on the way back from the store, dropped it into a paper sack and took it home with him.

And so, after the strawberry caper, the boys made their way through the village and stopped at a storage shed near the alley behind Hobo's house. One by one they climbed a ladder to the flat roof of the shed. The moon, still sliding in and out of cloud cover, spotlighted a paper sack lying on the roof. Vince opened it, shined his light on the contents, then withdrew the cat – which suffered a great deal from rigor mortis – and placed it on the roof.

Hobo, beaming with pride, hastily explained that he'd never seen the cat around before, and it must have been a stray – not somebody's pet.

Vince patted Hobo on the back, then stood over the cat, rubbing his hands together like a witch might do over a boiling caldron.

"Ah, perfect," he said. "Perfect, do you hear me? How long have I waited .... "

He withdrew a coil of string from the belt of his tunic, tied one end of it around the cat's tail, then dropped cat and string back into the sack.

"Now, my merry men," he said, picking up the sack, "let us proceed to the graveyard."

Tom felt the hairs on the back of his neck prickle.

They filed silently back down the ladder and fell in behind Vince on a quick pace. They went up the alley to the street and made their way up over the railroad crossing, heading for the highway and the hills.

Tom, bringing up the rear, his mind racing, grabbed Gale by the arm and stopped him.

"Wait a minute here," he said. "I thought we were going to the grave-yard. The church is back that way."

"We're not going to the church cemetery," Gale said, trying to pull Tom on along to keep up with the others. "I wish we was. Only good people buried in the churchyard. We're headed for Cemetery Hill, that old ceme-tery on the slope of Dead Man's Ridge. I know what Vince is up to, and I don't like it a bit. This shouldn't be a part of your initiation."

Vince led on in silence, across the railroad and the highway, up a slope thick with honeysuckle vines and underbrush, and on under the trees on the hillside overlooking School House Hollow. Tom, filled with trepidation and wonder, had no choice but to follow.

They stopped at an ancient, crumbling stone fence. The moon revealed a cemetery that seemed to be in about the same condition as the fence. It was nearly overtaken by weeds and briars and saplings. Here and there tombstones leaned at odd angles.

The moon ducked behind a black cloud. There was a flash of lightning, much closer now, followed by a roll of thunder. Tom felt some fat raindrops splatter on his head.

Vince handed the sack and its monstrosity to Tom.

"This is as far as the rest of us go," he said. "You're going to be on your own from here, 'cept, of course, we'll be backing you. Like Hobo has said, we're all for one and one for all. Now listen close to the instructions. And here, I'm gonna let you use my Captain Midnight penlight again."

The moon was out again and Vince pointed out over the cemetery to where a former great live oak – now a great dead oak – staggered up against the sky. He turned to Tom and said, "Right near that tree is the tombstone markin' the grave of Clarence L. "Buzzsaw" Baker. You can't see it from here because of all the brush, but you'll see it when you get up there. He was evil. Killed three men in cold blood. The state executed him, back in the twenties. He died cussin' his executor, even threw in an oath or two at God. The Devil claimed him, and up there he lies.

"He's the Devil's own now, and of course the Devil protects his own. Some folks say they've seen his old horned figure standing up there over that grave on moonlit nights, especially around midnight."

He searched the shadows and moonlight splashes on Tom's face for some indication of what effect this talk was having on him. Dale Riley jockeyed for position to where he could see Tom's face, too, but also where he could huddle in closer to the group.

Vince, who felt a shiver run up his spine, turned to Keith Richards and asked, "What time is it, Keith?"

"What time is it! How the heck should I know. You see any sun out there? You know I tell time by the sun, son," Keith said, then quickly added, "Let's get the heck out of here, Vince. Come back in daylight."

Vince ignored him. A bullfrog croaked from a long-forgotten pond off in the cemetery. "Come-on-over. Come-on-over." From the dark woods behind the cemetery a weirder sound chimed in: "Who-who, who-who, who-who-who-who-o-o-o." The group of six cringed, drew closer together.

"What in the name of Alley Oop was that, a spook? It was a spook, wasn't it?" asked Keith, grabbing Vince by the arm.

Vince jerked his arm free of the grasp. "Why, no! You dummy," he said. "That was nothing but an ol' hoot owl. They won't hurt you. They're good – eat rats and things."

55

"And Vince, what in the world is it you said we're doing out here at this old graveyard at this ungodly hour?" Hobo wanted to know.

Vince, ignoring the question, turned his attention back to Tom. "We've got to hurry, 'cause there's a storm movin' in. Now here's the whole deal. Listen up, 'cause this thing's got to be done right. This is the night we beat the old Devil. You, Tom Sycamore, are gonna slap him in the face and let him know we're not afraid of him in the least. There's no danger in it to you. I read all about the correct procedure in a book dealing with witch-craft."

Witchcraft!

The hairs on the back of Tom's neck definitely stood up now and took notice.

"And besides," Vince went on, "we're gonna be right here backin' you. Your test – and ho boy, is it a big one – is to go out there alone, stand flat-out on old Baker's grave, swing this dead cat around on the string 13 times, then fling it toward the woods yonder, shoutin' this verse: "Beelzebub, Beelzebub, you dirty old rat, your power over us is as dead as this cat!""

Tom had never heard such a tale. Well, something similar to it, for he knew the cat and the graveyard was something right out of Tom Sawyer. After he managed to get his lower jaw back up into place, he said, "Just a minute! Just a dadblamed minute here. There's something wrong here that's not right. The part about getting' rid of the Devil, I mean. I went to Sunday school a lot up in Ohio. I didn't pick up on everything, but I never heard anything like this taught. Witchcraft? No, no. There's a way you beat the Devil, and … "

"Yeah, but what I'm tellin' you, Sycamore," Vince interrupted, "is that doing it this way we beat the Devil once and for all and for good. You beat him at his own game, in his own element, and he don't show his face any-more. We'll be able to do the good deeds this here organization wants to do, free of hindrance.

"I go to Sunday school, too. All of us here do. There's a big revival in the church every spring. Folks team up on the Devil and slap him down good, everybody prayin' and shoutin' at the same time. Why, Aunt Maude once took a broom and ran all around the church whooping the Devil every step. Swept him right on out the front door. Every sinner and backslider in the place was up at the mourner's bench. It was a great victory over evil.

"Three weeks later, though, there was a big argument amongst the members over the color of the new fabric they would use to cover the pews. Quick as a copperhead, the Devil was right back in the middle of things. Wound up with five families pullin' their membership and joinin' the church down in Killin Hollow.

"That's the way the Devil operates, Tom. He keeps coming back around, tryin' to catch us off guard. There's never a minute's rest. But this way, the way we're doin' it ..."

"Go on, Tom," Gale broke in. "Don't argue with Vince. He's up on this stuff. Just go out there and swing that cat and say them words and quickly get this over with and let's get out of this God-forsaken place."

"Yeah, get jumpin'," said Keith, realizing he wasn't going to have to go into the cemetery.

"Wait much longer and this storm's gonna be right on us," Hobo said.

Tom crawled over the fence, sack in hand, and started out through the graveyard.

"Be sure now," Vince called after him, "to swing it 13 times. And say the verse as you fling it. You got the words?"

"Yeah, I got the words," Tom said. "But I'll tell you one thing for sure. I'd feel a lot better about this if I hadn't stole them strawberries."

"You didn't steal 'em!" Vince said. "You're good. You're a knight in shining armor. Go on!"

Tom was halfway through the graveyard when the moon turned off again. He bumped into a tombstone in the darkness, and felt the first stirring of genuine fear quiver along his backbone. But, flicking on the penlight, he plunged on. The owl called again, its sound seeming to come from the oak that spread its limbs over Baker's grave. The moon came out again and Tom plodded on, like a zombie.

Finally, under the dead tree, he shined the comforting light on the small stone with Baker's name on it. He pulled the cat from the sack and uncoiled the string, wrapping its free end a couple of times around his hand. It took all the strength he could muster to step up into the depression at the base of the stone. He tucked the light into a rear pocket. He started the cat into its arc, around and around. The moon went out like pulling the string on a light cord. Lightening flashed, thunder rolled. Raindrops splattered off his head. He kept the cat going as he counted, "Eight, nine, ten, eleven . . ."

Just as he was ready to fling the cat and say the words, a flash of lightening lit the sky. Suddenly something swooped low over his head, almost close enough to part his hair. Then, in the ominous dark that followed the lightening, the cat was no longer in orbit. The string was yanked from his grasp and the thing was gone!

For a moment he stood like the Statue of Liberty, his arm frozen over his head. Another bolt of lightening, so close he could feel his hair crackle, hit the dead tree. Bark flew. Branches cracked. Tom gave a flat-footed leap that must have propelled him six feet to his left. Part of the old tree crashed to the ground on the very spot he had been standing.

Then there was only fear, and fear gave birth to panic. His mind tried desperately to remain in control of the situation. But in its confusion, it transmitted only one message, and it was a direct command to the feet, which were pleased to receive it.

And down through the darkness he flew. He heard someone screaming, "He's after us boys! He's after us boys!" and realized it was his own voice. He stumbled over a gravestone, somersaulted, and sailed on. It was a record leap that catapulted him over the old stone wall. No one waited there. As another great flash of lightening lit the scene before him, he saw his five brave, former companions, all in a dead run, crossing the railroad tracks down below.

And then Tom opened it up. He fell three times going down the hill, once having to untangle himself from thick honeysuckle, but his legs never once stopped pumping.

CHAPTER 7:
DON'T BE A QUITTER

Tom had no problem climbing the post and bellying up onto the porch roof. He had plenty of incentive coming from the feeling that something was nipping at his heels. To get inside quickly was uppermost in his mind. Rain pounded the tin roof of the house as he opened the French window and stepped quietly inside. He heard Flint snoring as he stripped out of his wet clothing, kicked it under the bed, dried himself as best he could on a couple of T-shirts, slipped into his pajamas, and crawled into bed.

"I'm sorry, big brother," he murmured, "for what I might have brought in here on you. I hope whatever it was chased me out of that graveyard didn't come into Hooperville. But I fear it did. I think it's right outside the window."

His brother was lying on his side, facing away from him, snoring. Tom wished he would wake up and talk to him, but he decided against shaking him. He drew the cover over his head.

The storm passed on over the village. The sound of thunder was barely audible in the distance.

Tom replayed events in his mind, trying to figure out exactly what happened up there on that grave. Something had definitely yanked that cat out of orbit. He could still feel a burning sensation in his palm where the string was pulled from around his hand. He began to pray fervently, in Jesus' name. Finally, a fitful sleep possessed him.

———————

Sunshine was streaming in through the windows when Flint woke him.

"Up, Tom," he said. "Get your church clothes on. Mom's about got breakfast. Be careful, 'cause there's water on this floor. Rain last night blew in through this window, I guess. Hope the sun dries that hay enough that I get to work."

He went out, tucking his shirttail in. Tom rose quickly and went to the drawer where he kept his Sunday school clothes. He wanted to get to church. He needed to get to church.

He dragged his wet clothes from under the bed, went out the French window, and spread them on the porch roof, off to the left far enough that they couldn't be seen by anyone looking out the window. Deception. His life was filled with deception. Yes, he needed church.

His mother set before him a plate of eggs, bacon, big fluffy biscuits and milk gravy. Now, if only his stomach would quit churning long enough to enjoy it. Flint and his father were already digging in.

"James Thomas, what's the matter with you this morning?" his mother wanted to know. "You look like you've seen a ghost." She placed a palm on his forehead.

"I'm fine," Momma.

He forced down most of the food on his plate.

The church bell was sounding as he and Flint went out the door. Chopper followed them to the bottom of the church steps. Leader was already there. They sniffed each other and both lay down in the grass to assume their watch.

Tom and Flint found seats about halfway down on the right. Several people tossed smiles at them. A lady seated behind them patted them both on the back. Tom looked to his right and saw Dale Riley, sitting beside a woman he guessed to be his mother. Dale, before quickly averting his eyes, looked at Tom as though he was Lazarus raised from the tomb.

Continuing to gaze around the church, Tom saw Gale seated with his parents, grandfather, and sister, Gina. Gale turned and gave Tom a quick little smile, which Tom ignored. Now he saw Keith, Hobo and Vince, all seated together on the back row. Hobo and Keith did not acknowledge Tom, but Vince looked straight at him and nodded slowly, three times.

Flint elbowed Tom and handed him a songbook as the superintendent brought the congregation to its feet. "Page two eighty-three," he said. "'Rock of Ages.'"

Let the water and the blood,
From thy wounded side which flowed,
Be of sin the double cure,
Save from wrath and make me pure.

Then they broke for Sunday school classes. Two fellows about Flint's age greeted him and led him toward a corner of the sanctuary, where his class was assembling. Gale came alongside Tom and ushered him toward the steps leading down to the above-ground basement. The four other Braves bounded down the steps after them.

They crowded around him at the foot of the steps, intent on touching him. Tom scrunched his shoulders and turned aside, trying to avoid contact. After all, they had abandoned him, left him to die in that God-forsaken graveyard on the slopes of Dead Man's Ridge. Yes, he was lucky to be among the living, and it was no thanks to them.

Besides the five Braves and Tom, there were three other boys, all a little younger than the Braves, who took seats in a small room in a corner of the basement.

The teacher spoke a welcome to his nine pupils as he walked in to take his place at the podium. Jim Galloway was a portly, gray-haired man who walked with a limp. The wound to one leg had been caused by shrapnel that slammed him on a battlefield in Europe during the First World War.

He launched immediately into the lesson. It was on Satan, and his demons, and how they work to deceive.

"Who is it," he asked, "who roars about like a lion in the streets, seeking to devour whoever he may?"

"Satan!" Hobo responded. "And we ought to stay out of his way."

Hobo looked directly at Vince, who shot Tom a glance.

"That's right, Hobo," the teacher said. "And do you boys know that, according to Matthew, the devil's demons know all about prophecy, and of their inevitable doom?"

He went on to tell how Jesus tossed evil spirits – demons – out of an insane man in a graveyard.

Did this teacher know they were up in that graveyard last night? Tom wondered.

The Braves squirmed about in their seats more than usual. It was evident this was a topic they didn't want to pursue.

But they got a double dose. The Rev. Ottis Hackelbee, who some said preached more on Hell than he did Heaven, brought a message on how Satan had used Hitler and Tojo in his attempt to destroy not only God's elect, but all of mankind.

Flint had left after Sunday school, went home and changed, and headed for the hayfields on Farmer Matt's river bottom acreage. Tom's mother had told them they didn't either one have to stay for church unless they wanted to. Gale talked Tom into staying. He said he and the other Braves were already locked into staying.

"Please don't be mad at me and the boys," Gale said as they sat in the pew waiting for the church service to begin. "We seen you was all right there after the lightning hit the tree. It just seemed like a good idea for a full retreat, with you bringin' up the rear."

Tom didn't say anything, for the song leader had called for all to stand.

After the service, outside, Chopper leaped up on Tom, who rubbed his ears as they headed for home. But Vince caught up with him and stopped him. The others gathered around to hear what was being said.

"Tom, you did good last night. You passed the test," Vince said. "And please don't be mad at us. We should have held our ground and checked on you, I know, but it seemed a natural thing for us all to temporarily scatter and make our way out of that, uh, unfortunate situation. I wasn't scared, but I just couldn't seem to come up with a plan."

"Wasn't scared, eh, old boy?" said Keith Richards. "Well now, Vince, if I was you I'd at least get out of the churchyard before I told one like that."

Vince raised a hand as if to smack him one, but then dropped it. Keith had jumped back out of range anyway. Vince turned his attention back to Tom, placing his hands on Tom's shoulders and looking him in the eyes.

"Anyway, Tom, there's just one more test to go," he said. "You do as well on it as you did last night and I'm sure you're in. You'll be a Brave, son. Don't quit on us now."

The others encouraged him. Tom looked from one of them to the other.

62

Knowing how frightened he had been, he really couldn't blame them for bolting.

"Tell me boys," he said, looking off in the direction of the hillside cemetery, "what did you see up there last night? I'm telling you – lordy, lordy! – something grabbed that cat right out of midair. You can see the mark here on my hand where that string nearly blistered me."

They all examined the hand. They saw the reddish whelp. A shiver ran through them.

It was Hobo who finally spoke out on the matter. "Well, when the lightning flashed real bright there," he said, "what I saw was a big black something over your head. It was a creature of some kind. Whatever it was, it had wings. It was either the Devil or one of his chief demons, the way I figure it."

Gale looked sharply at Vince and added, "That was a crazy stunt. We should never have tried it. I told you I was against it from the start."

"Now boys," Vince said. "Let's not squabble. Remember our motto: All for one and one for all. There's no harm done here. Tom's OK, and everything is gonna work out fine and dandy."

After mulling it over a minute, Tom agreed to go on with the initiation. It was bad enough to be a stranger in a strange land, but to be there with no friends was unthinkable.

A little cheer went up from the others as they parted. Gale walked Tom to his front gate. "The final test is set for two o'clock," he said. "I'll call for you."

He turned for home, but turned back to Tom and said, "Oh, by the way, Tom. Wear something you don't mind getting wet. This test involves swimming."

Tom felt his heart leap up into his throat. He swallowed it back down as he went in through the gate.

he had seen puppies swim the first time they were tossed into the water. Surely to goodness he could keep his head above water long enough to "doggie" out to the edge of the willows and back to shore. If he survived the dive, that is.

"What's a matter up there? Not turning chicken, are we?" Keith Richards shouted up at Tom.

One thing for certain: Tom wasn't going to climb back down that tree. That would be worse than drowning.

He called down to Vince. "You say I can't go feet first?"

"Nope. Head first. Let's go now."

"Go ahead and do it, Tom," Gale whispered from the limb next to him. "Even if you hit a belly-whopper, it won't kill you. I want you to be one of us. You talk about a summer of fun."

It was the point of no return. Bravery was not required for the task before him; just stupidity. He released his death grip on the overhead limb, and leaped like a frightened frog.

"Ker-splat!" It was a belly-whopper. Tom was stung by pain and engulfed in total darkness. He fought his way back to the surface and flailed at the water with both arms. Then he went under again, his feet searching for a bottom that wasn't there.

He swallowed a half-gallon of river water before he popped to the surface again. He tried swimming doggie-fashion, his arms rotating in front of his chest like a paddlewheel. But his feet wouldn't come up. Everything was a blur. He realized he was drowning. Almost apologetically, he yelled, "Help-p-p!" He saw Chopper in the water, swimming toward him. Then he was sinking beneath the surface again.

Suddenly, though, someone had him by the hair of his head, pulling him back to where there was sweet air to breathe. It was Flint, good old big brother Flint to the rescue. Flint's friend and coworker, Bish, had one arm under Tom's arm, and he and Flint towed him ashore. Tom coughed, wheezed, spit up a sizable amount of the Ohio River as they dragged him up onto the bank. A yelping, tail-wagging Chopper licked him in the face.

Tom lay there on his belly, one cheek resting on the back of his hand. All he could see was the bare legs gathered round him. "Is he going to be all right?" he heard Vince ask Flint.

"Oh, yeah, sure. He's tough. He must have took a cramp," Flint answered.

Humiliation, defeat, dejection, rejection – Tom felt them all. He had failed miserably. Better had they let him drown.

Flint helped him to his feet. "Tom, maybe you'd better go on to the house," he said. "Me and Bish have to go back to the hay fields. Stay here if you'd like, but don't go back into that deep water again."

Head low, Tom started up the path for the village.

"He can't swim a lick," Flint admitted to the boys when Tom was out of hearing. "He's never had a chance to learn."

The five Braves stood silently as they watched Tom go. Then Vince, taking a couple of steps in his direction, shouted, "Tom! Come back here, Tom."

Tom turned and walked slowly back to where the others stood. Flint, who had headed up the path with Bish, turned and watched.

"That was a brave thing you did there, Tom Sycamore. I mean, knowing you couldn't swim, yet diving into that water," Vince said.

"Lordy be, yes!" Keith Richards said. "No way I would have dove into that water if I couldn't swim."

"Whatta the rest of you say?" Vince asked.

"He's one brave guy, in my book," Hobo said.

"A tough hombre, senior," chimed in Dale Riley.

"It's unanimous," Gale said. "We can teach you to swim, Tom."

Vince walked over to a willow tree and pulled something from underneath a chip of bark.

"Hold your hand out here," he said to Tom.

Tom stretched his arm out toward Vince. He took Tom's hand in his and pricked Tom's index finger with a straight pin. He did likewise to his own index finger, then pressed his finger down hard on Tom's.

Slowly, the other four, forming a line, stepped up and had their forefingers pricked. One by one, they came around and pressed the tips of their bleeding fingers against Tom's.

Blood brothers! Tom was a full-fledged member of the Hooperville Braves.

CHAPTER 9:
WAS SHE THROWING A KISS?

The two-story orange brick building that was South Shawnee High School actually housed grades one through 12, about 200 students in all. It sat up a narrow hollow off Route 10, about a quarter of a mile west of Hooperville. A small creek wandered down between the schoolyard and the base of Dead Man's Ridge. The bony, much lower wooded ridge on the other side separated the school from Route 10, from Hooperville, and from Shawnee across the river. To follow that ridge upwards from the mouth of School House Hollow would lead the wanderer to the top of the high cliff and the mysterious-looking cave Tom and Flint had wondered about from the back of the truck. The deep wooded hills to the rear of the school and on both sides were inhabited by hoot owls, whippoorwills, opossums, flying squirrels, grouse and a wide variety of wild songbirds.

Carrie Sycamore got her two boys out the door with their satchels and lunch bags just as Hobo, Gale and Dale stopped to get them.

"Tom, you stay close to your brother, now," she said as the five boys made their way up the slope of the railroad crossing. "Flint, you watch crossing that railroad, and watch for cars before crossing the highway."

"Your dog's gonna follow us," Gale said to Tom. "Leader knows better. He got bumped once by a truck and won't go near the highway now."

Carrie allowed Chopper to go in the house until the boys got away. Chopper seemed in a state of shock as he trotted in through the open door. Perhaps he was thinking that at last he was getting a measure of the respect due him.

They met Vince and Keith coming out of Gammons' grocery at the third crossing and they all continued on their way to school, along with half a dozen other kids of varying ages from the village.

"Hello brother," Vince said as he put an arm around Tom's shoulders.

"Get all that muddy Ohio River out of your head yet?" asked Keith.

At the school, they joined a bunch of students jostling about and yelling at one another on the side stoop and the three concrete steps that served it. The stoop was bounded by concrete walls on either side, walls just high enough and wide enough to serve as benches.

Vince introduced Tom to a group of students on the steps and the benches. "He's a Buckeye, but he's one of the good ones," he said.

"A good Buckeye? How's that?" someone asked. Vince ignored the remark.

Some of the students acknowledged Tom; others were too busy at horseplay to pay him much attention. It didn't matter to Tom one way or the other, for his gaze had locked in on just one person in the crowd, much as a hungry lion zeroes in on a particular prey. She was a blond with a pigtail that stretched halfway down her back. Tom's stare was so intent that she must have noticed, but she never averted her gaze from the girls she was having a conversation with.

Across the stoop on the concrete wall opposite where she sat, Tom, with his back turned to her and the girls, put one foot on top of the bench, which had the effect of making his baggy, hand-me-down overalls fit tighter across his buttocks. It was a move similar to one made by a wild gobbler as he strutted for a hen's attention.

He wondered if she was stealing a glance at him. It felt to him like her eyes were on him, but he couldn't be sure.

The bell rang and students filed in through the double doors. Tom followed Vince and Gale, Hobo, Keith and Dale to their homeroom. At the classroom door, Tom felt a hand on his shoulder and turned to face Flint.

"Everything all right?" Flint asked.

"Oh yes, Big Brother. So far so good."

"Here's your papers from Ashville. Your teacher will want them."

The room, filled with about 25 students from both the fifth and sixth grades, was on the ground floor. Four large windows overlooked the stream and the wooded slopes of Dead Man's Ridge. Tom stood at the back of the room as the others took their seats. At the front, the teacher, a chunky woman with graying hair, tapped the side of her desk with a yardstick and demanded quiet while she called the roll.

She motioned for Tom to come forward. "And who are you?" she asked. "I wasn't aware we were going to have a new student, especially this late in the year."

Tom gave her his name and handed her the transfer papers Flint had handed him. Her eyebrows arched as she looked over Tom's grades from the Ohio school.

"Very impressive, Tom Sycamore. Most impressive. You'll have no problem fitting in here. Matter of fact, you may be an over-fit. You may call me Miss Newberry."

She introduced Tom to the rest of the class and assigned him his seat.

Glory be! It was right behind the lovely creature with the golden pigtail. Providence must have taken a hand here. Tom smelled the faint aroma of lilacs as he sat down, placing his satchel and lunch sack on the desk. Cupid's arrow made his heart leap with joy.

Miss Newberry left and the room buzzed. Tom saw Keith fire a paper wad that struck Gale in the back of the head. The teacher returned, thankfully too late to see that. She placed Tom's textbooks on his desk, tapped her desk again with the yardstick, and the room fell silent. Serious education began.

The most important thing Tom learned that morning was her name. It was Jane.

Me Tarzan, you Jane.

Later, when Miss Newberry asked for the capital of Germany, she raised her hand. The arm sticking from her white blouse was like ivory. Even her elbow was beautiful. Her back was straight and she had such a firm set to her shoulders.

"Tell us, then, Janie, what is it?" Miss Newberry prompted. She did, and her voice was like the sound of spring stream water tumbling down over rounded stones.

The morning wore on and not once did she turn to look at Tom. Neither had she acknowledged him when he had walked by her to take his seat.

71

The recess bell rang and students leaped up. Tom stayed seated, waiting for her to get up and pass him. As she did so, Tom's heart leaped as he saw her daintily cover her lips with a cute little hand. She was going to blow him a kiss?

His spirit fell with a thud as he realized she was only smothering a yawn.

Outside, on the porch with the bench railings, Gale was talking to Tom, something about swimming lessons. Tom wasn't sure what Gale was saying, for he was gazing over Gale's shoulder to where Janie sat, on the opposite bench, talking to another girl. They were watching some other girls, out on the sidewalk, jumping rope. Tom heard Janie ask the other girl if she had any gum, which she didn't. Oh goodness, he thought, why didn't he bring some gum? He would never be without it again.

Well, he had to talk to her, say something, anything, at least let her know he existed. He left Gale in mid-sentence and started toward her. Each foot felt like it weighed a ton. His arms seem to dangle at his sides, like a gorilla. His mind tried to form some idea of what his words would be.

I'll just introduce myself, he thought.

I'm Tom Sycamore, the new boy. How are you, Janie. Fine, you say. Good, good. Say, can I walk you home after school today?

No, no. That might be rushing things a little too much.

She didn't appear to notice his approach. He was still six feet away from her when a truck hit him in the back. At least it felt like a truck. But it was Hobo. He spun Tom around by the shoulders and cradled the back of his head in his big paw.

"How are you, Thomas?" Hobo asked. "Get all that muddy water out of your head?"

By the time Tom looked back her way Janie was gone from the bench. She was out there with the girls, jumping rope. Only she didn't jump. She skipped, and ever so gracefully.

Tom's first day of school at South Shawnee turned out to be the last day of the war in Europe. Classes had no sooner reconvened than one of the high school boys from upstairs stuck his head in the door. "Germany's surrendered!" he shouted.

It took several seconds for the news to register. Miss Newberry started the celebration by tossing the book she held toward the ceiling. "Hallelujah!" she shouted.

It was the signal for the whole class to start tossing papers and books into the air. They jumped and shouted and leaped about the room. Hallelujah! they yelled, almost in unison.

Someone was swinging on the rope of the bell in the front yard. Miss Newberry threw open the windows. "Listen!" she said. Even though the schoolhouse sat near the head of the hollow, and there was that tall ridge, which held the cliff and the cave, between it and the city of Shawnee, they could hear sirens and whistles sounding off from there. The bells of the two Hooperville churches were also ringing.

Principal Wayland Rooker, who had two sons in the army somewhere in Europe, dismissed school at noon.

Tom and the Braves filed out of the hollow, eating their lunches as they went. Chopper met Tom at the foot of the crossing, leaping up on him as though it had been a week since they parted. Leader came loping up the street to meet Gale.

"Come on over to my house in a couple of hours," Gale said as they parted. "The boys are all comin'. Vince says we'll get into something."

He found his mother on her knees waxing the kitchen linoleum. The radio in the living room blasted out the news: "The surrender of the Reich to the Western Allies and Russia was made at General Dwight D. Eisenhower's headquarters at Reims, France, by the chief of staff for the German Army," the announcer was saying.

"The end of the European warfare, the greatest, bloodiest and costliest war in human history – it's claimed at least forty million casualties on both sides in killed, wounded and captured – came five years, eight months, and six days after Hitler's arrogant armies invaded Poland on Sept. 1, 1939.

"Joy at the news was tempered only by the realization that the war against Japan remains to be resolved, with many casualties no doubt still ahead."

Flint came through the door, rubbed his hand through Tom's hair, and went upstairs, either to write, or maybe to change clothes and head for the hay fields. His mother's gaze followed him until he disappeared at the top of the landing. Then, rising and acknowledging Tom, she said, "Don't come in here, Tom, not 'till this floor's dry."

She snapped off the radio. "They've said nothing at all about the draft," she muttered, more to herself than Tom. "They should end it now, Oh, how I pray they will."

CHAPTER 10:
VISITOR, OR OWNER?

Tom changed clothes, got the hoe from the building, and soon worked up a sweat in the garden. Chopper dozed between rows of potato vines, which were blooming.

Then came the visitor – or was it the owner, and Tom the visitor? This time there was more than just sensing a presence. Ten yards from Tom there was a misty swirl. He first thought it was a dust devil. But at the top of the swirl there appeared a marine combat helmet, like those Tom had seen in the newsreels. Below the helmet was a man's face! Definitely! Vivid blue eyes, and lips formed into a slight smile.

"Hello?" Tom called.

No answer.

He fought the urge to drop the hoe and run – run for the house.

As before, he shook his head violently from side to side. Still the image persisted. He was caught in the riveting stare of the eyes, imploring eyes, eyes that held some deep wisdom. There was a disarming honesty about them.

Chopper saw it, too. The little dog leaped up, barked, whined, and then scampered for his refuge beneath the building, tail tucked between his legs.

Tom turned his head to watch Chopper crawl under the building. When he looked again at where the image had appeared, he – or it, whatever it was – was gone.

Mystified, he put the hoe back in the building and headed for the house.

Too much sun. I'm seeing things that aren't there, can't be there.

Chopper scampered out from under the building and followed close on his heels. Tom had to shut the screen door quickly to keep the dog from coming in behind him.

He debated about whether to tell his mother what he had seen. Two years ago, he recalled, the day after Grandpa Sycamore had died and the family had gathered at his house for the funeral, which would be held there the next day, his mother had seen Grandpa standing at the fireplace, filling his pipe and smiling at her. Now when this happened, Grandpa's body was laid out on a daybed in the front room, where Tom's mother and father, and several other relatives, had stayed up late, keeping a wake. Tom's mother couldn't believe no one else had seen him. "He was standing right there, on the hearth, big as life," she told her husband later. Bruce Sycamore nodded, more in sympathy than belief.

Tom had been upstairs in bed at the time, but his mother had told him later of seeing the apparition. "I think he just wanted to let us know he was fine, and that death was not such a fearful thing," she had said.

Tom's response was to wonder aloud if his grandfather would be able to get tobacco in Heaven. His mother pondered that. "Well, I don't know," she said. "I think that at the time I saw him he probably hadn't crossed over as yet."

Now, in from the garden and still pondering what to make of what he had seen out there, Tom passed by his mother on his way to the pump at the kitchen sink.

"What's the matter with you, Tom?" she asked as Tom drank from the tin cup. "Your face has no color."

She placed her hand on his damp forehead. He assured her he was OK.

"Well, you stay out of that garden until the sun goes over."

She seemed glad when he left to go visit Gale.

The gang was all there. Grandpa Flanders was reading, out loud, from an extra edition of The Shawnee Times as Gale's mom looked over his shoulder. At the top of the front page, black letters three inches high spelled out two words: "Germany Surrenders"

The account that followed was much the same as the one Tom and his mom had heard over the radio.

As Gale passed close by Grandpa Flanders' chair, the old man reached out and got him by the arm. "I want to talk to you, young man, about an important matter," he said. He glanced up and backwards at his daughter-in-law, but quickly refocused his liquid, gray-blue eyes on Gale. "I want you to learn an important lesson here about how confession of our sins is good for the soul."

"What are you talking about, Grandpa?" Gale asked, grimacing as he searched his mother's face. He dropped his chin to his chest.

"I'm talking about the big galvanized tub that I take my Saturday night bath in," his grandfather said. "I brought it in from the side of the building where it's kept hanging, to take my bath, but when I put water in it, it ran out on the floor through a hole in the bottom – a hole about the size of one of those arrows I saw you shooting into a cardboard box, back there near the building. What we're interested in learning here is how that hole got there."

Gale squirmed to free himself, but his grandfather held him tight.

"Well, good garsh, Grandpa. I told Mom what happened. I just mis-fired. The tub was hanging on the side of the building, and I had put the box up against the building. I sure didn't think that bow was strong enough or that arrow tough enough to go through that tub. The bottom must have been rusted out, and you were going to have to get another one anyway."

"Uh huh. I see. Well, it wasn't rusted out. That's why they galvanize them, so they don't rust," said Grandpa Flanders. "Now, since you didn't lie about it, we're not going to punish you. But a word of warning is in order. If you pull another stunt like this, we'll have to get rid of you. Your mother and father can make us another little red-headed boy."

Gale's mom rolled her eyes up at the ceiling and held her mouth in a straight line. Tom and several of the Braves gave out with a little nervous laughter.

"The rest of you Boys take notice of this," Grandpa Flanders said, turning to face them. "If you don't turn out right, if you persist in destroying other people's property, we can just kill you and make new ones."

He wrapped one arm around Gale's neck and drew back his cane. "I think I'll just go ahead and kill this one now," he said. "What do you say, Lois?"

"No, no, Dad. I've already promised him another chance. We'll see how he works out first."

Grandpa Flanders gave Gale a Dutch rub before giving him a slight push toward the rest of the Braves. Then he threw back his head and laughed long and loud.

With the war in Europe won, Vince was ready to finish off Japan. That afternoon, he led the Braves on an assault on the Jap-held caves of Okinawa, in this case the clay bank bordering Farmer Henson's hay fields, downriver from Sherwood Forest. There was a narrow strip of sand between it and the river that served as the beachhead. The river had fallen several feet, but there was still too much water to allow for pulling out in the Reuben James and striking the sandbar on the Ohio side.

Mud squished between their toes as they filed out to the tree that held the tree house. Up there, rifles with fixed bayonets, grenades, bazookas, flame throwers and shovels with folding handles were handed out. Vince had drawn an elaborate map with crayons. He unrolled it on top of the orange crate and laid out the battle plans.

"Sergeant Hooper, you and Private Sycamore will bring your platoon of fresh recruits in from this angle," Vince said, drawing a sweeping arrow on the map with a red crayon. "You're going to draw fire when you hit that beachhead. You'll have to dig in and pound the mortars in there before you try to cross. PFC Flanders, you take your men and back them up. I'll land with another platoon a little ways up the beach and angle in. We'll meet up at this point, here behind this fallen tree."

They paused in Sherwood Forest long enough to pick leafy boughs and stick them in behind the strips of cloth tied round their heads.

"Gotta get us some helmets," Vince said. "One of these days somebody's gonna get their fool heads blowed off."

They parted company at the edge of the sandy strip of beach. Hobo, Gale and Tom crept on down a piece, then began shoveling sand like doodlebugs. "Good enough," Hobo said, before the foxholes were even knee deep. "Set that bazooka up. We're already taking fire." He slapped at the sand and made a sound like whining bullets.

The bazooka, a cardboard tube four feet long, worked to perfection and

Gale and Tom lobbed in one mortar round after another. As they charged toward the fallen tree, Hobo became the first casualty. He grabbed his midsection, staggered, and took a full 10 seconds to fall. But as the other dozen or so marines behind them charged by, he leaped up and rejoined the battle.

They linked up with Vince's platoon at the fallen tree. Withering fire from the caves kept them pinned down.

"Cover me, men!" Vince shouted. "I'm going in to the base of the hill and lob a grenade in on that Jap machine gun nest."

The five kept a steady stream of fire going as he dashed across the sand. He was hit twice, but crawled to the base of the clay bank and heaved an empty tomato can into the "nest." He waved for the rest of them to join him.

"There's Japs in that cave," he said. "Let's burn 'em out!"

Dale Riley and Keith Richards moved up with flamethrowers to blast the interior of the depression. Fifty or more Japanese soldiers rolled out, some in flames. The stench of burning flesh filled their nostrils. They turned a merciless rain of rifle fire in on them.

Then, from the hill, came the shouts of "banzai!" The enemy, a thousand strong, came at them like mad men. It was hand to hand fighting, bayonets flashing.

"Fall back! Fall back!" Vince shouted.

Regrouping behind the fallen tree, the good ol' U.S. Marines blistered the enemy with rifle fire, grenades, and mortars. Somehow they repulsed them, drove them back through palm groves and scattered them in the mountains.

As they sprawled behind the tree, Vince called for breaking out K-rations and took a head count.

"Only six of us left," he said. "Let's hope we get reinforcements in here soon. They'll hit us again at dark."

"Not me, they won't," Hobo said. "I'm going home for peanut butter and jelly. These K-rations ain't doin' a thing for me."

"I'm thinking about the chocolate chip cookies Mom made today," Gale said.

Keith Richards, squinting up at the sun, said, "It's right now five thirty-two. We need to go now anyhow if we're gonna find out how Superman gets out of that fix he was in."

"A bunch of deserters, is that what we have?" Vince said. "Well, OK. We can finish mopping up this island tomorrow. A little R and R will be good for the troops. Let's get out of here."

So they left the battlefield, not knowing that at that very time, far across the vast Pacific, Japanese children were emulating the soldiers of His Imperial Majesty, the emperor, in mock battles just like theirs, only they were leaving thousands of American and British soldiers dead and dying.

Nor did they know that, at the top of the bank overlooking their mock field of battle, their Sunday school teacher, hidden behind the trunk of a thick maple tree, had watched it all.

That night, for the first time in his memory, Tom had his own bed to sleep in. With the additional bed procured from Aunt Mary, Flint now had his own room. As Tom passed through it on the way to his room, he saw his brother hunched over a small desk, writing. He looked up and asked Tom, "Will you take care of my bicycle for me?"

"Take care of your bike? Why? What are you talking about?"

"I'm going to be leaving here pretty soon, Tom. Probably next week. Boyd Conley and I have already talked to the marine recruiter. All I have to do is get Mom or Dad to sign."

Tom, a bit dazed, knowing that his brother wasn't kidding, undressed in silence and climbed into bed. He took his mind off his big brother by mulling over his experience with the Marine in the garden. He had seen a face, and then it disappeared, which was impossible.

He had to talk to someone about it. Right now, though, he could hardly wait to get back in the Marine's garden, see how it played out.

And, too, he could hardly wait to get back to school. When he finally fell off to sleep, he dreamed that he and Janie were spending their honeymoon on Safari in Africa, in a tent at the edge of a dense jungle. Night creatures calling, a lion's roar off in the jungle, Janie moving closer to him.

"Don't worry, Janie," he said in his best Johnny Weismuller voice. "I have my trusty knife and rifle here handy."

He had left a lantern burning and, sometime in the night, they were yanked from slumber by a one thousand-pound lion ripping apart the canvas.

Tom grabbed his knife and confronted the beast, looking him directly in the eye. The beast turned its head sideways and roared, than backed off and turned tail for the jungle.

Janie smothered his neck with kisses.

Me Tarzan. You Jane.

CHAPTER 11:
THE SCRAP MAN COMETH

The next morning, on the way to school, Tom and Gale stopped in Alvie Gammons' little grocery and notions store, located down at the third crossing, between the railroad and the highway. Flint went on ahead, reminding Tom not to be late. Gale bought a Baby Ruth candy bar. Tom would have liked to have had one, but, with funds limited, he chose instead a pack of gum.

He went into the school before the bell and left a stick of gum on the pigtail's desk. As class took up, he watched as she took her seat. She picked up the gum and looked at it.

"Who left this here?" she asked the girl in front of her.

"I don't know. Don't you want it?"

"No, not my brand. I like Wrigley's."

Wrigley's? My lord, you couldn't hardly find that stuff. And this was spearmint. Good spearmint. What the heck's wrong with you, girl?

She handed the gum to the girl, who quickly unwrapped it and stuffed it in her greedy little mouth.

I'm not her brand, and neither is my gum.

But her rejection only drew him deeper in. His desire to please her grew stronger.

Outside, during recess, Gale noticed Tom watching Janie intently as she hop-scotched on the sidewalk with some of the other girls. He came to Tom, his face wrinkled with a worrisome frown.

"Methinks you're getting some ideas, Tom, and I mean to warn you," he said. "Forget about Janie West. She's way beyond your reach. Her dad's a big insurance executive. They live in that big house about a mile below

Thelma's Grill. They moved in at the beginning of the school year. If you watch when school's out today, you'll see a big Buick pick her up. That's how she got here this morning, too. Her mother chauffeur's her. She's too rich for your blood, kid. So come on now, let's go back there where some of the boys got a marble game going."

Tom went with Gale, but Gale's advice did not go with him. It spilled out the other ear as quickly as it went in the one.

The week was a busy one, with Miss Newberry reviewing subject matters and priming her students for final exams. The following week would bring graduation ceremonies for the seniors and the eighth graders, and then summer vacation would begin. Tom looked forward with sweet anticipation of adventures with the gang, yet he willed that time go slowly.

By afternoon Janie had abandoned the pigtail and her golden hair cascaded down past her shoulders. Once, unbeknownst to her, he touched it. It was soft as early summer corn silk.

On the way out the hollow with the other boys, he glanced over his shoulder and saw, approaching them, the blue Buick carrying Janie home. He quickly laid down his books and hand-walked, his legs crooked at just the right angle to maintain his position. He managed half a dozen "steps" before falling to all fours just after the Buick passed them. Had she watched? He felt like her eyes were on him. But, to his knowledge, she had yet to notice his existence upon the earth.

By Thursday afternoon the temperature outside had risen to ninety degrees. Students and teachers were glad to escape the muggy classroom. At home, Tom wasted little time in changing to his cutoff overalls and joining the gang at the river. With a car inner tube around his waist, he got his first swimming lesson. "Go overhand! Go overhand! Keep your feet up," Gale yelled. Chopper swam circles around Tom, whining and barking, behaving like a mother hen.

On Friday, Roscoe Hunt pulled into the village in his battered pickup with the high board sides, on his weekly drive for tin cans, scrap iron, paper. Tom was waiting for him. He had brought with him in the moving truck a bushel basket of stuff he had collected up in Ohio. It brought him one dollar and thirty cents. Wow! Gale was there, too. He came out to the street pulling the rusty pedal-car he got the Christmas when he was four. He had it loaded down with newspapers and pieces of scrap iron. Roscoe pressed eighty-five cents worth of coins into his hands. "What about that ol' car? Want to sell it, too?" he asked.

Gale hesitated a moment, but when Roscoe offered him a shiny quarter for it, he said, "Sure. Why not?"

Mr. Hunt gave him the quarter and tossed the car into the back of his pickup with the other stuff.

"What about that?" Gale said to Tom, "my old pedal car's going to be turned into a tank."

Back in his house, Tom showed his money to his mother, who gushed over it and bragged on his patriotism. He took the coins up to his room and put them in a cigar box with his other treasures.

CHAPTER 12:
TROUBLE AT THE THEATER

War times were good times. On Saturday, all six boys had scrap iron money jingling in their pockets as they walked Grand Bridge, skipping, frolicking, horse-playing, pausing now and then to peer over the rail at the river eighty feet below. They didn't grumble at the tool booth. Paying a nickel to cross was not a happy thing, but it was an accepted way of life.

As was putting up with the gruff. Strange it was how the residents of two states separated by a river forming the border between them were often hostile to each other. Sometimes they treated each other like visitors from another planet, not from two of the great states making up the United States of America. The war that had brought Americans together in a common cause had salved such feelings for a time, but still hostility reared its head, especially so among the younger generation.

"You Kentucky boys have to show me your passports too, you know," said the collector, keeping a straight face as long as possible before guffawing at his own joke.

"Yeah, and you Buckeyes should have to pay five bucks to get into Kentucky. Most would probably be glad to pay it, if we'd let them in," snapped back Keith Richards, who had actually been born in the U.S. Canal Zone as a military brat. The war had taken his father, as well as his brother. His mother had an emotional breakdown, leading him to wind up living with his grandmother in Hooperville, Kentucky.

They came off the bridge and ambled up Main Street, headed for the Garden Theater, four blocks straight ahead. Tom stopped abruptly in front of the window of W.T. Grant's. A pearl necklace displayed in the window carried a price tag of one dollar. He could see it on Janie's neck.

"Come on, Tom. Keep up," Gale said. Tom had tarried at the window while the others went on ahead.

"Can't we take time to go in here a minute?" Tom asked.

"No. Maybe afterwards. Movie starts in 10 minutes."

Hobo, Vince, Keith and Dale had all stopped, too, but they weren't looking in Tom and Gale's direction. Their attention was diverted to half a dozen other boys coming away from a hot dog stand and making their way up the other side of the street.

"Go back to Kentucky, you hillbillies, before you get lost in the big city," one of them shouted at the Hooperville gang.

Tom and Gale walked away from the department store window and galloped to join their compatriots. "How'd they know we're from Kentucky?" Tom asked Gale.

It was Vince who answered. "Oh, they know. Sometimes I think they've got scouts out watching for us and lay in wait for us. We've been into it with this bunch before. Let's try to ignore them. Come on, everybody keep together."

A few more insults were hurled at the Braves as they continued up the street. The Braves fired back a gutsy salvo. Less than a block from the theater, the Ohio boys crossed over and both groups broke into a run for the ticket line. The Braves won the foot race. Tom was the first of either group in line. After the four or five people in front of him had bought their tickets and filed into the theater, he plopped his dime down. "One, please," he said.

But no ticket was forthcoming. Instead, the ticket seller, hardly more than a teenager, demanded another five cents.

"You know the price of a ticket is fifteen cents if you're twelve," he said.

"I'm eleven," Tom said, making no move to produce the additional money.

"I'm eleven," the ticket seller mimicked him. "You probably don't even know who your mother is, much less when you were born."

Anger swelled up in Tom, but before he could respond, a voice from back in the line, from one of the natives, shouted, "Let's move it! What's the matter? Somebody have to count his money for him?" Another added,

"Why don't you hillbillies go to your own movies? Oh, I forgot. You don't have moving picture shows in Kentucky yet, do you?"

Hobo, in line behind Tom, glared back at the speakers threateningly, and said, "You hold your horses." Then he gently moved Tom aside and stepped up to the ticket counter, placing down a nickel and a dime.

"I'm twelve and there's my ticket money," he said. "These five boys behind me are all eleven. "Now, you sell them their tickets, or there could be trouble for you, even before I go in and get the manager."

Hobo, big for his age, was sized up quickly by the ticket boy. It was plain on his face that he feared Hobo even more than he did having the manager called on him.

The Braves got their tickets and, ignoring insults hurled at them from those still in line, made their way into the theater. They all stopped at the concession stand and each bought a nickel bag of popcorn and a nickel cup of Pepsi.

Nearly all seats were filled by the time the lights dimmed and the newsreel came on. It was followed by a public announcement that filled the big screen: "Fascist Italy and Nazi Germany have been defeated, but Japan is still to be reckoned with. Be quick to return to your war work. And buy war bonds."

Next came the serial: Chapter eleven of "The Phantom." It was of particular interest on this Saturday, because viewers were taken inside the Phantom's home. Vince leaned forward in his seat at the sight of what was in the Phantom's cave. The floor was littered with gold, silver, precious stones – some in overflowing trunks, some in loose piles. Tom thought Vince might choke on his popcorn.

After the serial, the boys rode the range with Hopalong Cassidy in "Call of the Prairie."

Coming out of the dark theater, where he had been transported into a world of adventure, Tom felt a great letdown as he squinted in the harsh light of reality. The Braves, quickly glancing around for signs of trouble, but seeing none, made their way into the Playhouse, which sat next door to the theater. They took a side booth and ordered refreshments, either Pepsi floats or strawberry phosphates. In the showcase near the bar, Tom saw they had a whole case of Wrigley's on display. Gale followed him over to the display case and watched as Tom bought a pack and stuck it in his pocket. But he withdrew it, slipped Gale a stick, and unwrapped one for himself. He felt badly about not sharing with Vince and the boys, but the rest of it was for Janie.

He felt Gale's hand on his arm. "Uh oh. Look who just came in," Gale said.

It was the six Ohio boys who had given them trouble in the ticket line. They didn't notice Tom and Gale, still at the check out register. They walked straight to the booth where Vince and the boys still sat. Hobo rose to his feet, his hands clenched in fists. The bartender, sensing trouble, moved quickly and shooed them all outside. Gale and Tom followed them out, and by the time they got out the door all heck had broken loose. A few insults thrown by both sides and the melee was on. Scuffling, kicking, fists flying. Tom saw Hobo bang two Buckeye heads together and both boys go down.

Vince squared off like a prizefighter and danced round and round another foe, but threw no punches. One boy with a butch cut and a pug nose shoved Tom in the chest with both hands. Tom toppled over the back of another who had gotten down on all fours behind him. Tom lunged, grabbed the feet of the boy who had pushed him, and yanked his legs out from under him. The boy hit the sidewalk flat of his back. Keith jumped onto his stomach with both knees and Tom heard the wind go out of him. Two fresh troops rushed to the scene from across the street and waded into the Braves, turning the tide of the battle. Vince, still circling in and out with his dukes up, was ready to sound retreat – and all-out mad dash for the bridge – when the Shawnee Police Department saved them their honor. A cruiser screeched to a halt at the curb and two patrolmen leaped out. They waded into the skirmish, pulling combatants apart by shirt collars and belts. They quickly set them apart and sent the warring parties off in different directions.

The Braves made their way back down Main Street toward the bridge. Tom examined a skinned right elbow. No other blood seemed to have been drawn.

"This is the first time we've ever actually exchanged blows with them,"

Gale said. "Must have been savin' up for you, Tom, which is what they call ironic – you being a Buckeye yourself."

"Ex-Buckeye," Tom said.

"They'll think twice before they jump us again," said Vince, skipping along and punching the air with his fists. Tom wondered if Vince had actually thrown a punch during the confrontation. If he had, he sure hadn't seen it.

They were in front of the W.T. Grant store again. Tom pulled his coins out of his pocket and counted them. He had just enough to buy the necklace. He turned to Gale and said, "Can you loan me a nickel to get back across the bridge?"

"I've got it, sure. You can get me next time," Gale said.

"What's he goin' in there for?" Keith asked Gale as Tom went through the door.

Tom was back out in two minutes carrying something in a bag. "Let's see what you got," Vince said. Tom held the bag behind his back. Keith snatched it, reached down inside, and held up the pearl necklace.

"Oh, I see," Vince said. "Girl stuff, huh? Then Gale was right. Tom Sycamore is in love, love, love."

As the others snickered, Tom grabbed the necklace from Keith and dropped it back into the bag. He stammered, then a sudden thought came to him.

"Tomorrow's Mother's Day. Don't suppose any of you thought about that? And you probably never think about what it means to have someone wash and iron your clothes and fix those hot meals, along with all the other good stuff moms do?"

The others fell silent for a minute, then into the store they went. Each came back out with some small gift. Keith Richards showed the candelabrum he had bought for his grandmother.

As they crossed the bridge, Tom thought about how he had put himself in a bind. But he could make something for his mother, or do her some special favor. He didn't have to give her Janie's pearl necklace.

The talk turned to finances, of how they were all broke, and how scarce scrap iron was getting to be.

"I'm not worrying about collecting scrap iron," Hobo said. "This river's getting' right for trotlinin'. I can sell all the catfish I catch to Mr. Herman at his store down on Market Street. I can become independently rich.

"In fact, we can start our own company and all get rich, if I can get you birds to help me. Always need skinners and bait-catchers. And, of course, I'll need to use the *Reuben James*."

Tom wasn't sure what a trotline was, but, after Hobo told him he would teach him to set a trotline and how to skin catfish, he volunteered to hire on.

At the Kentucky end of the bridge, the six adventurers abandoned the highway and took to the railroad, galloping along the right of way and replaying scenes from the Hopalong Cassidy picture show.

As they stopped to catch their breath, Tom, pointing over the trees and up to the cliff on the hillside, said, "What's the story on that cave up there?"

"Devil's Den," Gale said. "We went in last year, all five of us. Vince wanted to look for Indian stuff. Went as far in as we dared, but didn't find anything. Our folks found out about it, and now it's strictly off-limits."

"It's a spooky old place that nobody wants to fool around in anyway," Hobo said.

Vince pinched his lower lip with his thumb and forefinger as he gazed steadfastly up toward the cave.

Back at the tree house, the Braves broke out their weapons of war and spent the next hour clearing an airstrip for John Wayne and his Flying Tigers. They battled the Japs through the thick jungles and finally drove them out to a beach on the far side, where the Flying Tigers strafed them.

Later, after a swim to wash off the sand and the mud and the blood, they stretched their weary bodies out on the deck of the tree house. The leafy limbs of the big tree covered them with shade. A clean and cool breeze drifted up through the cracks in the boards. It was a wonderful place to be, this house in a tree – a place of security in a world that was not so secure.

Vince couldn't relax. He was up and pacing, finally rousing the Braves from their laziness by calling a "special meeting."

"I can't get my mind off all the treasure the Phantom had in that cave," he said, his blue eyes flashing. "We need money. People all around us need help, and we could do a lot of good with money."

"Hail, hail," said Dale Riley. "I got seven cents if that would help."

Vince ignored him and continued. "I know Devil's Den is not the Phantom's cave, but I was reading about how a Frenchman, Howard Le-Kain, something like that, sometime during the 1750s mined some rich silver deposits in this country. Somewhere in the hills, overlooking the Ohio, it's thought that he hid tons of minted coins in a cave. Also, some gold bars recovered from a sunken flatboat."

The Braves gathered in, eager to share the treasure, or at the least the dream of it. But Gale said, "You're dreamin' if you think it's in Devil's Den, Major. We've been in there, last summer, remember?"

"And we didn't find anything, except some old bones and mysterious-lookin' tracks. Probably an old wildcat lives in there," Hobo said.

"Yeah, but we only went in that front part of it," Vince said. "You remember we shined the light back through that narrow passage at the rear and could see what looked like another big room opening up? Back there, in that room nobody's been in for 200 years, is where Le-Kain's treasure is. I had a revelation while watching the Phantom."

"Yeah, Vince, but we couldn't get through there," Dale said. "Small as I am, I couldn't squeeze through there."

"But," Vince said, "those rocks that blocked our way looked loose to me. We go in there with a pick and shovel and we'll dig through."

The group fell silent, mulling it over.

And then the plans were laid for the extraction of untold riches from Devil's Den. It was scheduled for the next day, after church.

"Not a word about this to anybody," Vince cautioned as the gang filed down from the tree house and headed up the bank for home.

CHAPTER 13:
RINGING OF THE BELL

While Tom and his friends were at the picture show, Bruce Sycamore had caught several nice catfish from the river. He had skinned them and cut them into white steaks, which Carrie Sycamore had fried to a golden brown. Fish and hot cornbread with real butter. Wow! Could life get any better?

After supper, the family gathered in the living room and turned on the big floor model Philco. Carrie Sycamore tried to look on the sunny side of life. But these days she constantly worried that Flint would be involved in the alleged coming invasion of Japan. It had affected the very fiber of her being, so much so that she had reached a point in life where she couldn't enjoy the good times for worrying about the bad times to come.

Her favorite radio shows brought her a respite, however brief, from that attitude. As she shared the life of fictitious characters coming over the airways she temporarily forgot her worry of Flint being drafted and going off to invade Japan.

Tom was enjoying watching and listening to her and his father more than he was the antics of Fibber McGee and Molly. His mother threw back her head and let out a roll of laughter followed by short intakes of air. Tom's dad's laugh was a one-syllable "Ha!" followed by a wide grin and a shake of his head.

Then came the Saturday night baths. Water was heated and the tub brought in. Flint was first, and. before going up to his room, helped Tom carry out the tub and empty his bath water off the back porch.

Before Tom stripped out of his clothing, his mother came in to make sure he had enough water in the tub. "I know you, bud," she said. "Ankle deep and a good splash off you think is good enough." She added water until the tub was three-fourths full. "Cleanliness is next to Godliness, and don't you forget it."

"Mom, Flint didn't leave me much hot water! That's gonna be cold!"

"Too cold, huh? Well what about that river? I'd say it's cold. You think I don't know you were in it? You're gonna fool around down at that old river 'till you get yourself drowned. Now hunker down in there and scrub yourself good."

Flint was hunkered down over his desk as Tom went through his room on the way to his. Tom thought he was writing songs, but when Flint asked him to come over to his desk, he saw that he had been reading a letter. He handed the letter to Tom and Tom saw tears in his eyes.

The letter was from Ashville and it was from the mother of Elmo Coffee. Elmo Coffee, Flint's best friend, a year ahead of Flint in high school, had joined the Navy right after getting his diploma in the class of 1944. Now, ten days shy of his nineteenth birthday, he was missing in action and presumed dead. Three Jap suicide planes had struck Elmo's ship, one right near the five-inch gun mount he was helping to man. Elmo and two other sailors were blown overboard and into the blue-green waters of the Pacific.

The letter concluded, "I know, Flint, that you love him like we do, so I wanted you to know. Give our best to your family.

Love,

Janet Coffee."

Tom was stunned and speechless. He leaned over and rested his head on his brother's shoulder, gently patting him on his back. Without speaking, he trudged on into his own room.

He had so many heavy thoughts on his mind that sleep did not come easy. He pushed away the thought of Jap planes crashing into ships. There was the matter of the necklace. He could make some little gift for his mother, who probably didn't expect anything from him anyway.

And what about this Marine in the garden?

Spirits.

Too deep a subject for him. He had to talk to somebody about this.

As the tree frogs and crickets sang outside his window, his mind finally slipped into neutral. Sleep found him, and Janie was there, shouting for help from an upstairs widow as flames licked up around her and Tom raced up the stairs to save her.

Hooperville Methodist could seat about 125 people, and that Sunday in May of 1945 it was nearly full. In addition to it being Mother's Day, President Truman had declared it a National Day of Thanksgiving.

Three couples in the congregation found it difficult to enter in to the spirit of giving thanks. All had seen a son march off to war, never to return. A dozen other families in the village had loved ones still serving, either in Europe or the Pacific.

Two couples were kneeling at the altar even before the first song was sung. John Redden and his wife, Emily, had received word from the War Department that their son, Joseph, was missing in action following a battle on Luzon. Henry and Louisa Sharp had been notified that their son, John, had been wounded by shrapnel during fighting on Okinawa. The Rev. Ottis Hackelbee knelt beside them and asked the congregation to join him in prayer.

After the initial gathering service, the six Braves jostled each other as they tumbled down the steps to their basement classroom. Vince was all excited about the planned trip into Devil's Den. All the gear was assembled, and the exploration crew would meet at his house right after dinner.

Tom's ears perked up upon learning that Mr. Galloway's lesson dealt with spirituality – chiefly on the work of the Holy Spirit in the lives of believers.

At an opportune time, Tom popped the question: What happened to the spirit when a person died? Could it linger around on earth?

Mr. Galloway's white eyebrows arched as he studied Tom's face. This was unexpected serious business from an eleven-year-old. Finally, he said, "Well, now, Tom Sycamore – that's it, isn't it? – you're getting into some pretty deep and serious matters here on a beautiful May morning."

Nevertheless, he tackled the question head-on, and he immediately had the attention of every boy in the class, especially Hobo, who made no secret of his belief that spirits roamed about wherever they pleased, especially after dark and around old graveyards.

"The Scriptures, that's where we must always go to find answers to life's questions," Mr. Galloway said. "We know that the Bible says, speaking of the believer now, that the flesh returns to the dust, but the spirit to God who gave it; that to be absent from the body is to be present with the Lord. This would seem to indicate that, no, the spirits of the dead don't roam the earth.

"The Good Book also demonstrates that there are demons who pose as the spirits of the dead. That's why it warns us to stay away from witchcraft, sorcery, or mediums who allegedly consult with the dead.

"But, as I said in the beginning, there's a lot of mystery concerning the spiritual world, so much so that we can't comprehend it. God can do what He will. His ways are not our ways. We know that there have been many reports, from reliable witnesses, of what is believed to be the spirits of the dead making their presence known, hanging around for a while, at a particular location, sometimes to right some wrong, to bring about justice. It seems that some people can experience these things, others can't. From what I've read on it, it seems that ghosts are images without substance, yet they become visible to people who have some sense along these lines that others don't. Animals, especially dogs, again from what I've read on it, can always experience beings from the spirit world. Is it a sixth sense? I don't know."

The boys fell silent as they pondered the teaching. Finally, Hobo said, "There's houses what are haunted, and that's a fact."

Teacher Galloway cocked his head to one side as he studied Hobo's face.

"Do you know of a house that's haunted?" he asked Hobo.

Hobo launched without hesitation into a story about how his grandfather, out coon hunting, about midnight passed an old abandoned house out in the woods that he knew had been vacant for years, yet on that night there were lights in the windows and fiddle music drifting out over the hollow. He crept up and looked in the window. He saw a blazing fire going in the fireplace, and men and women waltzin' around to music of a five-string band. He even went in. Had a drink with them. Danced with one or two of the women. Said they had the coldest hands he'd ever felt. Next day, mid-morning, he went back up there to find out more about these folks. Why, the floor was covered with years of dust, he said, and there were no tracks in it either. Hadn't been a fire in that fireplace for years.

"It was ghosts. Ghosts havin' a party, Grandpa said."

"Your grandfather was fond of moonshine, wasn't he, Hobo?" Mr. Galloway asked, trying unsuccessfully to suppress a smile.

"Yeah, but he was stone sober that night. Never went within half a mile of that place again."

As the class ended, Mr. Galloway took Tom by the arm and pulled him aside as the others filed back up the steps into the sanctuary.

"I'm curious, Tom," he said, "as to why you're asking questions about the spirits of the dead."

Tom first told him of his mother seeing his grandfather after his death, then, after a little hesitation, blurted out his seeing the Marine in the garden – how the Marine had planted the garden, then gone off to the war in the Pacific and been killed; about feeling a comforting presence when he worked the garden, and how he had actually seen the Marine's face.

Mr. Galloway's eyes widened at the mention of the Marine. He was silent for a moment, then, rubbing his chin, said, "My, my."

For a moment he seemed to stare right through Tom, Then he spoke again: "Last week, right after we got word that Germany had surrendered, I headed over for the church here to ring the bell. As I started up the steps, the bell started ringing on its own! The front door was locked, as usual, since a few weeks ago some vandals did some damage to the Christian Church up the way here. I used my key to get in. The bell had stopped ringing, but the rope hanging down from the bell tower was still swaying back and forth a little. I could feel a presence. Someone had just been in that spot, or was still there. I climbed part of the way up the ladder, where I could see all the way to the top of the steeple. No one there. Nearly got stung by a wasp for my trouble.

"I came back down, and when I looked up toward the altar, there was someone kneeling there. I'm sure I saw someone kneeling there. But it was

99

only for an instant, then whoever, or whatever, I saw was gone. Then I thought I saw it again, heading down the basement steps. I went on up to the podium, looking all around, and finally came down here to the basement. There's no back door to this church. Just the front door, and the door leading out from the basement here. It was locked, from the inside, and there was no one here."

The teacher looked now toward the door. "Something's very strange here, Tom," he muttered.

"What, Mr. Galloway?"

The Sunday school teacher suddenly felt a bit ridiculous, talking to an 11-year-old student about – about what? A ghost?

He walked to the basement door and pulled the curtain back from the small window in the top half of the door. "I looked through here, into your garden, and I thought … I thought I saw a soldier there – a Marine, I guess, as you say – big as life, just standing there with his hands on his hips. I was squinting into the sun, couldn't see too well, but it seemed so real. Then, as I rubbed my eyes, it disappeared. He didn't walk off somewhere. He just disappeared."

Tom nudged against Mr. Galloway to peer through the bottom of the window at his garden, lying in the sunlight just beyond the fence that separated it from the side yard of the church. Both were silent for several seconds. Finally, Tom, backing away, said, "What does it all mean, Mr. Galloway?"

Mr. Galloway moved away from the door, rubbing his chin and shaking his head. "I don't know, Tom," he said. "We'll just have to watch and see. I know the Marine who lived there before you. He and his wife – can't recall her name just now – came to church one Sunday. She was, as they say, Tom, heavy with child. Very nice young couple. Reverend Hackelbee counseled her after she received word that her husband had been killed on Okinawa."

"Well," Tom said, "if she's still around here, don't you think we should get hold of her? I mean, shouldn't she know about this? Or should we just forget it, and say nothing?"

Mr. Galloway pursed his lips and rubbed his forehead with the knuckle

100

of his thumb. "I think you're right, Tom. And I think I might be able to reach her. I understand she's living over in Shawnee, with her parents."

———————

It was Mom Sycamore's golden fried chicken for dinner. Tom's father had the back and the neck and Flint and Tom each had a breast. Carrie Sycamore waited for what was left, if any. If necessary, she would satisfy her appetite with fried potatoes and biscuits.

Tom hung around the kitchen after dinner, helping his mother tidy up. He took the bones and what few scraps there were out to Chopper, then returned and started ridding the table of dishes. He washed them at the sink, while his mother, somewhat shocked, dried.

"You feeling OK today, Tom?" she asked.

"Just helping my mom on Mother's Day," he answered.

"Well, I didn't think you'd remember," she said. "Both my sons remembered. Flint, bless his heart, gave me two dollars from his hay money this morning. Wants me to spend it on myself."

Tom swallowed hard as he thought of the necklace. He dried his hands and ran up the steps to his room, got the necklace from the cigar box, returned and handed it to her.

She was flabbergasted. "A pearl necklace? For me? Oh, Tom, it's beautiful. How did you manage this?"

"My scrap iron money."

"Well, you shouldn't have. But I'm glad your did." She put the necklace around her slender neck and snapped it. "It looks real. Well, it is real. At least it will always be real to me." She kissed the top of his towhead.

And Tom began his getaway. "I got the weeds all out of the garden, for now at least. Gale and the boys are going hiking in thc hills this afternoon. I told them I would go with them. Can I?"

He had known he wouldn't mention the cave exploration.

After a while to study, she relented, but only after a stern reminder that he watch for copperheads and rattlesnakes. "Be careful, and be back by supper time."

101

CHAPTER 14:
OFF TO THE TOP

Chopper had become wise to his master's ways, knowing full well when he was to be excluded from an adventure. Tom had no intentions of taking him up around that cliff. He had to run the little dog down and capture him in order to lock him in the storage shed. Leader obeyed the command "stay!" when spoken plainly by Gale. Chopper pretended not to know what the word meant. He was cussing up a blue streak as Tom shut him in and latched the door.

Tom found the five Braves in Vince's garage, marveling at the things Vince was placing in the army backpack he had bought at the army surplus store in Shawnee. It included a shovel that folded neatly down against its handle and a short-handled pick. Hobo added a flashlight.

"We'll take it, but I don't think we'll need it," Vince said. "I've got these."

He pulled half a dozen long-stemmed cattails from a Fleetwood coffee can.

"Soaked them overnight in coal oil," he said. "Make wonderful torches."

Dale Riley had his Shawnee Times paper bag over his shoulder. "We'll carry the gold and silver in here," he said, "'case it won't all fit in the backpack. I've got a couple of peanut butter and jelly sandwiches in there, too. Sometimes I take a weak spell and have to have something sweet."

"We're not stayin' for the duration," Vince said. "We'll be back home for supper. Good idea, though, to have extra carryin' capacity. We might have to make three, four trips to get all the treasure out of there."

Check and double-check and up the street for the lower crossing they headed.

Alvie Gammons always opened his little grocery for four or five hours after church let out. Vince led the way inside. He bought a ball of stout string, the kind used for tying up bean rows or tomato plants to the stake.

"What's that for?" Gale asked.

"To make sure we find out way back out," Vince said. "We play out the string as we go in. That way, if we make a lot of turns and different passages, we just follow the string back out. All big-time cave explorers do that."

That last line got Mr. Gammons' attention.

"Cave Explorers?" he asked. "What are you boys fixin' to get into now?"

Vince winced. "Nothing. Nothing at all, Mr. Gammons," he answered. "Dad needs it for the garden."

"Uh huh. Well, I hope you boys are not thinking about going up around that Devil's Den place. You know full well Devil's Den is off limits. It's a very dangerous place. You couldn't pay me enough to get me to go in that place. So you stay out of there now, you hear? And be careful if you go messin' around that steep cliff."

Outside, Vince put the ball of string in a side pocket of the backpack.

"When we cash in the treasure, we'll buy his store. Let the old fellow retire," he said, patting the pocket that held the string.

They hiked along Route 10 a short way and, just short of the lane leading into School House Hollow, slipped in under the trees and began the climb up the bony ridge that led to the cliff.

CHAPTER 15:
STAY WITH THE LIGHT

The panoramic view from the top of the cliff was nothing short of spectacular. Grand Bridge was a ribbon stretching across the Ohio. The river disappeared around a distant bend turning between green hills to the west. In the other direction, a paddlewheeler pushing coal barges downstream around a bend above Shawnee looked like a toy. They could see the whole village of Hooperville and almost all of the city of Shawnee. The smokestacks from the steel mill on the upper outskirts of the town spewed gray smoke, even on this peaceful Sunday afternoon. The Charles River twisted off to the north from its mouth on the downriver end of the town, resembling a giant wounded snake.

"Wow! This is something," Tom said, catching his breath.

"I knew you'd like it up here, Tom," Gale said. He pointed to a flat rock where the Braves had chiseled their initials on a previous trip. He produced a hammer and chisel from a satchel on his side and handed them to Tom, who set to work adding his own to the collection.

Vince, though, already in his mind able to hear the jingle and clinking of gold and silver coins from the Le-Cain collection, was in a hurry to move along.

"You can finish it when we come back out," he said to Tom, who barely had "TO" chiseled into the rock before they were off. They followed Vince from the top of the cliff down into a swayback, then turned down a rocky, steep trail that led down under the cliff. They checked their descent by clinging to saplings and tree roots.

The great gaping hole seen from the highway on the upriver edge of the cliff was not actually the entrance to the cave, but a rockhouse. The ceiling and walls held chiseled initials and dates going well back into the past century.

The entrance to the cave itself was at the back of the rockhouse. It was a small tunnel that would require crawling on hands and knees to enter. Cool air wafted out from the entrance and carried a musty smell that was not at all inviting, yet still it carried the hint of adventure.

Vince lit two of the cattail torches and instructed Hobo to tie the garden string to a rock lying near the entrance.

Keith Richards looked longingly through the treetops at Hooperville and his grandmother's house. His claustrophobia was urging him to turn back, but he didn't want to admit it. All for one and one for all, he remembered.

"You've got to play that string out, now, Hobo, wherever we go," Vince said. "Hard tellin' how many twists and turns and tunnels we'll be going through, but all we have to do is follow our string back out. And everybody – once we're through the tunnel and able to stand up, stick close together. These torches don't throw a light very far."

They crawled in one after the other. Within twenty feet they were able to stand and the walls widened to give way to a room, maybe twenty feet by thirty feet square. Their shadows cast by the torches onto the ceiling and walls made the boys look like giants. They shriveled their noses at the dank and musty smell pervading the air.

Suddenly, Dale exclaimed, "Look! Over there! Whazat?"

Vince raised his torch high, stepped forward, and kicked at the small pile of bones, bones of some unfortunate small animal.

"These were probably left by a saber-toothed tiger," he said, glancing around to study the expressions on the faces of the others.

The boys responded by drawing closer together. They gave the bones a wide berth as they explored the room.

At the back of the room they spied a passageway, shaped like an upside down "V" leading off into the inky darkness.

"I tell you boys, this place ain't nothing but an old fox's den, and I'm already starting to lose interest in it," Hobo said. "What say we skedaddle, Vince?"

Vince turned on him and held the torch he carried almost close enough to Hobo's face to singe his red hair.

"You're some adventurer, Ain't 'cha? Been here 10 minutes and you're already wanting to turn back," he said. "Turn back, when down at the end of that tunnel ahead lays enough gold and silver to buy your mom and dad a new house?"

Again he held the torch high to study the faces of the others. He judged they all had a hankering to go back to the comforts of the outside world.

"Man oh man," he said. "What if De Sota had been like this bunch? There wouldn't have been no Mississippi River, that's what."

Vince walked brazenly on into the passageway, the torch held high in front of him. The others followed. Better to go with the light, no matter where, than to be left standing alone in the dark.

Soon they were crawling again on all fours. They came to a place where the roof and the floor came so close together that Tom judged Chopper couldn't even have crawled through.

"Looks like the end of the line," Hobo said.

"Maybe not," Vince said, asking Hobo to pass him his flashlight.

He directed the beam of light through the passage and into the darkness beyond. The walls of the passageway rose upwards again beyond this narrow place, and there appeared to be a large room straight ahead.

"It's back there, boys. I'm tellin' ya, it's back there – gold and silver, riches for us all," Vince said.

He broke out his shovel and pick and began clearing away loose dirt and stones from the floor. The others passed the shovel full of dirt back to the rear, and soon Vince had cleared enough of the material away to allow him to forge ahead on all fours. But not before Gale, looking up, sounded the alarm. "My gosh," he said. "Them rocks are just hangin' there. Looks like they could come down on us. Be still, everybody!"

They studied the low ceiling a bit before Vince said, "Those rocks have been that way for two hundred years, and they'll stay that way for another hundred. We can crawl through this passage and then you can see for yourselves it opens up again back in there."

And so they squeezed through the narrow spot, then were able to stand and make their way into a room even bigger than the first room – a cavern, actually.

"I don't like this place one bit," Hobo said as the torches sent weird patterns of light and shadow on the steep walls and high ceiling.

"Me either," said Keith Richards. "This place reminds me of a tomb."

It was Hobo, bringing up the rear and playing out string as they went, who wandered a bit off course and startled the others – even Vince – out of their wits as he suddenly stumbled over something in the darkness and fell.

"What is this?" he mumbled, fumbling to get his flashlight from the paper bag Dale carried. He flicked it on and cast its beam on something under his right leg.

Then he was kicking and screaming, pushing away from the odious something like a frightened crawdad.

"Oh, my gosh!" Keith wailed.

"My gawd, we are in a tomb," said Dale Riley.

Vince brought the torch into play. "Well, I'll be durned," he said. "It's a skeleton."

The rib cage was mostly intact. Leg and arm bones lay askance in the dust. The skull rested against the base of the wall, grinning up at them. A grinning skull of what had once been a human being.

"A human skeleton!" said Dale, stuttering over his words.

"A...a... a mummy!" said Hobo. "I'm picking up string. Let's get outta here!"

"And quick about it!" said Keith.

"Hold on a minute. You think a skeleton's gonna hurt you?" Vince asked. "This fellow's past hurting anybody. But somebody sure put a hurtin' on him. Look here."

He poked at the rib bones with the point of the shovel and they could see an arrowhead down inside the cavity.

"My gawd, Vince! Don't touch that thing!" Hobo fairly hissed his words.

Vince ignored him, moved closer, exploring the skeleton with his shovel and the flashlight. He could see two tarnished bracelets on the thing's wrist. He touched the arm bone. The wrist broke, and the bracelets fell into the dust. Vince picked them up.

The others wanted to make a fast retreat to the narrow opening and get back into the first room and outside, but their curiosity held them fast.

Vince rubbed one of the bracelets against the sleeve of his shirt as he held the other in his palm.

"Boys, if that's not silver, I'll eat this cattail, fire and all," he said. "This is pure silver. And there's no doubt plenty more round about here."

Tom got brave, moving one of the leg bones with the toe of his shoe. Hobo, too, moved in closer, then began looking around the base of the room with his flashlight.

Vince stuck the bracelets and the arrowhead in his pack and they continued their exploration, looking for signs of where the cave floor might have been disturbed, as in burying something.

In the back wall of the room, a crevice led farther into the mountain. Vince, satisfied there was nothing more to be found in the cavern, moved into this new passageway. The others protested, but followed, staying close enough to maintain near comforting contact with each other.

As they moved deeper into the tunnel they began to see their first stalagmites and stalactites. They wound their way around and between them as water dripped on their head and shoulders.

The ceiling turned downward and they were soon bending at the waist to continue on. The floor sloped downward and disappeared into a pool of black water. The ceiling continued its downward slope until it met the water and disappeared. The walls, too, plunged closer together. They were no more than two arms lengths apart where they disappeared into the water. There appeared to be a recess in the right wall that went back farther to the right than they could see, even with the flashlight. But it, too, was filled with the water.

It was evident that this was a dead end – the end of Devil's Den.

After exploring every crevice and ledge in the walls, and examining the floor, they knew for certain that this was the end.

And knew for certain that they were not going to find any treasure trunks filled with gold and silver coins like those they had seen in the Phantom's cave.

Disappointed, Vince and the others followed Hobo as he gathered in the string and coiled it around his forearm.

Back in the skeleton's tomb, Vince and Hobo debated about whether to gather up the skeleton bones and skull and put them in the pack.

"No, Vince, no." Hobo said. "Leave the dead lay. We take that thing out of its final resting place, hard tellin' what'll happen."

"Let's just get out of here with our own selves," Dale chimed in, "I tell you, I don't like the feel or the smell of this place."

They were at the entrance to the narrow tunnel connecting the two rooms when they heard a terrifying rumble: rock grinding against rock, slabs falling, smashing against each other.

One final loud thump shook the floor beneath their feet.

They heard the mountain groaning. A cloud of dust rolled back over them. They scuttled backwards like frightened crawdads, spinning back toward the skeleton's tomb, stumbling and falling over each other, Vince and Gale struggling to keep the torches they carried away from bodies.

They sprawled on the floor as a deafening silence engulfed them and the dust settled over them.

Tom stole a glance at the dust-flecked face of Vince in the light of the torches. The leader's eyes were wide and white, and Tom saw fear written there.

"What in the world..." Vince muttered. "Do you reckon..."

Then he and Tom made their way back into the tunnel. Vince led the way on all fours as they approached the point where they had dug out the loose rocks on the floor to squeeze their way through from the main room to the second room. They were greeted by a wall of jumbled stone, pressed down to form a wall of solid stone. Not only the loose ceiling stones they had been concerned with had fallen, but a larger portion of the ceiling had come down also. Vince climbed up the mountain of stone until his head butted against the roof. "It's all wedged in tight. Not even a piss ant could crawl through there," he muttered, as much to himself as to Tom.

They returned to the others, who read the lack of hope in their faces.

"We're trapped, ain't we?" Dale said. "We're trapped for the duration. Nobody even knows we're here."

CHAPTER 16:
THE TREASURE
NOW WAS LIFE ITSELF

Outside the sun was shining and people went about their daily lives. A mile to the west of Devil's Den, at the two-story West home, Janie West looked up from some homework she was doing and tried to comprehend why an image of Tom Sycamore came suddenly to her mind; why it caused a shiver to run down her spine.

Perhaps she was feeling guilt because she had ignored him, even though she felt something unusual in her breast when she looked at him – and she only looked at him when she knew he was unaware that she was looking at him. Knowing what she knew about the future, she knew she could not afford to let her feelings for Tom settle in.

In Hooperville, Carrie Sycamore was down on her knees waxing the linoleum on her kitchen floor. She was known among her very close friends to have the gift of sensing the goings on in things pertaining to the spiritual side of life. Yet she was unaware that her youngest son and his five friends were trapped inside the cave overlooking the village. This was perhaps because her thoughts were too much on her oldest son and Japan, and on the possibilities of his having to go there, and what she could do – short of praying, which she had done plenty of – to stop it.

In the garden out back, a sudden wind swept through the young vegetables. In the building, Chopper howled. In the Sanders yard, Leader paced back and forth and whined.

Meanwhile, inside the cave, the Braves tried to be brave, even though fear churned acids up in the pits of their stomachs. Dangerous situations were grand and glorious when acted out on the big screen in a darkened theater. There was, after all, the knowledge that normal lives awaited just outside.

But no play-acting here. They were trapped in a dark and chilly cave. To think about their situation was to let panic sweep over them.

Vince's mind was racing. He was entertaining no thoughts now about finding hidden treasure. The treasure sought now was life itself.

Finally, in slow and measured tones, Hobo spoke. "Well. Major," he said sarcastically, "what you've done with this stupid scheme of yours is to get us killed. Years from now, maybe, they'll find our bones in here, the same as that poor skeleton over there."

Vince looked Hobo in the eyes, shaking his head from side to side.

"That's foolish talk, Hobo," he said. "We're a long way from dead. Why, nobody's even hurt. This is just the end of a chapter. The Phantom and the Durango Kid always find a way to escape, and so will we. We're the good guys."

Gale reminded Hobo that no one had twisted their arms to get the Braves to accompany Vince on this cave adventure. "We got ourselves in this situation together, and we need to stick together to get ourselves out of here, however that might be," he said.

They took turns at crawling back into the passageway leading to the cave-in and digging with the pick and shovel. Gale even hit it a lick with his hammer and chisel. But such efforts were futile, totally futile.

Claustrophobia had to be dealt with. All of the boys were fighting the urge to panic, to scream out for help.

"When we don't show up for supper, they'll send somebody to dig us out," Vince said. "I feel like Mr. Gammons knew where we were headed."

The torches he and Tom carried began to burn lower, to flicker, prompting Gale to recall Miss Newberry's demonstration of the candle in the fruit jar.

"Remember how, when she tightened the lid on the jar, cutting off the supply of air, how the candle soon flickered and went out?" he asked.

CHAPTER 17:
SOMETHING ALIVE BACK THERE

But Vince said he believed the cattails were just using up all the kerosene he had soaked them in. He pulled another from his pack and lit it from the low-burning one. It ignited and put forth a healthy flame, but it did not burn as brightly as the first two did before the cave-in.

"We've got air in here, men. Air's coming in from somewhere," he said.

That was comforting to know, Tom thought. Comforting, too, was the light and heat provided by the torch. He said a silent prayer of thanks.

It was Gale who had a sudden inspiration concerning prayer.

"You know, Mr. Galloway has been teaching us for months on end about the power of prayer, and yet we haven't even tried it officially concerning our present difficulty," he said. "Let's form a circle and hold hands."

Vince laid the torch down on the ground and the Braves circled it.

"Tom, I think you ought to be the one to lead us," Gale said.

Tom's heart leaped. He had never said a prayer out loud before. Yet, without even taking time to organize his thoughts, he began:

"Our Father, which art in Heaven, hallowed be thy name, thy Kingdom come, thy will be done, on earth as it is in Heaven. Uh, forgive us for getting ourselves in such a bad fix. And we wouldn't mind at all comin' up there to be with you. But, uh, our folks would miss us something fierce. And we're so young we'd like to stay here for a little while, if you don't mind. Now we ask that if there be a way out of here, that you show us that way. We'll be eternally grateful. It's in Jesus name we ask these things, amen."

The moment of silence that followed was broken by Vince, who said, "And besides air, we've got water, too. I read somewhere where humans can go a month without food, but only three days without water."

Water was dripping from the roof back in the tunnel that led from the tomb and ended in the black pool.

They made their way back to that area, through the stalagmites and stalactites, and managed to catch enough water on their tongues to satisfy their thirst.

Vince stood studying the pool of water. He knelt down and stuck his hand beneath the surface. The water was cool and clear, not dirty and stagnant. Water was coming into the cave from somewhere, yet the cave did not flood.

"This water has to be going somewhere," he muttered.

He waded into the water, letting out a shriek. "Like ice!" he said.

But he waded on in. The floor sloped sharply beneath his feet. Suddenly he disappeared!

He surfaced, sputtering. "Drop off!" he said, treading water. He moved back toward shore until his feet were on bottom. He came close enough for Tom to reach him the torch. He held it high in one hand as he side-stroked out to where the roof disappeared under the water and the walls of the crevice moved to within two arms lengths of each other.

Steadying himself against one wall with the hand that held the torch, he reached beneath the surface with his other hand. He discovered that instead of continuing on its downward journey into the pool, the ceiling broke a foot underwater. Vince could feel its flat surface for as far back as he could reach.

There was a recess in the wall on the right, almost like a small room in itself, with its floor formed by the black water. The torch tossed eerie shadows on the surface. By pressing his body against the left wall and craning his neck, he was able to see around the "corner" of the wall.

And something around that corner caught his eye. And whatever the something was, it was moving!

"What in the world …?" he muttered.

Gale, startled by the tone of his voice, said, "What is it, Vince? What

114

do you see?"

Vince moved quickly back to join the others on the shore, so quickly that he almost drowned the torch.

"Just around that corner, boys, there's something ALIVE!" he said.

Tom felt a shiver run along his spine, a shiver not associated with the damp coolness of the place.

"Awww! What're you talkin' about? You're crazy!" Hobo said.

Vince invited them out to take a look for themselves. They joined him, shrieking at the coldness of the water, Tom scooting his feet along the bottom, being careful not to go off the step-off. Hobo flicked on his flashlight and handed it to Vince.

"See, see back there?" Vince said, shining the light back into the crevice.

The others, all except Tom, saw it, too. Some kind of creature with a serpentine head, which bobbed and swayed in the water, was staring at them.

"What in the name of holy hallelujah is that thing?" Keith asked.

"Doesn't matter one bit. Let's just get our skinny hind ends out of here quick!" Gale said, turning back toward shore and grabbing Tom by the arm.

"I think you're forgetting, Mr. Flanders, that's there's no longer a way out of here, not back that way at least," Vince said.

Then, still looking at the thing, he added, "It doesn't seem to be threatening us – just stayin' there in one spot, bobbin' up and down."

"It's sizin' us up, deciding which one of us to eat first," Keith said.

"Maybe it's friendly," Dale said. "Here, boy. Here, boy. Cluck cluck."

"Somebody hand me up one of Dale's peanut butter and jelly sandwiches," Vince said.

Dale protested, but nevertheless brought it from his paper bag and handed it over.

Vince tore the sandwich into several pieces and threw a couple of them at the thing. One piece struck it right on its head. It went under, but bobbed right back up, swaying back and forth but not moving any closer. The piece of sandwich floated on the surface under its chin.

"Well, it doesn't like peanut butter and jelly," Vince said, pondering his next move.

Tom picked a piece of slate the size of his hand from a shelf on the wall and handed it to Vince. Vince tossed it at the thing. It landed a foot from it, causing it to bob more furiously in the light of the torch. It still made no move toward the boys.

"Pass me the flashlight. I'm gonna see once and for all what that thing is. I don't think it's anything alive at all," Vince said.

Cautiously, he side-stroked toward the beast, holding the flashlight aloft with one hand and keeping the light trained on the monster as best he could.

"You're nuts, Vince!" said Keith, watching through the fingers of his hands, which covered his face. "That thing'll go under water and grab you by the leg. Probably drowns its victims before it eats them."

Hobo overcame his fear and swam out far enough to keep an eye on the goings on. Vince was close enough to reach out and hit the thing with the flashlight, which he did.

"Well, I'll be durned," Vince said, reaching out to take the thing by the "neck." He wagged it back and forth and gave out a nervous little laugh.

"Our monster, boys," he said, "ain't nothing but an old grapevine sticking out of the water. On back farther from its head it comes out of the water again and disappears through a crack in the ceiling."

"Hahahaha. I knew it wasn't nothing real," Keith said.

But there was nothing much to laugh about in that cave. Back on shore, they stood in the cold, dark dampness and shivered. Hypothermia, the silent killer, was coming in for a visit, and they did not even know it by its name.

Finally, Vince turned to Hobo. "Hobo, do you want to taste your momma's biscuits and gravy again?" he asked.

"Oh my, don't talk about that, Vince. Wish I had some right now," Hobo said.

"Well, then, perhaps you shall. Take and tie this line around your waist."

Hobo could hold his breath longer than anyone. He was the only one who had ever been able to dive down and bring up bottom in the middle of the Ohio River.

"Gravy and biscuits – and our lives – depend on what you can do here,

Hobo," Vince said. "When I put my hand under the water a while ago, I could feel the roof leveling off and running on back beneath the water, away from us. What you've got to do is to go out there, take a deep breath, go under and pull yourself along the underwater ceiling, keeping your nose close to the ceiling, and search for pockets where the water doesn't go all the way to the ceiling. I believe you'll find it within a very short distance. But maybe not. Time yourself and make sure you have enough breath left to get back. See if you can't see if this water's running off, out of here. If you run into trouble, give three yanks on the line and we'll pull you back, if necessary."

Hobo secured the line around himself and stood studying the water and the spot Vince indicated, where the ceiling disappeared. Then he plunged into the dark, cold water. Thoughts of his mother's cooking overrode any fear he might have had of the dark water. He swam to the wall, sucked in air, and disappeared beneath the surface.

The wait was a long one. Dale Riley, who had sucked in air at the same time Hobo did, expelled his breath, unable to hold it any longer. Tom thought it seemed five minutes had passed, though he knew it couldn't have been that long.

There was no tug on the line, but Vince told the others to begin reeling it in anyway. "Hurry up!" he said. He plunged into the water and was ready to dive under the ceiling himself when Hobo suddenly surfaced, spouting water like a whale.

"Hallelujah!" he sputtered.

"What do you mean? What did you find?" Vince asked excitedly as he helped Hobo back to shore.

After Hobo had enough breath to make normal talk again, he said he had pulled himself along under the ceiling for maybe 20 feet, keeping his nose close to the ceiling and checking for pockets of air between it and the water.

"Finally, I came to a place – a trough-like – in the ceiling, a place where there was just enough space for my mouth to be out of the water, with my head tilted back and the top of my forehead touching the ceiling. And I'm purty sure I heard water running, and I'm purty shore I saw a slither of light

117

out ahead of me."

A cheer went up from all. They embraced. They danced. Keith cried.

Their thoughts were becoming thick and heavy as their body temperatures dropped. But all realized that if straight ahead, through that cold water, did not prove to be a way out, then they were finished. The thoughts none of them dared speak told them that by the time a rescue effort was organized, and by the time heavy equipment needed to break through that solid wall of rock back there at the cave-in was in place, it would be too late for them.

A lifeline was formed. The garden line was tied around Hobo's waist. He would lead the way. The others would grasp the line, letting it run through their hands as they followed him. The lose end of the line was tied to a stalagmite back on the cave floor. If anyone felt they were running out of air, they could pull themselves back.

Tom was between Hobo and Vince. One would pull him, the other would push. Then came Keith, Dale and Gale bringing up the rear. Vince insisted on keeping his backpack on his shoulders. Hobo assured all it was probably less than a minute's journey to where they would find the pocket of air.

"Don't panic on me, boys," he said. "We can make it, believe me."

They swam out to where the ceiling met the surface, took deep breaths in unison, and under they went.

Thoughts of life and freedom kept the boys moving without panic. There would be no turning back.

Finally, after a long minute, Tom found himself bumping his head against the ceiling and gulping air. Vince surfaced behind him. Hobo pulled them along a short distance to make room for the others. Keith popped up and yelped as his head hit the ceiling. Sputtering and spitting, Dale and then Gale surfaced. All had made it and were sucking precious air into their lungs.

All were joyful and hopeful as they pressed on in single file, holding their heads above water and pulling themselves along with their hands on the walls of the enclosure. Hobo had been right. They could hear the gurgle of running water and see light up ahead. They moved steadily toward it.

Eventually their feet touched bottom and the water level soon dropped to below their chests. The distance between the floor and the roof decreased until they were bending at the waist, their backs scraping the roof. Soon the water was no more than ankle deep, a gentle stream flowing toward the light. The tunnel became so confining that they were forced to continue on all fours. Up ahead was that glorious light, and the sound of water falling and splashing on something.

Hobo crawled on ahead on his belly, and the rest of them wiggled along behind him. Sunlight was filtering in through vines and roots that covered an opening no bigger than a basketball. Vince passed up the shovel from the backpack and Hobo dug furiously at the loose earth and stones, like a beagle at a rabbit hole, enlarging it enough that he squeezed his head and shoulders through and was out! The others followed, tumbling on top of one another as they dropped two feet from the mouth of the tunnel to a place where the water ran out and splattered on the stones, pooling up before trickling on down the hillside. The joyful sound of songbirds welcomed them back to the outside world. Never had they sounded so beautifully. The late afternoon sun shone brightly. There was another outburst of jubilation. More backslapping. Keith and Dale held hands as they danced a little jig.

"I want you to look at that," Vince said, pointing down the slope and into the hollow below. Looking out over the tops of scrub pines and oaks and hickories and down the hollow, Tom could make out the school building. They were looking down on the roof of the school! They had gone into the cave on the north side of the bony ridge and came out on the south side, through a passage that they were probably the first to know of.

The boys quickly made their way down and into the side yard, then followed the little stream running past the school and on through the culvert under Route 10, through Henson's farm, and on to the river. The river seemed sweeter than ever as they washed the mud from their bodies.

Later, Vince placed the bracelets and the arrowhead in a secret place under one corner of the roof of the tree house. Before the following week was out, however, he and the boys took them to show to Mr. Gammons, who had a notable collection of Indian artifacts.

119

Mr. Gammons raised his eyebrows and whistled as he handled the bracelets. Taking his pocket knife, he shaved several slithers from one of them. Then he whistled again.

"Pure silver," he said. "Where'd you get these? You boys went in that cave, I'm pretty sure. Is that where you found them?"

After getting a promise from Mr. Gammons that he would tell no one of their little adventure, they told him of the second room of the cave, the skeleton, the cave-in, and their escape through the passage on the backside of the hill.

"Oh my Gawd," Mr. Gammons said. "You boys were lucky. I told you not to go in there, that the place was dangerous."

"Well, we'll not be going in Devil's Den again," Vince said. "In fact, no one will."

When they left the grocery, the bracelets and arrowhead were in the collection of Alvie Gammons, and each of the six boys had a dollar and twenty-five cents worth of credit with the store.

CHAPTER 18:
SCHOOL'S OUT; SHE'S GONE

Janie West, even though she sat right in front of him, close enough for him to smell the wonderful aroma she emanated, still had not acknowledged that Tom Sycamore existed on the face of the earth. And this was the last week of school. Something had to happen, fast.

Tom decided it was better to risk all-out rejection than to go on holding out hope where, sadly, it seemed, no hope existed. The next day in school, at the first recess, he caught her sitting alone on the concrete banister of the side steps. He removed the pack of opened Wrigley's from one front pocket of his overalls, moved swiftly toward her, and offered her a stick.

"O-o-o," she said, forming a beautiful little "0" with her lips. "That's my favorite brand. Yes, I'll have a stick. Thank you...uh, Tom? Tom Sycamore, is it?"

Wow!

She opened the gum with her long, delicate fingers, folded it, and stuck it between those marvelous white teeth. She scooted over and patted the spot beside her with her hand. Tom, feeling a bit dizzy, sat down beside her. Their forearms touched and he felt more like he was soaring than sitting.

Then she began to question him: Where had he moved from, who was in his family?

Well, wasn't she the nicest, most talkative thing you ever saw or heard?

Tom heard himself babbling on and on, telling her about his big brother, Flint, who was a senior upstairs and hoped to soon be a U.S. Marine; about his mother's fried chicken, and how his father kept the trains running and military supplies hustling along the C&O tracks.

He wanted to tell her about being trapped inside the cave, and of their daring escape, but Vince had led the gang into an oath not to share that. After all, the cave was off limits, and they had engaged in a bit of deceit in going there. No need to invite the wrath of their parents down on them.

The Marine in the garden. That was an interesting thing. He was thinking about sharing that with her when the bell rang and they followed the others back into the classroom. Across the aisle, Tom saw Keith Richards looking at him and making the "shame on you" gesture with the forefingers of both hands. Tom didn't care what anyone thought. Nothing else but his relationship with Janie mattered just now. True love comes with its own set of blinders.

He and Janie exchanged notes before the rest of the morning was over. As they filed outside on lunch break, he declined Gale's invitation for a game of marbles. Then Gale watched, a question mark over his head, as Tom and Janie headed up the hollow toward the ball field, she holding onto his arm while Tom carried their lunch pails. Tom no longer felt clumsy and awkward. It's hard to trip over your feet when you're walking on air. He ignored cries of "oh, look at lover boy" which came almost in unison from Vince and Keith.

Tom and Janie opened their lunch pails in the shade of the big walnut tree that grew at the edge of the woods. Tom swallowed a bite of his peanut butter and jelly sandwich, which made him think briefly about the cave "monster," then said, "I can't believe you're sitting here with me. It's hard to believe because, until today, you never spoke to me – never even looked my way. Why was that?"

Janie rolled her eyes at him as she nibbled a carrot stick. "How do you know I didn't look at you?" she asked. "Maybe I looked at you when you didn't know I was looking at you.

"And why would that be? Because I was afraid. Not afraid of you, Tom Sycamore, but afraid of the way you make me feel inside. I didn't want to become attached to you – can't let myself become attached to you."

Tom was silent. He wanted to ask her why this was, but he feared what the answer might be.

Janie drew a deep breath, then exhaled with a murmur that came both

122

from the lungs and the heart.

Then she blurted it out: "School's out Friday, Tom, and I'll be long gone from here."

Tom was startled. He dropped his sandwich back into his lunch pail. He thought of the irony, of how he had been forced to move off and leave Annie in Ashville, someone he thought he couldn't live without -- and who told him she couldn't live without him – only to become smitten here, and now this angel was going to leave him in the exact same manner as he left Annie?

Janie reached out and put her hand on Tom's arm and continued.

"On Saturday," she said, "we're moving to Cleveland, Ohio, away up on Lake Erie. My father's insurance company has promoted and transferred him. There's nobody here that I could stay with, and my mother would never permit that to happen even if there was."

She paused to let Tom's mind absorb all that she had said before continuing. "Oh, Tom, now do you see why I tried to ignore you. I didn't want to hurt you, but I didn't want to hurt me, either. Kind of selfish of me, I guess."

Tom closed his lunch pail. His appetite was gone. He saw the tear in the corner of Janie's eye, but he could find no words to speak. *What is this thing called love anyway? It's more about heartbreak than happiness.*

I'll never fall again.

The Hooperville Braves had all made it up the next rung of education. Now the prison doors were flung open, and it was good to be paroled. That last day of school was a happy day for the gang – that is, all except Tom. Gale couldn't get him to talk about it.

"Come on, Tom," he said. "Let's get home, get out of these school clothes, and hit that river. Three months of freedom!"

But Tom told him he would catch them at the tree house. Out of the corner of his eye, he saw Janie sitting on the front steps, waiting for her ride. If he had money, he could have gotten her a ring. W.T. Grant's had one for two dollars and ninety-eight cents. Might as well have been a thousand dollars. He moved up beside her and slipped into her hands a bag of his best marbles.

As the Buick came rolling up the hollow, she stood suddenly, grabbed Tom by the shirt, pulled him in close, and kissed him smack on the lips. Tom looked down to see if his feet were on the ground.

Then she was gone, waving from the window as the big car pulled away.

CHAPTER 19:
OFF TO THE WAR

Chopper met Tom in the yard and let him know that he was ready to head for the river and look for muskrats. Tom rubbed the leaping dog's head and then pushed him aside. As he stepped up onto the back porch, he heard voices coming through the screen door. His mother and Flint seemed to be arguing about something.

"No! No, I won't sign," his mother said as Tom walked in through the door.

Flint leaned over the table, his hands on a piece of paper. He tossed the pen in his hand down on the paper.

"Mom! You know I'll have to go. I'll be 18 next month. The army's going to draft me. By enlisting in the marines now, I get what I want."

Carrie Sycamore, seated in front of the paper, cradled her head in her hands and sobbed. The thought that had kept her awake at night for the past six months had leaped out into reality. Her first-born child was going to war.

Flint, along with fellow graduate Boyd Conley, who had driven his father's car to the county seat, had already talked to the recruiter. The marines wanted them both. They had passed their physicals and were to be at the induction center in Steelton, 30 miles upriver, the next morning with their papers in hand. From there they would catch a train directly to boot camp.

Mom Sycamore got up from the table, brushed by Tom with no notice of him, and stumbled clumsily from the room. Flint picked up the paper and stared blankly at it. "Dad will be home in a while. He'll sign it," he said, glancing at Tom.

Tom looked at the screen door and thought he saw someone standing on the other side of it, on the back porch. He moved quickly to open the door and step out onto the porch. He saw someone walking away – someone dressed in a marine combat uniform. Whoever or whatever it was disappeared around the corner of the house toward the garden. Tom hurried to the corner of the house, but although he had a full view of the garden, he saw no one.

Had it only been shadow and sun?

Flint left for somewhere. Tom's mother returned to the kitchen and busied herself at preparing supper. Tom, to tide him over, fixed himself a peanut butter sandwich and poured himself a glass of milk from the icebox.

"That's enough for you now," his mother said, putting the jar of peanut butter back in the cabinet. "Your father will be here in a couple of hours and supper will be ready then. Where did Flint go?"

"He didn't say," Tom said between bites. He finished the sandwich and told his mother he would be in the garden until supper was ready.

Gale came into the back yard as he was getting the ax from the building, but Tom turned him down on plans to join the others for a swim in the river. Using his garden work as an excuse, he also told the red head he wouldn't be over for the radio serials later. Gale seemed to understand that Tom's strange behavior had something to do with Janie West, and he left without trying to influence him.

The poor boy's heartbroken, but he'll be over it by tomorrow.

Chopper followed Gale and Leader off for adventure, while Tom picked up the single-bit ax and, from the nearby slope of the railroad bed, cut several sumac saplings and trimmed them down to make nice straight poles. These he drove into the ground at either end of the bean rows. He stretched a string from one pole to the other and tied three-foot strips of cloth to the string to dangle down over each bean plant. As they grew, the bean plants would climb the strips of cloth and crawl out along the string, making for easy picking. This trick he had learned from his father, who had never let a summer go by without growing a garden.

This garden, though, he had entrusted to the care of Tom.

Time had escaped him. His father was already in and washed up for supper. He and his mother had come out to the garden. While his mother picked lettuce, Bruce Sycamore stood with hands on hips, admiring Tom's work.

Someone else was admiring it, too. At the far end of the garden stood the Marine. He gave Tom a salute! Tom chuckled as the figure dissipated into the lengthening shadows.

His mother, standing with a mess of lettuce in her apron, had been looking down at that end of the garden.

"Who was that?" she asked Tom.

Tom stared at her. She had seen the Marine too? He shrugged his soldiers. She walked to the far end of the garden, looking this way and that.

His father, watching intently, said, "Who was who? Nobody here but the three of us."

His mother returned, looked out over the garden again, studied Tom's face for a moment, and then went into the house.

"She looked like she'd seen a ghost," Bruce Sycamore said.

"Maybe she did," Tom said, and headed for the building to put up the ax.

Finally his dad said, "You want to go fishing in the morning?"

"Like to, but I'm going to have to get on this corn. It needs hoeing."

"Forget the corn until later. That river's needs fishing. Got to keep our priorities straight here." He grinned as he wrapped an arm around Tom's shoulders. "Let's go in and get you washed up for supper."

Flint was already washed up and was seated. There was no mention of the papers until everyone had their fill of Carrie Sycamore's brown beans, cornbread and wilted lettuce.

Then Bruce Sycamore pushed his way back from the table, pulled a ready-rolled Bugler from his shirt pocket, lit it, exhaled a stream of blue smoke, and said, "So, Flint. Your mother tells me you're wanting to go into the Marines?"

Flint brought the papers down from his room as his mother cleared the table. He placed them on the table in front of his father, at the same time repeating his argument that he was bound for the military whether they signed these papers or not. There was a somewhat heated discussion

127

between Tom's parents. His mother lost. She seemed at last more resigned to reality than defeat.

Bruce Sycamore signed the papers, rose, and put his hand on Flint's shoulder.

"You should have picked the Navy, you know. That way you'd have a good bed to sleep in and hot meals to eat. But you go, son. I know how you feel about this. I've felt it, myself. You go with our blessing, and may God go with you."

He looked over toward his wife, who stood at the sink with her back to them, her head bowed, her shoulders shaking. He put an arm around her shoulders. She turned and buried her face in his chest.

"Mom, mom," he said, rubbing her back with both hands. "It's going to be all right. This thing will be over by the time Flint finishes his basic training. He'll not have to leave the states."

———————

Just after 8 a.m. the next day, Carrie Sycamore and Helen Conley, Boyd's mother, accompanied the two teens up over the crossing and out onto Route 10. Tom followed, staying as close in Flint's footsteps as he could. Bruce Sycamore had said his good-byes on the front porch, then went around the house to the building to assemble some fishing gear.

As the entourage made its way up the grade of the crossing, Tom had turned to look back toward the house. And just for an instant he saw him: the Marine, standing at attention, his right hand raised in salute.

They crossed the highway and Flint and Boyd sat their suitcases down on the shoulder. Flint rubbed his hand through Tom's hair. "I replaced the link in the chain and oiled it good, Tom. The bike's all yours now. Don't ride it out here on the road, OK?"

Tom's mom put on a brave front, but she could not stop the tear that trickled down one cheek. Helen Conley tried to comfort her, and herself, too.

The Blue Ribbon bus came around the bend and squeaked to a halt, right on time. The door swung open and the long-time driver, Jiggs Baldwin, looked down with tenderness in his eyes, for he realized immediately what was happening. He had seen a lot of scenes like this over the past three or four years.

The two inductees kissed their mommas goodbye. Flint rubbed his hand through Tom's hair again as he climbed the two steps into the bus. Tom, without realizing what he was doing, stepped up behind him, holding onto his big brother's shirttail. Flint laughed, then turned and guided Tom back off the bus. "I'll be back, and I'll bring you something nice," he said,

Tom's mother put one arm around Tom's shoulder. Flint kissed his mother on top of her head and went back up the steps. His mother leaned against the door so that driver Jiggs Baldwin could not close it with his leverage handle.

"Mam, you'll have to step back from the door," he said. "And don't you ladies worry about these boys. The military takes good care of them."

Flint and Boyd waved from the window as the bus pulled away for the induction center. Tom's mother was still waving after the bus had gone out of sight.

CHAPTER 20:
PATIENCE GETS THE FISH

The morning's thick fog bank still swirled on the surface of the river as Tom and his dad, loaded down with fishing gear, arrived at the water's edge. A towboat sounded its whistle straight out from them, but they could not see it.

While Bruce Sycamore cut forked sticks from the willows to be used as pole holders, Tom crumbled crackers into the glass minnow trap, screwed down the lid tightly, and tied a heavy string to the wire frame of the trap. Once the waves from the towboat had subsided, he waded out until the water rose above his knees, and submerged the jug, with its funneled mouth pointing downstream. Then he played out the string and tied it to a flat rock at the edge of the water.

"That's good, that's good," his father said, watching out of the corner of his eye as he stuck forked poles into the soft sand, about ten feet apart. "Just make sure you have no air bubbles in the jug."

Tom's father was in his element now. His work on the railroad, aligning rails and installing ties and ballast, was something he did to feed and clothe his family. And to buy fishing equipment. Ah, fishing, now this was life. There were catfish in this river that would weigh a hundred pounds and more. He never expected to catch a fish like that, but any fish he hooked gave him joy.

Bruce Sycamore broke out one of three bait-casting reels on steel rods he owned and handed it to Tom. The outfit had a two-ounce flat lead sinker tied to the end of the line and a hook on a six-inch leader tied to the line about a foot above the sinker. And about a foot above that hook, his father had tied a second hook. He would generally bait one hook with worms, the other with a three-inch shiner.

But before he baited the hooks, he showed Tom how to hold down the release lever on the reel, then place his thumb on the line in the reel, draw back over his shoulder, and come forward on the cast.

"Release your thumb when the rod is at this angle," he said, holding Tom's wrists. "But don't take your thumb off all the way. You've got to apply some pressure to the line, else you'll get a bad backlash."

Which was what Tom got on his first attempt at a cast. The line on the reel snagged on its own loose loops and the sinker hit the water six feet in front of him. Both baits were flung off the hooks and out into the river. Once the line became so hopelessly backlashed that his father had to cut it and retie the sinker and hooks. He had plenty of extra sinkers and hooks, which he carried in an old leather pouch. He made his own sinkers by pouring molten lead into molds, and he bought hooks by the box full and tied a six-inch length of leader line to each.

After half a dozen casts Tom had the line fairly singing off the old Pflueger, flinging the sinker and hooks 60 to 70 feet out into the river, the baits still intact.

Next his father broke out nine cane poles, each nine or 10 feet long, and each having a line of about the same length. He unwound the lines and placed the cane poles in the forked sticks, ready to be baited.

Hardly 15 minutes had passed before he had Tom raise the minnow trap. It was black with shiners and fat chubs.

"Oh my oh my oh my, will you look at that," his father said.

Tom poured the minnows into a live box – a rectangular wooden box made of slats and covered with screen wire, with a wire screen door that fastened on the top. The box floated in the river and the minnows could live in it indefinitely.

Sometimes his father hooked the minnows through the lips, sometimes through the tail. When they finished baiting, they had out altogether the nine cane poles and all three bait-casting reels. They had taken up more than 100 feet of shoreline.

His father dragged a log in close, lit a Camel, pulled a worn Zane Gray novel from his hip pocket, and sat down. Tom busied himself drawing pictures in the sand. Chopper was digging at a muskrat hole farther up the bank.

Fifteen or 20 minutes passed with no action. "Think I'll reel mine in, check the bait," Tom said.

"No, James Thomas. Not yet. The fish will check your bait. You'll know when one takes it. Patience. Patience makes for a good fisherman. Let the fish come to us. Good things come to those who wait."

An hour went by without a nibble. Now and then Tom's dad would look up from his novel, give the poles a good eye check, and continue reading. Tom couldn't take it. He wandered off with Chopper, looking for anything of interest to get in to.

Three hours passed. His father had caught one small sheep head, a "trash fish" that he threw back.

"Why don't you take the dog and go to the house and get your mother to make us some bologna sandwiches?"

Tom was glad to do that. He and Chopper scampered up the bank.

While his mother fixed the sandwiches, Tom asked her, "Momma, what did you see out there in the garden?"

She stopped wrapping the sandwiches and looked at Tom. "It was a soldier, saluting you," she said as she spread mustard on the sandwiches. "You saw him didn't you?"

"Oh yeah. I been seeing him since right after we moved in."

He went on to tell her how Mr. Galloway had seen him, too, in the church and in the garden.

"He thinks it's that Marine you mentioned, who lived here, planted the garden, and then went off and got killed in the Pacific. He said Leon Selby was his name. Mr. Galloway is hoping to contact the Marine's wife. Bring her over here. See what she makes of it."

His mother wrapped the sandwiches in newspaper and placed them in a paper bag. She looked Tom directly in the eyes.

"You take after your mother, and I take after my mother," she said. "Only a few people have the power to see such things as we saw here in the garden yesterday. My mother, rest her soul, said sometimes the spirits of the dead hang around, hoping to get something resolved, before moving on to their peace with God, or whatever fate awaits them on the other side. Judgment awaits all of us after death, according to the New Testament scriptures.

"She saw my father and his brother, Uncle George, both of whom died within hours of each other during the flu epidemic of '18. They were both horse traders, and Momma said she saw them within days, standing out by the barn and examining the teeth of a beautiful white stallion, which she had never seen before. It was just for an instant, just long enough to recognize who they were, and then they were gone, never to show themselves again. Them and the horse. A horse, now. That seemed doubly strange."

She went on to tell Tom again about how she had seen Bruce Sycamore's father the night after he died. This was basically the same story she had shared with him earlier.

"Frank Sycamore was standing right there by the fireplace, at the same time his body was over there in the pine box, in the same room. It was midnight and everybody else was asleep. He was standing there, lighting his old pipe, and looking into the fireplace. It startled me so that it was all I could do to keep from crying out. I think all he wanted was to let me know everything was all right. In just an instant he was gone, and there was just a peaceful feeling filling the room."

Tom shook his head in amazement. "I don't know what the Marine wants, Momma. But I feel like he likes how I've brought the garden along."

"We'll see," his mother said. "I believe he'll let us know what it is that's keeping him here. And I think we already know the answer to that."

———

When Tom arrived back at the river with the sandwiches, there was still no fish on the stringer. All the poles appeared to be in their original positions. His father was near the end of his book. Surely he would move the poles on up or down the shore when he finished the book.

"Fish have to eat sometime," his father said, bringing a bar of soap from his chest pocket and washing his hands in the river. He devoured his first bologna sandwich and reached for another. Tom broke off part of his for Chopper.

There was a commotion from up the path leading to the village and out of the willows came Hobo and Gale, loaded down with gear.

"Catchin' anything?" Hobo, sitting down his load for a rest and admiring the poles set up and down the bank, directed his inquiry toward Tom's dad.

"Not yet, but we will," Bruce Sycamore replied.

"Just been here 'bout four hours," Tom said.

"Well, we're going out where the big ones are. We're gonna set ourselves a trotline," Hobo said, picking his gear up and heading up toward where the Reuben James was tied off.

"We're gonna corner the market on catfish," Gale said as he picked up his load and started after Hobo. He stopped, turned to Tom, and said, "Why don't you come and go help us, Tom?"

"I believe I will. OK, Dad?"

"A trotline? Well, now, you boys be extra careful. That can be a dangerous thing – dangerous because of towboats, and dangerous because, if you're not careful, you could get a hook in your clothes as you're dropping that line back to the bottom. So be very careful," he said. "And when you get ready to bait, come here and get a bucket of these big chubs and shiners from our live box. We're sure not going to be able to use them all."

Tom took that as a yes and headed upriver after Gale and Hobo, Chopper scampering behind.

In the boat, Hobo played out line from the ball it was wound on, coiling it loosely on the floor in the bow. He tied the end of the line to a concrete building block resting on the deck of the bow. There was a similar weight resting on the deck of the stern.

They cast off, Gale rowing, Tom in the back, and Hobo up front. Chopper swam along side the boat, whining, moving Tom to bring the dog in by the scuff of the neck. Nobody complained about the shower of water the shaking dog sprayed them with.

"Keep him back there away from these hooks," Hobo said.

Gale rowed out to about seventy-five yards from shore as Hobo tied the end of the trotline to the concrete block on the bow. He pushed it overboard, holding onto the line, letting it slide through his hands until it went slack. Gale continued rowing on a slight upstream angle to compensate for the slow current.

After Hobo had played out about 50 feet of line, he stopped and tied a 20-foot lead line onto the main line. To the end of this line he tied a cork float about a foot square. Then he played out line as Gale rowed on, slightly upstream against the current, toward the middle of the river. When the coils of line were all off the floor, Hobo tied the end of the line to the concrete block on the rear of the boat and, as Gale held the line taut by continuing to row, pushed the weight overboard.

They rowed back to shore and Hobo went down to Tom's dad's minnow box and placed five dozen of the largest minnows in a five-gallon bucket.

"Thanks Mr. Sycamore," he said. "I'll be setting my trap later and I'll replace these."

"Don't worry about it. I won't get to fish again until next weekend anyway."

With Gale still at the oars, the three boys moved out again. Hobo picked up the cork and used the lead line to pull the trotline up off the bottom. As Tom used a paddle off the stern to keep the boat pointed upriver, Hobo pulled them along, tying on hooks rigged to two-foot leaders, about every four feet. At intervals along the way he also tied on an old iron and two window weights. These were to keep the line on the bottom. He had tied on 50 hooks by the time they reached as far as they could go with the line. Tom was amazed to see that they were out nearly in the middle of the river.

"Got to get your line out here into the channel to get the really big cats," Hobo said.

He moved the bucket of live minnows in between his feet and began moving back along the line, baiting each hook, being careful as he passed them over the bow to make certain he didn't let one of the hooks get into him. He hooked the shiners through the lower lip, then brought the leader on through the lip enough to allow him to hook the shiner in the tail. When he had baited the last hook and dropped the line back to the bottom, he said, "Boys, we are in business. We'll look 'er right before dark."

As they tied off the boat, Tom looked downstream and saw his father motioning to them. When they got down there, Bruce Sycamore held up a stringer of catfish so heavy he could hardly lift it. The boys' eyes bugged out.

"Wish you could have been here, Tom," his dad said. "When they started, it was more than I could keep up with. Three and four poles bending at a time."

He kept four of the fish, each weighing about three pounds, and gave the rest to Hobo to place in his live box, anchored in the river just out from the *Reuben James*.

Tom helped his dad carry the fish and equipment up the bank for home.

"Patience, Tom. Patience is what it takes," he said. "Whether it be fishing, or something else you're trying to succeed at. Patience, my boy. Patience."

CHAPTER 21:
THE CATFISH COMPANY

The sun was nearing the tops of the hills downriver, casting a glimmering, reddish-orange path on the water by the time Hobo reached the last hook on the trotline. The *Reuben James* was capable of carrying two riders on each seat, and all six Braves were present, eager to make money from this new venture. Vince had dubbed it simply the Hooperville Fishing Company. All who would chip in with catching bait, skinning and dressing out catfish, and whatever duties needed to be carried out to keep the firm viable, would share equally in the profits, of which 50 percent would go to help the poor of the immediate vicinity.

This first "look" of the line had put nine channels on the stringer, one of them estimated to weigh 15 pounds. The others were three- to four-pounders, which Hobo said were just the size Mr. Herman liked to buy for his market. These would be added to the live box anchored near shore, which already held the eight others donated by Tom's dad.

Now, as Hobo worked his way back along the line, baiting the hooks that were empty, he discussed company plans with the others. "We'll look it a couple of times tomorrow," he said, "and then come Monday morning we'll have to skin and gut what we've got, leaving the head intact so's Mr. Herman can inspect the color of the gills. He won't buy them if the gills have lost their pinkish color. We'll put a little ice in a tub and row them over to the Market Street Landing in Shawnee."

Behind him, mayhem was in the planning stage. The boys waited until Hobo had released the line back to the bottom of the river, then Keith devilishly hit him in the naked back with a bailer-full of water. The other four used oars and hands to douse Hobo. Very coolly and deliberately, Hobo emptied the bait bucket, set it afloat in the river, made sure the stringer holding the nine cats was secured to the gunwale, then leaped to one side of the boat, throwing everyone else off balance and over to that side, too. Water poured in and the boat overturned, dumping them all into the river.

Tom surfaced and dog-paddled over to grab hold of the side of the boat. The others were all busy trying to escape Hobo, who was ducking everyone he could catch. He started once to put Tom under, but then remembered that he was still not a qualified swimmer. "Hang on to the boat, Tom," he said. "I'll get you in."

Finally, nearly exhausted, they managed to right the boat, but it remained filled with water. Hobo pulled it by the front rope with a powerful side stroke. The others kicked their feet and pushed at the sides and rear. Gale began swimming alongside the boat. "Come on, Tom," he said. "Join me. It's only about a hundred more feet to shore."

Tom released the death grip he held on the boat. He began swimming overhand and kicking his feet. The others stopped and treaded water long enough to applaud him.

Before that summer was over, Tom would surprise himself by swimming that broad river over and back.

CHAPTER 22:
MONEY IS GOOD

It was a delicious feeling, Tom thought, waking up on a Monday morning and realizing he didn't have to be rushing around, getting ready for school. Summer vacation. It stretched on before him, forever and ever. Still, though, Tom's 11-year-old heart couldn't get into the spirit of full happiness. Not with Janie gone from his life, and no doubt forever.

These were crazy times. At the breakfast table, Tom's mom talked about trading her apron for overalls. Nearly 500 women were already on the payroll of Wheeling Steel and the company was advertising for more.

"I can help make the bombs that will end the war and keep Flint from having to invade Japan," she said. "And Lord knows we can use the extra money."

Tom went out to feed and water Chopper. The little dog was staying clear of the garden. He had no understanding of what happened out there from time to time.

Neither did Tom.

What was the story on the Marine anyway? What did he want?

He decided to put off garden work until later. The family had already enjoyed a mess of new potatoes and sweet peas. His mother called the garden a "thing of beauty," and talked about writing The Shawnee Times about taking a picture of it.

The Marine, Tom assumed, was still hanging around, although he had not seen him for sometime now. He went around the house, crossed the street, and made his way down to Gale's house. He found the redhead in the backyard, where it looked like he had been shooting his Red Ryder BB gun at a cardboard target tacked on the side of the storage building, the side that was just around the corner from the wash tub his grandfather used for his bath – a new tub that had replaced the one Gale had shot an arrow through.

"Hail, Gale Newt," Tom said.

"Hail to you, Jim Tom," Gale responded.

The two boys then decided to see who could put a BB closest to the bull's eye Gale had drawn with a black crayon in the cardboard target. Gale went first. Then he handed Tom the gun and walked closer to the target to see where his shots had hit. As he waited for his turn, Tom levered another round into the chamber.

Gale had made it almost all the way to where Tom stood – "yer goin' to have to do some shootin' to beat me," he was saying – when Tom accidentally hit the trigger. The BB struck Gale somewhere around the naked shinbone.

He grabbed his leg and hopped around on one foot, howling. Tom was amazed when Gale even uttered a few choice cuss words.

Tom ran toward Gale, apologizing. He handed the gun to Gale, saying, "Here, shoot me." It was just a gentlemanly gesture on Tom's part, never meant to be taken seriously. Gale held the gun in one hand and rubbed the wounded shinbone with the other. His face was screwed up into contortions of pain. Tom thought he saw justifiable homicide written there, and he knew he'd made a mistake in handing over the gun.

"Give me a head start!" he said.

He didn't understand how a man could cock and fire a Red Ryder with such speed. Maybe he had stupidly cocked the thing himself before handing the gun to Gale.

At any rate, he had managed to take only one step before Gale shot him pointblank in the rear. "Yawl-l-l!" He rubbed his left cheek as he rounded the corner of the house. Tears welled up in his eyes. It hurt.

"Hot damn-n-n!" Tom yelled.

Gale dropped the gun and chased after Tom, catching him at the front gate.

"Wait, Tom, wait!" he shouted. "I… I'm sorry. I shouldn't have done that. I know you didn't mean to shoot me. It just stung so bad I was temporarily out of my mind. Come on back. We'll be more careful, that's for sure."

Tom accepted the apology and offered one of his own. Both boys stood rubbing their wounds, neither of which resulted in broken skin – just whelps. They were soon laughing at each other.

It was a lesson in gun safety neither boy would ever forget.

Tom would joke years later that he also learned another valuable lesson from the experience. "After that," he would say, after telling someone the BB gun story, "whenever I inadvertently did something to hurt someone, I offered no chance at retaliation. I just started running."

Pretty soon Vince and Dale came along. Vince carried wooden, rectangular-shaped paddles, about four inches wide, with handles whittled out on one end, and a tennis ball. They went across the street to the churchyard and soon had a hot game of partners paddleball going on the wide sidewalk that led around to the basement door. A crack separating the two segments of concrete served as the "net." Similar cracks farther back on each side of the court served as out-of- bound markers. The game was played by the rules of table tennis. Vince and Dale on one side and Gale and Tom on the other went at each other with such vigor you'd never know they were in the same gang.

They had exhausted themselves and rested their sweaty bodies on the front steps of the church when Keith Richards walked up. He looked like he had come straight from his bed without splashing water in his face, or putting a brush to his shock of arrow straight yellowish white hair.

"Well. What have we here?" he said. "A bunch of hooky players? Perhaps I should alert one Mr. Wayland Rooker of this? Oh, what's that you say? You're on summer vacation? No more school for three long months? Ah, shoot! I miss it something fierce already, don't you boys?"

He broke into an idiotic laugh, leaped up the steps and slid down the banister. He sat down on the steps and squinted up at the sun. "It's 10:10 a.m., boys," he said. "Are we going to waste this whole day of our vacation sitting here doing nothing? Come on, Vince, what's on the agenda?"

"Doing nothing? No, we're gonna do something, something valuable for a change. There's more to life than play, boys." It wasn't Vince, but Hobo doing the talking. He had walked up unnoticed. He wore a pair of cutoff jeans and old tennis shoes. Water squeezed out of them when he walked. He didn't have on a shirt, exposing rust-colored freckles spread across his broad shoulders and chest. His stomach muscles resembled a washboard. "While you boys were snoozing," he continued, "I looked the line and took off eight more fat cats. They're down there in the box, with the others, waiting to be cleaned."

"You were supposed to come get me," Gale complained.

"Ha! Well, I did. Your mom said you were still asleep."

Hobo had all the tools and expertise needed to clean catfish. The other five had some experience. Tom had watched his dad clean fish. They stopped at Hobo's house to get the things needed, then made their way under the bank to where the Reuben James was nosed onto the sandy shore.

The boys lifted the cats from the live box one by one. Hobo took time to conk each fish on its broad head with a claw hammer, for all intents killing them, and leaving them oblivious to the skinning. He illustrated how to cut the skin below the head all the way around; pull the skin slowly off the length of the fish and over its tail fins, make the cut up the stomach, re-move the entrails and clean the cavities with buckets of water dipped from springs on the shore.

The fish were curled and stacked in the five-gallon buckets and cov-ered with icy spring water. Then they rowed as quickly as possible across to the foot of Market Street on the Shawnee waterfront.

"Good boys, good boys, I was getting orders for catfish but had none at all," said Mr. Herman as he removed the catfish one at a time, drained the water off each, inspected their gills, and placed them on his meat scales.

The boys rowed back across the river singing,

"Row, row, row your boat
  Gently down the stream,
Merry, merry, merry, merry,
  Life is but a dream."

They put the seven dollars and thirty cents Mr. Herman paid them in a Christmas candy tin, secured the lid tightly, and hid it in a cavity of the tree holding the tree house, just above the roof of the tree house.

Two more trips to Market Street that week brought the total to more than eighteen dollars. They were now wealthy fish merchants. To celebrate, Hobo held out one dollar and fifty cents and they all went to Miss Louella's little store by the tracks to treat themselves. Upon returning to the tree house, Vince insisted that they take out two more dollars and take bread and milk to a couple of families on the outskirts of the village.

"We've got two or three families here that are as poor as church mice," he said. "As long as the river gives up its catfish, we can do a lot of good for them."

Everybody felt good about this.

145

CHAPTER 23:
BURIED TREASURE
AND BACK TO BATAAN

Nothing about summer vacation was wasted. Each day brought a new adventure, thanks to Vince and his vivid imagination.

Tom got a blue bandanna from his dresser drawer and the cloth belt from an old bathrobe. He picked up Gale at his house and they made their way to the river. Gale carried a bandanna and sash in one hand. Leader and Chopper followed, wondering what was up.

They found the others at the tree house. Before going up, they tied the bandannas around their foreheads and the sashes around their waists. Today they would be pirates.

All four boys were bent over a map Vince had spread on the orange crate desk. He waited until Gale and Tom squeezed in. "We'll follow this dotted line here," he said. "The treasure will be buried here, where you see the red X."

They took up their swords from the wall and stuck them down inside the waist sashes. Vince wore a black patch over one eye and an authentic-looking pirate hat. Once on the ground, he tied a length of driftwood to his leg, and moved down the bank stiff-legged, nearly dragging his "peg" leg behind. They climbed into the *Reuben James*, which held two shovels, drifted down stream a short ways, then Hobo rowed the boat ashore. Vince stood at the front of the boat, the foot on his "good" leg poised on the front seat, and directed the landing.

"Keep a sharp lookout for headhunters, me laddies," he said.

Vince directed the digging. The boys dug several deep holes in the soft sand, but came up with nothing. Leader and Chopper joined in, making the sand fly between their legs in several locations.

Vince finally sat down, held his head in his hands, and mumbled something about being in deep trouble. He confessed to having taken a one-pound coffee can nearly full of pennies from his father's workshop three days ago, and bringing it down under the riverbank to bury. He hid all evidence of where he had placed it, but drew up the map, which he now had placed on the sand between his legs.

"It was supposed to have been there, at the base of that tree that forks," he mumbled. "But...it could have been down there, where that other forked tree stands."

By the time they dug one more hole there, the sun was high overhead and hot. Vince gave up.

Today, Vince's dad's pennies (it's not known if his dad ever missed them) lay buried deep along that stretch of river bank; or else bank erosion, brought on by the high-level dams, has allowed the rising water to scatter them along the muddy bottom of the Ohio.

The boys put their pirate stuff back in the tree house and hit the water.

———————

Tom worked the garden for half an hour, keeping a lookout for the Marine. He never showed. Chopper dozed in the shade of the storage building.

Speaking of the Marines, Flint was faithful in his letter writing. A letter came two or three times a week, telling the family of the misery of sand fleas and long marches in boot camp. Carrie Sycamore treasured each one and read them over and over again.

The gang gathered at Gale's house again in mid-afternoon. They played board games and munched on a fresh batch of chocolate chip cookies baked by Lois Flanders.

Grandpa Flanders shushed them as a special war report by Lowell Thomas came over the radio. The commentator told how more than 80,000 Japanese had been killed in the battle to take Okinawa, an island of just eight square miles.

"My good lord!" Grandpa Flanders exclaimed. "You couldn't cram that many into Yankee Stadium. Why won't those Japs give it up?"

The afternoon Shawnee Times also talked of statistics of the war. Altogether, it said, 8,000 military people were serving from the immediate region of Ohio and Kentucky.

Saturday came and the Braves fell into their home assignments of grass cutting, hedge trimming and garden work. Tom had done his yard work earlier in the week and he spent an hour in the Garden. The Marine did not show. Tom fed and watered Chopper and shut him up in the building.

"Sorry, ol' boy, you can't go. We're going over town," he said to the complaining, whisker-faced dog.

All six of the boys met at the tree house at a pre-arranged hour. Vince held a weapons inspection. Then they got money from their coffee can in the hollow of the tree, went home to dinner, combed their hair, and hoofed it across Grand Bridge for the matinee. They missed that week's chapter of the Phantom, playing at the Garden, because Vince wanted to go to the Laroy, where John Wayne and Anthony Quinn were starring in "Back to Bataan."

The highlight of the program was a live appearance of a former prisoner of war who had been rescued from Bataan. The soldier, standing on the narrow stage in front of the big screen, told the audience of the atrocities the Japanese committed against him and other prisoners in what had become known as the Bataan Death March.

"We were beaten. Many who fell out of line for lack of strength to continue were bayoneted or shot right before our eyes," said the former POW. "The man in charge was Lieutenant General Masaharu Homma. Remember that name. Let us pray that that dog will be made to pay when this thing is over."

Tom hoped they got him, but he thought that would be one tough name to remember.

He stole a glance at Vince's face and knew that the Japs were in for another butt-kickin' before the day was ended.

After the movie, the boys wound their way up the street to the Play House, where they found four of their "friends" from Ohio just making their way out the door. A few threats and insults were exchanged, but there was no physical contact this time.

Back in Kentucky the Braves struck out straight away for the tree house. They hung up their go-to-town clothes and put on their mud-caked Marine battle fatigues. They broke out their rifles and grenades and piled into the Reuben James. Hobo and Keith pulled hard on the oars for the "beachhead" on the far side of the river.

On the way into the landing, Vince acted as both war correspondent and the officer who would lead the platoon across that strip of sand into the face of enemy fire. "These brave young Marines, knowing that the survival of freedom and democracy could well rest on their shoulders, stare into the face of death as thoughts of home and loved ones sustain them," he said in his best newsreel voice.

Then, as the bow slid onto the sand, he shouted, "Drop the gates! Everybody out! Hit it! Hit it!"

Vince led the way, zigzagging as bullets whined and snapped the sand around them. Fighting, firing, falling, jumping up to charge again, they drove the Nips back through the willows and on into the jungle – which was actually a field of waist high corn plants.

As the brave young Marines were temporarily penned behind a huge log, Vince asked aloud: "Where's all the Filipino fighters? Thousands of Filipino Freedom Fighters were supposed to meet us here!"

Keith, raising his head up to peer over the log, scraped his forehead on a sharp snag. It was only a scratch, yet blood trickled down until it dripped off the end of his nose. He thought it was sweat.

Seeing the blood, Vince shouted, "Medic! Get us a medic up here fast, before this man bleeds to death."

Dale Riley dropped back, then scurried up, dodging bullets, and broke open a pouch containing a bottle of iodine and several strips of cloth taken from an old bed sheet.

"What's his chances, Doc?" Vince asked.

"I'd say fifty-fifty," Dale answered. "He needs surgery. We need to get him back across the strait, to the base hospital."

Dale wrapped the top of Keith's head from the eyebrows up. Keith continued to play the part. He was enjoying being the center of attention – until he wiped "sweat" from his nose and saw the blood on his hand as he withdrew it.

"That's blood!" he said. "My blood! Lordy be, boys, I am hit!"

"Get on the radio, Flanders," Vince said. "Call a PT boat in here. We've got to evacuate this man. Tell them to fetch a chaplain, just in case."

"I'm dyin'!" Keith said, leaping up and making a dash back toward the *Reuben James*. "Get me to Doc Meadows' before I bleed to death!"

The bandage slipped down over his eyes and he tripped over a log on the beach. Vince and Tom leaped on him and held him down as Hobo and Gale rushed to the boat and grabbed the old Red Cross stretcher Gale had pulled from a drift pile when the water went down. They managed to roll Keith onto the stretcher and make a dash for the boat, Hobo on one end and Vince on the other, as bullets spit the sand and whined around them.

"The Japs are coming out of the jungle!" Vince said. "Quick! Everybody into the boat. Shove off!"

The stretcher holding Keith was placed on the middle and back seats as the others scrambled in. Vince stopped long enough to rake the advancing Japanese with a machine gun: "Tut, tut, tut, tut, tut, tut, tut...."

As he leaped into the boat, he kicked the stretcher on one end and promptly dumped Keith overboard. Hobo grabbed him up, dragged him back into the boat, and threw him down on the stretcher. Keith, spitting river water, moaned, "I'm dyin! You're killin' me."

Vince shoved the boat off and leaped in. Hobo manned the oars. Vince turned back toward shore and, with one foot on the bow seat, shook his fist at the enemy and screamed, "I shall return!"

Gale cocked his head to one side and looked at Tom. "I thought that's what we just did," he said.

By the time the "PT boat" hit the middle of the "strait," Jap planes were diving in, strafing the boat. Everybody leaped overboard, except for Keith, who was still dying on the stretcher, and Gale, who bravely decided to take on the Jap fighter planes with his rifle. He emptied his gun, then dropped the weapon and grabbed his stomach. He was hit badly, and what followed was without doubt the most dramatic piece of acting ever demonstrated in the war games. He twitched, he jerked, he staggered the length of the boat, toppled from the bow, and floated on the surface of the water for a full minute. John Wayne couldn't have done it better.

"Look out! They're comin' back!" Vince shouted, smacking the water with his hands to simulate striking machine gun bullets from the enemy planes.

Keith, with his bandage off now and realizing his wounds were only scratches, got back into the spirit of things as the others climbed back into the boat.

"I'm riddled with bullets, boys," Keith said. "Get me to the base hospital. Cut the shrapnel and bullets out, but don't send me back home. I'll be ready for the next invasion. We shall return-n-n-n!"

Reaching the Kentucky shore, they carried him on the stretcher up through the horseweeds and hoisted him up on the roof of Hobo's shed. A blood transfusion followed and he was ready to fight again.

"But not today, boys," he said, squinting up at the sun. "It's ten after five and grandma's having new potatoes and brown beans and cornbread for supper. See you boys later."

CHAPTER 24:
OKINAWA FALLS

After supper, the gang came together at Gale's house, where they gathered around the big floor model radio to fly through the latest adventure of Superman and ride the range with Tom Mix. After that came Gabriel Heatter with the latest war news from the Pacific. Tom had taken an interest in such reports ever since Vince went off to boot camp. How would this terrible conflict with Japan end? Would Vince wind up as part of an invasion force of the Japanese home islands? The other Braves, though, got so rowdy that the white-haired Grandpa Flanders became hostile.

"Either pipe down or go outside and play!" he growled at Gale. They piped down.

The news was about Okinawa – not just the violent fighting going on, but on the unforeseen attacks on American ships by Japanese suicide planes. The Japanese fought desperately. Its air force launched about 6,000 kamikazes. And as the campaign wound down in mid-June, these suicide planes, overall in the Pacific Theater, had sunk 36 ships and damaged another 332.

Although organized enemy resistance on the island ended in mid-June, some of the fighting to secure the island would continue until late July. But Heatter reported the main battle had ended. This was coming 82 days after the first allied forces landed on the 67-mile long island – 82 days after the Marine whose victory garden Tom was tending had been among the first American casualties in that land so far from Hooperville, Kentucky.

It had been one of the bloodiest campaigns of the war. The Japanese had lost more than 110,000 men and 7,800 airplanes, Heatter said, and approximately 12,500 Americans and 60,000 Okinawans had died in the fighting.

"Okinawa, boys, is the last major stepping stone to the Japanese home islands," Grandpa Flanders said. "Now maybe we'll end this thing. The

Japs can't continue to fight much longer."

Tom thought that the Marine in the garden would be happy to know that the island he gave his life to liberating was close to being secured. He wondered if the Marine was still around. He had not seen him nor felt his presence in more than a week. Maybe it was all in his mind, Tom thought. Maybe one must concentrate with all the powers of the mind to see an apparition.

He need not have been concerned. Darkness had fallen and a near-full moon was rising above the hills as the boys said goodnight outside Gale's. Tom was crossing the street for home when he suddenly sensed that he was not alone. The Marine was evidently expanding his territory. He was beside Tom, in step with him. Tom could see him in his peripheral vision. He was wearing his combat fatigues.

Tom stood for a while at the back porch, looking out over the garden. The moon bathed the scene in a yellow-white light, illuminating the cherry tree at the rear of the garden and bouncing off the white church tower and the tombstones in the church cemetery. Not a breeze stirred the leaves of the trees and yet, all of a sudden, a wind rushed through the garden, rippling the corn and beans as though a wave from a towboat's paddlewheel had washed through it. Wow!

"You seem excited over something tonight, Lance Corporal Selby. What is it you want? How can I help you?" Tom said out loud.

No answer.

CHAPTER 25:
TERROR ABOUT TO BE LOOSED

The United States was being roused for the final drive against Japan. Fire bombing continued to sear Tokyo. Many Japanese suffered asphyxiation as they rushed toward Meiji Shrine for salvation. But the grinning Japanese stereotypes appearing on posters at the post office made it impossible to find sympathy for their plight. "Avenge December 7," one poster said, depicting the sinking battleships at Pearl Harbor. Caricatures pictured the Japanese as savage and still dangerous – as brutal, sneaky and heartless Japs.

Pidgin English was used in the messages aimed at workers in American war plants. One said, "To all Clysler men absent from jobs, thanks." Another took a shot at pleasure drivers with the message: "Tokyo Kid say – dwiving like sap helping for Jap. Thank you."

Wash Tubbs and Captain Easy switched their action in the daily newspaper comics from Europe to the South Pacific.

Military leaders got a taste in the battle for Okinawa of what it would be like to take Japan's home islands. On Okinawa, six battleships, six cruisers and eight destroyers rained 19,000 shells in on the Japanese, but they fought on, living on potato vines and mulberry leaves. Three American units that had advanced in the wake of the shelling were repelled with heavy casualties. On the sea, allied bombers knocked out twenty-eight more Japanese ships as the vessels tried to run a blockade.

Plans for a massive assault on the homeland were laid. If it came, it would cost America and the Allies dearly, Kaltenborn said. With their island strongholds gone, more than 25 million women, children and old men drilled with bamboo spears and pitchforks, planning a nasty reception for

Americans when and if the real invasion should come. The shorelines of Kyushu and Honshu were fortified with tunnels, bunkers and barbed wire. Some 5,000 planes, camouflaged on the mountainsides, were rigged for kamikaze missions, loaded with just enough fuel to reach the invasion beaches.

Flint wrote letters home from boot camp nearly every day, but they did little to ease his mother's mind. When his training was over, she just knew that he would be put on a ship and disgorged on Japan's front door.

Having lined a ride up with a neighbor, she had gone to work at Wheeling Steel across the river in Shawnee. She figured her efforts there in making bomb casings would help to end the conflict before Flint was called on to go and fight that awful end-time war.

She was one of some 500 women who had yanked off their aprons and donned coveralls to join the bomb-producing work force at Wheeling Steel.

She was showing less and less interest in the things of her household. She tuned in more and more to the radio reports of the war corespondents. She stared blankly at walls. She let Tom go off to Sunday school without checking his ears. She didn't always yell him in at dark.

Bruce Sycamore was handling things the only way he knew how – by maintaining the railroads and spending the weekends fishing the river.

"Don't go in after the Japs," Gale's Grandpa Flanders said one day as he listened to the radio reports while the gang was at Gale's. "Just keep them bottled up there on their islands. If they try to build a plane or a ship, bomb the daylights out of them."

Residents in the two-state region around Hooperville bought more than five million dollars worth of war bonds in the Seventh War Loan campaign.

"It's hard to tell whether patriotism or capitalism is the strongest," Grandpa Flanders said another time, noting a report in The Shawnee Times on how strikes by John L. Lewis' miners had left the steel mill with enough coal to last just sixteen more days.

The Hooperville Braves were certainly doing their part, sending wave after wave of fighting marines in on the *Reuben James* to battle the Nips in hand-to-hand combat.

In one invasion, the Braves' entire battalion was wiped out. All six of the combatants lay in the sand with the flies buzzing them, thinking of how much play their heroic deaths would get in The Shawnee Times.

At times like that Tom thought of Janie. Would she read about it in the Cleveland papers? Would she be sad, realizing that she should have stayed with such a brave fighting man, and how much she had missed in never having gotten to hold his buttery hand in the Saturday matinee?

Vince had the boys quit their island-hopping and tried an invasion of mainland Japan itself. Somehow he had gotten his hands on a three-foot by three-foot map of Japan. He hung it on the wall of the tree house and the Braves spent a good deal of time planning the attack on Honshu. They would go ashore on a point near Yokohama. To be sure, it looked like the same beachhead as that on Okinawa and Bataan – that is, the sandy shore across the river from Hooperville.

"Looked like a million Japs comin' at us," Vince said as the Braves re-grouped in the deep shade on the deck of the tree house. "We definitely must have reinforcements. I'm going to arrange a meeting with Harry as soon as he gets back from Potsdam."

Vince kept up pretty good on current events, for at about that very time Truman was in Potsdam, meeting with Churchill and Stalin. They were try-ing to figure out how to deal with the Japanese.

And as Truman toured the ruins of Berlin, another important event was happening in the New Mexico desert, near Alamogordo. A tremendous blast was followed by a great ball of light and a mushroom cloud rising two miles above the desert floor. Many who witnessed it would struggle for words to describe what they experienced. An Army news release called it simply "a revolutionary weapon destined to change war as we know it, or which may even be the instrumentality to end all wars."

Dr. J. Robert Oppenheimer, the physicist who established the labora-tory that produced the warhead on "Fat Boy," reached back to ancient Hindu texts for a line to describe what he had seen: "I am become Death, the shatterer of worlds."

157

CHAPTER 26:
THE GERMAN INVASION

One of the highlights of the summer came when Vince's brother, Charlie Royalton, got home on a short leave before he would ship out from the West Coast to the Pacific. He had been an Army gunner on a tank that blazed its way through the Battle of the Bulge and drove on toward Berlin in the closing stages of the war in Europe.

The Braves stopped their paddleball tournament and gathered around him on the church steps to plead for a story of what it had been like. He was reluctant to speak of the battles he had come through (in one of which, in a fight with one of the bigger, more powerful German tanks, his tank operator had had his head blown off.)

But he found himself telling the boys about the day he and his GI buddies helped to liberate a Nazi concentration camp. It was a memory that would never leave him, and perhaps he needed to talk about it. They were attached to the 4th Army Division when, in the days just prior to Germany's surrender, he and his fellow soldiers arrived at the Ohrdruf concentration camp.

"We saw that all of the prisoners – they were Jews, we found out – had been shot in the head. They had already been mistreated and starved, then as the Nazis were pulling out ahead of us coming in, they had shot them. Why, I don't understand."

His gaze traveled down the street toward the river, and Tom sensed that he had forgotten that he was sitting on church steps talking to some young boys from his hometown.

Charlie had made it home with a few souvenirs, including two German helmets. These he entrusted to Vince.

It was the day after Charles left his worried parents to report to a troop ship in San Diego that Vince came up with the idea for the attack on Shantyboat Bill's place.

Shantyboat's given name was William R. Lester and he was the town drunk. He lived all alone in an old houseboat moored just short of Sherwood Forest. He was a threat to no one. In fact, he often found it his duty to protect the good people of Hooperville. He used to go meekly, about every Saturday night, up to the Tip Toe Inn, then stagger through town in the early morning hours, singing the old church hymns he had learned as a boy at the top of his voice.

But on May 22, Turnip County had voted to go dry. The Tip Toe Inn had shut its doors forever. It wasn't that much trouble for Shantyboat Bill to walk on to Shawnee for his liquor, but after the Shawnee police locked him up a couple of times, and the city court took a sizeable chunk out of his pension in fines, he relied on a bootlegger who set up shop halfway between Hooperville and Killin Hollow. Things quieted down after that because Bill decided to do his drinking at home.

Now and then he would still appear on the streets of Hooperville to preach to the people to keep their firearms loaded and ready, for he was convinced the Germans would come up the Ohio River for an invasion of interior America. Never mind that Germany had allegedly surrendered. That was only a ploy.

It was with this theme in mind that Vince planned to blow ol' Bill's shantyboat out of the water.

It was an elaborate scheme. First, Vince had used watercolors or soapstone, or something not permanent, to paint swastikas on the two German helmets. Then there was a bicycle tire pump with a long length of piano wire attached to it. The other end of the wire was tied around a bundle of fusses Tom's father had brought home from the railroad.

They rowed the *Reuben James* downstream and pulled it into a thick clump of willows just upstream from Bill's boat. Four of them stayed with the johnboat to manipulate the plunger at the proper time and to keep the boilers fired up for a getaway. Vince and Hobo donned the helmets, fastening the straps under their chins. Vince tucked the fusees under one arm. He and Hobo slid under the water and surfaced again near the houseboat. Here Vince began talking to Hobo in a loud voice in German: "Vos, Franz. Der vouchits von frankels!"

They heard Bill's feet hit the floor and saw the boat shaking. As he came out on the deck to investigate, Hobo and Vince, keeping their heads down so that just the helmets with their swastikas showed, placed the signal flares on the deck and began wring them to the base of a handrail.

Bill stopped dead in his tracks, looked at the fusses, then stepped toward the rail to look down on the helmets. "What in the living..." he muttered. Then he let out a scream you could hear half a mile. "Ya-a-a! Germans!"

He ran back into the cabin and came out carrying quite a surprise – a double-barreled shotgun! Vince and Hobo ducked underwater. Tom and the others could only watch from their concealment as the two "Germans" resurfaced back under the recess of the deck. The old man couldn't have seen them without leaning out over the rail. He fired both barrels into the water where he'd last seen the helmets. The shots ripped open the surface and the recoil knocked him back against the cabin wall. He ejected the two empty shells and fumbled through his pockets for more. He let out a long string of curses. "All the shells I've got," he said in an agonizing voice. He ran around in a tight circle, one hand over his eyes, motioning at the water with his other. He kicked at the fusees, but missed them.

"You %#**& Germans!" he shouted.

Then he was off, bouncing across his board walkway and hitting the bank running. He cleared a new path through the underbrush and the horse-weeds. He hit the top of the second rise yelling at the top of his voice, "The Germans! The Krauts are here! I said all the time they would come up the river. Nobody would listen. Turn out! Turn out, every able-bodied man, woman and child. It's the @#%%$ Germans-s-s-s!"

Vince's father, busy trimming his front hedge, didn't even bother to look up. Neither did John Stephenson, who was working in his garden as Lester went screaming up over the crossing, headed no doubt for the boot-legger's place.

Hobo and Vince swam around the front of the houseboat and clamored up onto the shore, slipping and falling several times as they made their way along the clay bank toward the *Reuben James*. Then they found more sure footing in the sand and opened it up.

They pushed the boat off with the others in it. They scrambled in themselves, landing on their bellies in the bottom of the boat. Vince tipped his helmet back and immediately began to shout commands. "Head 'er back to port, men! Full speed ahead! We've got wounded!"

Then, looking down at Hobo, who had rolled onto his back on the bottom of the boat, he said, "My gawd, Hobo! We could have been killed! That was real buckshot the old man was firing!"

"I thought we would be killed, for sure!" Hobo said. "How'd I ever let you talk me in to a stupid stunt like that?"

Keith and Gale manned the oars with all speed, propelling the boat back upstream. Vince made his way to the bow, where Dale was on lookout, and slapped Dale on the back.

"Did you see it, Dale – er, Chief Riley? Did you see him fire that cannon right in where we was at? Me and ol' Hobo could'a been killed! Hot dang! This turned out better than I planned. I love it! Heh, heh."

Dale gave him a wide grin, but before he could say anything Vince started making machine gun noises with his mouth. "Cha-cha-cha-cha, tut-tut-tut-tut, tut-tut-tut." He fell into the bottom of the boat on his back. "Hit the deck, men!" he screamed. "It's a U-boat. The Krauts have surfaced and zeroed in on us."

Hobo, still on the floor of the boat, raised up and fired back a volley from the stern. "Cha-cha-cha-cha-cha-tut-tut-tut-tut."

Vince leaped up and slapped the water with his hand, making the sound of an exploding shell with his mouth.

"Dang the torpedoes! Full speed ahead!" he shouted.

Keith and Gale pulled harder at the oars.

"Keep a sharp lookout there, Chief Riley," Vince said. "Looks like a mine 30 degrees off the port bow! Bring 'er to starboard! Bring 'er to starboard!"

Tom looked for all he was worth in the direction Vince pointed, but all he saw was an empty Boscul coffee can, drifting along with the current.

CHAPTER 27:
WAR IS HELL

Unbeknownst to the Braves, Sunday school teacher Jim Galloway had set in on one of their mock battles with the Japanese. It was one of those assaults along the Kentucky shore beachhead when the force had landed and fought and used flame-throwers and hand grenades to roust the Japanese out of their caves. He had come to the riverbank intending to fish, heard the sounds of battle, and concealed himself in the weeds and willows near the top of the bank to watch and listen.

More than once the boys had tried to get him to deviate from the Sunday school lesson and tell them some stories of his World War One actions. But it was something he would never talk about.

Now, as they assembled for his class, he seemed troubled. He ran one hand through his thinning gray hair. His face was contorted in anguish as he looked not at them, but off out the basement window somewhere, as though reliving some painful experience.

"I know you boys like to play your war games," he said at last. "But I think you have the wrong conception of what war really is."

Again he paused, looking down and rubbing his forehead with the backs of his fingers on his right hand, searching for the words to carry his thoughts.

"When I fought, more than twenty-seven years ago its been now," he continued, "a battlefront commander would shout, 'Over the top!' and we infantrymen would climb out of the trenches with fixed bayonets and dash across no-man's land."

Immediately he had the boys' full attention.

"Rain filled the dugouts with water and mud, and rats swarmed through the venom-infested trenches. Everywhere there was the stain of blood and the stench of death," the teacher said, now turning his full gaze on his students.

"And there's one thing about war that you boys are not experiencing, probably have never even thought of. I'm talking about the day when the Germans unleashed a new weapon in their drive to the French coast. A greenish-white mist drifted from the enemy lines toward the French and British forces. The Germans had released poisonous chlorine gas, and there was no fighting back against that. Bodies were stacked everywhere. Where was the glory in that?

"And you boys, with your cartoon character war, have no idea of the full agony and pain suffered in this war we're fighting now, suffered by both the allies and the Japanese. And you won't see it on the newsreels – the terrible blood-letting that has taken place from Guadalcanal to the Solomons to New Guinea to Guam to Siapan to Okinawa – the stepping stones to Tokyo.

"You don't know about the landing craft filled with dead young Americans who never reached the beach and never fired a shot; of the failure of communications and the plans gone wrong; of the maggot-infested bodies of soldiers lying at the water's edge; of the smell of death, the sweetish odor of decaying flesh wafting across a thousand yards of lagoon water, sickening and frightening those who must go in; of the wild melee of knives, bayonets and rifle butts as the Japanese overrun Marine positions with shouts of 'Banzi! Banzi!'; of the Japanese who shoot, stab and blow themselves up rather than face the ignominy of surrender; of fighting in torrential rains and overbearing heat for twenty-four hours non-stop."

This was sickening, Vince thought, almost enough to turn a body against war. But no one dared interrupt as Mr. Galloway talked on.

"Oh, yes, to be sure, I helped put the Germans on the run at Argonne. More than one million of us Americans fought in that battle, and one out of every ten died. More than five million allies were slaughtered in that war to end all wars, one hundred and sixteen thousand of them Americans. And for what? Well, it's for freedom, we know, and it seems like the struggle never ends. Here we are, at it again."

He paused to look into the face of each of the Braves.

"I just hope and pray to God that you boys never have to experience the real thing," he said. "I hope you'll give up these war games and study your history books. Try to find out how to live peacefully with your fellow man."

The bell rang and it was a somber crew that left that Sunday school class. Everything, it seemed to Tom, was getting out of hand – out of control.

CHAPTER 28:
RIDING HIGH

Mr. Galloway's lecture on the evils of war had a profound affect on Vince, who seemed instantly weary of war games.

The war seemed far, far away as the six of them spent a day of summer vacation relaxing on the sandy shore of the peaceful Ohio River.

"Good lord, but I'm bushed," Vince said. "I wouldn't go look a trotline right now if I knew for sure there was fifteen cats on it."

A steamboat whistled on the bend downriver. Dale raised up on one elbow for a better look.

"That's the Omar, boys," he said. "She's pushing a string of empty barges and pouring black smoke."

The boat came into full view, pushing water out ahead of its lead barges.

"Man, look at the high, high waves she throws behind that paddlewheel. No wave-breaker," Hobo said.

"Oh, boy, yes! Look at them waves," Keith said. "I wonder if the *Reuben James* could take 'em …"

Vince raised up quickly. "That's an interestin' thought, Mr. Richards" he said. Then he was on his feet, running toward the clump of willows where they had tied the red johnboat. "Let's find out!" he said.

The others came running. They leaped in and pushed off. With Vince and Hobo manning the oars, they rushed out to meet the Omar.

The towboat was plowing almost up the middle of the channel. The *Reuben James* moved fast enough that they were in danger of getting in front of the twelve-foot high barges. They treaded water with the oars until the lead barges cruised by. The barges slid by just twenty feet from them. There was a long blast on the boat's steam whistle. A deckhand stood on one of the barges, watching them, shaking his head from side to side. The pilothouse loomed above them and a man rushed out of it with a megaphone in his hands.

"Hey, you dumb kids!" he shouted. "Get back! You wanna get yerselves killed? Get back!"

Keith, standing in the bow beside Gale, cupped his hands to his mouth and shouted back, "Up your hairy legs with a blow torch!"

The others roared their approval. His comments were a mask for the fear they felt as the thirty-foot paddlewheel moved up abreast of them.

"Pull, Hobo, pull!" Vince said, bent on plowing into the trough in front of that first mountainous wave. They settled for the second wave, shooting into its trough and climbing, climbing up a mountain of water. When they hit the top of that third wave, it was like being on top of the world. It seemed they were so high above the surface that they could see over the top of the bank and into the village. It was like a roller coaster as they slid down the lower side of the wave, into the trough, and rode high up onto the next wave. Water pouring down over the massive wheel made it seem as though they had come over a waterfall.

At the very crest of the wave, Hobo stood up and beat on his chest like Tarzan. He promptly lost his balance and fell overboard, grabbing the side of the boat as he hit the water. The boat flipped as it slid down the other side of the wave, plunging all of them out into the murky water. Tom clung to the side of the overturned boat, not too confident of his swimming ability in rough water like that. Up, up, on the next wave they went, and down again. Everybody was clinging to the sides of the boat as they rode out the last of the diminishing waves.

They pushed and pulled the johnboat in to shore, a half-mile downstream from where they'd started, bailed her out, rowed back upriver, and waited for the next towboat.

Later, when hunger drove them to the top of the second rise, they met Gale's mom on the way down. She had a switch in her hand. She applied it to Gale's bare legs a couple of times. Gale danced and the others scattered for home. Gale's mom had him by the ear as she marched him in through his front door. Out on the street, the four Hooperville girls – Yvonne Blitz, Betty Jo Hooper, Barbara Bellcraft and Gale's sister, Gina – were jumping rope.

"We told your mom, too," Gina said as Tom passed on the way to his house.

Sure enough, his mother waited on the front porch, hands on hips.

"Out on that river in that leaky old boat, messing around those big barges!" she said. "Your father will know about this. Now get yourself in the house."

There was no gathering at Gale's house for the radio serials that evening.

And on Friday evening, shortly after Bruce Sycamore got home, Tom was sent out to the cherry tree to break off a small limb suitable for a switch.

"Now you know why you're getting this, don't you?" Bruce Sycamore asked his son.

"Oh yes, I know," Tom said. "For riding the waves of the Omar."

He stung Tom's legs pretty good.

Then he said, "Now get the fishing gear. We'll eat some supper and have a couple of hours of daylight to try our luck."

And so they did.

CHAPTER 29:
BIRDS FLY, WHY CAN'T I?

When the Sunday school lesson ended, Mr. Galloway took Tom by the arm and held him back as the other boys filed up the steps for the sanctuary. He walked Tom back to the door leading out from the basement. He pulled the curtain aside and looked out toward Tom's well-kept garden.

"I just wondered if you'd seen our Marine lately?" he asked.

Tom told him about the Marine crossing the street with him coming back from Gale's on the evening that the news came over the radio about Okinawa falling. He told him about the wind rippling the corn on an otherwise calm evening when there was not a breeze moving the leaves in the trees.

"I've been in the garden several times since then but he hasn't shown up," Tom said.

The teacher fell silent for a moment, then said, "I visited his wife and her parents over in Shawnee."

He had Tom's full attention.

"Her name is Mary Ann Selby and his was – or is – Leon Selby. Lance Corporal Leon Selby." Galloway paused, rubbed the back of his hand across his forehead, and then continued, "I didn't handle things too well, Tom. I blurted out about you working the garden her husband had planted and how you had been visited by a, uh, apparition – looked like a marine – while doing so; and about my experience in the church – the ringing bell and all; that maybe she might want to come for a visit. She placed her hands suddenly on her stomach and remarked that she had felt the baby give a 'prodigious leap.'

"Her mother called me aside and told me her daughter was under strict orders from her doctor not to travel, or become overly excited, for that matter."

Mr. Galloway placed his hands in his pockets and limped away from the door window.

"At any rate, we made arrangements – I've since talked to Reverend Hackelbee about this – for her, as soon as the baby is born and she's okayed to travel, to come and have the baby dedicated at the church."

Tom could hardly wait to tell the news to his mother, who was working at the mill, Sunday or no Sunday.

After dinner, all six of the boys – anything, it seemed, that happened to one of them, happened to all six – met down at Vince's house, where he had assembled his "flying tools," and they headed out to Farmer Matt Henson's house, then down into the pasture to the barn, where the greatest experiment in flight since the Wright Brothers would take place.

Little doubt Vince would rather have tried his wings from the old diving tree, high enough to give him more flapping room, but the river was down to near normal and he wouldn't have any soft water for a landing spot anyway. He picked Matt Henson's barn loft as the taking off-point for his latest experiment in aerodynamics.

The barn stood in a draw along the small creek that wound past the schoolhouse and under Route 10 on its way to merge with the river. The barn couldn't be seen from the farmhouse. The Braves knew Farmer Henson was over in the bottoms planting a cornfield anyway, Sunday or no Sunday.

Really, though, it didn't matter if Henson had seen the boys. He didn't mind them playing in the barn lot, as long as they didn't let his cattle out. Vince presented an imposing picture, standing in the hayloft looking down on the mortals below, a wide, six-foot long sturdy cardboard wing tied securely to each arm; a piece of an old blue bed sheet tied around his neck for a cape.

"Birds can fly, so why can't I?" Vince said, making a few up-and-down motions with the wings.

Gale had his camera ready as Keith urged Vince on. "Fly up and around Dead Man's Ridge," he said. "See how things look from up there."

170

"I'm not going that far," Vince said. "This is just a test flight. I'm just going out over the creek and back."

"My turn next!" Dale Riley shouted.

Vince moved forward, his toes sticking out over the edge of the boards forming the bottom of the barn loft. For a minute it looked as though he might back down.

"Come on, Vince. Too far to turn back now. You can do it," Hobo said.

And with that, Vince leaped outward, his wings stroking downward at the air. He had time for two, maybe three, frenzied flaps before he crash-landed. He hit the earth toes first and pitched forward, thumping the ground with his chin and chest.

The boys rushed forward to assist their fearless leader, to see what might be broken besides the crumpled wings. Vince had a small cut on his chin. His breath had been knocked out of him on impact. It was a while before he managed to get out between gasps, "How far did I make it, boys?"

"As far as it is from here to up there," Gale said, pointing straight up to the entrance to the barn loft. "What, maybe ... fourteen feet?"

CHAPTER 30:
GIRLS! WHAT GOOD ARE THEY?

The temperature was in the 90s by early afternoon, and so the Hooperville Braves were to be found in the cooling waters of the Ohio River. They had a contest going to see who could locate a small bell tossed high to land somewhere on the bottom of the river. Whoever retrieved it first rang it above their head and was awarded points toward the championship.

As they tired of the game and sought new adventures, Vince called for a meeting to discuss plans for the day's activities. They headed for the tree house, sheltered in the shade of the big maple tree's branches.

As they walked down along the edge of the water and approached the tree, Keith was the first to sound the alarm.

"Girls!" he screamed. "Girls in the tree house!"

The girls, Yvonne Blitz, Barbara Bellcraft, Betty Jo Hooper and Gale's sister, Gina – yes, the same four who had ratted on them for riding the waves of the Omar – were scrambling down the wooden ladder rungs on the side of the tree. They had heard the owners of the house in the tree approaching and were trying to make their getaway.

"Hey, hey! What is this?" Vince screamed.

In unison the boys scooped up mud and clay from the water's edge and sent a volley of mud balls after the fleeing girls.

Vince was even more incensed when he saw what had been going on in the tree house. The crusty old blankets that had covered the windows had been replaced with frilly curtains the girls had no doubt rescued from their mothers' closets. After they climbed the tree ladder and made their way inside, they discovered a flowered table cover with fringes around the edges covered the orange crate. There was a setting of toy dishes on top of the crate. The guns on the side storage area had ribbons tied round the trigger guards and flowers stuck down in the barrels. There was a rag doll in Vince's seat.

"They've made a playhouse out of our clubhouse," Vince said. "Next time we catch them in here, we'll be forced to kill 'em. We'll drown them and weigh their bodies down. No one will ever miss them."

"Let's first hang them by their thumbs out there on the big limb," Dale Riley suggested. "We've got rope here."

Next day was another day for delivering catfish to Herman's Market on Market Street in Shawnee. A look of the trotline that morning had provided eight more catfish to the 12 already in the live box. They cleaned the fish and stored them in buckets of spring water.

Then, not wanting to make the delivery in wet clothing, they hung their clothes on the limbs of a willow and went skinny-dipping. They soon became engrossed in a game of water polo. Then, suddenly they heard a girl's frilly voice calling, "Oh, boys-s-s-s. Look here-e-e."

It was Yvonne. She and the others were waving the boys' clothing at them.

"Put them back, you dirty little rats. We've got fish to deliver," Vince said. "Right now!"

"Come and get them," Betty Jo said, a grin spreading ear to ear.

The boys, already in chest-deep water, waded out into even deeper water. All they could do was watch as the girls vanished into the willows with all of their clothing.

"We're gonna kill all of you!" Keith Richards screamed after them.

After a while and a short discussion, Gale said, "Now what do we do? We can't go to town. We can't even go home. Stupid girls. I'll skin that Gina alive for this."

The dilemma they found themselves in was solved by a makeshift diving platform and board the boys had rigged up just out from the shore. The heavy planks had been covered with pieces of an old tarpaulin to protect their bare feet from splinters. The sun had dry-rotted the canvas enough that Vince was able to rip off a big enough piece to wrap it around his waist like a sarong. Then he started up the bank in the direction he girls had disappeared.

There was a lot of giggling and guffawing from the boys who remained in chin-deep murky water as they watched their fearless Major go.

His hind end was shining in the sunlight.

In a short while he returned with all the clothing, which the girls, before vamoosing on home, had hung on some willow limbs, where they would be seen, at the foot of the second rise.

That evening, as they gathered at Gale's house for games and the radio serials, Gina stayed upstairs in her room.

CHAPTER 31:

A LESSON FROM THE WEAKER SEX

Down at the end of Tom's street was a "court" where the older men of the village gathered after supper to play horseshoes. Saturday tournaments, in which some money was exchanged, lasted into the darkness of the night.

Hooperville's blackouts had ended with the surrender of Germany, so electric light bulbs with tin shades over them again spotlighted the peg boxes. Wayne Hooper, Hobo's dad, who could ring the peg with the best of them, brought his table-model radio onto the front porch and turned it on high, so that everyone could enjoy the Grand Ole Opry. He evidently thought the whole village was as hard of hearing as he was, for he always had the volume cranked as high as it would go. Everybody along the street, with windows up and doors open against the heat, had no choice but to enjoy Earnest Tubb singing, *There's a Star-Spangled Banner Waving Somewhere, or When the warships left Manila, they went sailing ore the sea, bright blue sea, all the sailors' hearts were filled with sad regret; looking backward to that island where they'd spent those happy hours, happy hours, making love to every pretty girl they met. . .*

"Thankfully," Grandpa Flanders once said of Wayne Hooper, "he goes to bed early."

It was also a place where there was nice smooth dirt for a marble ring, and it was there that the boys often gathered on hot July evenings, after the radio serials, to test their skills against each other. They were all pretty adept at the game, but Hobo and Dale were clearly the best, with much greater power and sticking abilities than the others. They most generally played for keeps, but here they learned their first lessons of altruism: Sometimes the big winner would give marbles back to the losers – a percentage of them at least.

But that wasn't a thing you could count on.

Marbles was a boy's game. Everyone knew that. Girls sometimes played the game, though not in the boys' circle. Their fingers and knuckles, after all, were not made right for the game.

One sultry July evening all six of the Braves were concentrating their full powers and skills into a marble game. The shade from the maples on the second rise combined with a light breeze from the river to make for a comfortable setting. At least it was pleasant and comfortable for a while – until Betty Jo Hooper and Yvonne Blitz came along.

Betty Jo wanted in. Yvonne carried a one-pound coffee can half filled with marbles – Betty Jo's marbles.

The boys believed the girls had planned something in an attempt to humiliate them. They tried to ignore the two, but they kept stepping into the ring, even "accidentally" stepping on their marbles.

It was Gale who first sidled over to the girls and looked down into the coffee can Yvonne was carrying. To give them a better look, Betty Jo took it from her and poured the contents out on the ground.

"Holy cow!" Gale said. The others gathered round to look. Tom couldn't believe his eyes. She had rainbows, marines, peppermint stripes, cat's eyes – even a few moonstones.

"Where'd you get all these?" Vince asked, whistling as he picked up a First American.

"Won 'em," Betty Jo said, slapping Vince on the hand to make sure he dropped the marble. "What'd you think? Santa brought 'em?"

"We won't play with her anymore," Yvonne said. "She's pretty good, really. Too good for you boys, even, I'd say – I'd warn you."

"Ho, ho," Hobo said, looking at the marbles and then from one to the other of the Braves.

With much relish, the rules governing girls were suspended and the invitation to play was extended.

Twenty-eight marbles in all were placed on the cross in the center of the ring, four from each player. They lagged for turns. Surprisingly, Betty Jo won first shot. That should have told them something.

She knuckled down at the edge of the ring. Her taw struck a nib and knocked it out of the ring with five feet to spare. Her taw stuck, spinning right where it first struck the marble.

From there, it was knuckle down, shoot, ping, stick, and then a repeat of that process until every marble was gone from the ring and into her can. Nobody else even got a shot. Her last shot to clean the ring of the last marble was expertly handled so that her taw banked off and, like the nib, left the ring.

The boys looked at each other, making little nervous jokes. What she had just done had to be pure, unadulterated luck.

They anted up again. After zipping twenty straight out of the ring, Betty Jo's taw came to rest behind a wood chip that had somehow got blown in or knocked into the ring.

"No cleans! No roundesters!" Vince shouted. "And no hikes!"

Betty Jo, on all fours, frowned up at him. She put her nose to the ground, sighting over the obstacle toward a marble lying near the far side of the ring. Then she knuckled down. Tom still finds it hard to believe that shot. Her taw sailed over the chip, hit the ground two feet on the other side of it, picked up speed from its forward spin, knocked the marble on the far side out of the ring, and stuck right where it was, spinning.

Then she proceeded to finish cleaning the ring again.

The third game was about the same, except Hobo finally did knock two marbles out, and Dale one.

Eventually, both Gale and Tom went home for more marbles. Pretty soon Vince did, too, and so did Hobo.

Dale and Keith lost what they had, then wisely decided to watch from the sideline. Within forty-five minutes the humiliation was complete. Yvonne helped Betty Jo carry off what were once their prized and beautiful marbles.

"Hey, we forgot to tell you – we was just playing for funs," Vince shouted after them.

Both girls were laughing as they turned the corner and headed down the alley.

Tom walked home with Gale. He was concerned about his red-headed friend. He was acting strange. Tom had to jump back when he slammed the door behind him with much force.

He followed Gale on in and up the stairs to his room. His mother, hands on hips, watched from the kitchen door as they ascended the stairs.

"What in the world's wrong?" she called up the steps after the boys.

"What's wrong?" Gale said, slamming a pillow against the wall. "Betty Jo – a girl! – won all my marbles, that's what's wrong!"

Tom thought he heard Gale's mom giggle. Then she called up, "Do you want me to go win them back for you?"

Gale didn't bother to answer her, but to Tom he mumbled, "Having your mom win your marbles back for you is the only thing that could be worse than losing them to a girl in the first place."

Then, in spite of themselves, both boys laughed out loud.

After that, when they played marbles – which wasn't for a long time – they put a sign up outside the ring that matched the one on the side of the tree house: "No girls allowed."

CHAPTER 32:
MAD DOG!

After Sunday school, Mr. Galloway called Tom aside to question him again about the Marine in the Victory Garden. Was he still around? Had he seen him again?

Tom said he hadn't seen him since the night he crossed the street from Gale's house with him, followed by the wind rippling the corn in the moonlight.

Tom told him about his mother seeing the Marine on that day he threw him a salute in the garden.

"Dad was out there at the same time and didn't see anything. Mom says it runs in her family, on her mother's side – the ability to see the spirits of deceased people. You must have it too, huh?"

Mr. Galloway scratched his head and smiled before replying, "Well, I don't know. I was certainly sure I saw somebody, down there at the altar that day Germany surrendered, and then over there in the garden, too.

"But what I wanted to say is, I talked to Mary Ann Selby again. She called me, actually. She still plans to dedicate the baby, just as soon as it's born and they're both able to travel. She had asked me to ask you if you'd seen the Marine in the garden anymore."

After dinner, Tom went into the garden with the hoe. The corn was already sprouting young ears, and he wanted to loosen the dirt around the hills to encourage more growth. Chopper wasn't much help. He kept pouncing at the hoe with his paws.

Tom knew he should have stayed out of the garden on Sunday, since this didn't exactly fit the situation of having an ox in the ditch, for which the Scriptures allowed work on the Sabbath. But he wanted to encourage these stalks. He intended to have the biggest and sweetest roasting ears ever produced.

However, if he had stayed out of the garden, what was about to happen would not have happened at all.

Suddenly Chopper's hackles stood up on his neck and a low growl emanated from his throat. Then he whirled and was headed for the building. Was the Marine on the scene? Tom looked all around but saw no one. He did, however, feel a presence.

And it wasn't a comforting presence at all. It seemed in some frantic way trying to warn Tom of impending danger. He felt something tugging at his britches leg, as though it wanted him to move – to get out of that garden, quickly!

Then, looking down the cornrow he was standing in, he saw the dog, a scruffy black dog twice the size of Chopper. It was coming toward him and staggering like a drunk man.

"Hey, boy. Here. What's the matter?" Tom said, snapping his finger and thumb together several times.

The dog stared blankly at him. Its eyes were like two coals of fire. It regained its balance and came down the cornrows at a fast trot, right toward Tom, a low growl ripping from its throat.

Out of nowhere came Chopper, a blur of black and white. He bowled the black dog over, breaking several stalks of corn. The stray was too big for him. It leaped up, growling ferociously now, grabbed Chopper just behind the left ear, and shook him like a rag doll. Tom leaped over into the next cornrow as the dog loosed Chopper and charged on past him. It broke into a full run and disappeared around the corner of the house. It circled the house and started around again, Chopper after it like a beagle after a rabbit. Tom headed for the house, the hoe still in his hand. His mother came out onto the back porch as the two dogs raced around for the third time.

"What on earth, James Thomas, is going on?"

"It's an old stray dog, Momma. Acting crazy."

"Well, get in here," she said, grabbing a broom from the corner of the porch. "It looked to me like it was foaming at the mouth!"

As she stood holding the door open for Tom, the black dog came around again, veered off course, tumbled onto the porch, and brushed past her leg and into the house. Tom grabbed Chopper by the scuff of the neck. He noticed a spot of crimson on his white hair. He heard the black dog's toenails sliding on the linoleum. Carrie Sycamore still stood with the door open, not knowing what to do. Tom shoved Chopper aside, pushed his mom in, and charged through the door, slamming it to keep Chopper out. Thankfully, the stray dog didn't turn, but ran on through the living room, where Bruce Sycamore was in his easy chair, a newspaper spread over his face, napping. The dog rushed on by him and through the open door into the bedroom.

"What in thunderation?" Bruce said, shaking his head and letting the newspaper drop to the floor.

"My gawd, it's a mad dog, Bruce!" Carrie screamed. "It's in the bedroom."

Bruce Sycamore uncoiled like a threatened copperhead, leaped to the bedroom door, and slammed it shut.

"It just now went under the bed," he announced. "I saw it go under the bed."

Chopper was trying to push through the screen in the kitchen door.

"Where's your ball bat, Tom? Get it!" Bruce said.

Tom thought for a second, then went out the kitchen door, grabbing Chopper up in his arms. He carried him into the storage building, where he found the bat, dropped Chopper and, holding him back with one hand, locked him in.

He handed the bat to his father, who eased the bedroom door open a crack. He owned a shotgun and a rifle, and Tom wondered why he didn't get one of them. Maybe he didn't know where the shells were, or maybe he didn't have any. They heard the dog growl. Bruce closed the door.

"Now, I'm going in and shutting this door behind me," he said, his voice calm and steady. "Don't nobody open it."

"Be careful, Bruce," Carrie cried out. "That dog's got rabies for sure. I saw slobbers at its mouth."

She stood in the kitchen for a moment, wringing her hands. She trusted her husband's ability to do what was necessary to take care of the mad dog. She decided to go across the street to the Rileys and wait. She yelled for Tom to come with her, but he lingered outside the bedroom door.

"Dad might need me to get something, Mom," he said. "You go on. I'll stay outside the door."

There was a long, irregular crack in the bedroom door. Tom pressed an eye against it and could see his father, the bat cocked, like Stan Musial waiting for a fast ball.

Dale and Gale came in the kitchen door and on in to where they saw Tom at the bedroom door. Leader was barking outside the kitchen door. Chopper was barking in the shed.

"What's going on, Tom?" Gale asked.

"Mad dog," Tom said. "In there. Don't let your dog come in here."

He put his eye back to the crack in the door. With Gale crouching and Dale on his knees, all three boys could watch as the drama unfolded inside the bedroom.

Bruce Sycamore stomped the floor, then tapped the floor near the bed with the bat. The dog came out from under the bed crawling on its belly and immediately lunged for Bruce. He slammed the dog across the neck in midair. The impact knocked the crazed animal down and sent him scooting on his side across the floor and into the wallboard.

The dog regained his feet, lunged again. Tom felt fear for his father as he continued to watch through the crack in the door. But his dad swung the bat in an overhead arc and smashed the bat against the dog's skull. The dog shuddered and then lay still. Its misery was ended.

Bruce stood over it for a few minutes, poked it with the bat, and then opened the door as the three boys stood back. He dragged the dog out by one hind leg, leaving a trail of blood. "Get the shovel out of the shed, Tom," he said.

Carrie scolded Tom for not accompanying her across to the Riley home, then checked him all over as Dale and Gale watched.

"Did it bite you, Tom? Or scratch you?" she asked.

"No, Momma. It might have if not for Chopper going after it. I'm afraid it bit Chopper."

Chopper, who had escaped the building when Tom retrieved the shovel, was still looking for a scrap, even as Bruce patted down dirt over the black dog's grave, which he dug at the foot of the slope of the railroad tracks. Tom caught Chopper and held him while his mother poured disinfectant on the gash in the side of his neck.

"I'm getting Leader out of here," Gale said. "See you after while, Tom."

Carrie Sycamore stood back from her work, looking at Chopper, then Tom.

"I know how much this dog means to you, Tom," she said. "But you've got to get yourself ready for the worst. And your dog has got to be put up, where we can watch him."

Reluctantly, Tom locked Chopper back in the building.

Carrie Sycamore cleaned the floors in all three rooms, pouring the disinfectant into her work. Tom helped her move the bed out and she scrubbed where the dog had been. All the windows were raised and they stayed out of the house the rest of the day.

Tom and his dad built a pen, using boards and the side of the storage building as one wall. They also placed boards in position to prevent Chopper from going under the building.

"You'll have to keep him penned here, Tom, and watch him. That's about all we can do," his father said.

CHAPTER 33:
A MEAN, ANGRY MAN

There was a train on the tracks.

A freight train stopping on the tracks at Hooperville normally brought the ire of residents. They blocked all three crossings, making it impossible to get to work, or to the doctor offices or hospital in Shawnee – or even up to Davis & Harvey's grocery store out on Route 10.

But this was a coal train blocking the tracks. Some residents called it retaliation – certainly no one would considerate it thievery – when they rolled a few lumps of coal off the heavily-laden gondola cars and stored the fuel away against the coming winter.

Another train that blocked the tracks momentarily brought no complaints, either. It carried war equipment bound for the West Coast. Several flatbed cars were loaded with Sherman tanks, and everyone who owned a camera had it out to record photos of friends and family members posing by the side of them or even on top of them.

Tom was glad in this instance that Chopper was penned up and out of the danger zone posed by rail cars that could jump to life at anytime.

But all in all, keeping Chopper penned was the most difficult and saddest thing that had ever come about in Tom's young life. The little dog just couldn't understand why he couldn't go swimming with the boys or even get free to play with his friend, Leader. Tom never saw tears in his eyes, but he knew his little dog cried because of lost companionship.

One evening the Braves scheduled a paddleball tournament on the church's broad sidewalk and the competition lasted until it was too dark to see the line. It was still too early to go in on such a nice summer evening, and they sat on the church steps trying to scare each other with ghost stories.

The steps were close enough to the Sycamore outbuilding that Tom could hear Chopper whining and begging to join them. He thought once he would put him on a leash and bring him out. But he realized the dangers posed by an animal that might be carrying the rabies disease, and so he resisted.

It was Gale's mention of his mother having a bag of marshmallows that got the campfire going. They could have built the fire in his backyard, or in Tom's, but the gravel between the street and the three steps leading up to the church walk seemed as good a place as any.

A fire brings out the gathering instinct. Soon Yvonne and Betty Jo came out from their homes to see what was going on. The boys treated them civilly. Betty Jo's run of the marble ring had been forgotten, although she never did give any of her booty back to the Braves.

They had no great dislike for the girls. They weren't Janie, of course, Tom took note, but they were nevertheless girls, and as such were creatures of interest. Tom watched Yvonne showing off around Vince, and came to the conclusion that she was sweet on him. If Vince was aware of this he never let it be known.

There was some horseplay and bantering and hat snatching and chasing. Vince and Hobo cut some limbs from the weeping willow. The marshmallows were opened and with marshmallows speared to the ends of the sticks, they waited for the fire to burn down a bit so they could get close enough to roast them.

Suddenly Gale spoke in a low voice, "Uh oh, boys and girls. Don't look now, but old man Maxwell's watching."

"Where?" Hobo said, a note of fear in his voice.

"Out there," Gale said. "Out there in his back yard. He's looking right at us."

Tom saw the shadowy figure facing in their direction. He felt a pang of pure fear go down his spine.

He had heard about Leonard Maxwell. So had Carrie Sycamore. "Don't ever go about his property," she told Tom one day. "That old man has a mean streak down his back like a skunk's stripe. So don't you provoke him in any way."

Tom wasn't about to provoke him, but he wondered how a man could live in the middle of a civilized village and yet have no social connections with it.

Thick hedges grew around the front and down most of both sides of Old Man Maxwell's property. The remainder was guarded by a high fence of rusty tin. There was a well-kept garage on the river side of his house in which he kept his Hutmobile. He went out in it now and then, but never spoke or waved or returned any greeting that might be thrown his way, be it sincere or sarcastic. No one hardly ever spotted Mrs. Maxwell or even knew her name.

Tom had seen old Maxwell once, through his back gate while he worked the Marine's garden. Maxwell was dressed in bibbed overalls, long-sleeved shirt, and gumboots. Long, shaggy, dirty-white hair projected out from under his planter's hat. He took it off to wipe his brow and the sun glistened off his white, bald dome.

Once, during a revival at the church, Preacher Hackelbee had gone over to the Maxwells to invite them to the services. He was rudely escorted out the back gate by Old Leonard, called a hypocrite, and told in no uncertain terms not to return. The Reverend Hackelbee said Mrs. Maxwell watched from the front porch, wringing her hands.

The Maxwell Ditch incident happened before Tom's family moved in. Maxwell lived the first house down from the church. An alleyway, a public thoroughfare, connecting the street from the first crossing with the street from the middle crossing, ran the length of the block between his property and that of the church. One day, with pick and shovel, he dug a deep ditch across the end of the alley fronting on Tom's street. It wasn't intended for improving the drainage, but to keep anybody from driving up the alley and spreading dust on his property.

Of course, nobody was about to stand by and lose a public passageway. It was Dale's mom who took the problem to the attention of the fiscal court at its monthly meeting up in Turnipsburg. It seems Maxwell's reputation had spread even to the county seat, for when the county truck and endloader came to fill in the ditch, two armed sheriff's deputies stood nearby.

189

It was a sheriff's deputy, though not one of those two, who had ended the life of the Maxwells' only child, 21-year-old Leonard R. Maxwell Jr. That had happened some years ago. Junior Maxwell, described by some as a bully and a "born hell-raiser," had gotten into a drunken, knock-down, drag-out fight with another man at the Tip Toe Inn. In fact, he had stabbed his adversary in the groin with a hunting knife, and when the police came, he turned on the sheriff's deputy with the knife. He refused to drop the knife, and when he lunged at the sheriff's deputy, he took a .45-caliber slug point-blank in the chest.

At the inquest, the sheriff's deputy said he had intended to shoot young Maxwell in the arm, but didn't have enough time to really think much about what to do. Witnesses testified that Maxwell got what he bargained for. Leonard Maxwell Sr. went back home from the courtroom a broken, seething man.

As the youngsters prepared to toast their marshmallows, everybody was feeling a little uneasy, knowing he was standing there in the shadows watching them from just fifty yards away.

"He can't do anything to us," Dale said. "We're on public property. And he knows we'll douse this fire when we're through."

Tom was just turning his marshmallow to admire its golden brown crust when he heard it: "Frump, frump, frump." It was the sound of old man Maxwell's gumboots. They all turned their gaze in the direction of the sound, and they saw him coming up the sidewalk, carrying a five-gallon bucket, and listing a little to one side with the weight of it.

He came right up to the fire, spit a stream of amber into it, and poured the five gallons of water directly onto it. He didn't say a word. Neither did anyone else.

"Frump, frump, frump."

Steam hissed. The crowd hissed, but dispersed.

Maxwell really knew how to put a damper on a marshmallow roast.

"Well, you shouldn't have built a fire out there on the street anyway," Tom's mom said when he told her that night at bedtime about what had happened.

190

But she didn't like him ending the harmless marshmallow roast so rudely any more than Tom and his friends did. "Built that fire out here by the garden and that evil old man couldn't have done a thing about it 'cause he knows your father would go down there and teach him a thing or two."

Next day, when the boys met in the churchyard to resume their double-elimination paddleball tournament, there was some talk of revenge.

"Ah, let's just forget about it for now," Keith Richards said. "Come Halloween and we'll get him. Oh brother, we'll get him good! Hey, one thing we'll do is see how many rocks that tin fence of his will take."

"I was thinkin'," Dale said, "we could poop in a paper sack, set it on fire, and toss it up on his porch. When he comes out and stomps it out...ho, ho, ho!"

Soon they did forget about the incident, each of them intent on becoming the paddleball champ of Hooperville. Yvonne, Betty Jo and Barbara came around to watch. Gina tagged along. They wanted in, even thought they could win, but Vince told them they could either be cheerleaders or get their own court, "'Cause this is a man's game, honey."

It was Hobo who hit the wild shot, striking the ball so hard with a sideways swipe that it shot out of the churchyard, bounced in the alley, and sailed over Maxwell's gate and into his backyard.

As they stood stunned, looking at each other, Maxwell came from behind his storage shed, picked up the ball, glared at the boys, and dropped it into a crock on his back porch.

It was the only ball the boys had. Tennis balls don't fall from heaven.

Nobody was quick to volunteer to fetch it. But Will Flanders, who had taken a sick day off from work at the mill, had seen the whole thing. He came across the street, gesturing for the group to stay put. "You boys stay right there," he said. "I'll get your ball for you."

As he reached the back gate, Maxwell came out of his garden, a hoe in one hand.

"Come on, Leonard," Will Flanders said. "The boys didn't mean to knock the ball in your yard. Just bring it over here, and we'll see that it doesn't happen again."

Maxwell responded by cursing him, cursing the boys individually, and saying that "hell will freeze over" before that ball ever left his yard.

Gale's father didn't bother with the latch. He put one hand on top of the gate and sprung over it. He strode to the back porch, retrieved the ball from the crock, and started back for the gate. As he reached it, Maxwell punched him in the head from behind, not with the hoe handle, but with a fist.

Will Flanders' knees buckled. It had to hurt. But he recovered, said to Maxwell, "I'm not going to fight you, old man," and unlatched the gate and walked out.

Then there came a sound almost like a lion's roar! Grandpa Flanders was crossing the street at a half-run!

"Hold on there, Maxwell," he said, approaching the gate.

Will Flanders grabbed Grandpa Flanders by the arm and tried to turn him back. Grandpa Flanders, with one hand on the gate, shook his fist in Maxwell's face.

"My son won't fight you because you're such a decrepit old man, and a sorry excuse for a man at that," he said. "But I'm about your age. Step out here in the alley. Come on, if you're not yellow, you old bastard!"

Maxwell stumbled backwards, regained his balance, and turned and went into the house.

Tom thought for a minute Grandpa Flanders was going in after him. But Gale's dad, saying, "Dad. Dad, remember your blood pressure now. He's not worth it. Come on. Come on," got him turned and headed back across the street.

Will Flanders tossed the boys the ball and wagged a finger at them.

"Careful, boys," he said.

It was a while before anyone could get back into the spirit of the games.

CHAPTER 34:
THE BITTER TASTE OF MELONS

Another summer day started innocently enough for Tom Sycamore and friends. Little did they know that it would be a day remembered for years to come as The Day of the Melon Escapade – a day that would lead to the Hooperville Braves standing before a Turnip County judge as accused criminals. And a day that would bring joy to the wicked heart of Leonard Maxwell, for its events proved to his warped mind that these boys were and always would be a bunch of hoodlums.

It was turning out to be an unusually hot summer, hot but wet. The boys, tired of swimming, were lounging on the tree house deck in amongst the big water maple's leafy limbs. Not a breeze ruffled the foliage as Dale Riley, raising on one elbow, said, "You know what I'd like to have more'n anything else right now? Do you know what I'm cravin-n-n-n' for?"

The others waited.

"It's to sink my teeth into a big, sweet, juicy watermelon – let the juice run right down into my belly button."

Peculiar it is how mere words can make the human digestive juices flare up in anticipation of taking in some particular delight.

Vince raised up, spit out the weed he'd been chewing on, and wiped a fleck of slobber from his chin. "You do come up with some of the most interestin' ideas off and on, Mr. Riley," he said. "And I presume that you know that there's a whole field of what you crave just layin' and wastin' a short distance down the river from here?"

"Hey-y-y-y that's right," Hobo said. "I forgot about old man Turner raising all them melons every year. Say, let's do go down there and have us one."

He was already on his feet.

It was Tom who raised the question of price, at the same time wondering how much money remained in the can in the forks above the tree house.

And, just like in the initiation test in the strawberry patch, it was Gale who had snickered and said, "A bought melon wouldn't hold a straw to the taste of a swiped melon, Tom. Swiped melons are the sweetest melons of all."

"Commandeered. That's the word, Gale," Vince said. "The spoils of war. We could call it that."

"Sounds to me like it's called stealin'," Tom said. "And stealing, the last time I checked it out, can still wind you up in jail."

"Oh, my gosh, Tom!" Keith said. "Old Throckmorton Turner's got so many melons he would never miss one. Every year he lets some lay in the field and rot. Probably sells two-thirds of what he raises. He's too stingy to give one away."

Before Tom could offer any further argument, Dale added that old Throckmorton "deserves to have someone cart off the lot of 'em. I'm for going and gettin' one. Right now!"

It was Gale who revived the Robin Hood philosophy. "Can't we still be in the business of stealin' from the rich and givin' to he poor?" he asked, stealing a sideways glance at Vince.

Vince snapped his fingers. "That's right," he said. "Aunt Maud and Uncle Frank. They're not so poor, of course, but they are on Social Security. Boy, do they love ripe watermelon. And remember how she shared that taffy she made with us a while back, even let us help with the pullin' of it?"

Mercy. Now, with the mention of the taffy, there was a conflict of mouth watering.

Shaking it off, Vince said, "But two's all we're gonna take. We'll be careful not to destroy any vines. We'll just tiptoe into that patch, pick out the biggest, ripest two, and bring them back up here to the tree house. We'll eat one and then take Aunt Maud her's. No, no. We'd better take her's to her first."

"Why're we settin' here discussin' this? Gonna form a committee or sumptin? " Dale said. "I can taste it, I tell 'ya. Let's go-o-o-UH!"

194

It was Vince who had made the decision to include the *Reuben James* in the raid.

"We might be talkin' twenty, thirty pounds or more here. No use strainin' ourselves in this hot sun" he said.

As they made their way down the ladder, Tom silently resigned himself to thinking that perhaps swiping a melon or two in this situation would probably be striking a blow for justice.

The six of them piled into the *Reuben James*. Hobo and Keith shared the oars as they rowed downstream, nosed the johnboat into a clump of willows, pulled it lightly up onto the sandy shore without tying it off, then made their way single file up through the horseweeds to the top of the bank.

They parted some weeds and pulled in a collective breath as they gazed out over watermelon heaven. Dark green melons covered the field for as far as they could see, up to where they disappeared at a rise in the patch.

No one spoke as they looked up the field and then down. They held their breath as they strained their ears for sounds.

"This is the way thieves behave," Tom whispered.

"Hush," Vince said. "We ain't thieves. We're good guys. We're just re-distributing the wealth."

He tiptoed in. The others followed. Tom felt naked and vulnerable as he left the cover of the tall horseweeds.

Hobo made his way from melon to melon, examining each as though he was a jeweler in a storehouse of precious stones. He used his knuckles to tap a deep green melon that seemed too large for a man to carry.

"This is one we want, boys. This one's ripe," he said.

"Plug it, Hobo. Make sure," Vince said.

Hobo pulled his knife from his pocket and had cut one side of what was intended to be a small triangle when things quickly flipped out of control. A voice boomed out over the field: "What the hell's goin' on here?"

The boys froze in their tracks, like statues. They turned their heads in the direction the voice had come from. "It's old man Turner himself," Vince muttered as they saw a man in bibbed overalls advancing from the weeds at the edge of the patch. A huge, dirty-white dog was at his side. Tom could see the hair standing up on the back of the dog's neck.

Tom was too scared to talk. Vince knew no such bounds. "Well, Mr. Turner. What a pleasure to see you, sir," he stammered. "We, uh, was just going to cut across your field to the highway to get some gas for our motor."

"The hell you say," Turner said, he and the dog moving toward the boys, the dog uttering low growls from its throat. "Looked to me like you were cuttin' a melon. Looks to me like you boys are here to steal my melons."

He drew a long knife from a sheaf on his belt and, still moving toward the boys, said, "I know who you boys are. That bunch of Hooperville brats. Well, just stay where you are. Don't you boys run now."

Don't run? A man comes at you with a wolf and a knife and says don't run, Tom was thinking.

It was a crazy thing to say. Their feet threw clods into the air as they turned and headed for the river.

"Sic 'em Fang!" Turner said as the boys drilled two or three new paths through the tall horseweeds.

They came out of the weeds into the willows with the melon farmer and the dog in hot pursuit. Dale had tripped and fell and Tom stopped to help him up. Everyone realized there was no time to push off in the boat, so they left it. Vince, Hobo, Gale and Keith, out ahead of Tom and Dale, had turned upriver and opened the throttle.

Turner turned that way, and Dale and Tom, in their confusion, headed downriver, the ugly white dog close behind them, growling and barking. They hit a clear strip of sand and clay and tried to use it for a runway. But they couldn't shake the dog. He was near nipping at their heels.

The fleeing boys both spied the overhanging tree limb, and without missing a stride, leaped and grabbed it, swinging themselves upwards into the tree, hoping to catch their legs in another limb, higher up. But the dog had managed to get his teeth into the seat of Tom's baggy britches. Dale kicked sideways and landed a foot in the dog's side. The dog let loose and dropped to the ground. The two swung on up into the tree and pulled themselves up to the next highest limb, then slithered along the limb to the tree's trunk. The dog was going crazy. He reared up and put his front paws on the tree trunk, sounding off like a hound that'd treed a 'coon.

Tom and Dale were in that maple for what seemed a long time. Finally, from upstream, they heard old Turner calling, "Here, Fang! Here, Fang! Come on, boy."

The dog whined, growled, started off in the direction of the voice, came back to circle the tree, growled up at the two boys one last time, and disappeared into the willows upstream.

After what they considered a safe time had elapsed, Dale and Tom climbed down and made their way up along the water's edge.

"If they come after us again, we'll take to the river," Dale whispered. "Swim it if we have to. If the dog comes after us we'll drown him."

They could scarcely believe their eyes when they came to the *Reuben James*, pulled up on the sand as they had left it, but now the rope was tied to a willow tree.

And the boat was loaded down with watermelons!

"You see what old Turner's done?" Dale asked, staring at the boat. "Can you believe this? He's settin' us up...."

Tom grabbed him by the arm and shushed him as voices drifted down from the melon patch.

"Let's get outta here, Dale," Tom said. "I think we're in deep trouble."

But thirty or forty yards upstream from the boat their curiosity overcame their fear. They scrambled up into a tall tulip poplar, high enough to where they could see over the tops of the willows and weeds and over the top of the bank and into the watermelon patch. Turner was talking to a man in a policeman's uniform and gesturing wildly with his arms. At their feet lay a pile of melons, enough to half fill a pickup. Some were busted open, exposing their red innards to the sun.

"That's Sheriff Wilson," Dale whispered.

Their hiding place was close enough that they could hear most of what was being said. Turner's voice was high enough that you probably could have heard him on the other side of the river.

"They came in here, John, and did all this. And you saw their boat down there. The little hoodlums are going to pay for this! I know every one of 'em."

The sheriff scribbled notes as Turner added ... the Riley boy and the Hooper boy, that Royalton kid ... Flanders .... the Richards brat ... there's

197

another I don't know, but he's a blond kid with a tooth missing in front."

"That lyin' son-of-a-gun is settin' us up," Dale whispered.

The sheriff, folding his notebook and sticking it in his shirt pocket, said, "I know these boys, Turner. I just can't imagine them doing this kind of damage to a man's crops. They've never been in any kind of trouble that I know of."

"This younger generation's going straight to hell," Turner said. "And they're gonna pay for this. I want you to see to that. I want warrants for the lot of 'em."

The sheriff and Turner climbed into Turner's pickup and drove away. Dale and Tom slipped down from the tree and galloped upstream toward the tree house.

CHAPTER 35:
FORGIVENESS FOR FORBIDDEN FRUIT

On the way up the riverbank Tom and Dale met the four other Braves. They had decided to come back, cautiously, to look for them – ready to take flight again if necessary. After leaving the melon patch owner lagging far behind (actually, he had not even given chase, but had gone back to the melon patch to do his dirty work before calling the sheriff), Vince, Hobo, Gale and Keith collapsed on the sand under the tree house to catch their breath and still the beating of their frightened hearts. After a while, they voted unanimously to go back and find out what happened to Dale and Tom.

"They might have been ripped apart by that dog," Hobo said.

"Yes, and remember our motto: All for one, and one for all," Gale added.

Now the six of them huddled under the big trees in Sherwood Forest. Vince circled Dale and Tom. "I don't see any blood," he said, "so at least the beast didn't get you? We didn't know what happened to you."

Dale told of climbing the tree to escape the dog. "His name is Fang – can you believe that?" he said.

Then they gave the report about what had happened at the *Reuben James*, about the busted melons in the patch, and of overhearing Throckmorton Turner's lying report to Sheriff John Wilson.

"Sheriff Wilson! He was there?" Vince said.

"Oh yes," Tom said. "And he's got our names."

"We're in big trouble," Vince said, rubbing his chin and pacing.

Moving a little, stopping to listen, then moving ahead again, they made their way back to the *Reuben James* and dumped the melons out onto the shore.

"Think maybe we ought to take one of them, since we're gonna get blamed for the lot of them anyway?" Keith asked.

"Are you crazy? The one thing we don't want to do is take a melon," Vince said.

"I've lost my taste for watermelon anyway," Gale said.

They rowed back upstream past the tree house, tied the boat off, and scattered for their separate homes.

Later that evening, at Gale's house, the worried Braves got together in the backyard before going inside. They decided on their course of action. Being reasonably sure that sheriff's deputies would be arriving at their homes the next day with summonses issued on Turner's complaint, they decided to confess all before bedtime.

"It's all my fault," Carrie Sycamore said after Tom told her that evening about the melon escapade. "I never should have taken that job and left you here alone with too much time on your hands. I've been so worried about Flint and his situation that I have neglected my younger son, and now he's turned to a life of crime."

She apologized for the latter remark as she placed one hand on Tom's shoulder at the foot of the stairs.

"The eating of forbidden fruit is what got the whole human race into trouble. Thank God for forgiveness," she said. "You go to bed and say your prayers. It sounds like the villain here is this mean farmer, what-his-name, Turner? He'll get what's coming to him. Justice will be served, Tom. And you chalk this whole thing up to a valuable lesson."

As anticipated, a sheriff's deputy showed up in Hooperville before noon and issued summonses for the Braves. All were named on a summons except Tom. His name was not known by Turner, who simply described him as "the blond-headed boy with a front tooth missing."

They were to appear in Turnip County Court the next day, a Friday, before Judge Harman Bellman, to face their accuser.

Most people in the village believed the boys' side of the story concerning the melons they were accused of destroying and stealing. Most felt that

Throckmorton Turner was a stingy old man who cared for nothing but his own wellbeing. Grandpa Flanders tried unsuccessfully to get Will Flanders to drive him to the Turner farm and let him call him out and "talk some sense into his head."

Will Flanders took off from his work long enough to drive the boys to the county seat of Turnipsburg and enter the courtroom with them. He carried with him money from the parents of Hobo, Dale and Vince, as well as Keith Richards' grandmother.

Tom's mother went on to work, saying she would turn the matter over to Bruce Sycamore to settle when he came home from the camp cars that evening.

All witnesses were sworn in, all agreeing to tell "the truth, the whole truth, and nothing but the truth, so help me God."

All six boys told the same story about not touching one of Throckmorton Turner's melons, except the one that Hobo had started to plug.

"Well, then, I wonder who cut up a truckload of them in my field?" Turner said mockingly in his turn from the witness stand. "And they had that boat of theirs loaded down. You – here he turned to face Sheriff Wilson – saw it for yourself."

The sheriff clinched one fist and rolled his eyes toward the courtroom ceiling.

The judge listened intently to Turner's testimony. The farmer said he never drew any knife and did not sic his dog on the boys.

"Why, Fang wouldn't hurt a flea anyway," Turner said, bringing an uneasy snicker from Tom and a pounding of the gavel from the judge.

The judge seemed somewhat skeptical of Turner's entire testimony.

However, he said, the fact remained that, according to their own testimony, the boys admitted to being in the melon patch with the intent of taking a melon (they decided against sharing with His Honor that they intended to take one melon to Uncle Frank and Aunt Maud, too. "It might make them an accomplice," Vince had said.)

The judge even at one point admitted to having "swiped a melon once" when he was a boy. "But I was in the wrong," he said, "and you boys are in the wrong. As to the damaged melons in the patch and those in your boat, all we know for sure is that they were left in your wake. You admit to being in another man's melon patch with the intent to take a melon without paying for it. And for that, you must now pay. I'm sure you boys have learned your lesson."

The judge ordered each parent, along with Keith Richards' grandmother, to pay Turner nine dollars and fifty cents in damages, plus court costs of fifty cents each.

Gale's father paid the fines for each of the boys, except Tom. Throckmorton, after learning Tom's name and where he lived, said he would stop by there on Saturday to collect.

After supper Friday evening, Bruce Sycamore listened intently to Tom's account of Turner having cut up melons in the patch and having loaded others in the boys' johnboat.

"Sounds like Turner figured out a way to sell more than $50 worth of melons – melons that probably would have rotted on the vine," he said.

After lecturing Tom on never again trying to take something that did not belong to him, he canceled the scheduled switching.

"So this Throckmorton Turner says he'll be by tomorrow to collect his nine dollars and fifty cents, eh? Well, that's good. Let him come. I'll see that he collects a little interest, too. And while we're at it, we'll give him a little lesson about lying. And while we're at it, we'll teach him a thing or two about justice."

He pounded his right fist into his left palm.

Although Tom's father sent in the court costs of fifty cents, he never paid Throckmorton his money.

For Turner turned out to be a wiser man in some respects than most people thought him to be.

He never came by the Sycamore house to claim it.

CHAPTER 36:
DOWN TO THE SEA ON THE *INDY*

PFC. Flint Sycamore got home for a short leave before he would go on by train for the West Coast, where he would take a ship bound for the Pacific islands. He was wearing his dress blues and Tom thought he looked just like the Marine in the garden. And speaking of him, as Flint gave Tom a bear hug on the back porch, Tom looked around his big brother's shoulder and there, in the corn, stood Lance Cpl. Leon Selby, giving a sharp salute!

As Flint pushed Tom out at arm's length for a better look at him, he noticed the pleasant smile on his kid brother's face as he looked steadfastly out toward the garden. He turned to see what he was looking at. "You looked like you saw somebody, Tom. I don't see anybody. What is it?"

"Well, nothing, really…"

Suddenly they noticed Chopper, leaping against the cage wire, nearly turning somersaults in his attempt to get the two brothers to notice him.

"I was sorry to hear about Chopper," Flint said, going to the cage and stooping down to greet the little dog. "He looks fine to me, though. I'd say he's going to be all right."

"Momma says we have to keep him up for at least 10 days, maybe longer. It's been about that now."

Carrie Sycamore frolicked around like a young girl. She was happy to see her oldest son, yet not able to fully enjoy it for thinking about the future. She was still certain the Japanese would never surrender and that Flint would wind up as a part of an allied invasion force that would hit their home islands.

"My mother, the steel mill worker," Flint said as he waltzed her around in the living room.

"Yes, and since I started working," she said, "the Japanese surrendered

Okinawa, so you can see I'm making a difference," said Carrie, laughing.

Bruce Sycamore was not a man who showed his emotions, but when he came home from work that Friday evening to find his oldest son waiting, he put a bear hug on him, pushed him away at arm's length to look him up and down, then squeezed him hard again.

Upstairs that night, as Tom made his way down the hallway past Flint's room, Flint called him in and told him he had a gift for him.

"Hold out your hands, cup them together, and close your eyes," he said.

Tom did so, and Flint filled his hands with coins. It was the most money Tom had seen at one time. There was money for treats for the boys at Miss Louella's candy and notions store and at Mr. Gammons' grocery store. And there was enough picture show money for several weeks. He couldn't stop thanking his big brother for making him rich.

It was a wonderful week, but one that passed all too quickly. Tom didn't get to see Flint as much as he wanted because girls he had graduated high school with flocked around him, wanting to drive him here or there.

Will Flanders volunteered to drive Flint to the depot in Shawnee, where he would catch a train taking him to the West Coast.

As Flint, in uniform, stood on the front porch by his seabag, waiting for Mr. Flanders to pick him up, his mother tried to squeeze in as many last minute requests as possible.

She had one arm around his waist and was imploring him to "be sure now, son, and write. Write more often that you did in training camp. Write every day, tell us where you're at and what's happening." Flint promised to do so.

Didn't he have any idea where his ship was headed for, his mother wanted to know.

"All I know so far is that my orders call for me to report to a cruiser docked in San Francisco Bay. The ship is the *USS Indianapolis.* "

Tom was a bit startled when he saw the Marine of the Victory Garden standing at the corner of the house. Somehow he had about the same feeling that he had had when the Marine warned him of the mad dog in the garden.

Why was that, he wondered.

Flint had kept his promise to his mother about writing often. A letter came almost every day, sometimes two letters a day. Carrie Sycamore had rushed home from the mill to change out of her work coveralls and begin preparing supper for her and Tom. She sat at the kitchen table as she tore open the latest letter from her Marine son.

The war in Europe had ended two months previous and action in the Pacific Theater had slowed as preparations were made for an invasion of the Japanese homeland. The boys on board the *Indianapolis* were all talking about the pending invasion and whether they would survive such a battle.

"Dear Mom and Dad (and Tom)," Flint's latest letter began, *"we're sailing out from San Francisco July 15. That's coming right up, We don't know exactly where we're headed, but Momma I will write and let you know as soon as I find out."*

Flint and three dozen or so other Marines had their own quarters, away from the regular sailors on the big cruiser, which was as long as two football fields.

There were 1,196 on board, and all thought they were to be getting ready to take part in the invasion of Japan.

Little did they know that they would be carrying the weapon that would bring Japan to its knees and save perhaps as many as half a million lives of Americans and their allies by avoiding the invasion.

The rest of the letter Flint spent trying to assure his mother that the war would probably be over by the time the *Indianapolis* reached the other side of the Pacific. Since May the ship, under the command of Captain Charles McVay, had been docked for repairs at Mare Island, thirty miles north of San Francisco. She had limped back from Okinawa after sustaining a nearly fatal kamikaze attack. Now, having completed her sea trials, she was ready for her next assignment.

Flint was on guard duty the day the ship pulled into Hunters Point Navy Yard, just outside San Francisco Bay. He watched as two army trucks stopped on the wharf. A crane unloaded a wooden crate that appeared to be about five feet high, five feet wide and fifteen feet long. It also loaded onto the *Indy* a metal canister about 18 inches wide and knee high.

205

The crate was lashed down in the port hanger; the canister, holding uranium 235, was fastened to the deck near the captain's cabin.

The ship, under much secrecy, got underway early on the morning of July 16. Flint's next letter told of passing under the Golden Gate Bridge and clearing the bay for the open sea – destination still unknown.

On the same day the *Indy* left San Francisco Bay, a submarine, under the command of Lt. Commander Mochitsura Hashimoto, launched from a naval base on the coast of Japan.

Within two weeks, in the miles deep ocean between Guam and Leyte, their paths would cross – with most disastrous results for Flint and the others on board the cruiser.

CHAPTER 37:
CHOPPER, BEST FRIEND

"Looks like you'll get to meet the Marine's wife soon now, Tom," said Sunday school teacher Jim Galloway.

He had held Tom back after the class as the other boys scampered on up the steps to the sanctuary.

"Mary Ann Selby gave birth to a healthy baby boy last week, Tom. Can you imagine what she named him? I guess you could – Leon Richard Selby, Junior."

Tom's face beamed with delight. He couldn't have been happier or prouder had it been his own little baby brother.

"When's she coming? Is she still going to dedicate the baby here?"

"As soon as possible, as soon as he doctor approves travel for them. It might even be next Sunday. She wants to come by early, before church, so she can meet and talk to you, and see what you've done with the garden her husband planted."

Tom's eyes widened as his Sunday school teacher continued, "I went to her mother's house in Shawnee again and talked to both of them. Her doctor has her on bed rest. But as soon as she and the baby can travel, she wants to have it dedicated here at church. Preacher Hackelbee is making the arrangements."

"Well....uh, what did you tell her? Did you tell her about us seeing her husband and all, I mean?"

"I didn't go into any great detail about it, but yes, I mentioned it to them. Mrs. Selby perked up when she learned you had seen him several times out in the garden he had planted."

Tom thought how sad it was that he had not been able to communicate with the Marine. This would certainly be good news for him.

After dinner, Tom went out to Chopper's pen with some table scraps and a fresh can of water from the cistern. Surely, he thought, he would be releasing the little dog next week, maybe as early as the next day.

He opened the door of the pen and placed the food in the dog's dish, then poured the fresh, cool water into the pan. Chopper's appetite had been good, but this time he did not touch the food. He sniffed the water dish, then did almost a back flip, running halfway around the pen and cowering in the far corner. Tom hadn't heard Chopper growl like that since the standoff with Leader upon arriving in town. Tom called, but Chopper lunged against the back of the pen so violently that he fell back on his back. Tom was so shocked by this behavior that he didn't even think to close the cage door. He barely had time to leap back before the dog plunged through the gate and was off on a staggering run through the garden.

"Chopper! Chopper, come back here!" Tom shouted. Tom's father came out of the building to see what the commotion was. He saw Chopper crawl through an opening in the fence, run into the churchyard, and continue on an erratic course down the street toward the river.

"This is bad, Tom. Hold back now," Bruce Sycamore said. "That's a running fit. Your little dog I don't think is any longer your little dog. Wait here."

He came back out of the house with his .22 rifle, putting shells into the chamber. Carrie followed her husband out, a dishrag in her hands. She looked at Tom, saw the agony on his face. She put her arm around his shoulder and pulled him in against her side. "Oh, Tom," she said. "I'm so sorry."

She knew there was no need to try to talk Tom out of going with his father. The two of them went down the street in the direction the dog had gone. His father carried the rifle over his shoulder by its strap.

"We can't allow him to suffer, Tom. He has to be put away, out of his misery," said Bruce Sycamore, pausing to put his arm around Tom and pulling him into his side.

Tom tried hard to choke back sobs as they went down under the first rise. They met Hobo coming up, in a hurry. He was carrying three catfish on a stringer.

"Tom! It's happened! That dog of yours has gone mad!" Hobo said. "He came down the path toward me. I called to him, 'Here, Chopper.' He charged right on into me. I swung these fish at him, but he nipped me on the leg and ran on."

He stuck his leg out for Tom and his dad to see. Blood was trickling down from a flesh wound on his calf.

"Which way did he go, Hobo?" Tom's father asked. Hobo saw the rifle over his shoulder. His eyes met Tom's. "Don't worry about me," he said. "Take care of your dog. Remember, Tom, he's really not your little dog any-more. He's gone mad, and I'm so sorry."

A tear streamed down Tom's face as he nodded.

Hobo spoke to Bruce Sycamore. "He went into that clump of willows there, just under the bank, right about where we've got the boat tied, Tom."

Tom and his dad went on and Hobo scampered up the hill for home. Bruce readied his rifle in firing position as they approached the clump of willows.

Tom whistled for his dog and called his name, as though hoping that this was all just a bad dream. Maybe Chopper would come running out of there to him and be his old self.

But as they drew closer to the dog's hiding place, they heard the growls coming from his throat. Tom's dad cocked the hammer back on the rifle as they bent to peer through an opening in the willows. They saw the dog. He was snapping at the air, and gnawing and clawing at weeds and dirt. Tom turned and put his hands over his ears as he saw his father creep closer, the gun pointed straight ahead.

Tom heard the rifle crack once, then again.

Silence.

Then his dad spoke. "He never suffered, Tom. At least, his suffering's over. You go back up and get one of those empty potato sacks out of the building. We'll bury him out in back of the garden."

Tom returned with the sack and waited while his father went into the willows and returned, carrying Chopper in the sack.

"He was a good dog, Tom," he father said as they made their way up the bank. "He just happened to be in the wrong place at the wrong time. What you've got to do now is just be thankful for all the good times you and him had. And know that life is like this, son. Men and animals – the whole world – is under the curse. For now."

Tom would never forget how this little dog overcame his fears of the spirit and saved him from being bitten by the mad dog. That was the Chopper he would remember.

But, oh, why can't time be rolled back, and the dead brought to life again?

With some help from his father, Tom dug the grave, out near the cherry tree in back of the garden. Carrie Sycamore stood nearby, and when the work was finished, she hugged her damaged young son up close to her side. His father touched his shoulder. And Tom was not surprised when he felt the touch of someone, or something, on the top of his head, and felt warmth spreading down to his very toes.

His mother held a bouquet of red and yellow flowers she had picked from her side yard. She placed them on top of the little mound of earth. Tom added a stake with a board nailed across it. On the white board, with black paint, he had scrawled the words, "Chopper. Best Friend. July 1945."

Will Flanders had driven Hobo and his mom up to Doc Meadows' office, which was in a room off the side of the doctor's house. Hobo's dad had buried the catfish in the back yard, not certain if Chopper had bitten or slobbered on one of them or not.

Later, as the boys gathered at Gale's house, Hobo showed them the white patch on his stomach.

"Big, long needle, right in the belly," he said. "You talk about hurtin'… and thirteen more to go."

Bruce Sycamore offered to pay Hobo's doctor bill, but Thelma and Wayne Hooper wouldn't hear of it.

"I'm sorry about your dog, Tom," Wayne Hooper said. "But I'm real glad my boy's not gonna go mad – not any madder than he already is, anyway."

Tom, of course, was not the first youngster to lose a little dog whose one goal in life seemed only to please his master – to be by his master's side through life's ups and downs, and to remain loyal no matter what life dished out.

As for where such animals go when they die, Tom wondered and wondered, but found no sure answer.

But he did not believe Chopper's life ended finally beneath this mound of dirt under the cherry tree.

After all, how could Heaven be Heaven without the love of a dog?

CHAPTER 38:
THE GHOST ON THE BEND

With the Watermelon Escapade turning out as it did, the Hooperville Braves were not likely to involve themselves ever again in taking another person's belongings, even when the Robin Hood Factor seemed to fit into the scheme of things.

But two men in the village wanted to make certain the boys could handle temptation were it ever to put its loving, lying arms around them again. The hard-working Jim Galloway brought the Boy Scouts of America to the rescue. He talked the church into sponsoring a troop and enlisted the help of Delbert Blitz, a kindly gentleman who had two daughters but no sons and who had recently retired from the shoe factory across the river in Shawnee.

Making good scouts out of the Braves became the chief ambition of these two men. They set out to make sure they were trustworthy, loyal, courteous, obedient, reverent and all those other good and fine things that should inhabit young boys who must grow up to be good citizens.

At first, Vince wasn't so sure he would join. The Braves had all the good deedin' they could handle, he said, what with killing whole battalions of Japs, supplying several older residents with fresh catfish the river yielded up on the trotline, and just in general helping the poor and the oppressed.

Nevertheless, when Mr. Blitz and Mr. Galloway announced plans to introduce boys to the program at a wiener and marshmallow roast planned for the head of School House Hollow, Vince decided the gang would all go, just to check it out. The church, after all, was buying the hotdogs and marshmallows and it would be a shame to see them go to waste.

Notices of the event were posted as far away as Killin Hollow and to the section above the bridge, home of the "Upriver Boys."

There were about twenty-five boys who gathered around a big campfire under the trees that evening to fill up with food and fellowship. It was the first time the Braves had seen many of the boys since school let out.

Delbert had invited Dick Karens, an Eagle Scout from a troop in Shawnee, to explain what the Boy Scouts was all about and to help with the organization of what was to become Troop 160.

Karens was at least five years older than even Hobo. Vince thought he was "some kind of prima donna." He whispered his doubts that Karens had ever swum the river, tasted forbidden moonlight fruit, or killed a Jap soldier, for that matter. Besides that, he was a Buckeye.

But Karens knew some great campfire songs, and soon had all joining in. And he told a ghost story that had the boys all pushing closer to the fire; glancing over their shoulders at the darkened woods where the firelight cast eerie shadows.

He told them the story of the mysterious blue light that wiped out nearly an entire troop bivouacking in the hills of Shawnee County. They would learn more about it and learn more good songs when they spent a week at Camp Yoyo, the long-time Boy Scout camp in the southern Ohio hills of Shawnee County.

Hobo, who believed fiercely in spirits, was spellbound by Karens' story. And Vince seemed highly impressed when Karens left the meeting driving his own car. Maybe this scouting wasn't so bad.

It was probably 11 p.m. or later when the festivities ended and boys started making their way home, many saying they would attend a follow-up meeting planned for the following week in the basement of the Hooperville church. Some boys were picked up by their parents in the school parking lot. Others had ridden bikes or walked. Hobo and Tom and a boy from Killin Hollow, Emil Hardin, got the assignment of helping secure the site, making sure the campfire was out. They stirred the embers and carried water from the nearby creek in a small metal bucket Delbert had brought for that purpose. Tom noticed Emil wouldn't make the trip down to the creek unless Hobo or Tom was with him.

The three of them and Delbert Blitz were the last to leave the hollow. The hoot owls and whippoorwills serenaded them as they followed Mr. Blitz, who had the only flashlight, along the path through the woods, across the creek, and out onto the school grounds. Emil picked up his bike he'd left there and pushed it along as he walked out the lane toward Route Ten with the others. Emil kept glancing over his shoulder. He stayed as close on Delbert's heels as he could and tried to keep Hobo on one side and Tom on the other.

Hobo was still talking about the Dick Karens ghost tale. "Wasn't that something," he said, "how that blue light appeared and shot out beams, striking them poor boys in the forehead?"

"It was a good story," Delbert said, "but shucks and hello scissors, we've got a more notorious ghost right here at home – right out at the mouth of this hollow, in fact. Did you boys ever hear about the Ghost of Henson's Bend?"

Hobo said he'd heard his dad mention it, but he didn't know the full gist of the thing. He said his understanding was that the incident that brought on the ghost "happened right out there on Route Ten, where the road bends around and goes up and around Farmer Henson's pasture. Didn't it?"

"That's right," Delbert said. "My dad – rest his soul – experienced it one night. Of course that was some time ago. No one's heard anything out of the ghost for a while now. Maybe he finally gave up."

It didn't take much pleading from Hobo and Tom to get Delbert to tell the tale. Emil didn't say anything, but got so close to Delbert he brushed against his arm, and kept his bicycle on the outside. On the other side, Hobo and Tom jockeyed for position next to Delbert.

"Well, hello scissors now, if it's gonna scare you boys, I won't even tell it."

"No. It's all right. We're not afraid. It's just that we can't see where we're steppin'. Go ahead," Hobo said.

Delbert cleared his throat and the four all stopped in a wad as he looked down toward the highway and began the tale.

"It was my father who told me the story of the crash that took place on the curve there late one night; how the A-model Ford careened off the road, rolled over and over, and came to rest at the bottom of the ravine.

"The woman passenger was mortally wounded. Her male companion, the driver, crawled up to the top of the hill to try to flag down help. I don't know if it was that nobody would stop, or that no one came along. Probably the latter, for the accident happened around midnight.

"Anyway, next morning they found his body just off the shoulder and, of course, recovered the woman's body from the ravine.

"After that, so my dad said, people having to travel this stretch of the highway around midnight often experienced a strange, supernatural force. And, as I said, my dad had himself encountered the Ghost of Henson's Bend one moonless night.

"He had taken his old pickup to Shawnee to get supplies and tarried much longer than he intended, even stopping at the Cow Shed for a few beers with some boys he knew. It was close to midnight when he crossed the bridge and headed down Route 10. As he rounded Henson's Bend out here and started up the hill, it felt like something picked up on the rear bumper and lifted the wheels off the road. He pushed the gas pedal and the wheels were spinning, but – hello scissors – he wasn't moving!"

Tom stared off into the distance toward Route 10 and felt a chill run down his spine. Hobo was wishing they hadn't asked for the tale. Emil was touching Delbert's arm on the other side. He pulled his bike in close and looked down to make sure his wheels kept turning.

Delbert hurried on with the story: "My father said it was at least a long minute or two before he was able to break loose from whatever it was that held him in its grip. When it did, he burned rubber getting away from that place, and he said he never went around that curve again after dark."

Others, Delbert said, told of having the same experience if they rounded that bend around the midnight hour. "They would push down hard on the pedal. The wheels would spin and whine, but the cars were held in place for a brief time, as though some invisible something was lifting and pulling on the rear bumper."

It must have been near midnight by the time the group reached the mouth of the hollow, where Emil would leave them and go his separate way.

He was keeping up a continual barrage of small talk, all the time holding the handlebars of his bike and staring off into the darkness toward the bend.

"Son-of-a-gun, Mr. Blitz," he finally said. "I wish you hadn't told that story, since I have to pedal right up that hill and around that bend."

Delbert chuckled, then tried to fortify his spirits.

"Oh, it's just a story," he said. "Probably nothing to it at all. Except there

214

was a wreck there in which a man and a woman were killed."

Emil mentioned the possibility of spending the night with Tom. But there was no telephone at Tom's and it was far too late to try to use the one at Gale's house. Everybody would be asleep by now. Except Emil's mother. Emil knew she would be waiting up for him.

He finally climbed on his bike, said, "I'm gonna pedal around that curve and up the hill at fifty miles an hour," and rode off into the darkness.

––––––––––

The next day was Saturday and Tom and the Braves went to the Garden to help the Phantom out of his latest troubles, and watch Jimmy Wakely ride high and handsome in "Springtime in Texas." Gale's dad dropped them off and came back to pick them up in front of the movie house. Good thing he did, too, because a bunch of Ohio boys were really taunting them.

He dropped them off at Thelma's, where he knew they couldn't get into any trouble, and could walk home after they spent what little change they had after buying their show tickets.

Tom was playing the pinball machine when Jim Dempsey, a friend of Emil Hardin's who had been at the scout meeting, walked up to him and said, "What in the world did you guys do to Emil last night after we left? He was without a doubt the most disturbed boy I ever saw."

"Emil? Why, what happened to him?" Tom asked.

"Well, me and three or four other boys was standing out in front here, just jawing. It was about midnight and Thelma was getting ready to close.

"All of a sudden we look up the road and in the glare of a car's lights we see somebody runnin' like a madman toward us, packin' a bicycle over one shoulder. I mean he's really pickin' 'em up and layin' 'em down, right up the middle of the highway. Wonder he wasn't run over.

"He came up to the light here in front of Thelma's and we could make out it was Emil. We could see his face had lost all its color, like a man does when he's seen a ghost or something."

Dempsey went on to tell about how Emil had flung his bike down in the gravel and kept mumbling over and over, "I was pumpin' and pumpin' but I couldn't move. My gawd, my gawd! It was awful!"

He said Emil ran in to Thelma's, saying he needed a Coke for his nerves.

215

"A couple of the boys was really worried about him," Jim Dempsey said. "They'd never seen Emil act like that. They followed him in the restaurant, trying to calm him. I guess Thelma gave him a couple of aspirin. We never did find out what was wrong with him, though.

"But while he was inside, I found out what was wrong with his bicycle – why it wouldn't go. Why he was packin' it. And I fixed it for him. It didn't take much.

"It was just that his chain had slipped off the sprocket."

CHAPTER 39:
SCOUTS OVERCOME STATE LINES

Another Gold Star went up in the window of another Hooperville home. Joe Dunaway, 22-year-old son of Dick Dunaway, reported missing in action in the China-Burma-India Theater on July 4, was now confirmed dead, shot by Japanese soldiers who had captured him.

And in Shawnee, John Wayne's "Back to Bataan" got a repeat performance, this time showing at the Laroy. Despite their Sunday school teacher's shaming of their war games, Vince could hardly wait to get out of the theater and back to leading the Filipinos against the Japanese stronghold. At the tree house, he was quick to check out rifles, bean can hand grenades and flame throwers, and soon the marine brigade was wading ashore behind him to wipe the island clean of Japs again.

Somehow, though, the old satisfaction wasn't there. It was a lackluster performance, one Vince seemed to lose interest in before they even got into the thick of battle.

The Scouts filled a void. The church managed to come up with enough money to buy the members of Troop 160 neckerchiefs and caps to wear to a weekend Jamboree held at Camp Yoyo. Parents would have to come up with the money to buy the rest of the uniform. Only two or three boys in the troop wound up with a complete uniform. For the Braves, the neckerchiefs and hats were it. The coffee can in the fork of the tree, to which they had added some catfish money periodically, coughed up enough money to pay for two nights of lodging in the camp cabins and their meals for the three days of the Jamboree. Farmer Matt installed sideboards on his hay truck and drove Troop 160, which included the Braves as well as some of the Killin Hollow and

Upriver boys, the ten miles to the camp.

Dick Karens tried to salve over any coming disappointment by telling Troop 160 scouts they shouldn't expect to win much in the games against seasoned scouters in the various other troops. Well, he said, they perhaps could expect to do some good in the swimming competition.

And oh, did they. With the bleachers at the pool jammed with parents and siblings and other onlookers, Troop 160 took first place ribbons in freestyle, breaststroke, backstroke, sidestroke and any other stroke they wanted to match its eager scouters up in. Hobo was first in each category, with one or the other of the Braves taking second and third places.

But the diving competition went for the most part to the Shawnee boys, who spent their summer days at the public pool. Gale, Vince, Dale and Keith all tried their hand at it, but had not had enough time to master the skills needed for the springboard.

"It's not at all like coming off the limb in the tree," Vince said after his attempt in the one and one-half from the high board landed him flat of his back almost in the middle of the pool.

Hobo also whipped everybody in arm-wrestling and the standing broad-jump. Tom won the knot-tying competition.

In the tug of war, teams from Troop 38 in Shawnee and Troop 160 wound up in a tie in the finals. Neither team was able to drag the other into the mud hole between them. After pulling each other back and forth like a seesaw, officials called the tie.

As the two teams fell in the grass side by side, exhausted, Tom noticed that the Ohio team included the very bunch of Buckeyes they had exchanged fisticuffs with earlier in the summer. They were coming to recognize Tom and the Braves, too.

But an amazing thing took place – a testimony to the clean fun and very real sense of camaraderie practiced and enjoyed by members of the Boy Scouts of America. State lines no longer mattered. There was no division. With all sincerity, members of both teams shook hands and congratulated each other.

Because of what they had accomplished in the swimming events, Troop 160 came in first in the overall championship. The Ohio boys from Troop 38 were among the first to line up and congratulate each of the Braves.

And the very group of six or seven Ohio boys the Braves had done battle with in front of the Playhouse now set a date to meet the Braves for a matinee at the Garden. And they would not only buy their tickets but treat them to cherry phosphates at the Playhouse after the show!

Members of both groups hung together and enjoyed each other's company for the remainder of the Jamboree.

At a campfire sing-a-long as the Camp Yoyo Jamboree wound down, the most popular song included the verse:

We come from old Kentucky, and West Virginia, too; and from the state of Ohio, and here's the things we do ...

Once back home in Hooperville, the people in the village treated the members of Troop 160 like hometown heroes. Even the Hooperville girls, who had been in the stands, showed them respect.

But that wasn't something the boys could count on for the long run.

And in coming weeks, in the Braves' hikes across Grand Bridge, even the tool booth collector, no doubt reading in the Shawnee Daily Times of the Hooperville boys' success in swimming competition at Camp Yoyo, treated them with respect – no demand for passports nor any of the other usual insults.

CHAPTER 40:
HELL TO VISIT THE INDY

Dear Mom, Dad (and Tom),

We arrived at an island named Tinian, where we unloaded the mysterious cargo we carried. We still don't know what was in the crate. That was six days ago, and now we're out to sea again, this time headed for a place called Guam. But Momma, the Japs have all been driven out of there, as well as Okinawa, the last island where fighting took place, and it looks like smooth sailing for us until this thing's over, which can't be long. I'll write when I find out more about where we're headed.

Love,

Your son, Flint

Carrie Sycamore, still in her coveralls from having completed the day shift at the steel mill, read the letter twice more before storing it inside the shoe box where she kept the others. She was filled with worry, despite Flint's attempt to ease her mind. It was all on the news, about how America and her Allies were preparing for an invasion of the Japanese home islands.

Flint did not mention what he and every Marine and sailor on board the *Indianapolis* knew: the big cruiser, her special mission completed when the cargo was delivered, was now returning to her life as one of the Navy's fighting ships.

The ship pulled out of Guam in a few days and headed for Leyte, a journey of 1,300 miles, which the ship's officers expected to cover in three days. It would be traveling without an escort, a bit unusual for a fighting ship that was not equipped with sonar. It generally depended on destroyers in its convoy to warn of enemy submarines and go after them with depth charges.

Once on Leyte, Capt. McVay's plans were to begin training his men on the ship's objective. Upon leaving Guam, he gathered his officers and told them they were going to Leyte to take part in the invasion of Kyushu, Japan's outermost home island.

Three-fourths of the crew would never live to know that, on Tinian, they had delivered the instrument that would bring Japan to her knees, nullifying any such invasion.

Flint and the other marines got word of the plan for invasion training from the marine officer in charge of them. Flint did not mention anything about that in his next letter home; only that they were headed for Leyte and were anticipating no activity from Japan's navy forces, what few were left.

"Note to Tom: Today, July 29, I learned that we passed over the deepest spot on earth. It's called the Challenger Deep. One officer told me that if Mt. Everest was on the bottom there, it would still have a mile of sea water over top of it."

As Flint penned those lines, just 60 feet below the surface, out there in the *Indy's* path, Lt. Comm. Mochitsura Hashimoto, commander of the 356-foot submarine identified as *I-58*, fretted. He knew Japan was nearing defeat, and in his four years at sea he had never sunk one enemy ship.

But that was about to change.

The Japanese sub commander could not believe his luck. His periscope was filled with the image of a large ship steaming straight for his position, a ship identified from his charts as American.

At eight p.m. July 29 Capt. Charles McVay had ordered zigzagging – an alleged defensive maneuver against attack by submarines – discontinued.

Flint was still in his sleeping compartment continuing his letter writing. Even though the ship was traveling in "yoke-modified" position, meaning all hatches and doors had been opened to draw salt breezes inside, it was still an almost unbearable ninety-seven degrees below decks. Flint was scheduled for the four a.m. security watch. After finishing the letter, he took his blanket and joined several hundred crewmembers on the decks, hoping to get a couple of hours sleep.

At eleven p.m. the ship switched to "Condition able" and was buttoned up for the night. All seemed peaceful and secure.

222

But hell was about to visit the *Indy*.

At about the same time, on the other side of the globe, the six Troop 160 members from Hooperville were about to have a hellish experience of their own.

To qualify for Merit Badges in cooking and camping, the Braves had headed for an overnight camping trip in the wooded hills of School House Hollow.

More and more, whatever came up, it was these six boys against the world. Whenever one was out and about, the other five were close by. They constituted their own troop, a troop within a troop. They were all for one, and one for all. The three musketeers, doubled down.

To make the routine camping trip more of an adventure, Vince led the five Braves up the steep trail to the top of Dead Man's Ridge. They had pitched their pup tents on the very top of the ridge, where they could look off down one side and see the school, and look out straight ahead and see the wide river winding its way westward between the purple hills of Kentucky and Ohio.

The Shawnee Times had reported a chance of overnight thunderstorms in the area, and so Vince had the three tents pitched in the shadow of a huge, half-dead oak that had one side split away by a lightning strike it sustained at some point in the past.

"If it does storm," Vince reasoned, "this will be the safest place to be here on the ridge point. Everybody knows that lightning never strikes twice in the same place."

Nobody questioned his wisdom. They pitched the tents, unrolled their blankets inside, and set about gathering firewood and making preparations for supper.

The meal was water gravy made in one iron skillet and potatoes and canned lunch meat, sliced thin and fried to a golden brown, prepared in a second iron skillet. The biscuits, made from scratch by Keith from his grandmother's recipe, were baked on a piece of curved tin set to reflect the heat from the fire. They were brown on the outside and a bit doughy in the middle, but nevertheless devoured, as was the meat, potatoes and gravy.

After supper, as shadows lengthened and a cool breeze wafted along the ridge, they built up a cheery campfire. The sun set behind the hills away off down the river. Darkness closed in, and for anyone with any imagination at all, shadows of unknown creatures began to move from tree trunk to tree trunk.

The talk turned to how this particular ridge had come by its name. Hobo had the gist of the story from his father, who had served a term as a Turnip County constable.

"I was hoping nobody would mention it," Hobo said.

Everybody, except Tom, knew how a man's body had been discovered by a squirrel hunter a dozen years ago on the very point of the ridge, not much more than fifty yards from where the scouts had set up camp.

"Don't talk about 'im," Hobo pleaded. "They say he still walks this ridge at night. And I'd say he's ticked off at everybody in this county over what the county did to him."

Of course, none of the five boys were going to let him off with that. They pleaded with Hobo to tell them what he knew.

Finally, Hobo agreed to tell the story. Gale tossed more wood on the fire and the boys all moved in closer.

There had been a wallet under the body, Hobo said, and it held sixty-seven dollars, but no identification papers at all. The victim had a peg leg, which you would think would have made it easier to identify him. The county sheriff made an attempt to locate anybody who could identify the body. They checked military records from World War Two and One, but turned up nothing on him at all.

"After the judge waited out a couple of days, and nobody came forth, he fined the dead man sixty-seven dollars for vagrancy," Hobo said. "Then they brought him back up here and buried him in a shallow grave -- no casket or nothin', no words said over him, no marker for his grave. You know he probably had some people somewhere could'a used that money."

"I'd a been the squirrel hunter 'at found him I would have thought the money would have been mine, ahead of the County," Keith said.

Hobo said, "The scary thing about it is that several fox hunters have sworn up and down they've heard – around midnight – someone or something walking through the dead leaves, said it sounded like it was dragging one leg behind."

Dale put more wood on the fire.

A wind swayed the branches overhead. From downriver they spotted some fierce bolts of lightning.

"Looks like a bad one coming," Vince said. "Make sure your tent pegs are pounded in good."

Gale and Tom shared a patched-up pup tent that belonged to Gale. After raking leaves back from the circle of stones they had built their campfire in, all six turned in for the night, each one taking thoughts of the dead man with them.

Thunder rolled across the hills. The storm was almost upon them. All were still wide-eyed awake as they heard it: someone, or something, coming down the ridge toward them, from the point.

Step, drag. Step, drag.

Gale and Tom stuck their heads out of the tent. The fire had burned low and offered no help in the pitch darkness. Vince and Hobo were out of their tent. Hobo was shining his flashlight down along the trail toward where the noise had come from. Vince had a hatchet in his hand.

"What was it, Hobo?" Tom asked.

"Don't know. Don't see nothin'. Sounded like somebody walkin', draggin' one leg behind 'em."

That brought Keith and Dale out of their tent. Vince was dragging wood toward the fire. Hobo, shining the light back and forth among the trees, shouted, "Whatta ya want out there?"

After listening a moment or two, he added, "Speak up out there, sound off or we'll open fire."

"Probably just an ol' fox scratchin' around," Vince said.

Then the storm broke right overhead. Lightning. Heavy, wind-driven rain. Everybody jumped when a bolt of lightning struck the split oak.

"My gawd," Tom said. "The old Devil's at work here. He's come up from the graveyard down there on the slope, not satisfied that he missed me the time I was up there with that black cat."

Tom was never sure who bolted first. Suddenly there was a unanimous evacuation from camp. And then everybody was in a foot race down the trail they'd come up on. They took nothing with them. Their one goal was to keep up with Hobo, who had the only flashlight.

They stumbled, fell, sometimes on the trail, sometimes off. Briars ripped their hides. Limbs from the saplings swished back to beat them about the face and shoulders.

They hit the creek at the bottom of the hill, went through the culvert under Route 10, and scurried like mice into the loft of Farmer Matt's barn, diving under the fresh mown hay. Rain pounded the tin roof with a great roar.

They sounded like a family of chipmunks, chattering away about a ghost on Dead Man's Ridge; about how it was just an old wives tale, that story of lightening never striking twice in the same spot.

Finally though, sleep claimed them.

The sun was shining in the meadow where the barn stood before anyone stirred.

They made their way back up the steep ridge trail in the sunlight to get their waterlogged gear. In the brazenness of daylight they saw that the gravesite on the point was undisturbed. In the thickness of the leaves and brush, and everything beaten down by the rain, it was impossible to tell what kind of animal, if any, had been poking around out there in the darkness.

It didn't really matter, because none of them ever went near the point of that ridge again, even in the daylight.

CHAPTER 41:
THE SINKING OF THE *INDY*

It was shortly after midnight when Carrie Sycamore bolted upright in bed, covered her face with her hands, and let out a loud scream. Bruce's feet hit the floor as fast as a sprung mousetrap.

"What is it, Mom? What's happened?"

"Flint's in trouble! Something awful has happened! I just know it!"

Tom came bounding down the steps three at a time. He saw his father seated on the side of the bed with his arms around his mother. One window of their bedroom looked out over the garden and Tom glanced out to see a light moving in the garden, He moved to afford a better look and saw actually that the light was above the garden. It moved and darted erratically back and forth the length of the garden.

At about the same time, on the far side of the world, where it was just about midnight Monday July 30, 1945, Private Flint Sycamore, U.S. Marines, had awakened after an hour or two of fitful sleep. He had spread his blanket on the deck to escape the stifling heat of the marine quarters down below decks. It was still nearly four hours before he would assume his 4 a.m. security watch. He wasn't sleepy, so he fell in beside a Marine buddy who had just come on the watch and accompanied him as he checked some equipment lash-downs near the stern of the *Indianapolis*.

It was 12:05 a.m. when all hell broke loose.

A tremendous explosion shook the deck and knocked Flint down. Before he could regain his feet a second explosion blew him 10 feet off the deck.

At Captain Hashimoto's command, the I-58 had fired six torpedoes, each carrying more than 1,200 pounds of explosives. One hit the *Indianapolis* forward and blew a huge chunk of the bow skyward. Another hit the ship near its mid-point. The big cruiser was nearly blown in two. It would be only 12 minutes before it began its plunge to the bottom of the South Pacific Ocean, more than three miles below.

An estimated 300 died on impact and nearly 900, including Capt. McVay, were forced into the shark-infested ocean.

A Navy cruiser as long as two football fields had disappeared from the face of the earth, and the Navy did not even miss her.

At least a fourth of the 39-man Marine detachment died in the blast, in their quarters, where Flint had earlier been writing his letter home before deciding to sleep on the deck before assuming his watch.

Now, grabbing a life vest from a storage area on the stern, he felt the ship turning on its side, its port rail pointing straight up at the sky. He was close enough to the rail to grab it. He climbed over it and found himself walking straight up on the side of the hull. He saw others doing the same. He squatted down and slid down the curvature of the hull and into the water. He was smothered in a blanket of leaking fuel oil. He ducked under, raised his arms above his head, and began splashing the surface with his hands. He surfaced in a little cleared space, but already oil was burning his eyes.

Behind him, he saw men leaping off the stern. The ship's propellers were out of the water. One was still spinning. Some of the men hit the propeller blades on the way down and bounced off it into the sea.

Flint swam away from the sinking ship as fast and strongly as he could. All around him, in the black of the night and the oily surface of the water, he heard men screaming, crying out for help. He bumped into debris and now and then a body of a sailor less fortunate than he.

In the predawn darkness, Flint spotted a life raft and began swimming through the oily surface toward it.

CHAPTER 42:
HYENAS OF THE SEA

Carrie Sycamore returned to her job at the steel mill. She had to have something to keep her busy. Concentration on her duties on the assembly line kept her mind temporarily off Flint. She could almost perform her job with her eyes closed anyway, and she worked without threat of an accident that might harm her or her coworkers. This was about the only function she could perform until she heard something from or about Flint, one way or another. She knew only that something bad had happened and that her first born was in great danger.

Indeed he was. Every survivor from the USS Indianapolis was in a struggle to live. About 300 of the 1,196 sailors and officers who made up the crew were killed in the initial explosions. Many of the nearly 900 who leaped into the ocean suffered from wounds and burns. Most of them had had time to grab a life jacket, but they had to swim directly into black fuel oil spurting from the ship's exploded hull. It formed a scum on the surface as thick as sorghum molasses.

And in the darkness lurked a deadly danger that many of them were unaware of. Schools of sharks with insatiable appetites were coming up from beneath.

Capt. McVay, who had been blown out of his rack in his cabin by the second blast, had barely had time to make it over the starboard rail. He was pulled down by the suction formed by the sinking ship. But he managed to break from its grasp and pop back to the surface. He was still trying to figure out what happened. At first he wondered if he was the only survivor, but soon he could see others in the darkness, with darkened, oil-stained faces – floating in life vests, some dead, most alive, many wounded.

He immediately began to assume his role as captain. He called out loudly to those sailors floating around him, trying to assure and organize them, and telling all within the sound of his voice that help would arrive.

Actually a distress signal from the stricken ship had gone out and was received on Leyte, but navy personnel there dismissed it as a ruse by the Japanese to draw search vessels out.

Both Navy commands, the one at the *Indy's* departure point on Guam, and the one on Leyte where she had a birth reserved, by Tuesday assumed the *Indianapolis* had completed her voyage. Leyte was a port so busy with plans for the coming invasion that it did not know who was coming and going. Officials charged with such matters assumed the *Indy* was checked in, even though a quick check would have shown her berth was empty.

The *USS Indianapolis* was on the bottom of the Pacific, those who had survived the torpedoing were adrift in the shark-infested waters of the Pacific, and no one in officialdom had the slightest inkling of their fate.

Flint, after giving his life vest to a sailor who was staying afloat merely with the aid of a bucket, swam to a raft that held four other men. There were three other rafts in the group, each holding three to five men.

The sharks made their appearance the first night, but were not noticed by the suffering men in the darkness. At first the 10- and 12-foot carnivores fed on the dead bodies and body parts that drifted down through the depths and on those bodies still afloat in their life vests.

During the second night men whose legs dangled as they drifted in life vests began to disappear beneath the surface. Now and then there was a scream, but for the most part the work of the sharks was silent and unnoticed.

As daylight came the sharks turned out in greater numbers, and they were hungry. Flint, peering over the edge of his raft, looked down in the clear water and saw their gray bodies circling about 10 feet below the surface, hundreds of them.

One sailor drifting alone about fifty feet from the raft had been making his way toward Flint and the others. When he spied the shark fins protruding from the water all around him, he panicked. He went out of his head. He began screaming and kicking, calling for help. Flint and the others in his raft began paddling as fast as they could toward him, hoping to pull him into the raft, even though it was clear there was hardly room for another person. And the raft really did not provide much safety over those who drifted in life vests. One end of it was partly collapsed and a shark would have easily been able to nose over top and into the raft.

At any rate, just when they were about to reach the boy, he let out a final scream and disappeared beneath the surface.

Twice during the morning a shark tried to nose its way over the partially collapsed end of the raft. One that seemed intent on succeeding was kicked in the eye by Flint and quickly reversed itself.

Groups of sailors floating in life jackets were easy pickings. Sailors at the outer edges fared worse than those in the middle. Flint and the others on the raft watched in horror as one boy in a life vest was dragged through the water like a bobber on a fisherman's line when a big fish strikes. He disappeared with one final scream.

Others disappeared without a word. Here and there empty life jackets, their straps chewed off, would pop to the surface.

Looking around in the other rafts, Flint was happy to discover one of his fellow marines – Private Lance Otworth, the one he had been making the security round with when the first torpedo struck. Otworth had been blown off the ship and into the sea by the impact.

Flint did not recognize him at first because of the black oil covering his face. He had a nasty wound and was in much pain. One of his arm bones was sticking through the skin just below the elbow.

Yes, Carrie Sycamore's 18-year-old son was facing a strong possibility of never again seeing the little river village of Hooperville and the green hills that rose above it.

And all she could do was wait anxiously for a letter from Flint.

That, or an official notice from the War Department that would verify her worst fears.

CHAPTER 43:
FLINT SURRENDERS TO HIS FATE

There had been no communication from Flint for nearly a week. Tom's anxious mother had worked three days at the mill following that horrible feeling she had that something terrible had happened to Flint. But now she had quit. She could no longer concentrate on her work of turning out shell and bomb casings. She prepared Tom's meals. Bruce Sycamore had returned to work on the Big Sandy Division and lived and, save for weekends, took his meals on the camp cars.

She herself hardly ate anything. She had lost weight and her face was worn and haggard. Tom kept his vigil of two visits a day to the post office. She scanned the newspaper for news of the Indianapolis but saw nothing. Had his ship been sunk, or was he on a ship waiting to be put ashore as part of the invasion? Why could she hear nothing?

She was showing less and less interest in the things of her household. She tuned in more and more to the radio reports of the war corespondents. She stared blankly at walls. She didn't always come onto the porch and yell Tom in at dark.

The neighbors knew that she was anticipating that Flint would soon be announced as a casualty of the awful war that had taken such a toll on the village. Flossie Riley, Lois Flanders and Thelma Hooper visited her regularly. Vince's mother, Louise Royalton, also came by and brought her favorite dish – chicken and noodles. She was hearing regularly from her son, Charles, who was at a base in the Pacific and seemingly out of harm's way. But she, too, worried about the planned invasion of Japan.

The other five Braves gave Tom the space he needed to help his mother. They tried to comfort him and assure him that his big brother would be coming home.

"He's too tough to let the Japs get him," Gale told Tom. "Remember how he plunged in and pulled you out when you were going down for the third time?"

As sharks continued their sporadic feeding on the survivors and bodies of sailors from the *USS Indianapolis*, the line of men floating in the water became separated by miles by the winds and currents of the South Pacific.

Edward Parke, in charge of the marine contingent, along with Father Conway, Catholic priest on the ship, worked with the boys in their vicinities – though separated by several miles -- to try to bring groups together and to shore up hopes that rescue would come.

Capt. McVay and his group were still at least ten miles away. Since shortly after midnight Monday, July 30, they had drifted more than 100 miles from the spot where the *Indy* went down.

Even though the three officers warned as many men as they could, some, now into their fourth day with no fresh water, had begun to ease their parched throats and cracking lips by drinking saltwater, which brought a lingering death.

Men were beginning to hallucinate. Some saw white sand beaches with pretty girls on them, waving to them.

And each night the sharks came to feed.

It was near noon on that fourth day when a crew on a bomber patrolling for subs spotted an oil slick on the water. Flying low and following down the streak, they began to spot men in the water, some floating in life vests, some in life rafts, some holding on to floater nets.

"Who in hell can they be?" the pilot, Lt. Chuck Gwinn, asked his navigator. No one as yet knew that the cruiser, the *USS Indianapolis*, was no more.

Gwinn at first thought they might be survivors from a sunken Japanese submarine, but then realized that there were too many men to have come from a sub.

The bomber dropped marker dye in the water and then headed for home base, radioing for help on the way. Lt. Adrian Marks, back on the island of Peleliu, picked up Gwinn's message on the transmitter. The instant he heard Gwinn say, "am circling life rafts," he leaped into action. By this time word had circulated that the *Indianapolis* had not shown up as scheduled in the harbor at Leyte.

Quickly he and his crew had a Catalina in the air and headed for the location. They carried life rafts and shipwreck kits holding water and rations.

Marks spotted the men in the water and began dropping supplies. Soon after Gwinn had flown out of sight, a school of man-eating sharks, twenty to thirty in number, had staged a vicious attack and in about fifteen minutes taken about sixty of the survivors perched on a floater net.

Marks, spotting sharks still in the water, landed his big Catalina on the choppy surface and began picking up as many survivors as he could. These were from the group headed by Haynes. Any ship in the vicinity had now been radioed to head for the area.

Haynes himself was hauled from the sea with a rope tied around his waist by crewmembers of the *USS Cecil F. Doyle*.

He was asked by the captain who he was and who all these men were.

"We're all that's left of the *Indianapolis*," Haynes said. "We've been in the water four days."

The rescue effort went on all day and under the glare of searchlights through the night.

Flint and his group of four others in the half-submerged life raft had drifted miles beyond any of the others. They were all alone in that vast ocean. They had seen planes pass overhead, and the night before they thought they had seen searchlights against the clouds beyond the horizon. They were now into their fifth day adrift, and convinced no one was going to find them.

They had spent four and one-half days in the water without food, water or shelter from the sun. They acknowledged that the end for them was near.

All five men had now accepted that they were going to die. Of the whole ordeal this was the worst of all. The sharks were bad. Watching some of their buddies die was horrible. But accepting the idea that it was over, that you were going to die . . .

Partly submerged, they lay on their backs in the rafts, as though they were in their caskets.

On his way to his room for the night, Tom stopped in Flint's room to read again some of his brother's poetry and songs. Perhaps he hadn't given them the proper respect before, for now he found himself appreciating their messages.

The south window in Flint's room looked out over the garden. As Tom rose to go to his own room, he looked out the window and saw the light in the garden. It was going up and down and back and forth. It seemed Lance Cpl. Leon Selby was as anxious as anyone for news from the South Pacific of fellow Marine Pfc. Flint Sycamore.

CHAPTER 44:
A LONG TIME TO DIE

By Friday afternoon, Aug. 3, search planes had turned up no more men in the water and the rescue effort began to wind down. Some ships, however, continued to prowl in search of survivors, perhaps even one lone survivor. Flint and the other four had drifted farther than any of the others, about 120 miles since the night of the sinking.

That morning Flint heard the droning of airplane engines and roused himself to one elbow. Off on the horizon he could see the planes. The others saw them, too, and with what strength they could muster they sat up and waved. But the planes disappeared, and the disappointed men returned to their burial positions.

No one was coming.

It was taking longer to die than Flint had anticipated.

However, at dusk, another plane appeared. The Catalina passed over so close that Flint could see the face of crew members in the cockpit.

The plane circled, came back, and dropped a dye marker near the raft.

Then, so quickly as if it came out of Heaven, a ship appeared. A transport ship was soon right by them. A sailor tossed a line that Flint was able to grab.

All five of the men were covered yet with oil, their faces swollen, their ribs and cheekbones showing sharply through their skin. They were sunburned skeletons. Flint managed enough strength to bow down and kiss the deck.

They were taken to the island of Peleliu, where a hospital had been set up. The majority of the survivors were already there.

Of the 1,196 men who made up the crew of the *Indy*, sixty-seven officers and 808 enlisted men had lost their lives. Of the nearly 900 who were forced into the ocean, only 321 were left alive. And four of those would die within the coming days.

To this point, the sinking of the *Indianapolis* was still a secret. Only a few Military brass and some hospital workers on Peleliu were privy to the news.

But an Associated Press reporter stationed on Leyte got part of the news regarding the ship. It was not in its berth there and part of a message radioed from one of the rescue vessels implied that the ship had been sunk. His brief that went out over the wire subsequently made its way into a notice on the front page of that afternoon's *Shawnee Daily Times*. It read:

"The *USS Indianapolis* has been lost in the Philippine Sea as the result of enemy action. The next of kin of 1,196 casualties have been notified."

Carrie Sycamore, the newspaper in her hands, slid from her chair to the floor. Tom, fighting to stay calm, rushed to the cabinet drawer where the smelling salts were kept, broke one, and held it under her nose. Slowly his mother recovered and was able to rise.

"We'll hear something from Flint yet, Momma. Keep the faith."

Shortly just about every house on the street had a representative in the Sycamore front room or on the front porch.

Tom stayed close by his mother's side until bedtime, which didn't come until the last news station had signed off. There had been no further news about the *Indianapolis*.

Flint had regained some strength by early the next morning. Military officials had found out about the AP notice concerning the sinking of the *Indianapolis*. The decision was made to allow those survivors in the hospital, the ones able to communicate, to call their families to let them know they were all right.

Flint, with the help of a pretty nurse who instantly liked him, was one of the very first ones to gain access to the overseas service.

It was 9 a.m. when Lois Flanders pounded on the Sycamore front door. Carrie answered the door still in her pajamas and bathrobe. She looked like death warmed over.

"Carrie, come quick! You've got a phone call, long distance."

The two women ran across the street, Tom close behind. And behind them came Bruce Sycamore, pulling on his shirt and still barefooted. He and Tom held his mother upright as she was expecting the worse. The rest of the Flanders family, including Gale, leaned in to listen. They were smiling and clapping hands as Tom's mother recognized the voice of her Marine son!

"The crew of the ship fed me water from a spoon for an hour, Momma. It was so sweet, almost as sweet as that spring water on the banks of Hooperville. We found out we had spent 112 hours adrift without food, water or shelter from the sun. Now I'm being fed, Momma, and more food is on the way. And very soon now I'll be on my way home."

Carrie was so excited she could scarce think of anything to ask. She turned to Tom, and then her husband.

"Flint's safe and he's coming home! This is him!" She fairly shouted the words as she hugged Bruce and tousled Tom's hair, at the same time holding the phone to her ear with the other hand.

Flint could not talk long because others were waiting to use the line.

"You have all been so kind," Carrie told Lois Sanders as they went out the door. "Your kindness and concern have kept me from going crazy."

Tom rounded the house to go to the privy. Lance Cpl. Leon Selby was standing near the cherry tree dressed in his blues. He gave a sharp salute. And before the image faded, Tom had been treated, for the second time, to a look at the Marine's full face – the blue eyes, the white teeth. What a good-looking man he was – or had been. His body was buried beneath a white cross on Okinawa.

CHAPTER 45:
THE DAY THE BABY FLOATED

Hooperville, having won several battles over the years with the Ohio River for survival, will no doubt still be squatting there on the southern shore of the mighty river when Christ returns.

And, for as long as there remains on the earth a descendant of one of the people in the congregation of Hooperville Methodist on that early August Sunday in 1945, the story of what happened there that morning will be told -- forever to be recalled as "the time the baby floated."

Tom had finished breakfast and his mother was giving him his final inspection before sending him off to church. Suddenly there came a knock on the front door. Tom thought it would have been one of the boys. But when Carrie Sycamore opened the door, there stood one of the most beautiful women he had ever seen. In her arms was a baby.

She introduced herself as Mary Ann Selby.

"My husband and I lived here back in the early spring," she said. "This is our baby, born just ten days ago."

"Oh-h-h, oh! You're the Marine's wife!" Carrie Sycamore said. "Come on in. Let me get you some coffee."

The young mother, seemingly glowing from being referred to as "the Marine's wife," hesitated for a moment before saying she didn't have time to come in, that her parents were with her; and would it be all right if they parked there, in front of the house, while they went into the church?

With that settled, she turned her attention to Tom, who stood behind his mother with his mouth gaping.

"And is this the boy – Tom Sycamore – who's been taking care of the garden?"

She looked around at Tom, reached out her hand to him. He couldn't find his tongue. His mother answered for him. "Oh, yes, yes," she said. "He really takes care of that garden. And we're enjoying the fruits of your husband's labor. We'll soon have plenty to share, and I hope you'll come back and help us with that."

Mary Ann Selby continued to look at Tom and seemed not to hear his mother.

"And did you ..." she said, pausing to select her words, "see my husband? Mr. Jim Galloway said you did."

It was again Tom's mother who spoke. "Yes, Tom saw him. I did, too. Saw somebody ..."

Bruce Sycamore had put his newspaper down and came to see what all the talk was about.

"Saw who? When?" he asked.

Tom, ignoring his father's questions, said, "There's a Marine in that garden just about every time I go into it. I didn't know who he was, and I don't know why he's there. But I think he's real proud of that garden."

"Did you see him?" Mary Ann Selby asked again.

"I saw a Marine," Tom said.

She handed Carrie the baby while she rested her purse on her thigh and rummaged through it. She pulled out a photo and showed it to Tom. His heart and eyebrows leaped up.

"That's him! That's who I saw," he said, then paused to search for the words to describe his experience. "But you have to understand. I didn't see somebody you could reach out and touch."

She looked at Tom and smiled.

"I know," she said. "Mr. Galloway told me. And he told me about the church bell ringing, and about the soldier at the altar. And he said he saw a soldier in the garden, too."

She took the baby back from Tom's mother.

"I bet he is proud of that garden, Tom. He was when he planted it," she said. "And here's something else – someone else – he's going to be proud of, too." She held the baby on her hip and tickled him under his chin, eliciting a smile and a "goo."

242

"Can I go and see the garden?" she asked. "I think we've got time. The church bell hasn't rung yet, has it?"

"Oh, my, yes," said Carrie. "But no, the bell hasn't rung. We've got time. Let's go right around the side of the house here."

Tom led the way. Mary Ann and Carrie followed. The man and the woman in the car got out, and they followed. Bruce came out onto the porch, stood watching, hands on hips, then joined the line, mumbling to himself, "What's going on here? Will somebody tell me what's going on here? What're you talking about, a Marine?"

At the edge of the garden, Mary Ann Selby held the baby out from her body. He was smiling as the sun glistened off his face. Then, as had happened the night before, the corn and beans and peas began to sway back and forth, though there was not a breeze in the trees.

Mary Ann laughed out loud. A few people going up the church steps paused for a moment to stare at the group of people in the garden.

"Well, yes we will," she said, and it was plain that she was not speaking to Tom, or any of the others.

The church bell was ringing as they made their way back toward the front of the house. She thanked Tom and his parents and then headed for the church. She was excited. Her parents had trouble keeping up. Tom skipped along beside her.

His mother stopped at the edge of the Sycamore front porch. Bruce Sycamore still stood in the side yard, looking back toward the garden. He looked at the treetops all around and saw that not a breeze moved the leaves, and was left to ponder why the plants in the garden had rippled and waved as though a wind swept through them.

Both Jim Galloway and the Rev. Ottis Hackelbee welcomed Mary Ann Selby and her baby and parents at the front door. Galloway caught Tom's eye and directed a thumbs up gesture at him. As Hackelbee escorted Mary Ann and her baby and parents into the pastor's office, Jim Galloway put his arm around Tom and apologized. "She called late last night to ask if we could have the service for the baby today, and I just hadn't had a chance this morning to share it with you," he said.

243

Tom smiled and went on down the aisle and slipped into a seat beside Gale.

The Rev. Hackelbee shared the good news with the congregation about Flint Sycamore's phone call the previous day and how he was safe and would soon be coming home.

Seats had been reserved on the front spew for Mary Ann and her parents. Hackelbee introduced them and the baby to the congregation and told how there would be a dedication service for the baby following the morning message.

The Sunday school superintendent stood and raised his hands. "All stand please," he said, and the congregation behaved as though he had puppet strings on his fingers. "Turn to page three-fifteen, 'How Firm a Foundation.'"

Later, Vince, Dale, Hobo, Keith, Gale and Tom were all in class. Tom had not shared the Marine encounter with anyone other than his mother, Mr. Galloway, and now Mary Ann Selby, and so it was not mentioned by the Braves.

Back upstairs after class, Tom was delighted to find that his mother had squeezed in beside Lois Flanders. He and Gale joined them.

People were making over the baby and Mary Ann and her parents, seated on the front row, as they made their way back into the sanctuary. They scattered to their own seats as the Rev. Hackelbee entered the pulpit to lead in a song.

In the preaching service, Rev. Hackelbee, as usual, held the congregation spellbound with his message, which was about current events in the Pacific islands, about patriotism, and the evils of the Japanese Empire. He concluded with a message from First Thessalonians, Chapter Four, the portion dealing with how the spirits of those who have died believing in Christ are asleep in him, and how Christ will bring them with him when he returns, at the trumpet call, and they will be resurrected at that time with a heavenly body. Those who remain alive, he said, will be changed from mortal to immortal in the "twinkling of an eye" and be caught up together with them in the clouds.

"We'll be with the Lord forever, so comfort each other with these words, which come not from the Apostle Paul's opinion, but from the Lord's own word," the reverend said, pounding the podium with an open palm for emphasis.

The message was especially comforting for those who, like Mary Ann Selby, had lost a loving husband and father of the baby she cradled in her arms; or, like her parents, had lost a trusted and loved son-in-law, in that terrible war that had left so many tragic deaths in its wake.

Every seat in the church was taken, and it showed on the faces of many they had gotten much comfort from the message. Hackelbee had had a gift for that, and for swaying the opinions of people. Local anti-liquor forces credited his preaching and visits in the neighborhoods with defeating by a large margin the efforts of the "wet" forces in western Turnip County – a margin that helped the "dry" forces win the election by a narrow margin countywide.

"Now we're going to move right into a dedication service for the Selby infant, born just about ten days ago," the preacher said. "I'm sure most of you have had a chance to reacquaint yourselves with Mary Ann Selby, who attended here when she and her husband, Leon, lived next door. She has expressed the desire to have their son dedicated to the Lord here this morning. With us also are her parents, from Shawnee, Harry and Mildred Hardin. We're delighted to have them all with us this morning."

Then Hackelbee asked Mary Ann to bring her baby forward, to the side of the altar where the baptismal basin stood.

Mary Ann knelt at the altar briefly, then stood, holding the baby in her arms.

"Dearly beloved," said the Rev. Hackelbee, reading from a book of ritual, "for as much as this child is now presented by you for Christian baptism, it is your part and duty to see that he be brought up in the nurture and admonition of the Lord; and that in every way, by precept and example, you shall seek to lead him into the love of God and the service of Our Lord Jesus Christ.

"Do you solemnly engage to fulfill these duties so far as in you lies, the Lord being your helper?"

"We do," said Mary Ann Selby, smiling and looking to her right, where she held the baby on the altar.

We do? She must be including her parents, Tom thought.

The congregation, most of whom no doubt thought that, too, rose at the preacher's motion to do so. Then he took the baby into his arms.

"What name shall be given to this child?"

245

"Leon Richard Selby Junior," said his mother.

Hackelbee dipped his hand into the basin. The baby kicked as he allowed water to drip from his fingers onto its forehead.

"Leon Richard Selby Junior, I baptize thee in the name of the Father, and of the Son, and of the Holy Ghost. Amen."

The pastor then led the congregation in the recital of the Lord's Prayer. He turned and handed the baby boy back to his mother. She turned and lifted the baby out waist-high, to her right. The congregation sucked in its breath collectively as she removed her arms and dropped them to her sides.

The baby levitated.

There were murmurs of alarm and of awe, and people saying. "Look! Look!"

The baby smiled, goo-gooed.

Tom didn't know what anyone else saw, but, just for an instant, he saw Lance Corporal Leon Selby, wearing his full dress blues, holding his baby boy and smiling down at him. Carrie Sycamore, seated beside him, covered her mouth with her hand as tears flowed from her eyes.

As Mary Ann Selby took the baby into her arms again, the organist broke into an impromptu and lively version of The Marine's Hymn.

The Rev. Hackelbee was startled at first, but then he began singing the words of the song:

From the Halls of Montezu-u-uma
To the shores of Tripoli…

By the time of the second verse, the congregation got into the spirit of the thing. The windows of the little church were up, and the crew of a passing towboat could have heard those voices ringing out, bouncing off the hillside and drifting out over the river:

If the Army and the Na-a-avy
Ever looked on Heaven's scene-s-s-s,
They would find the streets are guar-r-rded
By United States Marines.

"Sing it once again," said the preacher.

And they did, with even more gusto than before. It was difficult to keep the feet from marching.

246

It was a service everyone seemed proud to have been in.

Later, outside on the steps, May Ann Selby was surrounded by well-wishers and people wanting to hold the baby. As Tom filed by, she caught him by the hand and followed him to the bottom of the steps. She looked deep into his very soul with those lovely, misty blue eyes and said, "I want to thank you, Tom Sycamore, for the work you've done on that garden, and for letting me know, in an indirect way, that Leon was here. All he wanted was to see this baby. He's happy now, and someday we'll understand why he was taken as he was, and how all things will turn out for the good. You heard the Rev. Hackelbee say how Leon is asleep in the arms of Jesus? I believe that with all my heart, and I know we'll be together again."

Tom stammered a bit, but managed to tell her how he hoped she would come back in a week or two and get some vegetables from the garden. She said she would.

Then he heard himself asking her the question, "Do you believe dogs have a spirit, and that Jesus will bring them with him for the resurrection?"

Tom had told her the story of how her husband had warned him in time for him to leap out of the path of the mad dog in the garden, and how Chopper had been bitten, and consequently succumbed to the awful rabies.

Mary Ann did not hesitate in saying, "Yes, Tom. There will be dogs in Heaven. Heaven would not be Heaven without the companionship of little friends like your Chopper. Oh yes, Tom. We will see them both."

She rubbed her hand through Tom's hair and kissed him on the forehead as tears of joy flowed down his cheeks.

At home, Bruce Sycamore pressed Tom and Carrie for details of the service. They told him everything, just as it had happened. He scratched his head as he looked from one to the other of them.

After dinner Tom went into the garden to tie up some bean plants. He looked down toward the end of the rows, and there, by the side of the little mound of earth where Chopper laid, stood the Marine. Tom sensed that he wanted to tell him something, to assure him of something.

Then Tom heard a sound that made his young heart thump against his chest, as though trying to escape.

It was Chopper's yelp and bark, no mistaking that. The sound came from right beside the Marine.

Chopper no longer feared the spirit.

The Marine gave Tom a sharp salute, and was gone.

Tom continued to work the garden that summer, and its bounty was great.

But never again did he see the Marine on patrol there.

CHAPTER 46:
WHAT'S AN ATOMIC BOMB?

The following day, bright and early, the Enola Gay lifted off from the airfield on Tinian Island. At 8:15 a.m. Pacific time, the big B-29 dropped Little Boy on Hiroshima.

Late that afternoon, back in Hooperville, Tom and the boys gathered at Gale's for their radio serials and found Grandpa Flanders with a special edition of the Shawnee Times on his lap, his spectacles high on his forehead, rubbing the bridge of his nose with thumb and forefinger.

"Merciful heavens," he uttered. "What have we loosed on the world?"

The newspaper slipped to the floor and Tom read the headline in bold black letters across the top of the page: "U.S. Drops Atomic Bomb on Japan."

Gale, looking over Tom's shoulder at the headline, said, "What is it Grandpa? What's an atomic bomb?"

The old man, after a moment to recover his composure, said, "Twenty thousand tons of TNT – that's what it amounts to."

Then he continued: "It's a nightmare. I know your teachers have read to you about Pandora's Box? This thing was tucked away down in there. Now it's out, and Pandora's Box probably will never be closed again."

Broadcast of the Superman serial was interrupted by a special broadcast from the White House.

"It is an atomic bomb," President Truman said. "It is harnessing the basic powers of the universe. The force from which the sun draws its power has been loosed upon those who brought war to the Far East. And if they do not accept our terms, they may expect a rain of ruin from the air the likes of which has never been seen on this earth."

Japanese newspapers urged the people to fight through until the last.

Tom continued to work the garden – the Marine's Victory Garden. During the week Mary Ann Selby and her mother, along with Leon Selby Jr., came for a visit and left with enough fresh vegetables to last for days.

The harvest was plentiful. Carrie Sycamore, while waiting for word that Flint was on his way home, busied herself at canning tomatoes and beans, as much as she was able to get jars and supplies to do with.

It was a garden that seemed to have no end to its supply of fresh vegetables. Two or three times a week the family enjoyed sweet corn on the cob – even had enough to share with Dale's and Gale's families across the street.

On Thursday, Aug. 9, Nagasaki became the victim of yet another atomic bomb, nicknamed Fat Man. It exploded a third of a mile above the city. The city was seared with a burst of heat exceeding 5,400 degrees Fahrenheit. Thousands of people simply melted into the ground, and thousands more would die within days of radiation sickness.

Just before that second explosion a Japanese youth named Koichi Nakijima and five companions, all about the same age as Tom and the other Braves, were playing in the Urakami River. Their game was much like the one the six Hooperville boys sometimes played in the Ohio River – tossing a bell out into waters over their head and seeing who could be the first to retrieve it from the bottom.

All six boys came up gasping for air. No one had recovered the bell. This worried Koichi. The bell belonged to his sister, and she would skin him if he lost it. Taking a deep breath, he dived for the bottom – an action that would see him live to tell his story of horror.

When he surfaced a minute later, he saw a world unlike anything he had ever seen. Everything was a swirling haze. No buildings could be seen left standing. Three of his friends were blackened corpses. The other two wallowed about screaming on the bank, soon to die.

On the newsreel at the Saturday matinee, Tom and the Braves saw for themselves the great mushroom cloud created by the Hiroshima bomb. After the movie ended and they headed into the Playhouse, Vince was sullen. Tom thought he must surely be coming down with something. His skin was pallid on an expressionless face. In fact, no one seemed to be themselves. Even Keith Richards was not cracking any of his jokes or snide remarks.

They walked the bridge in 92-degree weather and followed the railroad tracks to Hooperville. They climbed to the tree house and changed into their swim trunks. All except Vince. He stayed on the shaded deck of the tree house reading a book. It was the same book Tom had noticed him reading for the past few days in the gatherings at Gale's house: "The Adventures of Huckleberry Finn."

The other five enjoyed their relief from the heat almost in total silence.

It was Dale who first went inside and discovered that all their implements of war – the wooden rifles, the stovepipe flame thrower, the grenades, the old music stand that served as a machine gun support – had disappeared from the wall and corner where they had been stored.

"Where's all our war stuff?" Gale asked Vince.

"Huh? Why, they are, they're gone. I hadn't even noticed," Vince said. "Some of the upriver boys slip in here, you think, and played a prank on us? Or maybe them girls ...?"

The five looked from one to the other. Hobo shrugged his shoulders.

After a while, "Vince said, "Well, it's no big loss. It doesn't matter. The war's over, boys."

He turned his attention back to his book.

"This book is the finest thing I've yet to read," he said. "This Huck and Jim really have some grand adventures down there on the Mississippi."

He looked up from the book to gaze out over the river.

"You know, I wonder what it would be like, going down that river on a raft?"

CHAPTER 47:
THE END IS NEAR

The dropping of atomic bombs on Japan brought mixed feelings to the residents of Hooperville, as well as to Americans across the land. Surely Japan, now faced with terrible destruction, would be forced to surrender, thus ending any plans for invasion of their home islands America and her Allies were considering, and thus saving further loss of America's youth. Military deaths on the Allied side already totaled 405,399, with another 670,836 wounded.

The perpetuators of the war suffered far worse. The military death toll for Germany totaled 3,250,000, while 1,800,000 Japanese soldiers, sailors and airmen were dead.

But there was empathy for the suffering of human beings wrought by this horrible new weapon. The anticipated joy of ending the war was tempered by the apprehension brought on by this harbinger of death and destruction heretofore undreamed of. A single bomb that could level an entire city and kill one hundred thousand people could well bring the destruction of the world, were its powers to be controlled by the wrong people.

The good thing about the unleashing of the atomic powers, according to The Rev. Ottis Hackelbee, was that it would usher in the Kingdom of God. It was a sign that the Second Coming of Christ was near.

So many people were coming and going at the little church next to Tom's house that Rev. Hackelbee decided to call a weekend revival. He would preach it, taking the opportunity to warn all those who would listen to be ready.

Flyers were circulated and the church was packed on the first night. There were the saints and there were the backsliders. And there were sinners brought by fear of the great mushroom cloud pictured in the papers. Carrie Sycamore was there, requesting prayer for Flint to get home safely.

Out through the raised windows into the hot August air flowed the words to "Nearer My God to Thee" and "When the Roll is Called Up Yonder I'll Be There."

But the ushers were soon closing the windows as lightning flashed and thunder rolled over the village. A two-week summer dry spell came to an end. The rain pounded on the roof of the church, but the attic storage area absorbed much of the sound of it.

The plates were passed and then Hackelbee lost no time plunging into his message, predicting the atomic secrets would fall into the wrong hands and surely lead to the melting of the elements and the death of millions the end-time scriptures spoke of.

"What manner of people ought we to be, seeing the culmination of the ages spoken of by the prophets closing in upon us?" the preacher asked.

Never before in the history of mankind, he said, had conditions been favorable to fulfill the events spoken of by the Apostle Peter more than 1,900 years ago.

"Let me turn your attention to those passages," the reverend said, opening his Bible on the podium. "Peter warns us here that the Day of the Lord will come as a thief in the night, in the which the heavens shall pass away with a great noise, and the elements will melt with a fervent heat, the earth also and the works that are therein shall be burned up.

"This day Peter warned about could come before your head hits the pillow tonight. All that we know and hold dear could be dissolved."

One could almost hear the shudder that ran through the congregation, like a wave washing ashore from the big paddlewheelers.

"The Lord is not slack regarding his promises," Hackelbee continued, "as some men count slackness; but he is long-suffering to us, not willing that any should perish, but that all should come to repentance."

A chorus of "amens" sounded from the Saints Corner. Some in the congregation seemed to have difficulty rising for the invitational hymn: *Have thine own way, Lord, have thine own way. Thou art the molder, I am the clay.*

One or two started for the altar before another verse could begin, and soon it became a steady flow.

That night in his bed, Tom mulled it all over in his mind, trying mightily to sort things out as the rain roared on the tin roof. He didn't mind the ushering in of the Kingdom, since Chopper would be there. And his Grandpa and Grandma Sycamore. And he really wasn't too crazy about going back to that school, since there would be no Janie there.

But he'd hoped to see more of the present world than a hundred miles or so of the Charles River and Ohio River valleys. If a man was to see the world it would have to be soon.

His work with the garden was finished. His mother, unable to concentrate on matters of her home until Flint was safely back home, could get along fine without him.

All of this line of thinking was brought on by the new adventure plan hinted at by Vince, whose parents had heard from son Charles and knew that he was safe – expected to be discharged soon now that the war had ended.

Vince had talked up Huck Finn's raft trip until he had the Braves longing to taste such an adventure. He didn't know how long the trip would last, but he thought at least they should try to get down to Cairo, just to see where the waters of the Ohio met the mighty Mississippi.

"We'd be able to work out way back upriver on a steamboat," Vince said. "Deck hands, cabin boys, they make good money."

Hobo said there were "so many youngins at home" that he wouldn't be missed for weeks. Keith Richards, who was born in the Panama Canal Zone and came to live with his grandmother after his father was killed in the Battle for Leyte Gulf, wanted to get away from his possessive grandmother, who now had him on piano lessons. Gale dreaded returning to school because Miss Newberry didn't give him the grades he figured he deserved.

"I think she's got it in for me," he said. "She's always after me to reach my potential, reach my potential. Lordy be! It's a lot of pressure."

Dale said it didn't matter to him one way or the other; he would go along with whatever the majority decided.

Before noon the next day Vince was talking up the raft trip again as they reclined on the deck of the tree house looking out over the river, watching the drift go by. It had rained hard all through the night and early morning. It was a general, overall rain that extended all the way up to Pittsburgh. The river was already rising into the willows.

Tom couldn't help believing, and maybe they all thought the same, that such a trip was all just talk and wishful thinking. It was fun to hear Vince talk of it, and tell of the things that had happened to Huck and Jim, the runaway Negro slave, as they drifted down the mighty Mississippi.

They would never be able to build a craft capable of such a trip. And certainly the *Reuben James* couldn't sustain the six of them and their provisions.

Yes, Tom thought, it was all just talk.

Until, that is, the raft came by.

Vince spotted it first, floating high and handsome, just outside the willows. "Hallelujah, look at that, will 'ya?" he said, and leaped up to drop through the trap door and down the tree ladder. The others followed as he ran downstream far enough to get ahead of the raft. He plunged into the rising water and swam to the outer willows, Hobo right behind him. Down it came, plowing into willow limbs here and there.

Tom and the others watched as Vince and Hobo latched on to it. There was a rope hanging down from the bow. Hobo grabbed it and side-stroked toward shore. Vince made his way through the water to the rear of the raft and pushed by churning the murky water with his feet. Tom, Dale, Gale and Keith now leaped in to help and together they managed to guide it through a clearing and bring it in toward shore in Sherwood Forest. There, out of the swift current, Vince tied it to a tree.

Rather than just a makeshift raft, it appeared to be part of a boat dock. The thing was sturdy, measuring about twelve feet by eighteen feet. Lashed under the log and board floor were six steel drums to give her a beautiful buoyancy.

Vince leaped from the shore onto the deck and ran the length of it.

"We could have a square dance on here," he said, giggling.

The five other Braves joined him, Dale and Gale dancing a little jig together. *Grab your partner, pat her on the head, don't like biscuits, feed 'er cornbread,* Gale sang, while Keith played the fiddle.

Later, as they lay on their backs on the raft looking up through the treetops, Vince rose to a sitting position, looked around, patted the board deck, and said, "Yes sir, boys. This is an act of Divine Providence."

CHAPTER 48:
OFF TO SEE THE WORLD

With the raft tied off and waiting, the six boys set about immediately, before they backed out, to initiate this the most ambitious adventure Vince had ever come up with – a raft trip down river to the mouth of the Ohio to see the mighty Mississippi. They did not know for sure if the destructive power of the atomic bombs dropped on Japan was really a part of God's plan to usher in the end of the world, as Rev. Hackelbee seemed so certain of; but most certainly this was a way to see part of the world before it was gone.

"I hear Russia's already got it," Tom had overheard one man say to another in Gammons' grocery. "And you know what they're after – a communist dictatorship. I heard they got plans to drop one on Great Britain and America."

Vince said he did not know how long a trip it would be by raft from Hooperville to Cairo, but he expected it would take at least three days and nights. The plan called for gaining permission from their folks for a three-night camping trip with Troop 160 to work on qualifications for additional merit badges needed for advancement. Their scout leaders need not know of the trip, since it involved only the six members.

"We'll just tell our folks we're goin' on a camping trip with the Boy Scouts," Vince said. "We won't be lying, 'cause we're scouts and we will be camping. We won't tell them, of course, it's on the river. Tell 'em we're going into the beech grove up School House Hollow and work on stuff we need for merit badges."

"A Scout is … well, no, it doesn't say anything about bein' truthful," Tom said, then added, "Just trustworthy."

Vince gave him a pained look.

"Well, shut up, Sycamore, the world's conscience," he said. "We're just doin' what needs to be done here, in this particular situation."

The boys had begun that very hour they found the raft in making it ready for an adventure greater than anything they had ever dreamed of.

"We'll need protection from the elements," Vince had said as Tom helped him carry and drag down under the bank a folded tarpaulin Vince borrowed from his father's garage. Dale and Gale and Hobo and Keith had completed a framework of willow poles on the raft about five feet high and eight feet square. Two-by-fours were nailed to the bottoms of the four corner poles and then the two-by-fours nailed to the deck. The four of them helped Vince and Tom stretch the tarp over the frame, leaving one end of the "cabin" mostly open.

The legitimate camping trip gave them the opportunity to obtain some provisions for the raft trip. Vince said to get whatever they could from the kitchen, without, of course, taking anything their families would need to get by. A few potatoes, some left over cornbread and biscuits ....

"Of course, we'll have plenty of fresh fish, and we can stop in towns along the way and buy a few things," he said. "Which reminds me...."

He climbed up to the forked limb above the tree house and brought down the coffee can holding their treasury. He counted it. It came to $18.84. After counting it, they had climbed down the tree and Vince put the can in under the other stuff inside the shelter on the raft.

They had sat cross-legged on the raft and looked at their provisions, the shelter, the lard can stove on a flat rock, the cane poles and lines tied on the roof, and the long paddle pole steering apparatus they had installed on the rear.

The anticipation of the forthcoming event left a most pleasant taste in the mind, Tom had noted to himself.

"I tell ya, boys, now this is a great feeling, ain't it?" Dale had said. "This must be something, I guess, akin to how Daniel Boone and DeSota and Columbus and that bunch must have felt as they looked down toward the unknown."

"Or how Huck and Jim felt when they pulled out on their raft," Vince said.

Then they had sat quietly for a time, lost in their thoughts, thoughts about leaving home on a river raft. Probably all were wondering if somebody was going to back out at the last minute.

Keith Richards had broken the tranquillity with a bunch of his nonsense.

"One thing of concern here for me, Vince," he said in his most serious tone. "Granny's really hot on me practicing that piano for two hours every day now. I was wonderin' if you and the boys could help me to get that thing down here and onto the raft..."

"Why, sure," Vince said without hesitation. "Go on up there with him, boys, and help get that piano down here. He can play it when we round the bends and come into the towns, like the old steam calliope on the showboat, you know?"

Gale, continuing in the spirit of the moment, said, "Yeah, and I want to go see if Miss Newberry will go with us. She could school me on my math..."

Both of them were shoved overboard.

They had pulled the raft off farther out into the water, tied it off, and swam to shore. Plans were to push off by 4 p.m.

All six boys gained permission for a three-day camping trip. Tom's mother consented right off.

She had pulled him in close and held him tight. "I look for news of Flint any day now, and there's not a thing you can do. I know I haven't been much of a comfort to you here lately, but I just can't do anything right now, Tom. Not till I know for sure Flint is coming home safe and sound and whole, and that this war with Japan is really over.

"The Scouts have been good for you. In a few weeks you'll be going back to school, so if you'll promise to be extra careful and come back safe and sound, then you go and enjoy yourself. Enjoy yourself while you can."

She worried more about his father getting hurt on the job – because she knew his first-born son was constantly on his mind – than she did about Tom getting hurt.

His father had given his blessing on Tom's plans, too.

He had been listening to a report by Gabriel Heatter about the fate of Hirohito now that Japan had suffered defeat at the hands of the Allies. He motioned for Tom to come set down by him. He put his arm around Tom and cautioned him about several concerns, especially warning him to watch for snakes in the heat of late summer.

"And don't you worry. Things are going to work out okay with your brother," he said. "Come out to the building. I have something for you."

He handed Tom two railroad lanterns with wicks trimmed, globes cleaned and each filled with kerosene.

"You're going to need to have these lit in your camp. And here's you a small can of fresh coal oil for them."

A wave of guilt swept over Tom and for a moment he considered telling his father he was actually leaving home for a raft trip down to the Mississippi.

———————

An hour later, his mother kissed him goodbye as he went out the door with his pack on his back. He paused on the back porch to tie the two lanterns his father had fixed for him on either side of the pack frame.

He stopped to pick up Dale before they headed on down to Gale's. Hobo was on the way up the street from his house. The four of them walked the alley to the next street to pick up Vince and Keith. No one lingered. They feared callback might come anytime.

The six of them went up over the crossing and onto Route Ten and turned toward School House Hollow. Once around the bend, they scooted down the slope of the highway shoulder to Farmer Matt's barn, marched through his pasture, and followed the creek on to the river.

Tom wondered if the others were wondering what he was wondering: Were they really going to follow through on this Huck Finn trip? Or was it just a matter of seeing who would chicken-out first.

The raft rode high and steady. Keith was nominated to swim out and untie it and bring it ashore. The water had raised only slightly during the night and appeared now to be at a standstill.

Suddenly the thrill of the adventure they were about to embark on took hold. They chatted among themselves excitedly as they placed their bedrolls and stuff inside the cabin. Vince complimented Tom on bringing the lanterns. He had brought the oars from the *Reuben James*, but had decided to leave the boat.

"It'll be here, on the bank, when we get back," Vince said.

When would that be, Tom wondered to himself, and would it be? He couldn't push out of his mind thoughts of danger that circled like buzzards over a carcass.

Any second thoughts and convictions they were having about having fibbed to their parents in order to get away flew away like hungry sparrows once they poled the raft out of the last line of willow tops and into the current.

"Every man needs to discover what lies around the far bend," Vince said. "Gentlemen, we are about to do that."

"That's poetic," Dale said.

"Let's keep in close to the tree line for a while," Vince added. "No use advertising ourselves."

It was Keith who started the song, and the others joined in:

...he don't plant taters, he don't plant cotton,
And them what plants 'em are soon forgotten.
But ol' Man River, he just keeps rollin' along.

Dale, watching as Vince and Tom tied the lanterns to the uppermost front corners of the canopy frame, wondered aloud what their purpose was. "We're surely not planning on running after dark, are we? Big steamboats will run over a man in the dark."

"They'll come in handy for the camp at nights," Vince said.

Vince was laid back with his head resting on his folded hands, a willow twig sticking from one side of his mouth.

"Only one thing missin' from this trip," he said, "and I tried my best to take care of that. I almost had ol' Joe Johnson talked into coming with us. Would'a come, I think, but he lives with his aunt, and she's sick."

"Joe Johnson? You mean the big Negro who cleans up at the Playhouse? What'er you talking about?" Keith asked.

"I'm talking about Huck Finn had Jim, the big runaway slave," Vince said. "Jim made the whole thing interesting. If you'd read the book, you'd know. Can you read, by the way, Richards?"

"I can read better than you, if I wanted to," Keith said.

"Yes, we needed Joe bad," Vince continued. "I tried to tell him we'd get him a job comin' back on the river that pays five times what he makes pushin' a broom and cleanin' windows at the Play House. He would have come hadn't a been for his aunt. I really believe that."

"Well, lord almighty. Good thing he didn't," Keith said. "That guy's always hungry. He'd a eat up all our grub before we ever got to Cincinnati."

They were sliding past Sherwood Forest and coming up on the first bend below the village when Vince broke out a small paper sack half-filled with something. Tom went back to help Dale out on the sweep as Vince went into the tent. Hobo was in there, stretched out, resting a sore back he said he injured the night of the graveyard incident.

Pretty soon they heard Hobo's voice through the canvass: "What in the world?! What are you puttin' on my face?"

"Why, it's nothing, Hobo, won't come off after a while. Hold still, now. Let me finish."

"What…why, that's soot. Soot 'n grease, or something. Get out of here with that stuff!"

"Aw, come on, Hobo. Just wear it this first day, until we get to where we're gonna camp. It won't hurt you none."

"I'm not for one minute bein' your Negro slave. You silly goose! I've got red hair anyway. Now get away from me or I'm gonna throw you overboard, Vince. I swear I will."

Vince ripped out of the tent entrance with Hobo after him. The other four laughed at Hobo's black face as Vince ran around the cabin and Hobo lost his balance and went in.

He washed his face good, pulled himself back up onto the raft, and sat there, letting go with a belch you could hear on the other side of the river.

"The days of slavery are over," he said, pointing a warning finger at Vince.

After that they all fell silent, alone with their thoughts and the whispering of the current and the adventurous aroma of that river.

262

CHAPTER 49:
A NARROW ESCAPE

Feelings of bitterness surged through the Braves as the raft approached the site of Old Man Throckmorton Turner's melon patch. He had lied about them in court and sullied their reputation, pinning charges of crop theft and destruction on them. They seethed about it for days after the judge's decision but decided to take Mr. Galloway's advice on the matter. He had showed them in the scriptures that "vengeance belongs to the Lord," and that God would repay Turner for lying on the boys.

"Jesus said that as a man sows, so shall he reap, and I want you boys to remember that and let the Lord take care of the matter. Don't you ever go down around there trying to some way get revenge yourselves," he had warned.

The time for full harvest of the watermelon crop had arrived and Turner's truck and a couple of hired hands were poised to begin picking and delivering the ripe fruit to market.

As they came abreast of the spot, Vince motioned for quiet with a finger to his lips as he reached out to grab a willow limb and swing the raft in out of the current.

"Hold us here, boys," he said. "I want to do something, if I can get away with it. It'll just take a minute."

"What n the world? You're surely not...." Hobo said.

"Naw, I'm not gonna bother any of the old man's melons," Vince said. "Even though we really should. We paid for a bunch of 'em that we got no benefit from. But all I need to do is to dash up there right quick and then straight back out."

He went into the shelter and, from under his bedroll, retrieved a square of white cardboard with lettering on it, affixed to a three-foot tomato stake sharpened on one end.

The letters on the sign had been clipped from newspaper headlines of various sizes and pasted in place. Vince had put in a lot of work on the sign, clipping and pasting and looking up spellings in the dictionary. He turned the sign around to where the curious onlookers could read it:

WARNING! AT LEAST 3 MELONS
IN THIS PATCH HAVE BEEN
INJECTED WITH STRICNINE

A ripple of quiet snickering surged through the Braves.

"Don't tie off. Just hold 'er here. Be ready for a fast getaway if necessary. Just don't go off and leave me," Vince whispered. "If there's any activity out there in the field, I'll sneak on back and not even go in."

After a period of intense listening for any sound of any kind coming from up in the melon patch, Vince slipped into the water. Holding the sign high and dry in one hand, he side-stroked until he was able to wade the rest of the way ashore.

Making his way through the horseweeds, he stood at the edge of the patch, listening and watching. Then, satisfied that no one was around, he stole silently out into the field, being careful not to step on melons or vines, and, using a rock he had picked up at the edge of the patch, drove the stake securely into the ground.

As he turned to sneak away, temptation overcame him. The spirit was willing, but the flesh was weak.

Tom and the others, watching the edge of the weeds where Vince had disappeared, saw their fearless leader come out of them struggling under the load of a forty-pound egg-shaped, green striped watermelon on his shoulder.

He plunged into the water and pushed the melon ahead of him. Tom, unbelieving, turned away as the others helped bring the booty on board, no questions asked.

"We paid for it," Vince said as they released their hold on the willow limbs and pushed off into the current.

When they were off at a safe distance, Vince slapped his knee with one hand, grinned at the admiring five, and said, "I'd like to see just how many melons the old man can sell now," Vince said. "Maybe he'll just ignore the warning, but then again he'll think a long time before taking a chance on selling one that could cause a customer to die. That'd bring a lawsuit that could lose him the farm."

Keith rolled on the deck laughing. "None, I'd say," he said. "This is a good one, Vince. And it serves that old man right."

As they drifted on, they all glanced back a time or two toward the melon patch. They knew that old Turner, who knew he'd lied on them, would realize very much that somebody might well have actually put poison in some of his melons. To be safe would require him to examine each melon before loading to see if he could detect a difficult-to-find injection hole.

Then they turned their attention to the beautiful green orb lying on the deck.

And Tom had to admit it was the sweetest, most delicious fruit he had ever had the pleasure of tasting.

Travel on the Ohio River in the 1940s was regulated by a series of locks and dams located about every 20 to 30 miles along the length of the river. Dams were something Huck and Jim didn't have to worry about on their journey down the Mississippi a hundred years before. Vince knew that Lock and Dam 31 was only a few miles below Hooperville, but he was not familiar with what the procedure was for getting through. He had studied up enough on them to know that they were obligated to lock through any recreational craft as well as the large commercial tows.

As they approached the dam, a towboat and its coal barges passed them heading downstream. It didn't bother to slow or to point toward the locks, which were located on the Kentucky side. The river was high enough that it covered the lock walls. As the Braves, their raft still drifting close to the willows, watched, the steamboat plowed right over the dam through a navigable pass section, more than six hundred feet wide, where a maneuver boat had pulled the movable wickets. The only thing showing above water to indicate a dam was there was a flagpole or some such thing projecting from the water atop the beartraps in the middle of the dam. All the boys had to do was steer the raft toward the middle of the river and follow the path of the steamboat down. They passed over the dam as smooth as silk, cut back toward the Kentucky shore, and continued their westward journey, carried along by a healthy current.

The river was falling now; this they could tell from the waterline on the willow trees and the fact that there was little driftwood going down.

The current carried them along at a good clip and before dark they reached Lock and Dam No. 32. They could make out the current breaking over the lock walls, which were just below the surface. But the wickets were lowered, and over they went, waving to two men on a boat working with winches and capstan. They appeared to be putting some of the wickets back into place. They stopped to watch the boys as their raft slipped by them not more fifty feet away.

The boys sat cross-legged on the bow and watched westward as the earth turned away from the sun. Hobo broke out a cob pipe and filled it with dried cornsilk, lit it, and they passed it around.

"Ug, Indian make peace with white man," Vince said as he passed the pipe to Gale.

"How long you reckon it will take to reach Cairo?" Dale asked.

"I don't know how many bends there are between here and the Mississippi," Vince said. "I know it's a pretty good trip just to Cincinnati. Mom and Dad took us kids down there to the zoo, before the war broke out. We rode that train for probably two hours or more."

The mention of distance on the river brought Tom's mind on Flint more than ever. He thought of him being adrift on a much larger body of water, and of fish that tried to eat him. He prayed that his big brother was recovering OK.

"Flint said this river stretches nearly a thousand miles from Pittsburgh to Cairo," Tom said. "Course, Hooperville must be halfway down the river to start with."

"It don't matter how long," said Gale, lying on his back with his legs dangling over the side. "We ain't got no time schedule to worry with anyway. Man, is this nice."

That was a sentiment shared by the others. All seemed glad that Vince had worked up the plans for The Great Raft Adventure. There's nothing more peaceful or soothing to the soul than twilight time on a broad, still river. The western sky was a tranquilizing orange glow, fighting back the shadows that closed on the raft from the rear. This was absolute freedom from the demands of time and toil. Tom was living for the moment, and declined to think what the future might hold.

Soon the sunset's last glow was gone and shadows crept in along the banks. Here and there they could see the lights of a farmhouse. They heard the *George Washington* whistle for a crossing and saw her headlamp streaking along the rails through the trees.

There was no moon up yet, but a million stars filled the sky. Keith, who had relieved Dale at the sweep, said they were far enough from shore not to worry about snags, and joined the others on the front of the raft. Vince pointed out the Little Dipper. A shooting star blazed a trail away off there somewhere in the universe. A dog barked from the Ohio shore; its voice carrying plainly across the surface to their ears.

Vince noticed no one had taken the time to light the two railroad lanterns, which he and Tom had suspended from poles on the front corners of the raft.

"I didn't know if we should light them or not," Tom said. "They'll burn a long time on a little bit of coal oil, but we sure don't have much of it to spare."

"Well, you're right, Tom," Vince said. "We shouldn't be doin' no runnin' at night anyhow. Let's start looking for a place to tie up for the night."

He stood up to stretch himself. "Hey!" he said. "Do you see where in the world we're at? We're right smack in the middle of the river!"

He could make out the outline of hills at equal distance on both sides of the river. They had rounded a deep bend striking to the north. The current had bounced off the Kentucky shore and took the raft with it into the middle of the river, aiming toward the Ohio shore, where the next bend turned to the south.

"Better light the lanterns 'till we get back toward the Kentucky shore," Vince said.

Hobo was searching his pockets for his matches when Dale pointed down-stream and asked, "What's the lights down there? Somebody looking a trotline, you reckon?"

It was pitch black below the skyline and they were all standing, straining their eyes down toward the lights.

"Listen!" Gale said. "What's that? Sounds like water rushing around something – something big."

Tom felt terror tingling along his spine.

"Trotline-looker, my foot," Hobo said. "That's a towboat. And it's closer than we think. Get on the oars!"

Gale grabbed one oar and Hobo the other. Vince leaped to the sweep, pushing the long-handled paddle back and forth.

Hobo said, "Should we be paddling this direction? Seems like we're pulling in front of it."

"She is closer to the Kentucky shore," Vince said. "Turn around. Let's pull for the Ohio shore. The current's going that way anyway. Pull for all you're worth!"

They were able to make out the dark shadow of the tow now, see the red and green lights atop the barges distinctly. There appeared to be three barges abreast. They were empties, and they rose up ten or twelve feet above the surface.

They were in the thing's path!

"Row like maniacs!" Vince screamed. "They don't know we're out here!"

Hobo stopped rowing long enough to hand Tom his box of matches. "Here, Tom. Light the lanterns. Light your shirt, a poke, anything…"

Keith and Dale leaped up and down, whooping at the top of their lungs. "We're out here! Hey! We're out here!" Keith yelled over and over.

Tom ran into the shelter with the matches, found the paper sack of potatoes, dumped the spuds, and with trembling hands struck a match and put it to the sack. It caught fire quickly. He jumped back outside, waving the blazing bag above his head.

A long blast from the steamboat's whistle shattered the night. A beam of light shot out from above the pilothouse, sweeping the middle of the river in front of the barges. It came to rest on the raft. The sound of rushing water diminished. They saw two lights bobbing up and down on the barges and moving quickly toward the front of the tow.

"They've spotted us!" Tom said, dropping the remains of the potato sack as the flames burned his fingers.

For a moment no one could see anything in the white glare of the spotlight. Then they could make out the barges swinging slowly until the entire tow angled at about forty-five degrees toward the Kentucky shore. They were out of the tow's path and the raft drifted down alongside the barges and toward the towboat.

"Looks like a bunch of crazy kids on a raft," one of the two men who had made it to the front of the barges said to the other.

Call them crazy or whatever, the boys didn't care. They had been spared.

The glow of lights from the windows of the boat fell across the raft as they drifted just off the side of the boat. The great paddlewheel turned backwards. A man stepped out of the pilothouse.

"Is everybody all right out there?" he asked. His voice was trying to sound angry, but it trembled a bit.

"Yeah, we're okay. Everything's fine, Cap'n," Vince said, shielding his eyes with his hands in an effort to see the man behind the voice.

"Well, I'm gonna tell you crazy little idiots something," said the voice, now losing itself to anger. "You're lucky to be alive. You don't deserve to be alive. We didn't see you, didn't know you were out there until you lit that flame or something. Now get that piece of junk off the river and get yourselves home, wherever that is."

No one on the raft said anything. They just started paddling for the Ohio shore. Tons of water poured down off the paddlewheel as it stopped, then churned forward. The spotlight swung to the Kentucky shore and the tow slowly corrected its path.

In close to shore, the Braves sought to quiet their frayed nerves with agitated talk and nervous laughter.

"We came very close to being dead," Gale said.

"Naw," Vince said. "All we had to do, and the thing I was about to have us do, was to dive to the bottom and hold onto a snag until she passed over us. Huck got run over by a big riverboat, and that's what he did."

"I bet he didn't have no string of coal barges to go under," Hobo said.

They lit the lanterns. As the lights of the steamboat disappeared around the upstream bend, they came to the mouth of a small stream, barely visible in the darkness.

269

"We'll pull in here," Vince said. "Make camp for the night. I don't think we'll be traveling after dark anymore."

"Amen, Brother Ben. Shot at a rooster and killed a hen," Keith said.

They paddled the raft up in under the trees and about twenty yards into the stream and tied it off to a tree.

"Long-line it," Vince said. "This water's dropping fast. Don't want to wake up in the morning and be grounded."

They lit the lanterns and finished off two of their five loaves of light bread, each slice spread generously with peanut butter and jelly. They washed it down with their only gallon of milk, now warm but still good.

Then they broke out their blankets and rolled up in them inside the canvas covering. The crickets and jar flies sang their late-summer songs along the shore. A bullfrog and an owl joined in the chorus. Tom thought of home and Dad and Mom and Flint. Had they gotten any word from Flint yet, he wondered. Was he on his way home?

Sleep finally claimed him, and the others. Tom drifted into dreaming of river bends, bends that went on and on with never an end in sight.

CHAPTER 50:
DRIFTING ALONG WITH
THE RIVER OF LIFE

Tom awoke to the sound of a bluejay's scolding call from a tree. It took him a minute to recall where he was. Looking out to the mouth of the creek, he could see the slanting rays of sunlight sparkling on the river's surface. But the raft was still in deep shadows. A canopy of varnished foliage and festooning vines blocked out most light.

The raft was slightly askance. The front was out on shore. He stepped out onto the muddy bank, relieved himself, and gathered an armload of driftwood. Soon he had a crackling fire going on the hearth of the lard can stove. He found a bar of soap and washed his hands in the creek. He broke out an iron skillet and set bacon to sizzling on top of the stove. He placed two small flat rocks under one side of the skillet to level it.

After that harrowing experience with the steamboat barges on the dark river, he entertained the thought that some of his companions in this quickly conceived venture might be ready to turn back. He would welcome such a move himself, though he certainly wasn't going to be the one to broach the subject.

The aroma of frying bacon soon brought the others to life.

"Get up, get up, boys," he said cheerfully. "There's a new day dawning, the Mississippi is waiting for our discovery. We will claim it for America!"

Vince awoke, grumbling, and made his way to shore. After relieving himself and washing his hands with the bar of soap Tom had left on the deck, he broke out the eating utensils. He poured most of the bacon grease out of the skillet, saving it in a tin cup, and made lightbread toast in the skillet. Then Tom added some grease back in and stirred the skillet full of scrambled eggs.

"We should have set the lines last night," Hobo said as he stumbled out of the tent and knelt down to wash his face in creek water. "We could have had fresh catfish for breakfast."

"How about fresh catfish for dinner," Vince said, dishing himself up a mess of scrambled eggs and bacon and toast into his scout mess kit.

Then the other three were up and helping themselves. Tom felt like his mother at the meals back home as he waited until last to be served. But there was plenty to go around, although he warned the boys that bacon was for flavoring, not to fill their guts up with.

Tom couldn't help thinking, however, that such breakfasts would probably soon be nothing but a memory. Vince had a way of ignoring or overriding such realities. He cheerfully said the boys could go ashore and buy eggs and bread and such. If the money ran out before they got to Cairo, they could work around the farms or the towns for their food.

Dale and Gale got the skillet- and dish-washing chores. When they finished, with some huffing and puffing and the aid of a long leverage pole and a log, they slid the raft off the shore and poled down the creek to its mouth.

The river had fallen considerably and was still falling. A current of five to ten miles per hour carried them along down the wide river toward Cairo. On shore, they heard a tractor cough to life, and a farmer calling his pigs. A steamboat pushing a tow of oil barges rounded the bend downstream. They headed for the Kentucky shore, making certain to give the towboat a wide berth.

"Say, ain't this the life, though?" Vince said. "We should 'a quit fighting wars a long time ago."

He was lying on his back with his bare feet hanging out over the edge of the raft. He had tied a length of fishing line around one big toe and had baited the hook with one of the nightcrawlers Hobo brought along.

"That's a good way to lose a foot," Hobo told him.

"I'm not down enough to drag bottom."

"I mean to a big catfish."

Dale, the poet laureate of Hooperville, was waxing elegant, as he sometimes did.

"Ah, yes, just drifting along with the river of life," he said. "Let the teeming masses lift that barge and sweat for the land; to them goes the struggle

272

and to them goes the strife. They seek the means of a good future life, but the Hooperville Braves live it already."

It left the others speechless for awhile. Finally, Keith said, "Say, that's good. You ought to put that down – have it published."

"Somebody already has," Dale said. "I just can't remember who."

Yes, with the near-tragedy of the steamboat incident behind them, all six boys were again caught up in the exhilarating grasp of adventure. Free from all cares of life, they looked now to what new mysteries might await them around the next bend.

They passed a little village where church bells were ringing.

Mr. Galloway's not gonna have much of a class this morning," Gale said. "And if he finds out – and you know he will – we're supposed to be camping up in the beech grove, he's likely to come looking for us."

Sometime in the afternoon they pulled ashore and lunched on peanut butter and jelly sandwiches, washed down with some of the fresh water they'd brought along in a five-gallon lard can. The sun was bearing down. It must have been above ninety. They lay in the shade of the willows for a nap before shoving off again.

The river was theirs. Confident in their boat, they felt good about themselves. No one had mentioned the possibility of turning back. At least once in his life, Tom thought, a man should taste life on a raft on a wide, still river. It makes you feel you're a part of the universe, that you actually belong.

It was difficult to believe the world knew violence. Rich fields of ripening corn stretched back across wide bottoms to the distant hills, which looked more like giant green sponges than the steep slopes covered with brambles and vines and tall oaks and hickories that they were.

They lay on their backs and watched the clouds roll by. Except for Keith, who hit a lick on the sweep now and then to keep the raft drifting at about one hundred yards from the shore. He was also the lookout. Vince had put them on shifts to cover the watch.

"That's the way they do it on the big steamboats," he said. "Four hours on and four hours off. We need to get used to it for the trip back."

Suddenly Keith brought the crew upright with his cry of "Land ho. Land in the middle of the river."

They were bearing down on not one, but two, wooded islands.

"Must be Blanchester Islands," Vince said. "Pull out toward the middle. Let's check them out. It's getting along toward supper, anyway."

Drawing closer, they saw a sandbar projecting out from the upriver end of the largest island, and they began maneuvering the raft for a landing at that point.

"I'll bet that island's crawling with Japs – whoops! Forget I said that," Vince said.

"We don't have any guns or gear to fight with anyway," Gale said. "Somebody swiped all our stuff. Remember?"

Dale said, "We could just radio the Enola Joy, or whatever the name of that big bomber was, and have 'em drop an atomic bomb on 'em. That's the way wars are fought now."

They leaped off onto the sand bar and held the lines while the raft drifted on around the point, then they tied it securely in the shade of some overhanging willows and maples.

Hobo had managed to troll up three nice catfish during the float. While he and Gale skinned them out, Tom gathered some driftwood and got a good cooking fire going on the bank. Vince spooned some lard into the iron skillet and by the time Hobo and Gale had washed the solid chunks of white meat, it was bubbling. They rolled the chunks in flour and dropped them into the bubbling grease. They fried the fish to a golden brown and served it on light bread with catsup. It was an excellent supper.

Evening shadows were falling and Vince had already decided to spend the night on the island. They had barely passed Hobo's cob pipe around and started to gather in some wood when they heard the roll of thunder downstream. The entire sky there was blue-black, and jagged streaks of orange lightning zigzagged through it. Already the treetops over their heads were starting to bend with the wind.

"That's dangerous lookin'," Vince said. "We can't stay out here. We gotta find shelter."

Making sure the lines were doubled for added security before grabbing their bedrolls, they leaped ashore and headed in under a canopy of giant trees for the interior of the island. The rain was splattering on the leaves overhead as they climbed a steep hill and came to the base of a cliff. And there beckoning to them was a wide and deep rockhouse leading back under the cliff.

Lightning slammed into a nearby oak and sent a limb crashing down. The boys literally jumped into the safety of the rockhouse. The rain and wind roared so loudly that they couldn't hear what each other was saying. Rivulets poured down from the rock face of the cavern and ran off downhill. Inside, they we were snug and dry.

"I can't believe it," Vince shouted. "Just 'bout this very thing happened to Huck and Jim. I wonder if old Mark Twain is up there worrying with our circumstances right now."

Suddenly Tom sensed the hairs tingling on the back of his neck. He knew instantly that there was someone – or something – in that rockhouse besides them.

Then a raspy voice said, "You boys make a habit of busting into a man's home without an invitation?"

They turned and found themselves facing a grizzled, long-haired, whiskered man. The rifle he held in his hands was pointed straight at them.

CHAPTER 51:
THE CAVE MAN

The six boys stood transfixed, everybody's gaze trained on the rifle and the man who held it. No human stares down the barrel of a gun without thoughts of sudden death crossing his or her mind and fear surging through their body like an electrical charge, especially so for boys of such a tender age. They wanted to bolt, but prudence warned them not to try it. Dark eyes under bushy brows of the man holding the rifle squinted as they darted about from one to the other of the boys. His face, most of it covered by an unkempt, dirty-white beard that fell to his chest, showed a leathery, grimy complexion. He wore soiled bibbed overalls buckled over a ragged denim shirt. Toes stuck through the end of one of his black brogans. It was hard to tell how old a man he was. Seventy? Eighty?

"Are all of you deaf and tongue-tied?" he snapped. "Speak up! Tell me what you're doin' here on my island."

Vince's adventuresome mind whirred as he sought to come up with an answer. Just tell the truth, he thought, tell the truth and then hope to get out with nobody hurt. Outside, the rain slacked, but showed no signs of stopping. Vince stammered, found his voice, and began to talk fast.

"We're just passing through," he said. "We plan on bein' on our way right away. We're on our way to Cairo, traveling on our boat, and we pulled in here to fix a catfish supper. Then the storm hit, and we come lookin' for shelter. Didn't expect to find anybody back in a cave like this."

The old man studied his visitors for long seconds. Then, to the boys' relief, he slowly lowered the rifle.

"I don't know what you're up to," he said. "You're too young to be out here on this river, that I know. But that's your business. You're the first people I've seen on this island in who knows when. You're the first ones ever been in my home here. Don't expect you mean old Elzie any harm. Let's get some light in here."

He disappeared around the end of a rock wall rising from the floor to near the ceiling, which had the effect of petitioning the rockhouse into two rooms. In a few minutes, he said, "Come on back here."

Cautiously, moving behind Vince as if in one body, they made their way around the end of the wall. Behind it, the rockhouse dipped back farther under the cliff, forming another room, with a wide, level floor. The old man, the gun now gone from his hands, had lit two oil lamps. In the flickering, shadowy light they gave, the boys made out various pieces of furniture – a table and chairs, a cabinet, two bunk beds against the rear wall. There was a wood-burning cook stove with a pipe that rose to the ceiling and bent to make its way along the ceiling and vent itself near the entrance to the rockhouse.

"You wouldn't think to find anybody living back in a 'cave' as you call it, eh?" the old man said. "Well, this is home for me. It stays cool in the summer and wards off most of the cold in the winter. The temperature in here stays probably in the fifties or sixties. That's not bad. I've a plentiful supply of driftwood for the stove, and rabbits and squirrels and catfish for the claimin'. No icebox, but then the settlers of this valley didn't have iceboxes. Salt preserves my meat. I'm self-sufficient here. I don't want for nothing."

He went on to tell the boys he had lived in the rockhouse "for, I don't know, seven or eight years. What is this? Nineteen forty-five? I moved up here to high ground right after the thirty-seven flood took the house. We had 'er up on pillars, but the flood took her anyway. I moved these few things out before she went. I plan on rebuildin' one of these days. What a hellachious flood that was. You boys old enough to remember that one?"

Hobo told about his dad carrying him out of their house at midnight in hip boots.

"I was four or five, and the water was over my head right off the front porch. We ended up losing stuff, but the house stayed put."

"Well, anyway," the old man continued, "you boys ain't old enough to be workin' for the government. I thought you might be government people pokin' around here when you busted in on me like that."

He stirred a pot of brown beans cooking on top of the stove. They smelled delicious.

"Got no use for anybody from the government. I'd shoot government people if they set foot on this island."

The old man cut loose with a volley of curses. After he'd caught his breath, he invited the boys to come on in and sit down. The rain picked up again. Water came down over the rockhouse entrance like a waterfall before striking the ground and washing on down hill away from the entrance.

"You're not goin' anywhere anyway," he said. "It's rainin' hard enough out there to drown a hippo. 'Pears the wind has slacked off, though.

"I know they talk about me over on the mainland like I'm some crazy old man who lives in a cave like a bear. They're afraid of me, and that suits me just fine. But I've got more sense than most of them."

Tom thought to himself that they should make a run for the raft, get away from this crazy old recluse. Then again, he might come after them with the rifle.

Vince shrugged his shoulders and went on in, seating himself on the linoleum that covered the cave floor. The others joined him. The old man added a cup of water to the beans. He sat down in a straw-bottomed chair at the table and lit his cob. Hobo followed suit, bumming a match from their host.

Then the old man continued his tirade against the government.

"The government's supposed to be for the people, of the people and by the people – that's what old Abe said about it. But all the government wants to do is take from the people.

"I'd say you boys are runnin' from some kind of government. You're too young to be regular river travelers. The government makes you go to school, don't it? And if you don't go, they come and get you, don't they? A body ought to be able to decide if he wants to go to school or not. But the all-knowing government thinks it ought to make that decision for you.

"All they want is for you to mature – turn into little worker ants. They want you to be buyers and sellers and taxpayers so's the government can be fed. Well, to hell with it! To hell with the whole capitalistic system. I don't produce nothin', 'cept my garden, and I buy very little. But you can see how good I live here."

He fell silent for a moment, taking a long draw on his pipe. Then, pounding the table with his fist, he said, "My folks didn't want to sell the old home place over there in the village. The Peaotts had owned that place since their ancestors came down from Pennsylvania on a flat boat. All my parents wanted to do was to live there and enjoy life until it was ended, and pass it on to my sister and me.

"But the government decided to run a highway right through the middle of it. When we wouldn't sell, they took it. Con-dem-nation, they called it. Absolute dictatorship, I call it.

"We bought land over here – bought this whole island, where we knew they'd never build another road. But my dear old mother was never happy after being driven out of her home. She died not long after we finished the house here. My daddy grieved hisself to death a year later. I got no idea where Sis wound up."

The old man took time to stir the beans, then rambled on.

"And then come that flood. The only thing more destructive than the government is this old river when it goes on a tear. Like I said, I managed to save these few things and move them up here. The river's never made it up on this cliff."

Vince tried to work in a word sidewise, but the old man, getting up to stir the beans again, then re-lighting his pipe, continued his indictment of the government.

"Now I see the government's got us smack in the middle of a big war, away off in Japan or somewhere. I rowed over to the landing at Blanchester back around the first of the month – always go over then to get my Social Security check and pick up a few things – and Joe Blankenship – runs Blankenship's grocery up there on the main drag – told me how the government took his son, the only help he had, right away from him. Drafted the boy, put a rifle in his hand, and sent him off across the ocean to fight in this war – fight against somebody he didn't have any quarrel with. Fightin' for Democracy, Joe said, but there ain't no such thing, not here anyway, not when they can up and take your home right out from under you."

Tom felt like some comment was needed here. He at first decided not to say anything, then changed his mind. He cleared his throat and said, "Mister…uh…I'm sorry, what'd you say your name is?"

"Elzie. Elzie Peaott."

"Well, Mr. Peaott, surely you know that it wasn't our government that started the war. It was the Japs and Hitler. There was a sneak attack on our ships at Pearl Harbor. Hitler and Tojo wanted to take over the world. The United States is the main one that put a stop to that."

The old man looked at Tom and seemed to be studying his response.

"Yeah, well," he said, finally, "they're still over there buttin' in. Defend the country, yes. But they ain't got no business over there, except to help some fat government official sit up there in Washington and collect a big fat salary, plus whatever else he can knock down.

"You don't see none of their sons going off to some strange land to fight and die. It's always the sons of the Joe Blankenships, people that's just tryin' to make a livin', in spite of the government."

The old man picked up a rag and moved the pot from the stove to the table. He took a pan of cornbread from the oven.

"I've got enough beans for all of us here, boys..."

Vince thanked him, but said no, adding that they were full of catfish.

"Suit yourselves," he said. He spooned soupy beans over a chunk of cornbread he'd placed on a tin plate.

Outside the rockhouse, the darkness was thick and the rain had stopped.

"I think we'd better be goin' on down the river," Vince said. "We're on a kinda tight schedule."

"You're welcome to spend the night here," the old man said. " Don't have enough beds or covers, but I see you got bedrolls. You can sleep here on the floor. I'm enjoying havin' you boys to talk to."

Before they could answer, he was asking about the war.

"How's it goin'? I heard the Germans had quit. But what about the Japs?"

Didn't his eyebrows rise when they told him about the atomic bombs dropped on two cities, completely obliterating them.

He took a minute to ponder this information. Then he said, "Good God almighty, then this is the end of the world the Bible talks about. They'll destroy it. They'll put a place like mine here right in style. If anybody survives, they'll wind up livin' in the caves and the rocks. That settles it for me. I ain't never goin' off this island again, except, of course, to pick up my Social Security check."

The Braves said their good-byes and started off down the slope, Hobo leading the way with his flashlight. The old man followed them to the mouth of the rockhouse.

"Take my advice, you boys," he said. "Keep on goin' down that river. You go back and soon's you're a little older, the government'll put a rifle in your hand, send you off to fight one of its wars and be tellin' you what you can and can't do."

They heard him utter another string of curses as they made their way on down the hill and under the trees toward the raft.

Tom began to have second thoughts about leaving.

"It's pitch dark out here, Vince. Not even any stars," he said.

"Don't trust that old man," Vince said. "I think he's on the verge of losing it all. I'm not even stayin' on this island. We'll move on downriver a little, get back along toward the Kentucky shore."

"Serve that old man right if the Japs had got over here," Keith said. "Would've too, if everybody had his attitude. He'd have a real reason to cuss the givernment then."

The raft had held fast in tight against the willows. They untied the ropes and pushed off. Hobo shined his light to make sure they cleared the trees just downstream from where they'd tied off.

Suddenly he reached out and grabbed a limb, saying, "Hey, what's this? Wait a minute, what is this?"

In the spot of his flashlight, they saw a small driftpile holding in the limbs of some trees, slightly above the descending water level. Hobo reached out with an oar and knocked it down and pulled some of it toward the raft.

He said, "This looks like – it is! Here's my old rifle, and a couple more of our guns…and hand grenades. This is some of our stuff that disappeared out of the tree house."

Gale, casting a puzzled look at Vince, said, "Well! How do you suppose …?"

"That shouldn't be hard to figure out, Flanders," Vince said. "Whoever stole that stuff got to worrying and threw it in the river, that's all. Come on, let's get on down around this island. It's spooky."

As soon as they cleared the lower end of the island, the clouds cleared, the stars came out, and a three-quarter moon rose over the Kentucky hills. The lower island appeared as a great black hulk as they slid by it. They struck out for the Kentucky shore, Vince singing out, "Man the oars, me laddies. There's treasure awaits us at the end of the trail."

CHAPTER 52:
A DAM DISASTER

With the moon hanging low on the left horizon, and the fog not having moved in as yet, they broke their rule about night travel and drifted on for a while. Everybody was too worked up to sleep anyway.

The jar flies sang their late summer song from the trees along the shore. Now and then a hoot owl called.

They drifted along just far enough from the Kentucky shore to stay outside the shadows cast by the trees along the shoreline. The moon afforded enough light that they could spot any snags or sandbars that might hang them.

It was as though they drifted through time and space, with no real world to anchor them.

Tom would never let anyone know, but dark water frightened him. They passed within twenty feet of a sunken tree whose limbs projected above the water, the current swirling and gurgling around them. It seemed he could sense it trying to reach out and snare him and pull him down under that black water. If they had hit it with the raft he believed his heart would have stopped.

And Tom would never admit it but he was ready to go back home. He longed to see big brother Flint and wondered if he had yet made it to the states. He missed his mother, and her cooking. He yearned for the silent, comforting company of his father.

They'd almost been killed by a steamboat and perhaps nearly shot by the hermit of Blanchester Island. Tom was hoping he lived long enough to have grandchildren, so he would be able to tell them about his adventures, especially those of this summer of 1945.

Tom decided not to mention quitting, but he wondered what the others were thinking. Were they trying to figure a way to get back home?

It was about midnight when they pulled into the mouth of a little stream running in from the Kentucky side and tied off for the night. Hobo set a 10-

hook throw line off the back, baiting it with nightcrawlers.

They blew out the lanterns and settled in under the tent. The sides were rolled up to let in what little breeze there was. There was very little small talk and no joshing. Each dealt with his own thoughts as sleep claimed him.

Tom was first up again, just after the songbirds stirred to life. They had a supply of dry wood in the corner of the tent, and he soon had a fire going on the hearth. Everybody was starved. They finished off their bacon and eggs. Hobo skinned out the four catfish the throw line yielded, cut them up, and stored them away in a pan of fresh spring water.

Everybody's spirits seemed to lift with the fog. They traveled on with the morning sun on their backs. The river had fallen back to nearly summer pool. The current had slacked considerably.

"I'd say we'll get the experience of locking through the next dam we come to," Vince said. "You can tell by this lazy current that the wickets have gone back up."

"How many we got to go through, anyway?" Gale asked.

"There's a bunch of 'em," Dale said. "My Uncle Harvey worked on a towboat as a deck hand. He said it wouldn't have been a bad job if it wasn't for locking through all the dams."

The river lay before them without a riffle. They reclined on the deck and enjoyed the ride. The spirit of adventure rode high again.

"This might be something like the frontiersmen felt when they first went down this river on flatboats," Gale said. "Except now, thanks to the dams, we've got fifteen or twenty feet of water under us. In those days this old river was so shallow that they hung up on sandbars. Sometimes they'd have to lay up for days waitin' on rain. That's when Indians would come whoopin' out of the forest, robbin' and scalpin'."

The mention of Indians whetted Vince's interest. "Maybe we ought to have us a battle or two with redskins," he said. "Or we could be the Indians, wreaking vengeance on these land-grabbing white settlers. We've got string, and there's plenty of willow poles along the shore for bows."

But then he decided that he wasn't up to it – that it was far too peaceful out on the river "to start stirrin' up old wars again."

He yelled back to Keith, on the sweep. "But anyway, keep a sharp eye out for Injuns, watchman. We'll protect ourselves if we have to."

"How'd you know so much about them early settlers and flatboats and all?" Keith asked Gale.

"Miss Newberry," he said. "Don't you remember all that history lesson she had last fall?"

"Yeah, but I didn't know you was payin' all that much attention," Keith said, then, after a pause, added, "She's not a bad teacher."

"What about these dams, Vince?" Dale asked. "How'er we gonna get through them?"

"Why, you dummy, how do you think? We'll lock through, just like any other boat. They have to lower us down. That's what they get paid to do."

Then he added, more to himself than to the others, "Huck and Jim didn't have to worry about lockin' through no dams."

In mid-afternoon they rolled the catfish pieces in flour and fried them in the bacon grease left from breakfast. They ate as they drifted on, each of them with a great feeling of self-sufficiency.

After that, they had a swim, diving off the raft and bellying back up onto it to go again.

Evening shadows were lengthening as they passed a sycamore grove fronted by a smooth beach. Vince said it would be a great place to pull in for the night.

"But it's a little too early, I think," he said. "We want to make all the distance we can while it's light. We pass a town we'll have to go in for supplies."

It wasn't long before they saw a dam coming up.

"The locks are in tight against the Kentucky shore," Vince said. "Better start bringing us in there, Jim – er, Keith."

Soon they eased the raft up against the head of the guide wall. Hobo and Gale grabbed the iron ladder rungs imbedded in the concrete wall and held the boat steady.

"Open, sesame," Vince said, facing down the lock with his arms raised like Moses with the staff.

"The upper gate's already open," Keith said. "That's the lower gate we're looking at."

"Well, by golly, let's go," Vince said. "Shove off, me laddies."

They hadn't reached the point where the upper gate was rolled back into its recess before they saw a man running along the top of the wall toward them.

He raised his arms. "Hey, hey. Hold it," he said, coming up and looking down on the motley crew. His eyes swept over them and up and down the raft.

"What are you boys doing out here?" he asked.

"We just want to get through your dam," Vince said.

"In that thing?"

They tied to the wall and for five minutes they gave him answers to his questions, being careful not to reveal who they were and where they were from.

He listened, shook his head, then said, "Now I'll tell you boys very seriously, we can't waste government machinery and manpower to lock through a tent on a bunch of boards."

"We have to get through," Vince said. "We're goin' down to help my uncle get in his corn crop. He's dependin' on us."

"Who is he and where's he live?"

"Well, it's my uncle Josh, and his farm's down almost to Cincinnati."

"Well, this is a stupid and dangerous way to get there. Your folks should'a sent you down on a train or bus."

But he finally acknowledged that they did lock through pleasure boats, and noted that the raft did seem to be seaworthy.

"I'll tell you what we can do," he said. "There's a towboat comin' down. We've got the lock ready for him. We can lock you through with him.

"But we've got to be very careful, and you've got to do what I tell you. We'll put you in first, and you paddle that contraption down to the lower gate. There's a ladder in the wall there, like the one up there, where you can tie. But you've got to leave plenty of slack line so the raft can lower as the water level drops. And I want you boys off there while this is going on."

A steamboat whistle sounded upstream. The boys looked upstream and saw the barges coming hard around the bend.

That's her comin' now," the lock worker continued. "When he's in and we drop the water level, we'll open the gate and let your raft out. You boys walk it down along the guidewall until you get around the end of it, out of the way. Then let the tow go on and get out of the way, then you'll be all right. Understood?"

Even as they agreed to his orders and thanked him, the steamboat gave another long blast on her whistle. She was fast approaching. A small tow, actually, pushing a single line of two barges, which were riding low in the water with their loads of coal. Before the raft reached the lower gate, the towboat was already easing into the lock – barges, towboat and all.

"All the way down to the lower end, now, hurry, and then you get yourselves off that thing," said the dam worker, following them along the wall.

Two deck hands stood at the front of the lead barge, ready to loop a line around the stanchion imbedded on the top of the wall when the time came.

"Why don't we ask them if they need any help on there?" Keith asked. "We could make money on the way down. My uncle said they really feed, and I could sure go for something besides catfish about right now."

"I'm not ready to go to work yet," Vince said. "Our time will come."

There was a spooky silence inside the lock chamber as the tow slid in, filling the lock from wall to wall.

The boys eased the raft up to the ladder near the lower gate.

"Come on, get off there," the dam worker said.

Tom long-lined the raft to the ladder and Keith and Dale started up while he held the raft in place.

"What'a we got here, John? A bunch of Huck Finns?" the deckhand with the line in his hands called over to the man on top of the wall.

"Looks like it, buddy," John called back. "You boys hurry up now. Climb up off of there."

The barges were within twenty yards of the raft and still moving. The towboat itself was also within the lock now. "Buddy" tossed the line to John. His aim was poor. The line dropped into the water. Quickly, he began pulling it in hand-over-hand for another toss.

"Hurry!" John said. "You're getting past the stanchion. Let me get it around it!"

The second deckhand was trying to signal the pilot to reverse the paddlewheel. Tom followed Gale up the ladder. Vince was behind him. Hobo ducked back into the tent, saying he had to get his pipe. John had the line from the deckhand now and was frantically looping it over the stanchion.

Too late. The barges were still drifting downstream, looming over the raft.

287

Vince and Tom hadn't reached the top of the ladder before they heard the sick-ening, splintering sound. Tom looked back to see Hobo leap for the ladder just as the floor of the raft buckled upward in the middle. Hobo scurried on up to the top of the wall. They watched as the barges pulverized the raft against the gate. The barrels under the decking broke loose. Two were crushed and promptly sank. The tarp followed them.

The boys stood at the top of the wall and looked down on floating boards and barrels.

"Everything's gone," Vince said, holding his head in his hands. "Food, lanterns, stove -- our eighteen dollars. We never got to spend a dime of it."

John the dam man showed both sympathy and anger.

"I knew I should never have let you boys in here on that contraption. But looks like none of you got hurt. You're not hurt, are you? Thank God for that. I should have pulled you in behind the towboat, but I didn't want you to be too close to that paddlewheel."

He left them and began checking the gate. The upstream gate had been closed and the water level was dropping.

"Buddy" the deckhand stood with hands on hips, looking down at what was left of their once beautiful raft.

"Looks like you modern day Huck Finns will have to find another way to travel," he said, and snickered. "You wouldn't have made it very far in that thing, anyway."

Keith shook his fist at him. "We'd have made it as far as we wanted to if you wasn't such an idiot," he said. "Come over here and I'll whip your hind end to Cincinnati and back."

He picked up a piece of driftwood and threw it at the deckhand, who promptly whizzed a lump of coal at them.

He seemed in the mood to cut loose with a volley, and the Braves were looking around for things to fire back. John the dam worker came running and put a stop to hostilities, telling the boys to move away, and threatening the deckhand with a "report."

"Somebody might want to smell your breath," John said to him.

The deckhand cut loose with a few curses and busied himself with letting out rope as the towboat and barges were lowered.

Vince tried to soothe things over. "Don't suppose it'd do any good to ask the captain if he needs some workers?" he said to the other deckhand.

"Buddy", overhearing the remark, laughed. "We don't hire kids," he said. "Go on back home to your mommas."

"I'll own that boat some day and you'll be on the street looking for a job," Keith told him. "Buddy" laughed all the louder.

John motioned the Braves on across the wide expanse of concrete stretching back from the lock, toward the long line of steps leading up the bank.

"I'm sorry, boys, for what happened," he called after them. "Can you get back home okay?"

Vince told him they had relatives nearby.

"I've got an uncle in the state legislature," he lied. "I'm reporting this to him. You can bet we'll be filing a complaint against this dam and against that boat. One of you boys write down the name of that boat, the John Delmar. We'll be getting our money and our boat and our stuff back, you can bet on that."

John the dam man stood hands on hips shaking his head, then turned and walked back toward the locks.

At the top of the bank, they looked and saw that the lower gate had opened, so the damage inflicted by the coal barges had been all to the raft; none to the gate. The tow was under power again, pushing on through the locks.

The boys made their way down the tree-lined street past a row of company houses.

"I didn't know you had an uncle in the state legislature," Gale said to Vince.

"I didn't either," Vince said.

"Whatta we gonna do, Vince?" Dale asked. "We're a far piece from home, and no money and no food."

"Simple," Vince said. "We'll just hitchhike back home, set some trotlines and sell some more fish, and build ourselves another raft."

CHAPTER 53:
HELLO HOME; GOODBYE HOME

The bedraggled six adventurers had the look of defeat about them as they made their way out the lane away from the settlement of company houses at the location of an Ohio River locks and dam. They did not even know which dam they were at, just that their river adventure had fallen far short of their goal to reach Cairo and see the mighty Mississippi.

They had lost everything – their Boy Scout gear, Mr. Royalton's tarp, Bruce Sycamore's two railroad lanterns, their life savings, the raft they had called home for the past three days ….

Confidence in their leader was shaken. The only plan Vince now had in mind was to reach the highway and hope to thumb a ride back home, sell more catfish to rebuild their treasury, and lay new plans for The Great Escape – the seeing of things unseen before they were gone.

Gale had suggested knocking on a door of one of the houses to ask to use a telephone. He could call home and his dad could come and get them. But how would they explain being where they were, wherever that was, Tom wondered.

"Yeah, Gale," Vince said. "We're still on our camping trip, remember? We're still covered. Actually be getting home a day early. We can make up the lost gear by the time it's missed, and be home free. No, let's not call your dad. We'll get home."

The double tracks of the C&O Railroad lay between them and the highway. And there was a train on the eastbound tracks. A stopped freight train. As they stood looking up and down and deciding whether to crawl under or climb over, they heard the sound of "buk, buk buk, buk" as cars were being jerked to life up along the line.

"The thing's startin' up. It's movin'!" exclaimed Gale.

One car and then another sprang to life. The boxcar right in front of them had a sliding door that stood half-open, exposing the straw-covered floor.

"You're durn right it's moving, and it's moving toward home!" Vince said. "Come on! Let's hop in!"

The next thing they knew Vince had scrambled in and turned to extend a helping hand to the others.

"Come on! Come on, boys!" he yelled.

As the car began slowly moving forward, they walked alongside, leaping up one by one, the ones already on pulling and the ones behind pushing. Finally, Dale, the shortest of them all, was the only one not on. He was jogging alongside now, a look of panic crossing his face. Hobo grabbed one of his arms and Vince the other and they pulled him in.

"Hey, hey! All right, all right! We're traveling in style now," Keith said, sitting back in the loose straw.

Tom felt the excitement mounting as the train picked up speed. Soon telephone poles were whizzing by. He looked over the edge of the doorway and saw the crossties become a blur. The "click click, click click" of the wheels on the tracks beat a steady tune. The car bucked and swayed back and forth like a beast alive.

The air was stuffy. They slid the boxcar door almost all the way open and managed to slide the one on the other side halfway open before it stuck.

Long hours had passed since their catfish dinner. The boys' thoughts were centered on some home cooking.

The sun went down and still the train rolled eastward. As dusk fell, they gathered near the open door as Vince announced some familiar sights coming into view.

"There's Thelma's!" he said.

Soon they passed the mouth of School House Hollow.

And then they saw lights in the windows of some very familiar houses.

They were passing Hooperville.

At sixty miles an hour!

"Fellow jump off this train it'd rip him to pieces," Gale said.

They waved goodbye to home sweet home with an appetite gnawing at

292

their hearts and their stomachs.

"Well, boys, we've all gone to bed at one time or another without supper," Vince said. "We're not going to starve before this thing stops. Then we can work us out some breakfast."

"My throat's parched," Hobo said.

Tom could not make out the features of Vince's face in the near darkness, but it seemed he could hear the cogs of his mind turning as he tried to work out a plan of some kind that would turn all this into a game.

But there had always been a quitting place for his games, one that he controlled.

Now the big steam locomotive chomping coal and belching smoke and pounding the rails with its great drive wheels was calling the plays.

They all fell silent; no wise cracks even from Keith. Finally, Vince said, "I declare if this ain't the best idea I've had yet. My uncle John lives in Baltimore, and the shipyards there are boomin'. We'll look him up. Baltimore ain't all that big a place. He'll put us up until we can work out a paycheck. Then we'll come back home on the George Washington."

Tom wondered if he really had an uncle there. And if the train would even wind up in Baltimore.

No one bothered to quiz Vince on the matter. They continued to stare out the door in silence, watching the tops of the telephone poles whiz by.

Suddenly they were startled by a voice from the darkened recesses of the car: "Hey, Harry! Wake up. We got company."

293

CHAPTER 54:
RIDING THE RAILS

After some groaning and grumbling from the dark at one end of the box-car, two men stepped forward into the evening's last light that filtered in through the open doors. Rather than being frightened, Tom almost giggled as he looked at the two. He immediately thought how much they reminded him of Mutt and Jeff, two characters from the funny papers. One was tall and skinny, the other short and heavy.

"Well, Jonesy, what have we here?" one said to the other. "A bunch of lit-tle men. Draft dodgers, every one, I'll bet." Both laughed.

Any humor Tom felt was not shared by the others. The boys huddled close. There was strength in numbers.

The tall one, presumably called Harry, wore bibbed overalls and a dirty-white pullover, short-sleeved shirt. He had a long chin. His eyes were razor slits under thick gray eyebrows.

The other – Jonesy – wore a long-sleeved denim shirt buttoned at the col-lar. A length of rope held up his pants, the legs of which reached halfway up to his knees and seemed to be held together with patches of various colors. For the life of him, Tom could not help but see a circus clown before him. His face was round and his eyes resembled black buttons.

Neither had gotten close to a razor for a few weeks. Hair hung down from under the slouch hat Harry wore, and also from the ballcap Jonesy wore. Their brogans were worn and scuffed and one of Jonesy's had a rag tied around under the instep and over the top. Harry was probably sixty, Jonesy maybe a dozen years younger.

Vince apparently didn't trust either of the two, for he came out right away, in one quick breath, with a tale about how the boys were traveling to meet his uncle, and how his uncle had killed three men who crossed him, and that he would hunt down and do the same to anybody who messed with his favorite nephew or any of his friends. He managed to get all this out in one breath, he really did.

"Why, we don't mind you boys bein' travelin' companions," Harry said. "What you're doing out here is your business. There's room on the rails for everybody, and it's not a bad life. See a lot of different country. Sometimes these old freights rumble on all through the night and day. Don't know why this one stopped back there a ways, unless one of these cars has a hot box. Let's hope they pull over in the Brussells Yards for service. Don't know about you boys, but we've not et supper. Some of the boys are sure to be there. And we'll have supper waitin', my guess."

He searched the pockets on the front of his bibbed overalls and came out with a package of Bugler rolling papers.

"Don't suppose you boys would have any baccer? I been dyin' for some nicotine since we pulled out of Paducah."

"Got any of your stuff left, Hobo?" Vince said.

Hobo reached into his pocket and brought out the cob and a sack of dried corn silks. "You're welcome to some of this," he said, filling his pipe and tossing the bag to Harry.

"What in the world is it? Don't feel like baccer."

"My own special blend. Ain't bad," Hobo said.

Harry examined it closely, smelled of it, wrinkled his nose.

"One of them foreign blends? Sort of elongated baccer."

He proceeded to roll himself a cigarette. He lit it, blew out a plume of blue smoke, took another drag, inhaled it, and broke into a coughing fit.

"Better than nothin, I reckon," he finally managed to get out, beating his chest with a closed fist.

Introductions were made all around. Immediately Jonesy asked Hobo how he came by his name. Tom listened for the story, too, because he'd wondered how Hobo got that name.

"When I was about two years old," Hobo said, "my dad set me up in the doorway of a boxcar on a train that had stopped. When it started up, he let me ride along for a little ways before he grabbed me off again. Somebody took a picture of me ridin' that train, and I've been Hobo ever since. Don't even recognize it when somebody calls me Harold."

Pretty soon the train slowed. Harry leaned out of the doorway.

"Sure enough," he said, "we're pullin' into the yards. That's good."

"Could be good and could be bad," Jonesy said, looking from one to the other of the boys. "The place is usually crawling with railroad dicks. The great and mighty railroad company don't think anybody should ever get so far down on his luck that he can't afford to buy a train ticket."

"He's right," Harry said. "They carry clubs and sometimes guns and they don't think twice before using them on a man. When we stop, we want to move on out of here, fast!"

The boys were excited to learn the train was stopping, for no one had swallowed Vince's tale of working in the Baltimore shipyards. They might have wound up on the East Coast had the train not stopped. Vince figured the Brussells Yards couldn't be much more than 30 miles upriver from Hooperville.

The train slowed more now. They began to see other rail cars parked on sidings. The Braves two emissaries cautioned them to stay back away from the doors.

"We wanna all get back here in a corner and pull that loose hay up over us," Harry said. "We'll lay there 'till we know all's quiet. Them dicks watch these empty boxcars. They might come lookin' in here with a light. Too late to try for closin' the doors."

"I wouldn't mind too much goin' to jail for trespassin," Jonesy said. "The eatin's better in there than out here. But some of them dicks enjoy roughin' you up with a billy."

The boys pushed loose hay along the floor, piled it up in a corner, and all of them got under it.

Harry hushed them as the car rocked to a halt. After a long minute of hearing nothing, the train bucked to life again, and they were going backwards.

"Musta overrun the spout," Jonesy whispered.

Back they went, until the train finally stopped again. They heard footsteps crunching in gravel, then a sound that must have been the car's coupler being lifted.

297

Then a voice asked, "Seen anybody tonight, George?"

"Nope. Seen or heard nothing."

"Too bad. Been a dull shift. We'd like to bash a head or two before we get off – liven things up a bit."

More sounds of feet crunching gravel. Then they heard the train clickety-clacking off up the line. Their car stayed put.

A beam of light cut the darkness. The boys and the two hobos didn't dare draw a breath as they saw through a slit in the hay the spotlight travel the length and breadth of the car.

"Nobody in here," a voice said.

"Close her up," another said. "Padlock the doors."

One of the side doors was pushed along its track and shut with a thud. Then they heard the door on the other side of the car sliding. It stopped.

"Stuck tight," the first voice said. "Help me."

A series of grunts and a banging sound, then the first voice said, "Let it go. We'll turn it in to the shop people."

It was a long minute after the sound of their footsteps faded away into the night before anybody spoke.

"Oh, lordy," Harry said. "I thought for a minute we would be locked in here for sure."

"We've been sidetracked," Jonesy said. "We can grab another train out of here in the morning though, no trouble. They're in and out of here around the clock."

They paused at the doorway, listening for sounds. Jonesy and Harry leaped down and the six Braves jumped down and followed them. They ran as quietly as possible through the gravel, between two trains, looking for an end to get around.

CHAPTER 55:
IN THE HOBO CAMP

There appeared to be no end to the lines of trains in the Brussells Yards, which at the time were the biggest and busiest single line yards in the nation. The boys followed their two tramp friends, Harry and Jonesy, as they crawled under one line of cars and then continued on between trains until they came to the end of tracks.

Soon they were confronted by a high wire fence topped by several strands of barbed-wire. It appeared to be a dead-end, but then Jonesy was pulling back a two-foot by two-foot section of wire at the bottom of the fence. He held it open while the six boys crawled through, followed by Harry and then him. He closed the section of cut wire behind them.

Now, finally outside the yards, they trudged behind the two men down-river on a roadway covered with cinders. Presently they came to a huge concrete structure that jutted up into the treetops. A concrete ramp, partially hidden by vines and saplings, led up to an open double-wide door in the front of the building.

"This is an old pump house," Harry said. "They built a new one upriver and this one is abandoned. We call it Hotel Hobo. Nobody comes around here, except us men of the road – traveling businessmen who can spend the night before making connections out."

Jonesy laughed at his friend's comments. "Yes, yes. Businessmen we are. Our business is travel and loafing and anything to stay away from work."

"And the draft board," Harry said. "Not me and not Jonesy. We're too old for the draft. But you'll see a few men out here on the rails who just have no desire for boot camp."

Jonesy, lifting his head and sniffing the air, said, "Smell that aroma? Supper's on, my men. Let's go!"

The two hobos started up the ramp. Halfway up they turned and motioned to the boys, who were hanging back.

"This time of year, when the harvest is in, there'll be plenty of food for all. And everybody's welcome. Come on!" Harry said.

Tom could smell a delicious aroma of what his nose identified as corn on the cob and pork and beans.

The boys stood grouped at the bottom of the ramp. "What do you think, Vince? Should we?" Gale asked.

"Whatta ya mean, what does he think?" Keith asked. "I'm starving to death, and I smell food coming from up there. Let's get our starved butts up there."

"Come on boys, nothing to fear," Harry called to them. "And the kitchen's open to all."

Vince looked up the ramp, then turned his gaze downriver. Finally he said, "Well. OK. Let's go. I'm starved, too, and we'll need something to give us strength for the journey home."

Inside the building it was all one big room. An open fire burned in the middle of the concrete floor. Concrete blocks on either side of the fire supported an iron grill, which supported a large pot that steam arose from. Several opened No. 5 cans of pork and beans also simmered on the grill. And corn roasting with the shucks still on covered one side of the grill. The scant smoke the fire generated went out through an open skylight.

There were three large windows, one on each side and one in the rear wall. The one on the upriver side, facing the yards, was covered by a heavy tarp. The window at the rear had a leafy tree limb projecting in through it.

Two railroad lanterns provided enough light that the boys could make out seven or eight men sprawled on nondescript bedrolls spread on pieces of cardboard along the wall on the upriver side.

A heap of discarded wine bottles was piled in one corner.

One man got up to stir the pot, which held yellow, tender ears of sweet corn. He also turned the roasting ears, greeting Jonesy and Harry as he did so.

"Wasn't expecting you two along this soon," he said to them. "But you've hit it lucky. Unlike old Dan Tucker, you're not too late to get your supper. Most of the boys already eat and conked out for the night, but as you can see there's plenty left. The beans is compliments of the railroad – heh, heh – and the corn's a bonus from somebody's patch of sweet corn down the way here."

He turned his attention to the six boys standing partly in the shadows, as though he'd just discovered them.

"You and Jonesy traveling with your kids now, Harry?" he asked.

Without waiting for an answer, he walked back to his bed and picked up a bottle and took a swig from it.

"Good blackberry wine," he said. "Well-aged ... at least three days old." He laughed again.

He walked back and handed the bottle to Harry. He took a long swig and handed it to Jonesy. Gulping sounds emerged from Jonesy's throat as he took three big swallows.

"That is good stuff," he said, looking at the bottle as he wiped the corner of his mouth on his sleeve. He handed the bottle back to the bean-stirrer.

"These are young friends of ours who hopped the train a ways back," Harry said. "They say they're making their way east to see some family. Maybe they're running from something. We don't know. But they seem to be mighty good boys. And, like us, they're hungry. We've invited them for supper."

There came a voice from among the bodies sprawled along the base of the wall.

"They're just kids," it said.

"We're older than you think," Vince shot back. "We're going to Baltimore to work in the shipyards."

"Well, that's OK boys, er, men," the voice continued. "I was 'bout your age when I decided that my drunken old man wasn't gonna hit me again. I hit the rails and I been living the good life ever since. Come on over here and get yurself a swig."

"I think we're all more interested in food right now," Harry said, looking toward the fire and rubbing his hands together.

"Eat all you want," the bean-stirrer said. "Like I told you, I was getting ready to move it off the grill 'till morning."

Harry and Jonesy led the boys over to the makeshift shelves on the wall. There they found a bucket of water and several empty bean cans with sticks wired to them for handles. After Harry assured them the water was from a clear, cold spring just upriver from the pump house, they drank their fill. It was sweet to the taste.

There was a bar of Lifeboy on the shelf by the bucket. They took turns pouring water over their hands while washing them with the bar of soap.

Hanging above the bean cans were quite a few hollowed-out wooden spoons. When the boys looked them over but hesitated, Jonesy said, "You can be sure these things are clean. I know our friends here look a little unwashed, but nobody wants to come down with the heebie-jeebies or something. We practice good hygiene when it comes to food. All these utensils are washed in boiling water after they're used and before they're ever hung back on this wall. Same way with the can cups. And anybody using the bathroom does so outside, on the downriver side of the hotel here."

Each of the boys got a can and a spoon, examined them closely, then made their way to the grill where the man who had been stirring the beans ladled them out. They squatted down at the top of the ramp. The beans were hot and juicy, and now and then contained a small chunk of pork.

"Glory be! I didn't even think I liked pork and beans," Keith said as he headed back for a second helping.

The corn on the cob they polished off was sweet and juicy. It would have been better with some butter, but they at least had some salt to flavor it with.

Most of the men were snoring by the time the boys finished eating.

From somewhere toward the back Jonesy gathered up some pieces of cardboard and spread it along the wall away from the others.

"It's warm enough you won't need any covers, but you boys will have to start carrying some kind of bedrolls if you're gonna travel the rails," he said. "Get some sleep. In the morning we'll hop an eastbound freight outta here."

Harry and Jonesy spread their own bedrolls off a piece from them, between them and the others that were sleeping.

Vince and the Braves huddled near the top of the ramp.

"We're going to get on out of here," Vince said. "I know we're all dog-tired, but I don't feel comfortable here. We don't know who some of these men are or what they might do."

Tom, with his belly full of corn and beans, knew that making it to the Baltimore shipyards was a thought as far away as Cairo and the Mississippi had been. He wanted to go home. Hobo, Gale, Keith, Dale – even Vince, felt the same as he did, of that he was sure, in spite of the fact that Keith and Dale were already conked out on the cardboard.

As soon as their hosts, Jonesy and Harry, seemed to be asleep, Vince roused Keith and Dale and they headed for the door, being careful not to step on anybody.

At the top of the ramp, they were startled to see, in the light that spread dimly over the pump house from the lights inside the yards, a man running frantically. He came down the cinder path and up the ramp, screaming "They're coming! Get 'em up!"

He passed the confused boys as he ran inside. "The railroad dicks are coming. Come on, get up, get outta here, everybody!"

Harry leaped to his feet. "Railroad dicks! Are you sure? They've never bothered us here. This is not even railroad property."

"They've got clubs, chains, probably even guns. Sheriff's deputies are with them, too. They've got trucks to haul us off in!"

The other men were roused and were up and stumbling around. They headed for the doors, but they were too late. Men piled out of a truck parked at the foot of the ramp and charged up the ramp, with flashlights in one hand and clubs in the other. Even the messenger was trapped.

Blows were falling on the heads and shoulders of the men as Vince pushed Hobo ahead of him and yelled to the Braves, "Quick! To the window on the back wall."

Ever scheming, he had earlier checked out the tree limb sticking through the window there.

He walked the limb, holding onto a smaller limb above his head, and the Braves followed. Tom was the last. He turned, facing the wild melee that was going on behind them: men screaming, cursing, the sound of clubs slamming into bodies, men being grabbed and dragged out the front entrance. He wanted to help Jonesy and Harry, to repay them for how they'd helped them. But it was too late to help them or any of the other men who had been sleeping peacefully just moments earlier.

"This is railroad property now, and we're cleaning this rat's nest out!" one of the attackers screamed above the sound of the one-sided battle.

There were more sounds of clubs on flesh and bone. Cursing. One man pleading for mercy.

"Come on, Tom!" yelled Vince, who was already climbing down the trunk of the tree, with the four Braves scrambling behind him. Tom moved quickly out the limb to the trunk and started climbing down from limb to limb.

The last thing he heard from inside the building was the voice of either a railroad detective or a sheriff's deputy shouting, "You thieving bums! Draft dodgers! Let's move it!"

There was nothing the Hooperville Braves could do for their newfound friends of the open road.

CHAPTER 56:
HOME AGAIN, HOME AT LAST

Tom hit the ground running, close on the heels of the others. It was dark under the trees along the riverbank. They ran, paying little attention to the limbs that slapped them. Tom fell, tumbled, but leaped to his feet again and continued running. For all he knew, the horrible force of men who had swept down on Harry and Jonesy and the others might have spotted them going out the back window. They might have sent men on the ground around the base of the building to catch them.

Hah! Fat chance of catching they had!

The boys angled down the slope until their feet touched the familiar waters of the Ohio. They hit a stretch of sandy beach relatively free of stumps or other obstacles. A near-full moon slid in an out of cloud cover and helped to light the way. They opened it up, Vince in the lead, and down the bank of the river they flew.

At last, exhausted, they fell on the sand, gasping for breath, and, over the thumps of their beating hearts, listened – listened for the sounds of anyone that might be coming after them.

Nothing. The sounds of the attack at the pump house, if it wasn't over, were too far distant to hear. The jarflies and the katydids serenaded the late-summer night.

Downriver they spotted the flash of lightning and heard the roll of thunder. Tom wondered if the devil was still after him.

"I can't go any farther, boys," Vince said. "My legs feel like they're filled with lead sinkers."

"I can't go any more, either. Not with all them beans and corn in my belly," Keith said.

"That's a storm coming up the river, boys. We've got to find shelter for the night," Gale said.

"We'll build a lean-to back under these trees," Vince said. "Hurry now!"

The darkness was illuminated from time to time by flashes of brilliant lightning. It was no problem to find long poles lying about where high water had left them. They angled them up from the ground and lodged them in forked poles pushed into the soft earth, and laid another pole across the front, bracing it in the forked poles. Groping about in darkness, they dragged in more driftwood and added it to the roof. Hobo and Dale broke off willow branches, enough for the roof and bedding.

The lightning was over them now and the wind increased. They had no sooner crawled into the makeshift shelter until the rain came down hard. The tall maples and sycamores helped shelter the lean-to.

Lightning cracked against a tree maybe twenty feet behind them. A limb big enough to kill a horse came crashing to the ground. Lightning, Tom thought, was never his friend.

It's always looking for me, wanting to teach me a lesson. Some day it'll probably get me.

The rain roared. The roof leaked, but not too bad. And it wasn't long before the rain slacked, and its pitter-patter on the leafy roof had a mesmerizing effect. Huddled together, dirty and wet but too exhausted to care, they somehow found sleep.

The sun was already up when a bunch of jays quarreling in a treetop woke Tom. The others began to stir.

"I feel like I've been rode hard and put up wet," Dale said, rubbing his head in his hands.

"I feel like somebody puked me," Keith said, rising up and looking around.

"Where's Vince and Hobo?" Gale asked. "Lordy, I wish I had my toothbrush and a big tube of Ipana."

They crawled out from under the lean-to and stumbled down to the water's edge to splash river water in their faces. The water was dingy and the level had risen two or three feet during the eight hours they had slept. Drift was running by on a good swift current. Vince and Hobo were waist-deep in the river. They were using grapevines to lash several logs together.

"Well, look at the sleepin' beauties," Hobo said. "Good mornin'. You just missed a fine catfish breakfast. Look here."

He held up a piece of line with three fat channel cats flopping about on it. He had found an old line with a hook attached. He tied the line to a willow pole and baited it with worms found under logs back in the bushes, and caught the fish one right after the other.

He had found some loose driftwood in the crotch of a maple and took great care in building a teepee of sticks and fine bark, just like they'd learned in the scouts.

"But I had one match and it went out, with no fire. Everything's just too wet," Hobo said.

"Don't make no difference anyway," Vince said, grunting as he wedged poles in between the grapevines and the logs to strengthen the tie. "Throw 'em back, Hobo. Before this day's over, we'll be eatin' home cookin'."

He stood up on the logs and pranced around. Hobo pulled the logs and him ashore as the others danced about, whooping it up in full joy mood.

The last whisper of fog had lifted as they pushed off, kicked their way into the current fifty or sixty yards out, and began a drift toward the distant bend.

The makeshift raft didn't fully support them. Their bodies were as much in the water as out. Some took turns drifting along at the back kicking their feet for propulsion, while others lay on the raft and side-armed or used a couple of boards for paddles for added speed.

It wasn't a bad way to travel, considering that the temperature had risen probably to ninety degrees by the time the sun was straight overhead.

Hunger drove them ashore in the afternoon to search for food. They discovered a garden there in a narrow bottom. The harvest had taken place and weeds and vines were moving back in to take over, but here and there hung a few tomatoes, sweet corn and bell peppers – enough to satisfy their hunger.

Then they pushed back into the current and continued their westward journey.

"How much farther, Vince?" Gale asked as he rested from paddling.

"Can't be far. Some of them hills downriver are starting to look familiar, I think," Vince said.

By late afternoon a cheer went up as they rounded a bend and saw Grand Bridge connecting Shawnee and South Shawnee in the distance. Somehow or other they found enough energy to start a game of Bunker Hill to see who could stay atop the logs. Hobo, of course, won out, throwing even Vince for a somersault into the river.

"Ats the way lumberjacks do," Vince said. "Which is a thought. Next summer, we'll hitch our way up to the North Woods and get us jobs in a lumber camp. We can prospect for gold on the side."

The boys converged on him, dousing him in the face until he was forced under to come up on the other side of the raft.

Vince said they didn't want to come into Hooperville from the river, since they were supposed to be returning from a camping trip up School House Hollow. He wasn't sure how they'd explain about not having any gear. Probably would just imply that they were going back after it later. At any rate, as soon as they passed under the bridge, they abandoned the raft at the shoreline.

As they stood on the shore, Vince, hands on hips, looked at the raft, and said, "Are you boys sure now that you don't want to just add a few logs and get back onto our original plan for Cairo?" Then he laughed and took off through the willows for the railroad tracks, the others giving chase.

They made their way along the tracks, passing to the rear of Davis & Harvey's, and soon were looking down on the Christian Church and the first houses in the outlying area of Hooperville, where a single row of houses line the second rise between the tracks and the river.

As they approached Main Street, the street where Tom, Dale, Gale and Hobo lived, the Middle Crossing, they found themselves looking down into the village where a great crowd of people was milling about. Suddenly the bell in the Methodist Church steeple began to toll, as did the bell in the Christian Church steeple. Whistles and sirens were going off across the river in Shawnee. Out on the river, a steamboat idled and gave long blasts on its steam whistle.

And the high school band was on the church steps and walk, blasting out a lively tune. Heretofore the boys hadn't heard the band play anything but "Go tell Aunt Mary her old gray goose is dead," but now this tune sounded a little like the one that was so popular during World War I: *Over there, over there...and we won't be back 'till it's over over there.* Some townspeople danced in the middle of the street, keeping time with the rhythm. People were going in and out of the church. People hugged each other.

The boys looked at each other incredulously. "What in the dog wooie's going on?" Keith asked.

"Looks like they've missed us," Vince said. "But I sure wasn't expectin' anything like this."

But nobody even seemed to notice them as they made their way from the top of the crossing down into town. Tom saw a discarded copy of a special evening edition of The Shawnee Times lying face-up on the gravel sidewalk. Across the top of the page, letters four inches high spelled out: WAR IS OVER!

A little farther down the street, Shanyboat Bill reclined in the grassy ditch, only a swig or two left in the bottle resting on his stomach.

As the boys passed, he looked up and waved the bottle.

"I jush knew we could do it," he said to nobody in particular. "I'm real proud our boysh. Merica! I love it!"

Grandpa Flanders was leaning on his front fence, smiling and puffing his pipe, taking it all in.

Now Tom's mother was running toward them from the Sycamore front porch. She spun Tom around by the shoulders before he even saw her.

"Tom! James Thomas! You dirty-faced urchin. Where have you been? I expected you boys home this morning. You keep me worried sick."

Before Tom could answer she hugged him up tight against her.

"Well, it doesn't matter," she said. "You're safe. And so is your brother. Japan has officially surrendered. Truman's on the radio in there now. Flint's arriving at the train station in Shawnee at ten in the morning. Aunt Mary is picking us up to go meet him. Mary Ann Selby and Leon Richard Selby Jr. are coming with her."

What a relief, what a relief, Tom thought.

"That's wunerful, Mom," he said. "Uh, is there anything on the back of the stove from supper?"

She continued to hug Tom as they made their way to the house. On the porch, he paused to look over his shoulder. He didn't see Vince or any of the boys.

He went on in. His mother sat him down at the table and waited on him hand and foot. He filled his belly with brown beans, fried bologna and corn-bread.

Back on the front porch with his mother, he watched the happy towns-people milling about on the street.

He couldn't stop the thought that flashed through his mind how that, just a few days ago, they had been sick with worry that the atomic bomb, which ended this war, would fall into the wrong hands and start a war that could spell the end for mankind.

That night though, following the adventures by river and rail, as Tom Sycamore lay on clean sheets in his own bed, mulling over the events of the past three days, the future somehow did not concern him.

He was too busy thanking God for his present blessings.

EPILOGUE

But now the future is here, only it's called the present. The old man standing on a limb in the diving tree continued to shade his eyes from the sun with the palm of his right hand as he stared steadfastly downriver toward the bend.

But the showboat never rounded the bend. The sound of the steam calliope fell silent. And as suddenly as they had come, the splashing, the laughter… and the boys … and Chopper, were gone.

He suddenly thought of something Miss Newberry had shared with them in a history lesson: "No moment of history stands alone. Each little chunk of the present echoes the past and foreshadows the future."

He recalled how, on that day, August 14th, 1945, time had stood wonderfully and delightfully still as Hooperville joined the nation in celebrating the end of the mightiest struggle that mankind had ever seen – a war that was now a part of the past. Three years and nearly nine months after their country bombed Pearl Harbor, the Japanese – for the first time in their history – had been conquered.

Now bombs hundreds of times more powerful than those that fell on Hiroshima and Nagasaki lie nestled and hidden in their birthing places on both sides of the Atlantic. They rest atop powerful rockets that can carry them anywhere on the earth, ready to spring when someone pushes the button.

The melting of the elements that the Rev. Ottis Hackelbee was so sure was at the doorstep had only been postponed.

As the elderly gentleman in the diving tree gathered himself for the dangerous descent before him, he suddenly felt an urge to cry.

And it was because the moonlit strawberry patch, the cave, the steamboats, the war-torn beaches along the Ohio's sandy shores, the tree house, Janie's pigtails, Chopper's steadfast love, the brave Marine of the Victory

Garden ... all were lost back there somewhere in the fog along the river.

With some difficulty, he made his way slowly down from limb to limb until his feet reached the ground. Head bowed, he made his way back up the path through the horseweeds.

At the top of the second rise he turned for one final look. And there he saw him one last time. The towhead waved to him from the limb of the old maple. The old man's heart leaped up, but his mind told him the chase was over.

He raised his hand and waved goodbye.

"Thank you, Youth," he said. "And thank you, Ol' Chopper. Thank you both for taking the time to remind me.

"And now it's time that I must move on.

"But, a-h-h ... how I wish I could stay."

AUTHOR'S NOTES

When I met J. Tom Sycamore he was in a nursing home, waiting for the Death Angel to pay a visit. His wife, Elizabeth, had gone on to wait for him. She had been barren, and the conditions for adoption had never quite presented themselves in an acceptable way.

G. SAM PIATT

His parents, of course, as well as his older brother, Flint, had also passed beyond the veil. So he was the last leaf on the tree.

I was there that day visiting someone else and when I passed Tom Sycamore's open door he called to me. I went in and drew up a chair.

He had read my book, "Men of Valor," a collection of World War II combat stories, and wanted to tell me a story that took place during the last year of that Great War. Sycamore was not yet a teenager during that summer of 1945, when America and its allies defeated Nazi Germany in Europe and had Japan's Imperial military forces on the run in the Pacific.

Sycamore's little Ohio River village had contributed to the war effort above and beyond the call of duty. He and the other five members of the Hooperville Braves, gaining inspiration from John Wayne in "Back to Bataan" and other such war movies on the big screen at the Garden, battled the Japanese hordes along the sandy shores of the Ohio.

As I listened to his story over the next few days, heard him try to explain the mystery of the Marine who showed up in the Victory Garden in his back yard while his body was buried on Okinawa; heard him tell of the thunderous cave-in that trapped him and the other Braves in Devil's Den; of the "demon" that ripped the black cat from his grasp; and of the danger-ridden raft trip down the broad river – I realized we had a boy's adventure story worth the telling.

I believe young readers will enjoy reading about the adventures of J. Tom Sycamore and friends. Then, too, so will those of us who are reaching the end of the journey with a nostalgic yearning for the golden friends we had, and the good times we had with them.

I am indebted to writer Doug Stanton for his great 2001 book, "In Harm's Way," the story of the sinking of the USS Indianapolis and the struggle for survival of crewmembers adrift at sea amid schools of man-eating sharks.

Sycamore got the story he told me from big brother Flint, who was a U.S. Marine serving on the big cruiser when two Japanese torpedoes nearly ripped it apart on that black late summer night in the South Pacific.

But Flint did not recall many of the incidents and details, and it was Stanton who told the story.

Stanton has such an excellent way of reporting the facts and in such an interesting way that it's difficult to rewrite his sentences into words of your own.

I have tried to do that in the chapters dealing with Flint Sycamore's hopes of getting pulled off that battered life raft and returning home to Hoopeville. I hope I haven't plagiarized Doug Stanton.

I'm thankful for boyhood friend G. Newt Sanders who encouraged me – badgered me – to write this book, and ditto for Betty Jo Cooper Bauer and Yvonne Fultz Lyon, whose memories are so much sharper than mine.

John Vinson Euton's artistic talents were appreciated.

I thank Amanda Gilmore, a former colleague on the reporting staff of the Ashland Daily Independent, for her editing help.

I say thanks to my wife, Bonnie, and to our extended family of 25 to 30 for allowing me those long hours of solitary confinement at the computer during the long, cold winter of 2013-14. I probably should have taken them all to Florida fishing.

To the good Japanese people of this generation, what can I say? I cringed at the boys' use of the words "Japs" and "Nips," but that's how it was in 1945.

It was a pleasure to turn my manuscript over to Adam VanKirk of Right Eye Graphics in Ashland, Kentucky, and have him turn it into a book I could be proud of.

And last but certainly not least, I thank my Lord and Savior Jesus Christ for, well, everything.

ABOUT THE AUTHOR

G. Sam Piatt is a retired newspaper reporter who lives with his wife, Bonnie, in the hills of northeastern Kentucky, with a view of the Ohio River.

Other books by G. Sam Piatt:
Men of Valor

CPSIA information can be obtained
at www.ICGtesting.com
Printed in the USA
FFOW05n0435160514

9 780988 731936